A

KING'S

TRUST

A KING'S TRUST

A Novel

S.E. McPherson

METALTAIL
PRESS

Map illustrations © Jennifer Bruce 2025

Cover design by Nicole Caputo

Cover image © Magdalena Wasiczek / Trevillion Images

ISBN 979-8-9922543-1-0

Library of Congress Control Number 2025900951

For my tulip family

For a full list of content warnings and ending spoilers for anxious readers, visit semcpherson.com/books/a-kings-trust.

WHAT IS REQUIRED

"Tf you keep ignoring every summons from the king, he's going
to have your head, you know," the young guard said. "Or more
likely, he'll have my head."

Prince Beauregard lengthened his strides, speeding toward a
side exit of the palace, the quickest escape to the stables. "He'll have
to catch us first, Elias. And I won't make that easy."

"Well, *he* won't be chasing you, will he? He'll expect me to
drag you back."

Beau threw a sideways glance at his old friend. "Whose guard
are you, anyway? Some loyalty you have."

"Just because you added me to the prince's flight doesn't mean
I don't answer to His Majesty," Elias said. His hand closed around
Beau's arm, and Beau's skin tingled under the warmth of his palm.
"Please, head back and hear him out, Highness. I'll get shin splints
keeping up with you all the way to the horses."

"I know exactly what he'll say," Beau said, huffing out an
annoyed breath. "You've got *responsibilities* now, Beau. You've got to
step into the shoes that—" He choked, his throat unwilling to form
the name that had been about to fall from his lips: *Charmant.*

1

His late brother, who'd left behind such big shoes to fill.

Beau couldn't afford to think about Char now. He needed to get out of the palace and as far as his loyal mare could carry him.

Elias sighed, and Beau knew his guard would've ridden faithfully out with him, complaining all the way, if the two other guards from Beau's flight hadn't emerged breathless from a doorway ahead to cut them off.

"Your Highness," Oria called, her constant scowl deeper than normal as her pale eyes flashed, "your father insists on your presence. We will bring you to him. *Now.*"

The third guard, Jude, said nothing. With his hulking form braced for a fight and his arms outstretched to catch the prince should he try to run past, he made his position clear. Beau groaned in exasperation and slowed to a halt.

"Fine," he snapped.

He let them bracket him, Elias trailing silently behind. As they plodded toward his father's chambers, the stone walls with their tapestries and sculpture niches closed in around Beau. The silence of his guards was oppressive, the air too thick to breathe. He didn't want to be here. He shouldn't have been. If Char hadn't slipped off his horse, that stupid, *stupid* accident, Beau would still be breathing the free air on the islands northeast of the capital.

Beau's eyes no longer heated with the threat of tears at the image of Char's blond curls, just visible as they had been through the column of nobles on horseback, vanishing from sight. The intervening months had cooled his grief somewhat. But a knot of pain remained under his ribs if his thoughts lingered on Char too long.

When they reached the ivory-inlaid doors to his father's chambers, Beau tried to paste a cocky smile on his mouth. "You wanted to see me, Father?" he said, nodding briefly to the servant who held the door for him.

King Fortin looked up from his ledgers, deep lines graven into the skin around his mouth and eyes, close-cropped hair more grey than brown. He hadn't looked this old four months ago, but of course four months ago he had a glorious golden son as his heir: well-spoken, intelligent, skillful with a blade and a horse, respected by every noble who met him. Now, he had only Beau.

"I see your guards managed to catch you before the stable-hands had to turn you away," Fortin said. "And yes, they would've turned you away. No one in this palace is going to let you run for the isles, no matter how often you act like a common child."

Beau kept quiet, though his smirk dropped into a mulish, flat expression. The king continued, "Your mother and I have been discussing how best to address your preparation. We weren't as diligent as we ought to have been in your education. Your mother especially has always been too quick to allow you to wallow in mediocrity."

"Why would you be diligent?" Beau asked, voice deceptively mild. "You had an heir and a spare. I wasn't supposed to get this close to the crown."

"Beau, please. This is a hard time for us. Please, don't make it harder. You have responsibilities now, and—"

Beau snorted and glanced at Elias, who was doing everything in his power not to make eye contact. "Do you really want *me* on the throne?" Beau said. "You've told me time and again what I am: a prodigal bird of passage, a sot, a philanderer. I'm nothing like Char. I can't be what you were training him to be."

"No, you can't," the king said flatly. "But you must be better than you are. I'm sorry to drag you out of your cups and into some semblance of respectability. But the loss of whatever wayward plans you had for your life is the least of our tragedies." His father only ever got that sharp, sardonic tone of voice when he spoke to his second son. "You've dodged this long enough. You *will* sit with the tutors. You *will* attend when I hold court. And you *will* talk to your mother about the marriage prospects she's arranged."

Beau shook his head firmly. But the king rolled on, stabbing toward Beau with a pointed finger. "You're twenty-five years old. You're not a child anymore. You are the crown prince."

"Then I'll abdicate," Beau said. "This kingdom would be better off with no one at the helm than with me. I don't want—"

"Beauregard." The queen's clear, quiet word sliced through her son's protests, silencing the room. She took a halting step into the parlor from the bedchamber. Wrapped in a dressing gown despite the late hour of the morning, Queen Acier commanded attention even in her grief-weakened state. Her once-beautiful face had greyed and thinned to that of a wraith and the gold of her hair had faded into a pale, silvery blonde like morning mist, but the strength in her reddened eyes spoke to a core of steel in her. "Come here."

Beau was loath to argue with his mother. He approached her reluctantly, eyes on the floor so she couldn't stare reproach into them. She set a gentle hand on his arm and squeezed, but her words were firm. "Look me in the eyes when I'm speaking to you." Beau obeyed, though her piercing green scrutiny made him sweat. "I know it can't be easy to lose Charmant and your freedom in one fell swoop. I—" Her voice broke, and a tear slipped free to track down her cheek.

The prince started to speak, but his mother shook her head, swiped at her face, and said to the guards, "Leave us. I need to speak to my family alone."

The three from Beau's flight filed out first, Elias casting Beau worried glances, followed by two from the king's and the queen's sole guard. Stripped of the minute movements of a half-dozen people shifting from foot to foot, the room seemed very empty.

Into the silence, the queen dropped the words, "Your father is in poor health."

"What?" Beau spun on his father. "You're sick?"

Leather creaked as the king leaned back in his chair. "Yes."

"How sick? How long?"

"I've been monitoring the situation for a couple of years. In recent months, it's gotten worse. My personal physician has impressed upon me the importance of having my affairs settled. My *heir* settled."

Beau absorbed this with a long, slow exhale. Like Char had been, his father was tall, broad-shouldered, perfect-postured. His brown eyes were sharp and clear. He didn't look sick. But perhaps the fresh grey in his hair and the lines on his face were not just from grief and age.

The queen's hand tightened on his wrist until he looked back at her. "There's no clear *next* in line. If you abdicate, your father's uncle Gereux will press his claim, as will the Macabrie and Courdur families. They will fight. There will be civil war, and our neighbors will take advantage of the chaos to carve strips off Granvallée, allies or no. You'll have assassins on your heels until the day you die to ensure you never come back and seize the throne for yourself."

Her voice softened and she released him. "You must know this, even without the teaching you should've had. You're fighting the inevitable because it doesn't seem fair. But facts cannot be changed, however much you dislike them."

Beau crossed the room to sit heavily in an antique armchair. Of course he knew these things. That's why the cavernous rooms of this place felt so small, why the hallways threatened to collapse and crush the air from his lungs. That's why he had to run.

He knew what Charmant would do if the situation were reversed. Ever dutiful, Char would be comforting their parents, offering up ways to improve and hasten his instruction, studying the names and positions and politics of all the lords and holdings in the realm. In short, he'd be the perfect crown prince that he was.

Beau couldn't do that.

He looked at his father, withered by the loss of his golden boy, his pride and delight. He looked at his mother, barely holding together the scraps of her noble dignity around the molten core of mourning and anguish.

Closing his eyes, he swallowed down his own grief and anxiety. He hadn't been trained for this. He wasn't equipped for this. He didn't have the talent or the charm or even one-tenth of the perfection his brother had had.

But if he was truly all there was…

"Fine," he said. "I'll see the tutors. I'll sit in court."

"And you'll marry as soon as a suitable match is made," his mother added.

A jolt of horror ran through him. "Mother, please. I don't need a wife. I don't *want* a wife, certainly not the sort of woman who'd tie herself to the crown prince."

"You don't have a choice," Acier said sharply. She closed her eyes, moderated her tone, and said, "When you ascend to the throne, your wife should already be at your side, with her own training in how to be queen. How to deal with nobles. How to run a nation."

Beau could hear the silent reasoning: if they found a woman skillful enough to rule through him, they wouldn't have to depend on Beau to be a good king. He pretended that didn't hurt. "There's no urgency for that. Any woman you'd deem a suitable match has already been trained. Every parent in the kingdom must've been angling to put their daughter in front of Char, ready to sit at the king's side."

Acier shook her head in calm disagreement. "It *is* urgent. The training is different; it takes time to build connections. If you would *consider* Lady Penamour—"

"I will not marry my dead brother's fiancée," Beau said flatly, not for the first time. "I refuse. It's sick."

The queen tried and failed to suppress her eye roll. "She was Charmant's best option by a mile, Beauregard. Duchess of Veritelutte in her own right *and* with strong ties on her mother's side to the Courdurs—stop making that face, for gods' sake. They had a political agreement to be married, not a romantic attachment."

Beau threw up his hands. "That's worse! You don't see how that's worse? What kind of woman agrees to marry a man and then just moves that engagement over to his brother when he dies? It's psychotic. How could anyone be that cold? I could never trust her." If she controlled the second-largest holding herself and had close ties to the largest, she was the most powerful and probably most conniving noble in the country; he couldn't trust her anyway.

"Beauregard—" the king began sternly, but the queen raised a hand to stop him.

"I understand," she said. She crossed the room to look down at him. "You picked up all sorts of common notions about love in the isles. I'll endeavor to find someone you can trust and come to love, but—"

"That's not good enough!" Beau said, anger welling up in him. Now tears did threaten, to his mortification, and he fought them down. "I've lost *everything*. My brother, my life in the isles, my future. I'm not agreeing to a lifetime in some cold contract with whoever offers the best deal for me."

The king slammed his hands down on the desk. "You will do what is required of you!"

"If you try to force me, I will abdicate," Beau said, staring his father down glare for glare. "I'll choose a successor and take my chances with the assassins. At least I'd die free."

A tense silence held the three of them in stalemate.

Queen Acier broke it. "Fine, Beauregard. Fine." She looked so, so tired. "I'll make arrangements for you to meet the ladies starting next week. So you can find yourself a love match." The last two words twisted in her mouth. "But you will choose someone by the end of the season, or one will be chosen for you. Is that understood?"

She was furious, Beau could tell, but he rose from his chair to kiss her cheek anyway. He ignored her flinch. "Thank you, Mother." He straightened, tugging the cuffs of his sleeves down more comfortably against his wrists. "Father, I'll see you tomorrow in the assembly hall."

He left before his parents could speak again. If he lingered, his father would keep the fight going and one of them would say something to further fracture their fragile relationship.

Elias was by his side in an instant as he shut the chamber door behind him, and the other two guards of the prince's flight fell into step behind them. "Are we making a run for it, Your Highness?" Elias asked lightly.

Beau sighed. "No." He scrubbed a hand over his face and sighed again. "No."

The march from the king's rooms to Beau's in the south tower was long. When he'd been called back from the isles for Char's wedding, he'd insisted on a guest room instead of his childhood suite in the royal wing. He wanted to be as far from his father as possible.

When tragedy struck and preparations for the wedding became preparations for a royal funeral instead, Beau was even more grateful to be away from all the reminders of Char there—or worse, where the reminders would have been, the spaces now empty, trinkets and toys long since packed away into storage, hidey-holes now free of dust and draped with soulless décor.

He sincerely hoped the steward didn't notice his still being in the small guest suite now that it seemed he was trapped at the palace for the rest of his life. If he had to move to the royal wing and pass his parents in the halls every day, he'd lose his mind.

Elias preceded him into his room, giving it a cursory inspection before nodding for the prince to come in. As they had since he'd inherited them from Char, Oria and Jude stayed in the hall to guard the entrance. Beau was glad of the distance; they made him uncomfortable.

He watched Elias stoke the fire in the parlor's fireplace, long, dark hair tied half back as it always was, with a swell of deep gratitude for his long-time friend. Elias was the guard of a second son with no ambition: skilled and alert, but quick to crack a joke or have a drink with Beau in his downtime.

The crown prince's flight wasn't like that. Jude and Oria were the intense, stoic, duty-and-honor type who got assigned to a future king. They weren't thrilled by their new charge. They'd been unhappy when Beau kicked a third guard out of their flight to make room for

Elias. They'd been *furious* when he bumped Oria down in rank to make Elias the First of his flight.

With them outside and Elias in here with him, he could relax back into someone more like himself. He let the tension fall out of his body, kicked his boots off by the door, and threw himself face-down onto the down mattress of his ostentatious bed.

"Fuck my life," he said directly into the stuffing, muffling the words into incoherence.

Elias understood the sentiment anyway. Unbuckling his sword belt and leaning his weapon against the wall, he sat in his chair next to the bed, stretched his legs out long before him, and said, "Well, Highness, what do we do now?"

With great effort, Beau turned his head far enough to the side to see his guard, the rest of him sprawled like a starfish. "I pretend to be a king-in-waiting long enough for you to figure out a plan to get me out of here," the prince said with a smirk that said he was—mostly—joking.

"And what does that look like?" Elias's hazel eyes were reassuringly steady, calm.

"We'll hold court with my father once a week. The tutors will come here to teach me. And…" He let out a long, frustrated sigh through his teeth. "My mother will be arranging for me to meet every eligible lady in Granvallée until I find myself a bride."

Elias's eyebrows rose as he teased, "You? Married?"

"Me, married," Beau grumbled. "I got my mother to agree that I can find someone I actually care about, but I don't know how long that'll hold."

"Were you planning to test how long it would hold?"

Beau shot El a wry look, then dragged himself up the bed with his elbows and flipped heavily onto his back among the too-numerous pillows. "She said I had until the end of the season. Knowing her patience, I might get half that time."

Elias yawned and stretched, and Beau looked away from the taunting inch of skin that appeared beneath his shirt hem as it pulled free of his waistband. "Maisie's heart'll be broken."

At this, Beau reluctantly laughed, fingers tracing the scars on his forearm absently as he stared at the wall and not at his guard. "Maiz probably doesn't even know I'm gone. She'd already dropped me from her rotation before we left the isles in favor of that popinjay who wears his captain's hat to bed."

Elias chuckled, and they settled into an easy silence, lost in private thoughts. Beau pictured Maisie, one of his occasional lovers, full of laughter and light and frivolity. There was no one like that at court. They came to the palace guarded, buttoned up, and politicked.

How could he possibly fall in love with one of these sly, power-hungry people?

"You're going to need a few new suits made," El said. He held out his hand like he was offering a dance, and Beau followed his train of thought: the balls. The dusty, insufferably dull dances he'd endure night after night for the six months of the season. There'd be brunches on the lawn, card games, trail rides, salon evenings, and a thousand other entertainments, but at the balls, he'd be on constant display. He almost leapt out a window at the thought, but defenestrating himself sounded like too much effort.

"Should I teach a few nobles Toothy's famous reel?" Beau asked, summoning a grin.

Elias chuckled at the thought of Granvallée's finest joining hands and kicking their feet at each other. "I'd pay good money to see their faces when you start bouncing around on your toes like Toothy. Maybe it's a good test? Any noble willing to shuck his or her dignity long enough to dance *that* with you in public is probably worth getting down on one knee for."

"I'm afraid this particular position is open only to women," Beau said. It was no secret that Beau dallied just as enthusiastically with men as women, but as heir, he'd be required to marry someone with whom he could make pretty royal babies. "And, having met this kingdom's noblewomen, I know not one of them would spend an ounce of dignity even to win a crown."

"Pity," Elias said. "Whoever you marry, you'll have to laugh enough for both of you. When does the season open?"

"Night after tomorrow, which I'm sure was the prompting for my dear father finally cracking down on me," the prince said, elbowing the pillows until they reshaped to cradle him.

"Want me to send for a barber?"

Beau raised an eyebrow at Elias. "Why, you think I need to clean up? Not good-looking enough to win a wife?" He said it jokingly, but he was altogether too invested in Elias's answer.

The guard was focused on loosening the straps of his leather vambrace. "I can't speak to the taste of noblewomen, but the other lords all seem to have the same idea of grooming."

Beau frowned. It was true. Beau's close beard didn't fit the fashion of the mostly clean-shaven nobles, and the unruly brown waves falling in his eyes lay somewhere between the young lords' fashion of long hair tied back at the nape of the neck and the older lords' preference for shorn hair like the king's. With a sigh, the prince shrugged. "Folk on the isles liked my look well enough. The highborn'll have to put up with it."

"Hmm," Elias said, a neutral sound of acknowledgement. "Whose ball is it?"

"Lady Abadie's black-and-white ball is always the season opener. Bland as hardtack, but everyone shows up."

"Well, it's been a few years since *you* did," Elias said, tugging off one arm's bracer and setting it neatly on the bedside table.

"Seven glorious years of freedom," Beau said wistfully. "Almost eight! I need a drink to toast the best days of my life, now gone."

Elias sobered, working the straps on his other vambrace. "Do you? Need a drink?"

Looking down at his callused, thick-fingered, very un-royal hands, Beau traced a scar across the back of his thumb before saying,

"I…don't know."

He wanted a drink. Badly. He'd wanted to drink himself into a stupor since Charmant fell. But Char didn't drink to excess, and Beau wasn't great at moderation. Char was always in control of himself, as a good crown prince ought to be. And if Beau was going to make any attempt to fill his brother's shoes, he'd have to try not to be a drunken lout.

"I think I'd better not. At least for now," he said at last. He pointed a finger at his First. "And don't you tempt me!"

"Wouldn't dream of it, Highness." Elias said it almost mockingly, but it was a kind, indulgent sort of teasing, and El's hazel eyes were soft and sad above his smile as he dropped the second vambrace on the table.

Gods, Beau was glad to have him here. Elias understood. The prince didn't need to explain why he was raging one moment and sniveling or cackling or staring blankly into the ether the next. He didn't have to tell Elias how badly he wanted to be *good* and *right* and *proper* and at the same time how awfully all of those things chafed. There was no need to describe the dizzying cycle of grief and fury and panic and warm fondness and manic energy that Beau's mind spun through constantly. The guard just understood.

"Thank you," Beau said quietly.

Elias stood, rested a callused hand on Beau's for a moment, then crossed to the fireplace to poke the smoldering embers back to life again. "Any time, Highness."

NOT EVEN THE GOOD TALL TALES

If one more waiter offered him the godsdamned champagne tray, Beau was going to lose his entire mind.

It was bad enough to be wearing itchy new clothing, stiff with embroidery, sweating through layers of fabric in this too-warm, too-loud room. Even worse to be confronted by lady after lady with cunning light in her eyes and a fake smile plastered across her mouth, each introducing herself with grating mock-humility and elaborate curtsies. Adding to all of that the insult of the constant temptation to drown his sorrows was too much.

A woman approached, his age or slightly older, her dark hair piled so precariously on her head he wondered how it didn't topple off as she swayed closer. In his mind, he ran through the portrait cards his decorum tutor was making him study in excruciating detail until he matched one to her pretty face. "Lady Roben," he muttered to himself. She was on the short list of marriage contenders.

"Your Highness," she said, dropping into the deepest curtsy of the night, her long neck bending in a way that reminded him strongly of a water bird. "Lord Arshakuni told me I simply must ask you about your time on a merchant ship. Is it true you were accosted by pirates?"

Beau bit down on a sigh. This made the fourth version of that question tonight, not to mention the number of times he'd retold the tale at the last three balls. But she couldn't have known that. It must be the only interesting story to make its way off the isles. At least she wasn't talking about the weather or the ball itself or any other inane small talk.

Summoning a smile, he said, "Yes, I sailed on the *Siren's Lament* for several months. It wasn't quite the adventure people imagine, but it was honest work and I learned a lot. We were boarded by pirates as we passed through the Evenstar Strait and had to fight them off."

She gasped with the theatrics of a trained actress, and Beau fought heroically against a smirk. "Was it terribly frightening?"

"It wasn't exactly a lounge in a hot spring," he said dryly. He lifted his left arm, showing her the pink scar along his thumb that traced up the outside of his forearm. He pointed, too, at the top edge of the scar peeking above the collar of his coat along his neck. "I'd been in the captain's quarters. I was late to the fight. A member of the boarding party gave me a few good swipes, as you can see. But I prevailed in the end."

The now-well-practiced summary. No need to get into the gory details of how many people he'd had to kill; how deep the blade had cut into the meat of his shoulder to chip his shoulder blade; the screaming as the cook sewed him back up, sprawled on his face on a galley table with a wooden spoon between his teeth; the unceremonious dumping of the dead off the sides of the ship when the wounded had been tended; the detached horror of swabbing up blood and bits of flesh off the deck. They didn't want to hear those things. They wanted just enough excitement in their small talk to flavor it, not enough realism to spoil the taste.

Talking about it always brought back the sound of the chain-and-bar shot from the oncoming ship as it tore through their rigging, and the feel of the captain's hands on him as he shoved Beau into his quarters and told him not to come out under any circumstances. Captain Ahirrim had raised the flag of no contest. Pirates would take their spoils from merchant ships and go; it didn't have to be a fight, and Ahirrim didn't want his crew killed.

But once they boarded, someone said 'prince.' And when the captain wouldn't hand Beau over to be ransomed to the crown, all hell broke loose. Beau couldn't bear it. He'd tried to give himself up, but by then the copper tang of blood was in the air and men slipped in their friends' entrails trying to reach their enemies. Beau knew how to fight with a sword; he'd been trained. But he'd hesitated when pirates spotted him. He tried to speak first, to surrender.

The cuts the pirate made in Beau's body hadn't even registered as pain at first, just cold shock. And when his sword rose to protect him by instinct, by training, flesh parted like silk. His hands twitched, remembering the force it took to slice through muscle, the twang of tendon snapping under a sword edge, the horrible, buzzing shock of hitting bone.

He'd killed at least four people. No one had given him the final count. The *Siren's Lament* sailed right back to the isles and put Beau off the ship, which was fine by him. He'd lost his taste for sea adventure. Lost his taste for all violence, in fact, and hired Elias to do his fighting for him not long after.

Lady Roben noticed the twitching of his fingers and smiled as though he'd done it on purpose to draw attention to them. "You must be an exceptional swordsman," she said, fluttering her eyelashes. He found the calculated flirting immensely off-putting. "I suppose the skill runs in the family. Prince Charmant was always happy to show off his bladecraft at my exhibitions—"

Her eyes widened slightly then, almost as if she hadn't meant to say that. But Beau was certain she weighed her words too carefully for a mention of his brother to have been accidental. Beau's pretense of a smile dropped, and he narrowed his eyes at her.

What was her game, exactly? Why bring up Char? Did she think to ingratiate herself to Beau by suggesting she'd been close with his brother? The idea that she could come over to him, a scant handful of months since his brother's death, and use Char's name to gain access to him prodded the prince into almost incandescent fury.

At that moment, a grey-robed waiter appeared at the prince's elbow with a tray. "Wine, Your Highness?"

Beau growled at the man in frustration before he checked himself. The waiter stumbled a step, trying to bow and back away hastily at the same time. Raising his hand as though he could physically smooth over his reaction, the prince said, "No, thank you. I don't want wine. *Please* don't send anyone else over here with wine!"

"Of—of course, Your Highness," the man said, ducking into another deep bow before fleeing with all haste and dignity.

"No wine?" Lady Roben sidled closer, dropping her voice like a co-conspirator. "From the stories I've heard of you, I'd never have expected to hear you turn down a glass of something as fine as what the Duchess of Untillia provides."

"You don't know anything at all about me, my lady," Beau said flatly, holding steady eye contact so she couldn't miss his seriousness. "Not even the good tall tales. Whatever you came over here to get from me, it seems unlikely you're going to get it."

She flushed pink, dropped her eyes, dipped into a much shallower curtsy, and fled.

Beau sighed, pinching the bridge of his nose in the hopes of preventing the building headache. Was this to be the rest of his life? Standing around meaningless, boring parties, conversing about nonsense with people he cared nothing about? *Married* to one of them?

Elias nudged him with an elbow, and Beau straightened, trying to look less bored and irritated. "I was under the impression you were attending balls to get to know the noblewomen who are *trying* to be nice to you," his First said under his breath. "Not to growl at anyone who got close like a feral dog."

"Maybe I should go full feral?" Beau whispered back. "Howl at the moon, bite a lord or two? At least then they'd have an interesting story for the next ball so they'll quit asking about the fucking ship."

"As much as I'd love to hear you explain the bite marks to His and Her Majesty, I don't think it would do much for your image of 'dutiful son doing his best to fall in love by season's end.' Undo your top buttons. You're always irritable when your clothes are too tight."

Beau nodded, loosened the neck of his shirt, and set off into the ballroom in search of someone—anyone—with whom he wouldn't mind dancing. Halfway through his circuit of the candle-lit grand hall, he caught a flash of beautiful fawn skin, a dark tumble of curls, and two deep brown eyes watching him with a cold, uneasy expression: Lady Penamour.

His feet stuttered to a halt. He'd spoken to her a handful of times in the lead-up to the wedding, always perfectly politely. Beau had managed to evade interactions with her at the previous balls, despite his mother's ham-handed attempts to shove him into conversation, but he'd already swung too close to her. If he changed course, it would be obvious he was avoiding her, and everyone was watching. He took a step closer, staring at the way her fine emerald silk skirts pooled on the floor around her.

Flicking a glance up at her, he offered a brief, polite smile. "Good evening, Your Grace." He should've said more, but his mind was empty of words that fit the shape of this silence.

She was a stunningly gorgeous woman, but so entirely un-approachable. He didn't remember her being that way before Char died. Her full lips pressed into a flat, tight line before opening to say, "Are you enjoying yourself, Your Highness?"

"Uh…" Beau half-laughed. "Sure." She watched him so intently, so unhappily. Had he done something to anger her? Was she upset he hadn't picked up his brother's pledge where Char had dropped it? "Are you?"

She flicked her head to toss her curls over her shoulder, and it made her nose ring flash. That was interesting; he hadn't seen many other ladies with piercings anywhere but their ears. "The Duchess of Untillia throws a beautiful event." It didn't really answer his question, but perhaps the unhappiness of her face was answer enough.

"Would you care to dance?"

Now where the *fuck* had that come from? His mind scrambled for a reason his mouth might have formed those words, but by then it was too late to call them back. Belatedly, he bowed his head and extended a hand in offer.

Her face tightened, hardened—not from fear or anger, but a skepticism so deep it almost made him doubt his own intentions. Despite the expression, her voice was honey and smoke as she said, "Of course, Your Highness. I would be honored."

Something about the combination of sultry voice and the elegance of her hand as she set it on his made him wish she was someone other than his brother's fiancée, the savvy politician and frigid conversational partner.

He guided her to the dance floor as a new song began and stifled a sigh. This particular dance had fussy steps, and he and the lady would only be within speaking distance every two or three turns. He missed dancing at The Powdered Hops on the isles, swinging people around, clapping, the genuine delight when the musicians played an old favorite. No steps to memorize, no rigid forms, just taking hold of a partner and twirling.

He'd give his left hand to dance that way with someone who looked like Lady Penamour.

Not *her*, of course. Not the most intimidating woman in the kingdom, who'd been engaged to his brother. But someone who looked like her.

They began a foot or so apart with a low bow and a curtsy, which she twirled gracefully out of as the music picked up. Beau's part had him making a statelier turn in place, the anchor she'd return to, so he was able to watch her and plan what he intended to say. He hadn't quite decided when Lady Penamour spoke first.

"I'm curious, Your Highness," she said as their turns brought them closer. "What have I done to tick to the top of your list of obligatory dances this evening?"

Beau's head cocked to the side. In a sea of dishonesty and pretense, here was someone who said exactly what she meant—albeit with open disdain for him. The dance swung them away from each other, circling around another pair of dancers before they returned face-to-face. "It was happy happenstance. You see, I was in the mood for something genuine," he said, smirking into her distrusting brown eyes. "And here I've found very honest dislike for me. Would it be too presumptuous of me to ask the cause?"

She blinked, brows drawing down like he'd confused her. The music carried them through the steps, and they each lifted a hand to almost touch, his left hand mirroring the motions of her right. They rotated in place, and his fingertips buzzed strangely where he didn't quite touch her.

Then she turned her face away and the dance spun her around another couple again, and he had to watch his own step to avoid collisions on his circuit.

"Does the interest and admiration of the entire court bore you so much?" Lady Penamour said, speaking before they were quite close enough. Again, they lifted their hands, though now they did touch, the back of her hand resting against the back of his as they turned. He was hyper aware of the smoothness and warmth of her skin against his knuckles.

"Only their scheming and dishonesty. I prefer to be openly despised over false kindness."

Her smile held syrupy sweetness. "I'm always happy to oblige."

"What have I—" His question cut off as they spun away again, more quickly this time, two couples sweeping in between them. Beau rushed his steps to get back to her and say, "What have I done to you, Lady Penamour? We barely even had a chance to speak during the wedding preparations, and we haven't said a word to each other since Char—"

"*Don't.*" The word came out harsh. Swept away by the dance, Lady Penamour visibly braced herself, jaw tight as she ground her teeth. Why was she on guard with him?

It was their turn now to dance as a unit, bowling through the other couples on the floor. As soon as she was in reach, Beau set a gentle hand on the lady's hip, extending his other hand for her to rest her fingers on; instead, she gripped it like an iron vise, and the hand on his shoulder could've been trying to break his collarbone for all the pressure she used.

He danced her through the couples, eyes mostly on her, since he knew the others would be twirling out of their way. "Will you answer a question for me honestly, Your Grace?"

"If you answer one of mine in return," she said, eyes cold. She didn't need to watch what went on around her, since he led; she could stare into his soul, weighing and measuring.

"A fair trade," he said, looking up to make their turn at the corner. He lifted her hand to turn her, and she obediently spun in his arms, resettling with no loosening of her grip as they swept back to the other side of the room. "Your hatred of me…do you associate me with my brother's death? Or resent me because I lived and he died? Is it something else?"

An emotion, dark and raw, passed over her face, curling her lip—grief or scorn or disgust, he couldn't say. "I…" Her voice grew husky as she said, "I do *associate* you with your brother's death, yes."

They reached the opposite corner and Beau released her. She sprang away, trading curtsies with the ladies dancing on either side of her. The three of them rotated in their own ring while Beau danced a few steps with the men. Eyes on her, he flubbed the forms.

When she returned to him, they raised both hands and stood palm to palm—so *hot*, the air between their hands—in a line alongside all the other dancers. The whole group took mincing steps sideways, bouncing on every third beat.

"My question now," she said, and Beau nodded.

With quiet, burning intensity, she asked, "Now you've gotten Charmant out of the way, do you have everything you wanted?"

Her eyes bore into him like augers, and Beau stumbled back a step, breaking the line of dancers. Each word struck him like thrown rocks. Stunned into stillness, he became an inconvenient island in the dance, couples edging around him uneasily or breaking away altogether as they watched to see what was the matter.

Lady Penamour danced on as if she'd said nothing, but she watched him. He couldn't breathe. A whole storm of grief thundered its way onto his face.

Is that truly what she thought of him? That he'd be pleased his brother was dead? That he wanted a throne more than he wanted Char beside him? Or…the words played back to him: *now you've gotten Charmant out of the way.* Did she think he'd had something to do with Char's death? How *could* he have? It was an accident. Going hawking hadn't even been Beau's idea; it'd been Char's, and the other nobles who'd gone along had seemed pleased enough, until Char slid out of his saddle and his neck made that sound, that awful sound.

He was going to be sick.

Elias stepped onto the floor, concern writ all over his face, but Beau waved him away. This was already turning into a spectacle. He tried to pull himself together.

As the dance trickled past him again going the other way, he stepped into the gap in line and put his shaking hands against Lady Penamour's slightly damp palms. In a strangled voice, Beau said, "Char's death took absolutely everything from me, Lady Penamour. If there were any way to trade places with him, I would."

Her eyes narrowed, suspicion alight in every curve and feature of her face. He couldn't bear to see her not believe him, to see her think he'd manufacture public grief and privately rejoice in the loss of Granvallée's best and brightest son.

Thank the gods the dance was winding down. He made his bow and fled the floor, sensing Elias's return to his shadow. He didn't stop and say his goodbyes to the hostess, didn't meet anyone's eyes as he marched down the drive.

A footman sprinted ahead, trying to bring his carriage up before he reached it, but it met him only a few feet from where it'd been parked.

"Take me home, El," he said to the guard as the carriage began to move.

"We're headed that way."

Beau shook his head. Not to the palace. Not to the soulless, empty rooms full of expensive shit from all over the world. Not to the whispers and lies and scheming and bowing and belief that Beau had wanted his brother dead so he could snatch a fucking crown.

Elias switched seats to crowd in next to Beau, shoulder to shoulder, hip to hip. He was so steady, so solid. It took every scrap of energy and will Beau had left not to rest his head on El's shoulder. That was too intimate; not his right. Instead, he drew strength from the quiet reassurance Elias's presence always gave: *I'm here, I'm never leaving, and I will protect you.*

"Do you think I'm secretly happy Char is dead?" Beau asked, needing to hear Elias's steady, solid answer.

Elias breathed out sharply, a quiet scoff. "No, I don't think you're 'secretly' anything. You loved your brother. You grieve his loss. And you grieve the life you would've had, had he lived. Anyone who believes otherwise simply doesn't know you."

"Take me back in time," Beau said, hardly loud enough to be heard over the noise of the carriage. "Put me on his horse instead."

"No." Elias's refusal was so firm it felt like a rebuke. "Not even in your imagination, Highness. You were meant to live. You were meant to lead. Even if it breaks your heart to be the one to do it, you're going to make this kingdom better than it was."

Beau closed his eyes and tried to soak in Elias's belief. But all he could hear were those baffling, hateful words again and again: *you've gotten Charmant out of the way.*

3

RUFFLING FEATHERS

B eau staggered under the weight of yet another folio of notes stacked in his arms. "Was Char really responsible for all of this?"

His father raised an eyebrow at Beau before licking his finger and shuffling through the stack of papers in his hand. "No," he said absently, "some of those are the things you were managing by correspondence and haven't touched since Char died. The mourning period is over; take care of your business."

Beau scowled down at the stack. He didn't recall managing *anything* by correspondence. He'd sent exactly one letter from the isles, a short explanation to his brother of why he'd left and wouldn't be coming back, to which Char hadn't replied; Beau had hoped to be entirely forgotten. Dreading the lecture he'd receive from his father if he asked, Beau elected to investigate the stack for himself. Hefting it higher in his arms, he carried it to the long table in his parents' sunroom. Elias trailed behind and caught the papers that spilled across the table.

With a heavy sigh, Beau settled into a chair and pulled sheaves of notes into heaps he could sift through. He threw a pleading look up at his guard. After a quick glance toward the king's desk, out of sight, El sat next to him, wordlessly lifting a few to read.

Petitions for marriage licenses from minor nobles, commissions for statuary in the capital, inventory lists of dinnerware or horse tack, detailed reports from ambassadors or spies in foreign courts—the papers were wildly varied and invariably dull. And there were so, so many.

Beau sorted as best as he could, but Elias had to recall him multiple times from staring blankly at the far wall instead of reading. He scrawled a signature at the bottom of each as he finished reviewing it and gradually built a teetering stack. None of it was remotely familiar, and an anxious stomachache grew by the minute as he wondered whether he'd been *supposed* to manage these things for years, and they'd piled up somewhere, waiting to be discovered.

In desperation, he ducked his head back into his father's office. "Why isn't this being done by your army of scribes and secretaries? Couldn't Dormont or Ferrial have reviewed these?" They were the seneschal and the pursekeeper, respectively—surely better eyes on these papers than Beau's. And if there was a shameful backlog somewhere, *they* could handle it.

King Fortin set his pen down with a sharp snap, sighing noisily. "Playing the idiot will not get you out of a crown prince's responsibility, Beauregard."

Beau bit the inside of his cheek, his questions sticking immovably in his throat, but when his father looked up and saw Beau looked genuinely confused, his anger sharpened. "Are you incapable of intelligent thought? These *are* the compiled reports of those people. They manage the day-to-day. All that's asked of you is to occasionally review their reports to keep people honest and hold them to the royal standard. Can you be trusted with *one godsdamned responsibility*, Beau?"

Beau shrank. "Yes, I'll handle it."

When he fled back to the table, he could only stare incredulously down at the documents spread before him. Reviewing everything happening in the capital city alone would employ his every waking hour if the reports were always this robust. How would he ever hope to look beyond the palace and know anything of what happened in his nobles' holdings, or in their neighboring kingdoms? More urgently, how could he avoid dying of pure tedium?

Elias gently shook his elbow to bring him out of his maudlin, spiraling thoughts, a faint smirk on his handsome face. "It won't always be this much. I'm sure it's piled up in your brother's absence."

Swallowing hard, Beau nodded. "I'm going to put out my own eyes if I have to read this many lines of numbers every day for the rest of my life."

The guard exhaled an almost-laugh through his nose. Beau wished they weren't in the royal apartments. Normally, El would've been cracking jokes, maybe doing a dramatic reading of a report to shake Beau out of boredom and refocus him. Here, though, he was on his best behavior, keeping a proper stoic distance like the First of the king's flight, who'd been standing still as furniture against the wall since Beau entered the room. He could've been a corpse.

"Beau," the king said as he stood and lifted his crown from its velvet-lined shelf, "it's time to hold court. I'll have the rest of the papers delivered to your study."

"*Wonderful,*" Beau said dryly. "I wouldn't want to miss a moment of this."

The prince and king swept out ahead of their Firsts, each picking up a second guard from outside the door as they walked. It was Oria who accompanied Beau today. He knew from the aura of her disapproval, so heavy the air smelled of it. He wasn't sure if it truly got stronger each day or if that was his imagination.

Many lords and ladies were already arrayed in pairs and chattering knots throughout the half-moon of the petitioner's chamber when the king and prince entered. A few more straggled in, taking pains not to seem to rush, as the clock tower began to ring its mid-afternoon chime.

Six weeks of this so far, six court sessions, and Beau was still running through the portrait cards in his head to match names to faces. He tried to find the most powerful people.

There, Lord Courdur, Duke of Suteneir, speaking sternly with his eldest son in the corner while his wife and Lady Macabrie swanned through the center of the room like this was their hall, their palace. Lord Macabrie, Duke of Arbrefront, laughed with two marquesses from his holding and a man who hovered obsequiously like a poor relation. Lord Lamont, Duke of Estforet, had cornered Lady Andremiere, who was technically *not* the Duchess of Untillia since she was widowed, but everyone called her that while she served as regent for her grandson until he was out of leading strings.

And of course, Lady Penamour, who was giving a man Beau couldn't name the most charming smile, touching his arm lightly with her fingertips as she leaned in to speak. She wore a purple gown today with an iridescence that caught the light with every movement, and Beau stared for much longer than he could justify before his father waved for those gathered to take their seats and eased himself onto his carved wooden throne.

Beau hesitated between taking the seat on his father's right, where custom indicated he ought to sit, and the one on the left where he'd have a decent view of one of the gardens through a narrow window. Every now and then, a gardener would walk through and prune flowers, and on occasion, birds or butterflies would be visible through that window.

Elias moved to stand behind the chair on the right, ending Beau's wistful longing for anything other than this room to pay attention to. The slight roll of the guard's eyes as Beau passed him to sit said Elias knew perfectly well what was going through his head.

With a simple raise of his hand, King Fortin began the audience, and arguments rose. In theory, there were rules to formal court hearings. Nobles were to submit their requests to be queued by the bailiff and present their claims one by one, holding the floor until the king delivered judgment or requested opinions from others.

In practice, it was rare for any lord or lady to speak more than two sentences together without another noble standing and saying,

"If I may intercede, Your Majesty," and launching into a speech on whatever need of their own was most related.

His father let them verbally trample over one another until Beau could hardly understand a word. The hum of their nonsense was soporific, and the prince fought hard not to yawn.

"—up to our ears in Paibons along the entire border. They've *destroyed* my grape harvest. What am I to do without my vineyards?" This came from Lord Courdur, whose intensity made his square-jawed face and sharp, dark eyes seem to burn from the inside. He spoke in a way that suggested he couldn't be interrupted and couldn't be disobeyed, much like Beau's father.

Nevertheless, Beau raised his hand to interrupt and was pleasantly surprised when the room fell silent.

"Lord Courdur," he said, shifting in his seat to avoid the sharp glances from his father, "are you speaking literally when you say these raids are happening along your *entire* stretch of the border with Paibona? Your lands cover nearly seventy leagues of it, if I recall." *If I recall from last week, when I learned that,* Beau thought, faintly amused that they were letting an imposter like himself speak in this room at all.

Courdur's chin rose, whether from pride at the size of his duchy or offense at being questioned, his blank face gave no hint. "Yes, Your Highness. Just over half the border, and every inch of it under constant, needling attack."

"How are you protecting your people?"

The silence in the room deepened, broken by the rustle of silks as nobles shifted uncomfortably. Beau caught Lady Penamour's eyes in the audience and his stomach jolted at how intently she was staring at him. No one attempted to interrupt Lord Courdur as he frowned and said, "I'm not quite sure what you mean."

"You've come seeking recompense from the crown for your grapes?" Beau said. "I assume that means you've already called your liegemen to arms and found a way for your outlying farms and villages to signal need for aid. You've already emptied your coffers to ensure their crops and livestock are replaced or that they have alternative ways to acquire food? If all you need from the crown is help with your vineyards, you've done incredible work protecting the rest of your holding. Not many could do so well. Please, share it with us, so other peers can follow your example."

The question had begun in earnest—Beau was truly curious how he could protect such a large stretch of border, even with the usually peaceful Paibons on the other side—but as the man's face grew colder and stonier, Beau's voice hardened. Lady Roben, Marchioness of Monteilais, the march in Courdur's duchy that would've taken the brunt of these attacks, shifted in her seat, mouth falling slightly open as she stared Beau down, but she said nothing.

Lord Courdur's eyes swept over the rest of the petitioners as though looking to see who found this as ridiculous as he did, and he did meet quite a few concerned and sympathetic faces.

"Your Highness," he said, infusing the title with gritted-teeth patience, as though Beau were a rude child on the edge of a tantrum, "I can hardly be expected to pay for every stray chicken and bad harvest in my lands. I'd be a pauper in a week."

Beau took a deep breath, preparing to say something scathing, but the faint pressure of Elias's fingers against his shoulder reminded him to rein himself in. "It's clear we need to speak to Queen Almeida about how seriously we're taking her people's aggression at the border. In the meantime, if direct aid is too onerous, you'll at the very least refrain from collecting taxes this season."

Murmurs susurrated through the room, and Lord Courdur's eyes went wide, then narrowed again dangerously. Behind him, Lady Roben and Lady Penamour exchanged surprised, silent glances. The king pressed his steepled fingers to his face to hide his mouth as he said, "*Beauregard*," in a low, warning hiss.

Incensed, Beau scowled at his father, then at Courdur. How could anyone think *he* was the unreasonable one? This man was charged with the care of the people on his land, the largest duchy in Granvallée. If he was going to stand aside and let their livelihoods be wrecked without lifting so much as a silver penny, the least he could do was not add to their misery.

He studied Courdur for a moment, wondering whether it was wise to voice his thoughts and ratchet up the tension in the room further. *Perhaps if I keep this up, Father will ban me from these gods-awful court sessions altogether.*

A thought occurred to him, and he tried to relax his face out of its scowl. "What would the loss be, Your Grace, if you forewent tax collection in the affected areas for this season?"

"Nearly ten thousand dorin," Courdur growled.

Rushing so his father couldn't interject and redirect the conversation, Beau asked, "My brother would typically hold summer court at your castle, wouldn't he?"

Courdur blinked, his commanding confidence shaken by the change of the wind. "Yes? For the last eight years."

"Were you planning to host the court this summer as well?"

Pursing his lips in thought, Courdur spoke slowly, verbally edging a foot forward in search of traps. "Yes, even with His Highness's tragic demise, I thought it prudent to ensure we were prepared in case you wanted to continue the tradition."

"Quite an honor, hosting the court. And no small cost, I imagine. How much do those few weeks set you back?"

Courdur's face was hard as flint as he sensed the snare pulling tight around his ankles. He looked to Beau's father to speak, but Fortin was watching Beau, eyes narrowed, not looking out at the crowd of nobles. "I don't have those figures in front of me, Your Highness," Courdur said dismissively. "I couldn't say for certain, and it's not relevant to the matter I brought—"

Beau ignored him, sitting tall enough to see Ferrial, the purse-keeper, at the back. The man lifted his long, narrow nose from his dutiful note-taking and met the prince's eyes. "Master Ferrial, what would you estimate the cost of hosting the summer court to be?"

The man scratched idly at his brow with a dexterous finger before saying in his dry, matter-of-fact tone, "It couldn't be less than fifteen thousand dorin, Your Highness. I'd wager closer to twenty."

Beau struggled to keep the smugness off his face. "Well, I have the perfect solution, Lord Courdur. The court will suffer the minor loss of a change of scenery and spend the summer right here. The cost I've just saved you should more than make up for the taxes you're not going to levy." When the man started to protest, Beauregard rolled right over him, saying, "Ah, yes, of course, you'll already have spent some of it to stockpile supplies ahead of our arrival. Perfect for distributing to those tenants who've borne a loss as a result of these skirmishes."

Courdur opened his mouth, closed it again, and turned the full force of his glare on King Fortin. Beau swallowed as the king cleared his throat before he spoke, brow creased in thought. The burning anger in his eyes when they cut over to Beau said he was prepared to undo everything his wayward son had done.

"A very neat solution, Lord Courdur," Lady Penamour said, and Lady Roben nodded intently beside her. "Should you need any help with the distribution, my sister was already planning a trip to Suteneir in the next few weeks. I can send hands with her."

The king's eyes flashed, then softened. To Courdur, he said, "Give the pursekeeper a good account of your vineyards' losses, and we'll address that as well."

Beau exhaled in relief, and Elias's fingers nudged him again, this time in congratulations. The session continued without issue. In fact, many of the nobles ceded the floor when their turn came, perhaps fearing Prince Beauregard's attention would turn to them.

Fortin called an early end, stepping down to chat with dukes, marquesses, and counts, smoothing feathers. Beauregard made his escape before anyone could capture him in conversation.

"I see you kept your mind with you today, Highness," Elias said as Oria joined them. "I've been wondering if something about the air of the petitioners' chamber caused it to wander off."

Beau laughed, then chuckled even harder at Oria's scandalized expression. "I'm sure Courdur would prefer it had taken its usual stroll in the gardens."

"He did not seem best pleased," Elias agreed, exchanging a glance with Oria, who nodded and tapped her sword in response to his silent question. "Back to your study for paperwork?"

The prince's sigh started in his toes. "Ugh, Watchers take me."

Elias's gait stuttered slightly as he missed a step. "What?"

"Oh, something Char and I used to say when we wanted to be elsewhere." Beau waved a dismissive hand. "He made up this secret society when we were kids, 'the Watchers,' to scare me. Said if I wasn't good, the Watchers would take me away." He chuckled.

He hadn't thought about that in a very long time. Being in the palace brought peculiar things back.

"Hmm," Elias said in response, picking up his pace again. "Kids are funny."

A flash of shimmering violet silk turned the corner ahead of them, and Beau jogged to catch up, calling, "Lady Penamour? A moment, please?"

She stood stiffly in the hall when he turned the corner, as if she'd frozen exactly where she was when he called. "Can I help you, Your Highness?" she asked, the cords in her neck tight.

"I wanted to thank you for speaking up in the hall." Beau stopped a few paces from her, since his proximity drew her even tighter. "Your offer of aid softened the edges of my proposal. I doubt we'd have landed on something so beneficial without your help."

"I didn't do it to help you." Her scowl was scathing. "My mother was a Courdur. She would want her people protected."

"Oh," Beau said. She'd worn a different nose ring today, this one lined with amethysts to match her dress. It sparkled when she turned away from him to look up the hall. "Well, regardless, thank you. If there's anything I can—"

"There is," she said too abruptly, then cleared her throat. "There is something I need from you. I went to Master Dormont first, but he told me that since you're back in the palace, these requests have to go through you."

"I'm intrigued."

Penamour opened a dark leather folio and pulled out a sheet of paper, which she handed over reluctantly. Beau read aloud, "'Formal request for the loan of one Maurilel relic'—how could I possibly give you a Maurilel relic?"

Everyone in the capital knew, of course, about the palace clock tower, powered by ancient magic that kept it steadily chiming with no maintenance, no winding. Very few other artifacts remained from the Maurilel civilization built on the now-lost secrets of magic. The only ones Beau knew of were the unadorned rings his mother and father wore: twin items of power that allowed them to sense each other's emotions. Magic was a mystery that had fascinated him as a kid, but even a prince didn't have opportunity to play with it.

The duchess bristled and snatched the paper back, cheeks reddening. "You might've at least read the request to the bottom before rejecting it. I'm sorry to have taken—"

"Wait, *wait*. I'm not rejecting the request, Your Grace." He tried to take the paper back from her without grabbing her arm to hold it still. "I just don't know what you're asking for. Does Dormont think I have some secret stash of magic artifacts?"

She went still, eyes dark with suspicion, and he was able to pluck the request letter from her fingers. "From the vault," she said, as though it were painfully obvious. "Don't play the fool with me, Your Highness. I don't have the time or patience for it. I need that relic urgently."

Beau scanned the entirety of the page and pulled at his lower lip in thought. "Of course, the vault," he said vaguely. "I'll do what I can for you, Lady Penamour."

She opened her mouth to say more, then snapped it shut audibly and gave a cursory curtsy. "Good day, Your Highness." She swept away before he could respond at all, and Beau stood bewildered in the corridor with his guards.

Her letter requested a Bounty Flask, which meant nothing to him. But the idea of hunting down a piece of magic in a vault *full* of magic somewhere in his palace was infinitely preferable to more paperwork. He changed course, heading toward Dormont's office.

"We have a great deal to do today, Highness." Elias's voice was strained. "Perhaps detours to visit magical relics could wait?"

"You heard her. She needs this artifact *urgently*. And you never know; maybe there's something in the vault that can do paperwork for me?" His steps grew lighter the further from his rooms and the waiting stacks he walked.

Dormont was easy enough to find, though he seemed surprised to have an office visit from the crown prince. Looking harried, he unlocked several nested drawers and produced a very large key ring, which he hastily shoved in his pocket before gesturing for the prince to precede him into the hall.

Despite his clear vexation at the interruption, he was cordial enough in leading Beau, Elias, and Oria to the vault. In the center of the palace, two floors below ground, an unassuming door was set into a recess in the wall. Patting his glistening brow with a handkerchief, the seneschal gestured for the prince and his retinue to stop a few feet from the door.

"When we pass through, we will have to leave some of the vault's security magics open, awaiting our return," Dormont said in a crisp, patient voice. "I would recommend your flight remain here to guard against any followers."

"Oria, stay here and watch our backs, please." When she flicked her gaze to the other guard, Beau said, "Will you need Elias's assistance with that?"

She narrowed her eyes slightly. "No, Your Highness, I can manage alone."

With a single nod, the seneschal lifted the ring of three keys.

The first was heavy brass like many others in the palace, but the other two were strange: one, all rose-colored filigree, put off more light than it could possibly catch and reflect in this subterranean hall, and the other was made of something like sea glass.

Dormont put the brass key in the brass lock and turned it with a thunk, swinging the heavy door in. When Elias stepped past the seneschal, alert, Dormont said, "We do not make a habit, master guardsman, of locking people into our vaults."

Elias didn't turn away from his perusal of the small room beyond the door as he said, "I will do my job, and you will do yours."

"Just so," Dormont acquiesced, letting Beau past him and shutting the door behind. He glided past to lead again, pulled the rose-gold key off the ring, and hesitated. "Your Highness, I will next show you how to take down the Rose Ward. Anyone who knows the pattern and has access to the key may do this, so I must ask—do you trust your guardsman to learn it as well?"

Beau almost laughed. "Of course."

Dormont pursed his lips, but gave his efficient single nod again and began tracing a pattern onto the wood door before them, carved with a simple grid of squares about the size of Beau's palm. Each one he touched with the key glowed and smoldered like coals. When the last one lit, a keyhole burned itself into the center of the door, flames licking bright up the wood.

The seneschal seemed quite unbothered by the fire, sticking the key—and his fingers—in to turn the lock. As soon as the door swung open, the flames guttered out, though the surface remained charred. Dormont left the key in the lock, and as he waited for Elias to do his usual checks, Beau recounted the steps of the pattern in his head, muttering under his breath and tracing the line in the air with his fingers to solidify it in his memory.

"Clear, Highness," Elias called, and Beau followed them into the next chamber, where Dormont stood before a beautiful, twelve-foot-tall entrance made of semi-translucent, multicolored crystal. Its opalescent surface flowed as he looked at it, more curtain than door.

He breathed out a, "wow," and reached to touch it. It *begged* to be touched. He wondered if it felt as smooth and cool as it looked. The seneschal laid a light restraining hand on the prince's arm. "This door demands a price of blood, Your Highness. I do not recommend giving it more than it requires by touching the door itself."

Beau withdrew his fingers, though the call to stroke the ever-changing face of the door didn't die away. "A price of blood?" He was unable to tear his eyes from the gentle prismatic shifts.

"Each who passes must pay a small ransom of blood—very little, but enough for the door to recognize and remember." The seneschal rolled one sleeve of his jacket to the elbow with careful, precise folds. Then he lifted the pale green, glass-like key and pressed the teeth, sharpened to a razor's edge, to his forearm. He made a tiny cut, barely enough to bleed, and then lifted the key again.

For a moment, blood smeared the sharp edge, and then, like rainwater drunk down by thirsty earth, the blood sank into the pale glass. Dormont tilted the key, and the blood moved within it as if it were hollow, a dark bead rolling back and forth.

Then the seneschal handed Beau the key.

Immediately, Beau's chest tightened with anxiety. The key was not a razor or a knife, but it nevertheless felt familiar in his hands as he shoved his sleeve back and held the key over his skin, already traced with faint, practically invisible lines of scars. He bit his lip; he was past this. He didn't hurt himself anymore, but as illogical as it was, he was terribly afraid this key would make him pick up the habit again. The possibility yawned in front of him like a chasm.

Frowning, Elias plucked the key from Beau's fingers. He took Beau's arm in one warm hand and made the tiniest cut, hardly a nick. Again, the key swallowed the drop of blood whole, and Elias swiped it along his own arm less carefully. He returned the key to the seneschal and ran his eyes over Beau, who smiled gratefully.

Dormont accepted the key without comment. Then he nodded once more and held the key at full extension from his body, the bow pinched between forefinger and thumb, inching it forward until it brushed against the surface of the door.

Suddenly fluid, the opalescent barrier lapped over the key, drawing it in and rippling with vivid, violent color before calming again. It didn't open. Instead, it dropped from the ceiling like a torrent of water, splashing to the floor. All three of them leapt back to avoid being touched by it before it pooled and seeped into the stones beneath their feet. All that was left was the key, resting innocently on the floor.

"Touching that again will cause the gate to reseal," the seneschal said, waving a hand toward the now-open walkway. "I will wait here for your return."

"Thank you, Master Dormont," Beau said, fascinated by the magic on display in this vault entrance, more wonders than he'd ever seen. Finding Maurilel magic intact was a rare thing; kingdoms scraped and gathered whatever artifacts existed, hoarding them. So many people in Granvallée traveled to the capital just to lay eyes on the clock tower so they could tell their children and grandchildren they'd seen it. To have *touched* magic sent a thrill of excitement through Beau that buoyed him as they left the key behind and delved further into the vault.

Preceded as always by Elias, Beau marveled at the tiny glass globes set into the walls as they lit before them: more Maurilel sorcery. His heart pounded in anticipation of what more would be found down here. How many miracles could this vault hold?

There was a faint hum in the air as they walked, and it buzzed in his chest, throwing off the rhythm of his breath. He felt heat gather in his torso, in his arms, in his hands, a strange warmth like he was absorbing the ambient magic. When the hallway opened into a large room, low-ceilinged and lined with shelves around all four walls, Beau lurched in excitedly.

He stopped, frowning. The shelves were empty.

"What?" he said aloud, turning on his heel. Though there were three, four, or sometimes five shelves running the full length of each wall—enough to store hundreds of artifacts—nothing sat on most of them but dust and scraps of paper.

Elias frowned intently at the walls with a concern that bordered anger more than confusion. "Seems a bit large for five items, doesn't it?"

Blinking, Beau followed Elias's gaze to the small cache of objects. On a shoulder-height shelf set into the same wall as the doorway sat a small butterfly pin, a clear glass orb wrapped in gold wire, a beaten tin cup, a gaudy green-stone pendant shaped like a bird in flight on a thick chain, and a single, large feather which, while it looked to be natural, proved on closer inspection to be made of unbelievably finely carved stone.

Any one of them could've fit neatly into Beau's hand, and the five together formed an unimpressive line in the too-large space.

The prince picked up the small piece of paper next to the butterfly pin. "The Deceptive Brooch," he read, "with which the wearer can alter their appearance at will." That was interesting. He picked up the next card. "The Orb of Tethering: sustains life alongside a committed partner." The other cards all read "Designation & Usage Unknown."

He did another spin, scanning all the shelves. "Is this really it? Two artifacts, three fancy knick-knacks with no known use, and a bunch of dust?" He picked up the tin cup, which didn't look magical at all. It looked barely serviceable as a cup. "Any chance this is the 'Bounty Flask'? I don't see anything else that might fit the bill."

His First gave the cup a doubtful look, but Beau pocketed it anyway. Elias picked up the butterfly and turned it over in his hand, examining every inch. He claimed the card Beau had left, reading smaller text on the back the prince hadn't noticed.

Beauregard studied the empty shelves intently, running his fingers along them to find places where the thick dust was lighter in circles or squares, like something had been removed.

Leaving Elias to his detailed perusal of the objects, Beau ducked back out to the seneschal. "Master Dormont," he said, "is there an inventory of all the artifacts that belong in the vault? I'd like to see if we've moved some things elsewhere or lent them out."

"Lent them?" Dormont said, incredulity cracking his calm facade. "Not likely. Half our trade bargains were struck favorably because we had the threat of that stockpile behind us. No other kingdom can boast even a quarter as many artifacts."

Beau blinked, swallowed. Something clearly wasn't right here. "Do you often go in there to clean up, do inventory and the like?"

"Oh no," the seneschal said, shaking his head. "No one but the royal family in the vault, unless they're specifically invited by a royal, as your guard was. I'm sorry if it's dusty—no servants in and out. Your brother had the keys, but I imagine he didn't come down either, since the vault was yours to manage."

Beau's chest vibrated like a struck gong. Another task that had been expected of him and not done. "Mine?" he asked, words choked by his heart in his throat. "The vault was my responsibility? Oh. Okay."

So it was Beau's fault the stockpile of relics they depended on was gone. Wonderful.

Elias reemerged, face neutral, and they maneuvered away from the vault silently as Beau's mind raced. They exited as they'd entered, the seneschal reapplying the wards behind them. When they reached the hall, he set the keys in Beau's hand, bowed, and left.

Bouncing the keyring in his palm, Beau tried not to look as uneasy as he felt. With Oria looking on, he drew Elias out of earshot and said, "Okay, the question of the hour: how bad did I fuck up and *who* do I tell that all our magical artifacts seem to be missing?"

Elias shook his head. "It's up to you, Highness, but if *I* were in your shoes, I think I'd keep it to myself until I knew more."

Beau nodded, a breathy laugh escaping him. "You have high hopes of my actually knowing more eventually."

"Or high hopes for you being able to keep your mouth shut indefinitely," Elias said lightly. "We should leave. Oria's concerned."

Beau nodded. "Paperwork awaits," he said airily at a more normal volume. "We'll just, uh, swing by Lady Penamour's apartments and see if this is what she needs."

A servant directed them to the duchess's palace apartments. When he knocked, a woman in loose trousers and long tunic with several braids converging into a single plait answered the door. "Is Lady Penamour in?" Beau asked. "I'd like to talk about her request."

The woman bent her head and said, "The duchess doesn't wish to be disturbed this evening, Your Highness. I can take a message—"

"No, Nilah, I'll talk to him," Lady Penamour said, appearing behind the woman. "Was something unclear in my request?"

"Not unclear, no. Could I come in? I'd rather not discuss it in the hall." Beau saw Elias's concerned eye flick and returned a small gesture of calm; he wouldn't mention the missing items.

The duchess studied him and then his guards for a moment before nodding and stepping aside to allow him in. Elias entered first, as always. The receiving area was not large or ostentatious, but the decor was luxurious and feminine and distinctly different from what Beau had seen in any part of the palace. Plush rugs in rich colors made him want to take his boots off and dig his toes in; when Lady Penamour turned to lead them into her parlor, he saw a flash of bare foot and realized she'd done exactly that.

"I went to the vault," he said. "But—"

"What, already?" she interrupted. Why did that cloud of suspicion always darken her face? *Now you've gotten Charmant out of the way...*

"You said you needed it urgently, didn't you?" He tried to keep his voice light. Nilah and Penamour watched him as though he were going to leap at them with a knife, and it made him hyperconscious of every move. "The artifacts were not as well labeled as I might've hoped. I wasn't able to find anything called a Bounty Flask."

Her frown deepened. "Then where is it? The inventory records in the archives listed it in the vault as recently as twenty years ago. So few artifacts are moved, and the Bounty Flask isn't one I would've expected to be used in that time."

Beau shrugged, debating how much of his ignorance to show. "I don't know. I'm still trying to get a handle on everything I'm responsible for now. It all changed so suddenly when Char died."

Char's death was absolutely the wrong thing to mention; Penamour shut down, so cold the air between them chilled. He scrambled for something to ward off the winter. "I wasn't sure what you needed it for, so I brought you…something. It was unlabeled. I wonder if it might help with whatever it is you're trying to do?"

He held the tin cup out to Lady Penamour. After a pause, she lifted it out of his hand and tapped it gently with a fingernail. It rang with a sound so unlike tin that Beau's head cocked to the side like a baffled dog's. She held it between her palms, putting pressure on top and bottom to still the sound, and squeezed until her hands went white between red knuckles. Then she blew across it, hummed, whistled. She set her mouth to the lip of it and pretended to drink. Her face lost its detachment, lit with curiosity, and that gave Beau enough encouragement to speak.

"What are you doing?"

"Shh," she whispered, eyes intent on something unseen in the middle distance as she bent an ear to the cup. "Listen, can you hear it? The echoes, like it goes on and on."

Beau strained to hear and realized the crystalline ringing from her first strike thrummed on, though deeper now and faded, like it had been reflected from cliff wall to cliff wall for miles. "What does that mean?"

"It means this is not a tin cup," she said dryly. "And certainly not the Bounty Flask." Penamour lifted the cup in the palm of one flat hand and said, "Could you be a whistle, please?"

The thing that lay in her palm was a whistle. There was no transition from tin cup to tiny metal instrument, no in-between phase, no stretching or theatrics. It had been a cup. It was now a whistle. Beau snatched it from her palm.

Cool hard metal, notched in the appropriate places to make a small, four-note tune. He put it to his lips and blew; it whistled.

"What?" he said, holding it back out to her.

Pinching the whistle between thumb and forefinger, she twirled it so it caught the light. "This is one of the more common artifacts the Maurilel made. They called them 'Useful Things.' They'll become whatever practical object you need, to a limit." Her face lit so stunningly as she spoke of magic, a warm inner glow that broke through the ice. "Some can only be a thing made of the same material as the original, or within the same dimensions. Some can only become things worth a certain monetary value or below. You have to figure out the rules of each one in particular."

Beau marveled at the perfectly mundane-looking object. Useful indeed. "So, can it be the Bounty Flask?"

"No. It can't take on any magical effects beyond the one that makes it change its nature." She glanced at him, hardened again, and sighed. Stiffly, she said, "Thank you for looking. I'll have to figure something else out."

"Sorry I couldn't help more," he said, suddenly wishing he could hand her more artifacts, just to see the way she lit up when she started explaining them. Studying magic must be a hobby of hers; she spoke with the confidence of expertise. He accepted the whistle and stuck it back in his pocket.

He ached to ask her what she'd meant at the ball, but three pairs of eyes from the guards watched him so intently he could feel their gazes like pinpricks of fire. "You said there was an inventory in the library?"

The duchess made a noncommittal sound in the back of her throat. "Nothing as current as what the royal family's kept, I'm sure. Have a good evening, Your Highness."

He took the hint and left. On the walk to his rooms, he pressed his hand to the whistle in his pocket, feeling its shape. Did he need to speak to change it? As clearly as he could, he shaped the words in his mind: *Be a spoon, please.*

He reached in and ran a finger along the smooth curve of a metal spoon. Wonder drew an almost silent laugh out of him.

Back in his rooms, the papers had multiplied in his absence, though whoever had brought them to his desk had taken great care to stack them neatly in the semi-order he'd imposed on them. Beau's small bubble of elation popped.

"I think I'll go to the library and see if I can find that inventory," he said. If he had to sit at that desk, he'd light it on fire.

Elias stepped into his path. "Highness. That inventory is twenty years old and won't tell you a damn thing about where those artifacts went. I understand it's a much more interesting problem to solve, but if you go another day with this much paperwork unfinished, things with your father are going to get ugly."

"I'll do it tomorrow."

Elias blocked him from the door again, setting a hand on each of his shoulders. "Tomorrow you have to play nice with the Macabries. Your mother said Lady Macabrie is the best candidate besides Lady Penamour for queen."

Beau squeezed his eyes shut, smacked his fist against his forehead a few times. "All right. Fine. I can do that. I can…focus."

"I'll make you some strong tea," El said.

The prince sat, picking up the first thing on the stack and staring blankly at it. He reread the top line at least a dozen times without taking anything in. He slammed it back down on the desk. "Come on, you lazy fucker," he muttered to himself. "Quit being an idiot and *focus*."

El's hand closed on the back of Beau's neck as he sat, steaming tea in his other hand. He squeezed, only hard enough to warn, not hurt. "You're not lazy or an idiot; you're simply not designed for paperwork. Hand me one; I'll read it out loud."

Beau sipped his tea and answered Elias's questions and thanked all twelve gods for the one person he could always trust.

4

ACQUIESCING

Beau yawned, scratching idly at his chest as he eyed the two outfits he'd laid out. Both needed to be pressed, if he were honest, but he hadn't thought about it until a few minutes ago, and he wasn't sure there was a maid alive who could make these presentable before he needed to leave for the Macabries' capital estate.

Three days with perhaps the most powerful noble family in the kingdom, and he'd left off packing until the morning of. The only thing he could possibly dread more was staying in his rooms and poring through more reports.

The door to his suite swung open, and he turned, fully expecting to beg a servant to do their best with his attire, but Oria's announcement of, "Her Majesty, Queen Acier," came just as he recognized his mother sweeping in. She gave Elias a dismissive gesture of her hand that sent him, hastily excusing himself, into the hall.

"Isn't this a surprise," Beau said, trying to sound casual as he ducked into his dressing room to snatch up a robe and throw it over himself. He could happily go his entire life without ever finding out his mother's opinion of his tattoos. "Good morning, Mother."

"You've been avoiding us," she said by way of greeting. When he emerged from behind the door, she levelled a flat stare at him, arms crossed over her stomach. "I shouldn't have to issue a formal summons for you to come speak to us when so much is at stake."

"I haven't been avoiding you. I see Father every week in court, and you even more often at your friends' *delightful* little parties."

The queen's flat look sharpened. She raised one eyebrow slightly at him, a movement that spoke volumes: yes, of course he was avoiding them, and she knew it, and he knew she knew it. He'd literally sprinted away to avoid talking with his parents when they crossed paths.

"The visit with the Macabries must go perfectly, Beauregard. Since you refused to be sociable of your own accord, I've had to go to incredible lengths to facilitate appropriate meetings with the ladies. You *cannot* offend Lady Macabrie as you have the others."

Her eyes darted past him to the rumpled lines of clothing laid on the bed. "What is that?"

"Uh, you caught me getting dressed for the trip," he said, willing her not to examine the garments more closely.

A futile wish; she picked up the sage green coat and ran a finger along the crease marring the lapel. "Not in this, surely?"

She blinked around the room as if seeing it for the first time, taking in the small pile of towels and clothes to be washed, the heap of ashes in the fireplace that needed sweeping, the books fallen off the stack on his bedside table to splay facedown, pages bent.

"What is this mess?" she demanded. "Where is your valet? He should be dismissed for letting things get in such disarray."

"I'm already ahead of you, Mother," Beau quipped. "I don't even have to dismiss him, as I never had a valet to begin with."

"You assured me when you moved in that you were bringing all your own staff!" Queen Acier said, eyes widening.

"And I did. I brought Elias."

"Elias is a *guard*. Who is taking care of you? Your clothing? Your baths? Who brings your meals? Who on earth were you planning to take with you to the Macabries'?"

"This palace has a *thousand* servants. If I really need something, I can always flag someone down to ask. And most of the time, I do it myself."

The queen folded her hands together in front of her face, tapped her fingers against her lips, and sighed before lowering them again. He could see her wrapping herself in patience. "Beauregard, those people have jobs that you're pulling them away from when you flag them down. And yes, of course, most of them are happy enough to help you—you're the prince. But you're being immensely selfish with your time."

"Selfish?"

"Yes, selfish," his mother insisted. "When you could've been spending your time considering how to affect hundreds or thousands of your subjects, you're instead focused on how you'll dress or feed or clean up after yourself. Do you understand? Your time is meant for other things, bigger things."

"I hadn't thought about that," Beau said, a blush creeping up.

"Not to mention the embarrassment you'd bring on the crown dressing like this, or showing up like a pauper without a proper staff. I wish you would *think*, Beauregard."

Beau scratched at the back of his neck, the heat of his embarrassment making the skin itch furiously. "I'm sorry. I...don't even know how to go about finding a valet."

"Fortunately, I know of one in need of employment who knows exactly how to serve a prince of Granvallée," she said crisply.

Dropping his weight heavily onto the bed, Beau sat. "Char's, I assume." He didn't want to be waited on by Char's staff; more people to see all the ways he was less than his brother, more reminders of the ill-fitting remnants of the life Char left behind.

"Yes," the queen said, the word richly marbled with grief. "I'll send Mistress Dubois up to determine what other staff you'll need." Her eyes swept his room, the faintest sneer curling her lip. She left without looking at Beau again.

When Elias returned, Beau threw him a frantic look. "Help me clean before the steward sees this!" They scrambled to straighten the suite, though there was little to be done about the ashes and they only had time to stuff the laundry into his dressing room before Mistress Dubois was announced.

Sweating, Beau finished tucking his shirt into his pants and nodded for Elias to let her in.

Mistress Dubois had been the palace steward for as long as Beau had lived, a fixture of these halls as unchangeable as the stone and glass of the building itself. When she walked in, it was as if the palace itself had come alive and swept a judgmental glare over the room and its contents—including one shabby-feeling crown prince.

He watched her circle the space, peeking through doorways and behind furniture, pausing to curtsy formally when she drew close enough before she scoured him with the same up-and-down scan the room received. He had the sense she knew everything he'd ever done wrong.

At length, she came to stand before him, folding her hands in front of her. "You're not a slob, Your Highness," she said, the first words she'd spoken. "I imagine you'll give your staff more interesting problems than can be solved by simply following you with a broom."

Beau wasn't sure how to take that. "I suppose. Though I can't imagine what kind of strange things you're anticipating from me. If I'm not at some event, I mostly just…stay here."

She nodded as though he'd agreed with her. "Underfoot, yes. Conducting your business here means you'll need staff that can keep your secrets, as your guards do. Especially this one." She inclined her head toward Elias, who startled at being spoken about. "He's well known among the servants for being too close-mouthed for even the most superficial gossip."

Beau laughed. "You'll never make any friends in the palace that way, El. At least make up some juicy stories about me."

Elias chuckled and shook his head. Internally, Beau glowed with warmth for Elias. He'd never asked the man to keep any secrets, but Elias had always respected Beau's privacy immensely. It was why the court had no good stories about him from the isles.

Mistress Dubois's eyes flicked between them. She pulled out a small book and pencil, scribbled a note, and slipped it back into her apron. Beau was rabidly curious what it said. "Your mother requested that, if appropriate, I recommend Master Uriel to your service as a valet. I do think he would suit the position well, although…"

She studied him again, that stare that took in everything. "Although?" Beau prompted.

"He has two chambermaids he prefers to work with," she said. "Do you anticipate any problems with young women cleaning and serving here?" Her eyes were sharp as knives.

"No?" Beau said, shrugging as he tried to imagine what problems she'd be referring to. "Are you worried about my modesty? I guarantee it's all been seen before. Or…are you worried *they'll* be uncomfortable? Seems like more of a question for them than me."

Dubois smiled ever so slightly, and it vanished quickly enough he might've imagined it. "I'll ask them, certainly. I've taken the liberty of calling them here, since time is of the essence. They should arrive presently."

"I don't know why my service would be so different from Char's, so if they were comfortable with him, I'd hope they'd be comfortable with me."

The steward went still except for a slight tightness around her eyes and purse of her lips. "They were only in the late prince's service for about a week before they were replaced with more senior attendants," she said shortly.

"Oh." Beau frowned. Had they not met Char's standards? He couldn't recall his brother being particularly finicky, but it'd been years. "Is that all the staff I'd need? A valet and two chambermaids?"

"For a minimal staff, I'd recommend a page. I'll find you someone suitable. It'll be good to see Aloise and Capucine work alongside Uriel again. I've had a hard time finding a good place for them. They're both very competent and very discreet. They'll give your First a run for his money."

"If they're so good, why have they been hard to place?"

She hesitated, then glanced toward Elias. His guard raised his eyebrows and nodded slightly, an answer to a question Beau hadn't understood. "Aloise and Capucine are very beautiful young women," Mistress Dubois said.

She stopped there, as though that were an answer. When Beau didn't respond, she made a small sound in her throat and said, "There are quite a few people of considerable power in this palace who I do not feel comfortable placing pretty girls within reach of."

Another knock at the door announced the arrival of Master Uriel and the two chambermaids, and curtailed any response from Beau. Mistress Dubois waved them in.

As the three new people filed into his rooms and stared around, Beau was lanced with painful awkwardness. He hated having people in his space, and this was so many people.

A plump, well-groomed man in his middle years, Master Uriel said in a reedy voice, "Hello, Your Highness. I am Enrich Uriel. This is Aloise Degland."

He waved forward a short, curvy, dark-skinned young woman whose twists of black hair fell just past her shoulders, each ending in a carved bead of a different color. She curtsied politely and then shook Beau's offered hand.

The second woman didn't wait for her introduction, but said, "Capucine Availe, Your Highness." She curtsied but never dropped her eyes, watching him almost confrontationally with brown eyes that stood out starkly from her pale face and red-gold hair.

"Lovely to meet you all," Beau said. "Master Uriel, I'm told you're the best valet a prince can ask for. And both of you come highly recommended, Mistress Degland, Mistress Availe."

Uriel's smile was very kind. "Always a pleasure to hear one's work is appreciated. Shall I get started with your packing? The girls can do a tidy-up now and a deeper clean once we've returned from the Macabries'."

"Oh—um. Well, I suppose..." His anxiety spiked as he realized they planned to stay, to accompany him both away and at home. "Is this all happening a bit quickly? It feels quick."

Master Uriel nodded in an understanding way. "It is quick. Mistress Dubois made clear the urgency of the situation. I understand you've not kept a staff up to this point. We'll adapt to your routines and preferences over the next few weeks. In the meantime, if you want anything specific or wish us to do things differently, you have only to ask, of course."

Beau nodded. It wasn't as if he'd never had servants, but he'd all but banished them from his rooms as a teenager because of how uncomfortable he was with someone always around, and in the isles, he'd had no one at all until Elias.

As if Beau's thoughts had summoned him, El crossed the room to stand next to him, arm brushing Beau's elbow. "His Highness and I have some work to do, so we can stay out of your way while you prepare."

The prince escaped to the study gratefully, shutting the door that connected it with his bedroom. He'd barely sat down when the front door of his suite opened again, bringing Mistress Dubois back in accompanied by a child of perhaps twelve, red-cheeked and panting, having apparently sprinted to his rooms.

"Good morning, Your Highness," the kid said with a cheerful grin and an eager, wobbly bow—not a curtsy, interestingly. The hair cut short around the ears and the boots instead of slippers sticking out beneath the palace dress and apron made Beau rethink his initial guess of how to address the kid.

"Good morning," Beau said, the child's enthusiasm tugging his lips into a grin despite the chaos of the morning. "What's your name, young...runner?"

The child bobbed on their toes and hesitated before saying, "My mother calls me Chloe Moulin, Your Highness."

"Nice to meet you, *Chiv* Moulin," Beau said, and his smile grew when the child positively vibrated with excitement. It wasn't palace protocol; it was what they called deckhands in the isles, and the only polite form of address he knew that didn't evoke male or female. "Sorry to make you run all the way here. My *urgency* seems to have set everyone running today."

"S'all right. My mother says if I don't run myself ragged, I turn into a right terror."

Beau chuckled. "So, your mother calls you a terror and Chloe. What should I call you?"

Moulin's eyes flicked over to Mistress Dubois. Beau realized he might be overstepping some etiquette line, but the steward only watched. "I like to be called Theodore."

With a nod, Beau said, "Ah. Very good, Master Theodore." The boy's smile could've lit a ballroom. "Is Theo here to be my page, Mistress Dubois?"

The steward rubbed an affectionate hand over Theodore's hair and smiled genuinely at Beau. "Yes, he's got all the energy needed to keep up with you, Your Highness."

"Very good. While I've got you, please tell me more about the 'quite a few' nobles you can't trust with our servants." Mistress Dubois seemed surprised to have the topic raised again. He flicked through faces in his imagination, guessing at which of the nobles she meant. "Have these individuals done anything that could be brought as a formal complaint against their House?"

Theo clicked his tongue. "Servants can't make complaints against nobles."

"They most *certainly* can," Beau said. "The complaints are open to anyone who can present trustworthy testimony."

"Trustworthy," Mistress Dubois repeated in a low voice.

Beau leaned back against his desk, propped his elbow on his knee, and chewed on his thumbnail as he thought. "The testimony of servants isn't taken seriously? Hmm. And I suppose it's a considerable risk to come forward. Even in a best-case scenario, you lose your job, and who's to say another household would take on a servant who's filed a complaint against a previous employer?"

Dubois nodded once, crisply.

He hummed under his breath, drumming fingers against his chin. A hint of a plan tickled the back of his mind, but he'd need to let it simmer there before it would take form. "Would you give me a list, Mistress Dubois?"

"A list?"

"Of noble names."

She considered it, then shook her head. "No. Forgive me, Your Highness, but I don't think this is your problem to solve."

"My nobles are misbehaving in my palace," he said incredulously. "I challenge you to find a problem that is more 'mine' to solve. If you're worried about my intentions, I promise I only want to make the palace safer for everyone."

"I don't doubt your intentions, Highness. Only your wisdom. There are names on that list who could trace the complaints right back to individual girls. You're stepping into a mire where you don't understand the consequences."

Beau nodded, thoughts racing. It *would* be hard to predict the consequences if he did something *en masse*. He needed more information. He needed the list and an understanding of what had made Dubois move those servants out of reach, so he could determine what the response should be.

"Give me the list, Mistress Dubois," he said at last, "and I promise to take no action on it without your approval."

"Approval?" she repeated, eyebrows shooting to her hairline.

He spread his hands. "You're right—I don't understand the consequences. But I don't want any of my people afraid to go to work if I can change it. So work with me. Help me fix it."

She tapped her notebook against her palm as she studied him. "You'd have me direct your actions?"

"In this situation, yes. Why, is there someone who'd be better?"

Mistress Dubois ran her thumb over the pages of her notebook, then nodded to herself. She flipped it open and began to write, one line after another. He watched, unable to read names from his vantage but able to see when she filled the entire sheet—and then turned it over and continued writing. He made a choked sound of alarm, and she paused to look up at him.

"How many names are going to be on that list?" he asked. "Will I have any nobles left?"

"There are one hundred sixty-two Houses with permanent or semi-permanent living quarters in the palace," Mistress Dubois said. "I have written…" She mouthed a count silently. "…twenty-four names. If you don't have the stomach, I'll simply work as I always have and kindly request that you forget this conversation, Highness."

"No, no, continue."

Elias stared at him expressionlessly. At the sound of paper tearing, Beau turned back to see Mistress Dubois creasing the page before pressing it into his palm.

"I am trusting you, Your Highness," she said as she folded his fingers over it.

He could see how afraid she was, though he didn't fully understand why. He supposed these things had happened in secrecy and darkness for a long time; bringing them to light bore a risk of making things worse. He wanted her to feel secure in his intentions.

Beau raised his hand palm-out. "I, Beauregard Mylan Adelard Tristain Highput, Duke of Verdmont and Crown Prince of Granvallée, do solemnly swear to aid you as I can and, by your advice, to do no harm."

Her eyebrows climbed again, and that faint smile returned. She said, with an undercurrent of wry humor he hadn't heard before, "With any other man I'd assume you were being a pompous ass."

Beau dropped his hand and laughed. "Maybe I am?"

She curtsied again, not answering, and then turned to leave.

"Come on, Theodore. You're not needed here for the moment."
As she passed El, she poked the First in the chest and said, "You
should've been gossiping, Master Elias."

Dropping the paper on his desk, Beau stared without opening
it. "So I have servants now. I can stop being 'selfish with my time.'
The question is, which of the ten thousand problems to solve first?"

"You get married," Elias said.

"Surely this is more important?" He flicked the folded paper.

El picked up the torn-out page and unfolded it. "Everyone is
going to have more to worry about than handsy nobles if you kick-
start a civil war by fucking up the succession," he said bluntly. "Get
married. Get your crown. Then worry about everything else."

He scanned the list, mouth flattening and brows drawing
down into a frown. "Hmm. No surprises here, but it is going to be
ugly if you hand out consequences."

"What do you mean, no surprises?" Beau snatched the paper.
"You knew about this?"

Elias exhaled a completely humorless bark of a laugh. "I know
nobles." When Beau met his eyes, he added, "Present company excluded. Probably only present company excluded."

"Only me?" Beau said, rolling his eyes.

"Yes. You're the only titled man I've met on this continent
who didn't feel entitled to every person, place, or thing his eye be-
held. Even your fa—" Elias practically swallowed his tongue cutting
himself off, laughter extinguished like a candle flame as he started
shaking his head at himself.

"My father wouldn't do this," Beau said seriously, intently. "He
would not do this."

"No, of course not," Elias said immediately. Too quickly.

"He *wouldn't*, El."

"I'm agreeing with you."

"You're not agreeing, you're acquiescing," Beau pressed.

Elias gave him a sickly grin. "I think you'll find those are synonyms, Your Highness."

His guard took the list back and read loudly, forestalling further argument. "Lord Hugh Abadie, Lord Lyam Cellier, Lord Auguste Harcine, Lady Nadia Kinasha…I know the stories of some of these from kitchen gossip—and yes," he said, cutting Beau off before he could speak, "I don't contribute to the gossip, but I do listen. This list is going to be very bad for your relationship with the nobles."

"Well, sure, now I know twenty-something names of people who are willing to hurt their own staff," Beau said bitterly.

"I'm not talking about the nobles on the list. I'm talking about all the rest of them. You're already so contemptuous of them, the way they speak, the way they spend their time. You don't bother to hide it. And now you're going to be suspicious of every one of them."

The prince scowled at him. "I am not *contemptuous*."

With a snort, Elias said, "If I say 'of course you're not,' am I agreeing or acquiescing?"

Beau chewed on his bottom lip. He was about to be trapped with those nobles on the Macabries' estate—though no Macabries on the list, at least, thank the gods—for days. He already had such a hard time relating to these people, and now this. Elias was right. The list was going to be terrible for his goal of falling in love with a noblewoman. "Fuck. I need Char's damned Watchers to be real so someone can make all the unsalvageable nobles disappear."

Elias breathed out a laugh, going to the bookcase and running his finger down the spines. "The trouble with imaginary secret societies is you never know quite who they answer to. Who can say whether they'd find the same nobles disagreeable?"

"Well, it was *Char's* imagination, so presumably he and I could agree on this set, at least," Beau said, jabbing the scrap of paper.

"Hmm." When Elias turned back from the bookcase, his face was blank. "Should we check in on your valet? We need to leave soon, and you'll want to be better dressed for the ride."

5

INK TO THE ELBOWS

"This can't possibly be the dress code for a picnic." Beau plucked at the thick fabric draping him from shoulder to waist, leaving at least half his chest bare before cinching under a belt and trailing loosely to his knees. Though his breeches beneath kept it from being completely indecent, the drapery exposed the tattoos on his chest and back, which were not for the court's eyes.

Elias stared for several long seconds, face entirely blank, before saying, "Uriel said Lady Macabrie was very clear. The whole thing's themed after ancient senatorial traditions."

"Call him back in," the prince said. "He has to redrape it or something. I can't go out like this." He moved a self-conscious hand over the black-inked swirls on his chest.

"You'll be late if he has to redress you," Elias reminded him.

"I'm the crown prince. They'll wait."

With some convincing, Uriel created a new outfit from the provided fabric, similar in spirit to the original, but fully covering his torso. He insisted on banding Beau's biceps with gold bangles shaped like laurel wreaths, and though the process of dressing up annoyed him, Beau had to admit the effect was nice, all together.

He arrived at the picnic on the lawn only a half hour late. Some nobles murmured at his deviance from the dress code, but most accepted it as part and parcel of the rebellious-younger-son persona the court had built up around him.

"Your Highness!" The high, trilling voice of Lady Macabrie drifted over the lawn as she descended upon him, clutching his arm with both hands as her own senatorial robe threatened to reveal the fullness of her endowments. "I'm so glad you could join us. We have room here on our spread for you, if you'll follow me?"

"Of course, Your Grace," he said, bending his head politely.

The duchess settled the prince at one end of a large spread of blankets on which lounged the entire Macabrie family, as well as a few other noble guests, including Lady Penamour at the far end. The themed garb complimented her tawny skin beautifully. He willed her to look up and say hello, but she was deep in conversation with the man next to her.

Beau was seated next to the eldest daughter of the Macabrie family, a slender young woman who spoke interestingly enough about her entertainments and pursuits but whose words always carried an edge of cruelty when talk turned to other people.

"It's good to see you again," he said politely as he took the plate offered to him by one of the servants. The servants, he noticed bitterly, had been permitted to wear their normal attire. "And what a pleasant day for dining on the ground."

The young Lady Macabrie smiled at him with narrowed eyes, catching the thin layer of sarcasm. "You mustn't mock, Your Highness. We dine as our noble ancestors did."

"Before they had the common sense to use chairs?" he muttered. But at a conversational volume, he said, "You're right, my lady, I apologize. It is indeed a time-honored tradition."

As they ate, he allowed Lady Macabrie—Haydée, she insisted, too familiar by half—to draw him into orbit around her monologue, making the right sounds to keep her rolling onward so he wouldn't have to respond. She wasn't uninteresting; it was only that every time he started to feel even the slightest bit sympathetic toward her, she'd casually throw in a story that made him grit his teeth: firing a maid for stealing, only to find the missing earrings in a drawer, or inviting a young lady arriving in the capital from a country estate to an event that evening knowing full well she'd have to attend in out-of-fashion clothing and be embarrassed in front of the court.

At one point, feeling desperate, Beau picked up an empty wine glass, running his hands back and forth along the stem to spin it, and smiled when one of the servants caught the movement and bent to offer him wine. One glass wouldn't hurt, and it would make this conversation go a lot more smoothly.

When the servant handed the full glass back, Elias plucked it from his fingers before Beau could take it. El raised an eyebrow at the prince, who scowled good-naturedly back. Lady Macabrie watched the interaction with a wicked sparkle of interest in her eye.

"He's pretty," she said, watching Elias step back into his watchful stance. "And willful, looks like. Did you tell him to keep you from drinking? Right after your brother died, the talk of the court was how surprised we were to find you sober for every event. Rumor put you deep in your cups; does your pretty guard keep you from losing control?"

"Their future king died, and the court was talking about what I *drank*?" Beau asked, voice too sharp for the circumstances, for how much he needed this conversation to go well. He remembered Elias calling out his contempt for the nobles and tried to control his face and tone, but he was incensed. "I was mourning my brother."

"Exactly," Haydée said, taking a sip of her own wine, her auburn hair catching the light as she tossed her head. "That's why we all thought you'd be drunker than a sailor on shore leave. I mean"— she giggled—"you *are* a sailor."

The note of disdain in that comment made Beau want to start a fight. Let her think of him more as a drunken sailor than a prince; maybe she'd lose interest and he could move on to less politically advantageous but kinder potential partners.

With lazy scorn in his voice, he drawled, "Oh, I get up to all sorts of things besides sailing and drinking. Blacksmithing, needlework, table dancing, barbery. And every now and again, preparing to be the most powerful man in Granvallée."

Her brows rose at his tone, but she leaned in, too close to him, as if intrigued by the crack in his usual placid, practiced small talk. "I'm glad you're over it finally. You were impossible to talk to for the first couple of months. So raw all the time. You *needed* a drink."

Over it? Beau's lip curled as he fought the urge to simply walk away, get in his carriage, and ride back to the palace. Out of his control, his mouth spoke. "By the fucking Twelve, you could sour ripe grapes just talking near them, couldn't you?"

Lady Macabrie's ash-darkened lashes left small smudges on her upper lid as she opened her eyes wide. "Excuse me?"

"Are you intentionally venomous, or do you not *understand* how unkind you are? You're glad I'm *over* it? My brother's death?"

Her mouth opened and closed for a moment, fish-like, before she found her voice again. "Your Highness, I…" Her pale, freckled face began to grow red as she fought down whatever words instinct had brought up, swallowing them with a queasy expression.

After a moment, she said in a saccharine voice, "I'm sorry if I've offended you, Your Highness. It wasn't my intention. I only meant I'm glad you've found some peace about it. Your grief was clearly painful."

So she was capable of speaking like a decent human being. She just wasn't in the practice of it. Beau took a deep breath and mastered himself, too. *This visit has to go flawlessly, Beau,* he could hear in his mother's voice. "I also spoke too harshly. I apologize. As you said, my grief is…raw. Talk of my brother is still hard for me."

"Then let's change the subject," she said, taking a too-large swig of wine and holding the glass out for a servant. Above the lilting ebb and flow of conversation from the blankets all around them, Beau heard Lady Penamour's voice, heated in argument, though she was smiling at Lord Arshakuni as he argued back with her.

Beau tried to hear what they were talking about that made Penamour's eyes light up like that, her cheeks warmly pink as she spoke too fast, hands moving to strengthen her points, gold rings flashing. He caught the word "Maurilel," and then fragments: "poorly understood even in their own…have one to study but…and you thought *that* was the end of the…"

"There they go again," Macabrie said with a roll of her eyes and a smirk.

"Again?"

"Lady Penamour and Lord Arshakuni get into *spirited* arguments every time they're in range of each other," she said, laughing unkindly. "They all but come to blows."

"What are they arguing about?"

"Oh, who knows." She took a dainty bite and swallowed, then said, "Some Maurilel nonsense. It's all nothing more than dry stories in dusty books. Gods know what Lady Penamour finds so fascinating about it. A lady worth her salt would be finding another engagement instead of getting ink to her elbows." She looked at him as though she expected him to share a joke, but he wasn't sure what she was laughing at. Lady Penamour not being engaged? Her fiancé died. Where was the humor in that, even with as cruel a sense of humor as Lady Macabrie's?

Or perhaps, given the context, she was laughing because Beau hadn't picked up the engagement. Had it been expected that he'd marry her without question? Had he shamed Lady Penamour by refusing her, exposed her to the derision of women like Haydée? He hadn't considered the fallout when he said he wouldn't have her.

He…regretted it. He wasn't sure, now, why he'd been so against it. He'd certainly rather be arguing Maurilel history with her than mucking through this miserable conversation with Haydée. "She's already a duchess," he said. "Perhaps she prefers to spend her time exploring things that interest her, rather than expanding her power? It'd be nice to be able to spend your days wearing ink to your elbows and studying magic if that's what you enjoyed."

"Yes, I suppose she's *technically* a duchess," Haydée said sourly.

"What do you mean, 'technically'?" Beau laughed. "You're either a duchess or you aren't. Your mother is. You aren't. Lady Penamour is."

"Sure, because she blackmailed her cousins who ought to have inherited it when her parents died and then got special dispensation from the king. It's not exactly the proper way to go about things."

Ah, right. *That* was why he'd been so against the marriage. Because Penamour was a cold political player. As much as it made him nervous to consider being tied to someone capable of so much strategic deception and power play, he had to admit there was something intriguing about a woman who could claim and hold her title through sheer force of will.

He hadn't realized his eyes had wandered back to Penamour again until Lady Macabrie touched him, bringing him sharply back to the present. "Lord Abadie and Lord Lamont promised to show us some swordplay after lunch. Are you a fencer, Your Highness? You have a swordsman's hands." She ran a finger along the back of his thumb, tracing the scar, and Beau jerked at the unexpected contact. Lady Macabrie was undeterred. "I'd love to see you go toe to toe with some of the lords."

"I've had enough of the real thing to lose my taste for playing at fighting."

"Oh, you need a little danger to spice it up?" she said, eyes sparkling. "Well, perhaps we can find a way to raise the stakes and make it exciting enough to entice you."

He shook his head. "That's not what I meant. I don't like swords much anymore."

Macabrie pouted for a moment, clearly looking for her next way in, some way to turn that into flirtation. "Pity," was all she managed. She launched into more stories about herself—now tailored to include danger to 'entice' him or syrupy and probably fake acts of her own altruism. At least she learned and adapted.

Beau's eyes drifted across the blanket and found Lady Penamour, still arguing some contentious point of magical history by the looks of it. She was interesting. Obviously not to be trusted, given her political bent, but interesting.

But then, wouldn't a savvy politician have been pursuing Beauregard from the day of the funeral? Penamour hadn't flirted with him or even really spoken to him. She'd ranged from quietly suspicious to openly hostile. And unlike most of the court, she never seemed to have prepared for *him* specifically. She was simply beautiful and graceful and impeccably dressed all the time. Even now, engrossed in her exchange with Lord Arshakuni, there was an unconscious grace in the way she held her head and how she used her hands when she spoke.

"Don't you think, Your Highness?" Lady Macabrie's fingers on his arm made him jolt again, more visibly this time.

He cleared his throat. "I'm sorry, I missed that last. What were you saying?"

Though her face stayed smooth, her throat tightened and then loosened again as she took a deep, calming breath. "I said, I've had quite enough to eat, and I'm more than ready to have a walk in the gardens. Don't you agree?"

Beau stared into the sharp, beautiful eyes of the woman most of the nobles expected to be their next queen. If he married her, he'd never know a moment's peace. She'd watch him exactly like this, constantly manipulating. He'd be on his guard every moment of every day, trying to undo the unkindness she spread so naturally. He wondered if it would infect him as well, making him harsher, crueler.

He'd prefer to stay gentle. Maybe he'd corrupt her instead.

"I haven't quite had my fill yet," he said, chewing and swallowing a mouthful of small, herby finger sandwich. "I told you some of my hobbies. What are yours?"

Her brows frowned but her mouth smiled, a confused expression. She had a very expressive face, made more so by the way she'd highlighted her features with makeup.

"Reading, singing, playing the piano. I like to play cards. I like to go riding. I like to dance."

"What's your favorite dance?"

She laughed like she was uncomfortable, though he couldn't think why. "I like them all."

He quirked an eyebrow up at her. The longer he looked, the more expressions he began to see in her face, the more emotion in her eyes. It was not all manipulation and mask, perhaps. "All of them? You must be a good dancer if the steps don't matter at all. Who taught you?"

Lady Macabrie turned her face away, and a pink flush began to rise up her neck like dawn. "What's wrong?" he asked.

"Nothing," she said with another laugh, her eyes flitting back to his and away again like dragonflies. "It's just—when you're actually looking at me, you're very intense."

"Oh." He studied the weave of the blanket on which they sat. "I'm sorry."

"It's…" Haydée sounded uncertain for the first time. "Not bad. Just a surprise. I had a tutor who taught me to dance. Two tutors, actually—one taught the steps and the other taught me to follow. I was fond of my steps tutor, Francois. And yes, I'm very good at it."

Beau asked questions, desperately steering the conversation toward harmless things that might make him like her even a little. It wasn't working, but he continued to try through the rest of lunch, through the small garden party that followed, through the formal dinner at which he was seated next to her again that night.

He fought *not* to pay attention to Lady Penamour.

And failed.

6

SEEING PEOPLE

The bed he'd been given at the Macabries' was too soft, worn in the middle where bodies had shaped a comfortable hollow. He lay cradled in it on his stomach, head tucked up on one arm so he could watch Elias doing his morning practice in the open space of the room. The sun lit up a comfortable patch of floor, and he was cozily warm under his blankets.

Though he'd seen Elias do the same exercises every day for years, it continued to astonish him how much strength could be packed into that lithe form. The control, the balance, the utter stillness when the man wanted to be still and speed when he wanted to move—it was poetry. Every muscle of his back, his shoulders, his arms was displayed, every scar, all the smooth planes of deeply tanned skin.

Some days, Beau did drills alongside his First to build his own strength, but on days like today, he simply enjoyed the show. When El set weapons aside to stretch, Beau caught his breath, an almost inaudible sound that nonetheless made the guard pause like he'd heard.

Beau closed his eyes, turning his face into the pillow. *Don't be a creep. You're not permitted to be turned on by your guard doing his job. You will not, under any circumstances, make the best guard in the kingdom and your only friend uncomfortable just because he is a beautiful, beautiful man.*

"Good morning, Highness," Elias said, humor in his voice as he dropped to the floor and began smooth, easy push-ups.

Into the pillow, Beau mumbled, "Morning, El." As he started to sit up, Master Uriel walked in. "Ah! Gods!" He clutched the blankets for a moment before remembering the man had seen his tattoos. "Uriel. Hello. Sorry, still getting used to you."

"My apologies, Your Highness, I didn't mean to startle you. I spoke with Master Elias and he suggested you'd prefer to wake up of your own accord and not be woken at a particular time, unless you have pressing morning business. Is that to your liking?"

"Um." Beau pressed his fingertips into his forehead, missing the sleepy, slow-moving, cup-of-tea-and-comfortable-silence warmth of mornings alone with Elias. Another thing lost with Char's passing. "Yes, that's fine."

"Wonderful. I've laid out two options for today: one formal and one more casual. Would you care to weigh in?"

When he emerged from his dressing room in the less formal attire, Elias chatted with Aloise as she made the bed and Capucine sat in a chair, repairing a tear in one of his shirts with the tiniest stitches he'd ever seen. Though he'd learned needlework in the isles and practiced enough to be decent, he knew he'd never match that.

"That's really nice work," he said, bending over her chair to look more closely. "I never had the patience or dexterity to sew that neatly." She didn't move, but her hands froze, tightening on the fabric, and he felt a sense of her withdrawing in on herself. He shifted back immediately.

Her eyes reminded him of a fighter's, tracking an opponent's body language to predict their next move. Beau took another step back. "I'm sorry," he said. He smiled at her, hoping it was reassuring since he seemed to have unsettled her. "I don't like to be bothered when I'm focused on a task either. Carry on."

The prince drummed his hands on his thighs, feeling thoroughly in the way in his own rooms. "Have I been given my agenda for the day yet?"

Aloise spoke. "Yes, Your Highness, and good morning to you." The copper of her skin glowed in the golden morning light and her smile was cherubic. She unfolded a gold-embellished letter. "I've got the itinerary from your hosts. There's a quick-partner brunch this morning in the greenhouse and then a fighting exhibition. And, of course, the ball tonight."

"A quick-partner brunch?" Beau shook his head, laughing at the absurdity of it. "Gods, this is all such an inane distraction from the actual problems of Granvallée."

"*Your* most pressing problem is lack of a bride," Elias said. "Eating small bits of expensive food while eligible partners parade past you gets you closer to a solution."

Beau huffed a sigh. "Yes, fine. Let's go before I lose my nerve."

The brunch was exactly as Elias described except that instead of partners streaming past him, Beau was among the handful who stood up from one small table and moved on to the next each time a chime rang. The food was delicious, though there was barely a mouthful at each table. Conversation was a nightmare, starting fresh every few minutes. Beau took to asking bizarre questions to avoid the painful small talk.

"Where'd you get your favorite scar?" he asked the young Lord Nathan Abadie, whose name Beau recalled from Dubois's list. As the man described some duel with a childhood friend, the prince couldn't stop imagining what had put him on the list, and what the room would do if he asked Elias to get rid of him.

His next partner, Lady Ovanne, seemed scandalized when he asked, "What breed of dog do you think you're most like?"

She wasn't nearly as offended as Lord Lamont, who received, "If you could wish one person dead and they'd drop dead immediately, who would you choose, and why?" He declined to answer, and Beau was darkly amused that it was probably *him* in that moment.

When he sat at the next table across from Penamour, he expected to be rebuffed again. "If you could have one task done instantly with magic for the rest of your life, what would it be?"

"Brushing my hair," she said without hesitation. "I despise it." Her face said she despised him, too, but since she alone had given an earnest answer, he grinned at her anyway.

Her hair made an elegant halo around her head, all loose waves. Today it was held back from her face with gold combs that matched her nose ring. "What makes it such a chore?"

"It curls. Very difficult to detangle. My arms get tired."

"Why not have someone else do it, then?"

Her eyes narrowed. "I have a sensitive scalp, and other people always pull when they brush it. Have you been asking questions this odd at every table?"

"Yes," Beau said. "You're the first one to properly answer, though, so I suspect you're nearly as strange as I am."

Lady Penamour took a deep breath, pressing palms to table and straightening her arms so her chair tilted back. "I don't think you and I have anything in common at all," she said quietly.

"Don't be ridiculous," he said, choosing to ignore her darkening mood. He popped something round and eggy in his mouth and chewed. "We're both Granvallée nobility. We both spend too much time in ballrooms. We both want to see the people of Courdur's holding taken care of, apparently. We both have an interest in Maurilel magic. And I, too, despise combing my hair. Although I actually like my hair pulled a little, so that's one thing different."

Her face contorted as a surprised laugh tried to make its way out of her mouth against her will, which seemed to infuriate her. He pressed his luck. "And we are both, you have to admit, a little strange. I heard you spent most of yesterday arguing about minutiae of Maurilel history, which is decidedly not what most ladies do at garden parties."

"You do not know me," she said.

"No, I don't," Beau agreed. "Isn't that sort of the point of this little mixer?"

"The point, as designed by Lady Macabrie," she said dryly, "is for you to suffer through conversations you'll detest with everyone else and therefore be relieved when you finally get to sit with her. This is all—" She spun her finger in a circle to take in the entire room. "—for you."

"What do you mean? This was designed so that I, specifically, wouldn't enjoy it?"

"You've made no secret of your distaste for small talk," she said, sipping her glass of chilled juice. "It's a smart move on her part. She looks gracious and accommodating, giving everyone a chance to speak with you at *her* event instead of dominating your time for herself, and you're all primed to be relieved when she uses the bits of intelligence she's gathered to make your conversation better. I don't know why she's working so hard, honestly; you've not paid attention to a single other lady, and if you have no genuine interest in anyone else, she wins the ring by merit of her family's position."

Beau turned that over in his head, fumbling at his own glass of juice and taking a hefty swig. "Am I also supposed to hate the fighting exhibition?"

"No, I don't think she understands how much you'll dislike that. Not paying enough attention to the stories you tell and how you tell them," Lady Penamour said. "If I had to guess, she just wants to see you in the gladiator outfit."

"The *what?*"

The chime rang out, and the rotating group began to stand and say polite goodbyes. Lady Penamour smiled darkly into her glass and gave him a mocking wave before morphing the smile into a much warmer welcome for the next person. Beau settled at another table, so lost in thought he missed his new partner's first attempt at a greeting. "What? Oh, sorry, Lady Roben, I was…um. I have a question for you: if you had to stand up right now and sing a song all the way through without missing a word, what song would you choose?"

When he did eventually reach Lady Macabrie, she'd seated herself with the large, stained-glass feature window of the greenhouse behind her, casting her in jewel-toned light. Her white dress hugged her like a second skin. She looked gorgeous, but Beau couldn't stop thinking about the way her eyes weighed and measured his reactions to calibrate her next move.

An urge to tease her rose up in him. Grinning widely, he sat down at her table with comfortable ease he didn't feel. "What a lovely event you've arranged, Lady Macabrie," he said. "I don't think I've had the privilege of so many delightful conversations so quickly before. Some of these ladies I'd never gotten a chance to be properly acquainted with. Fascinating women."

The tightening around her eyes, the pinching of her lips, and the way her inhale tightened all the cords in her neck before she smiled lent credence to Lady Penamour's theory. "I'm delighted to have been able to facilitate so many wonderful chats. I believe we're at the end of the rotation. Have you had enough to eat? If you'd like, you and I can have a walk around the grounds while we talk instead of sitting in here if it's getting stuffy."

"Sure," he said, standing again. "I'd like to walk."

To her credit, she tried to tell kinder stories. She just didn't understand what the hell kindness was. He wondered if it was immaturity that made her humor so vicious and the scope of her altruism so small. He guessed she was five years or so younger than him, though he couldn't tell for sure and couldn't ask. At that age, he'd been doing hard labor for whoever in the isles would give him a task, but if he hadn't had that opportunity, Beau thought he could've easily been an asshole. Plenty of people probably thought he was an asshole *now*, so he ought to extend her some grace.

As they climbed to the top of a small hill behind the Macabrie manor, he saw more carriages disgorging passengers in the front drive. "Who's arriving?"

"Oh, other guests for the ball," Lady Macabrie said dismissively. "We wanted a more selective attendance for the rest, but for the ball, I've invited some fun attendees. Lesser Houses, second and third sons, you know. Not marriageable, but good for a turn around the room." Beau watched them exit with moderate interest. At least there would be fresh faces in the crowd.

"Ah, it looks like everyone's gathering," Macabrie said, looping her arm through his and tugging him down the hill. She hugged his arm against her curves, giggling excitedly as they descended.

A twenty-foot circle was marked out on the lawn with stanchions and rope, and the nobles gathered around it. A small table hosted an A-frame board on which a man marked chalk lines. As they mingled with the others, Beau asked, "Are we making wagers?"

"Oh yes," Lady Macabrie said gleefully. "And I've already committed a sizeable bet on you to win your first round."

"On me?" Brunch sat queasily in his stomach. "Oh, I don't...I don't want to fight. I'll watch and I'll wager, but—"

"But you must!" she cried, attracting the attention of those around her. "All the other lords are competing! And everyone wants to test themselves against the crown prince. Especially a prince who's proven his skill on the high seas."

"I..." There were so many eyes on him. It was a harmless enough request that he couldn't find the words to say no without revealing more about himself than he wanted to. Two lords emerged, laughing, from changing tents along the tree line in a strange half armor, half...dress? It appeared to continue the theme from the previous day's senatorial robes, though this was closer to battle attire. The top half was nothing more than a leather harness holding up gold-inlaid pauldrons. Beau *would not*, under any circumstances, wear that.

As he panicked, Elias's deep voice cut through the chatter insisting the prince join in. "Could he select a champion instead?"

Lady Macabrie's eyebrows shot up at being spoken to by a guard, but when Beau didn't call him down, she scanned Elias head to toe. "Interesting. Typically, I'd say no, but you would fit the costume nicely, wouldn't you?"

Nodding to herself, she clapped her hands and raised her voice. "All right, a change of plans. Any lord—or lady—is welcome to appoint a champion to enter the ring in their stead."

"Much more my style than yours," El muttered, and when Beau gave him a grateful smile, he said, "Go on, tell me I'm the best that ever lived. Give me a little magic."

Beau smirked. Elias always joked about Beau's 'magic,' like El hadn't brought skills and protective instincts any guard would've killed for all on his own. "You're the best who ever lived," Beau said, and he meant it, and Elias's grin widened. He squeezed Beau's arm reassuringly and waved for Jude to take his place. After several minutes of jostling and chatter, the combatants were dressed and lined up to receive their red-painted practice swords. They were paired off randomly, with the first to three hits claiming the win for the round.

When Elias stepped into the ring, a hum of approval ran through the crowd from the gathered ladies and at least a few of the men. The costume *had* to have been designed specifically to show off the man's every attribute; there was no other explanation. Beau made an absolutely outrageous wager on Elias.

As the bell rang for the first round, Elias left the wooden sword at his side while Lord Cellier took a formal fencing pose. Though the audience muttered at his not being ready, when Cellier lunged, Elias barely seemed to move as he sidestepped and slashed a long line of red paint across the man's stomach. Gasps and scattered applause erupted.

Cellier, angry at how quickly the first touch had gone, went red to his scalp through his thin blonde hair. He lurched toward Elias again, and El neatly parried, then circled the man and lifted his wooden sword as though to slash again. Instead, he looked up at Beau, winked, and kicked the lord a stumbling step forward.

They fought, and Elias dragged it out, entirely in control. He could've ended it a half-dozen times, and he made sure the crowd knew it, but instead he showed off. Beau chuckled madly, fist pressed to his mouth so no one could see how hard he was biting his lip.

This had no right to be so attractive.

When he finally did finish it, Elias grinned and made two slashes appear across the lord's chest so fast it took a full breath before the audience realized what had happened and reacted.

"Gods above," Haydée Macabrie breathed as everyone cheered the winner. One hand clutched at her chest. When she met Beau's eyes, her pupils were huge. "How do you get *anything* done with him around? And what are you paying him? I'm going to offer him double and steal him away."

Beau laughed. "I sincerely doubt that."

She raised a brow at him, cruelty back in her face. "I've never known a commoner who wouldn't jump for twenty dorin a month."

"I thought you wanted to double what I'm paying?" Beau said, mirroring her raised brow. "You're not even close." Beau bet more money on Elias to win it out, tipping the woman taking bets generously. Penamour did the same, which surprised Beau, since she'd entered her own champion, Nilah.

In the next round, Elias's opponent, another champion, was more competent, but El barely broke a sweat beating him. The third round was the same, though it featured Lord Lamont, who'd been training passionately with the sword all his life. Elias seemed to delight in flaunting his prowess; Beau had never seen him show off. If he'd been a scrap less talented, his cocky, showy style would've been obnoxious, but he was so obviously better than everyone else in the ring that he could be forgiven for acting superior.

The finals pitted Elias against Nilah, and Beau found Lady Penamour's eyes in the crowd, grinning expectantly at her. As soon as the bell rang, Elias's cocky face vanished as he focused. He and Nilah circled one another, feinting, watching each other's bodies. When they moved, it was immediately clear they'd both been holding back in their previous rounds.

They fought almost too fast to track, blades flashing red arcs of paint as they clacked and clattered. Nilah was a blur, braid trailing like a whip. But Elias was something else entirely. He was almost dancing, off hand leading Nilah where he wanted her. Always a step ahead, always anticipating her strikes. And he was speaking; Beau leaned forward, straining to hear El's words.

"…good, but you don't want to leave that wrist open for me," he said as he circled Nilah's arm with his fingers, jerking her off balance. His sword painted a mark across her throat almost casually. "Get your feet under you before—good girl. Ah, almost had me there. Are you pulling your swings? You're not going to hurt me. Swing hard."

Elias was coaching her.

The barest glance up at Beau, and then his First smiled and said, "All right, I think that's enough." He drew a line across her thigh and went for a quick slash to her belly, but Nilah dodged and scored a hit on Elias's forearm, striking him hard enough that he had to shake out his hand. El laughed. "*Good*. Much better."

Nilah threw herself into combat harder, and to her credit, she made El actually defend. But he was still smiling, still laughing, still *playing*. He grabbed the end of her braid as it whipped past him and wound it around his hand, and Nilah jerked, stabbing blindly toward him since she couldn't move her head as she wanted. Elias bent slightly to let the blade pass him and then pressed the point of his to the middle of her back. "That's three."

They separated, and Elias bowed to Nilah with genuine respect. She responded with a slight bow of her head, but as she panted, catching her breath from the whirlwind fight, she eyed him like an alien, dangerous thing. It was the first time Beau had realized Elias was dangerous. He'd never seen anyone swordfight like that. El wasn't even winded. Nilah's eyes found Penamour's in the crowd, and they shared a brief frown.

"Perhaps a fairer bout would be Elias against everyone else?" Lady Macabrie said, half joking, but others picked up the idea. Beau could sense an edge of darkness in the audience's calls. Elias was common, and he'd embarrassed lords. They wanted to see him fail and know he did have limits.

Beau wasn't worried about Elias; based on what he'd seen, El could take on all fifteen of the other competitors. He was more concerned about how ugly things might get when they didn't get the failure from him they wanted.

"No," Beau said, "someone will get hurt if we do that." *And it won't be Elias.* "Let's end it here and go have a drink and a dance."

Elias ducked under the rope and took his usual spot next to Beau, no more than a glance necessary to make Jude back up out of the way. "What do you think, Highness?" he asked, eyes dancing with amusement as he spread his hands at his sides. "Should I replace my usual attire? I have to admit, this is very easy to move in. And breezy."

Beau fought with every fiber of his being not to stare at the drop of sweat drawing a ponderous trail down Elias's bare abs. "It might draw more attention than you're looking for."

"True." His First laughed, nodding toward the woman distributing winnings. "How'd you make out in the betting?"

Beau accepted the sacks the woman dropped into his hands. "Like a fucking bandit." It was unbelievable how much money was thrown around at events like this. Any one of these sacks could re-roof every house in the isles and have more left over to put in some windows. He pocketed three of them and tossed the fourth to Elias. "Here, you earned that."

Elias's laugh was sharp, dismissive. He threw the sack right back. "What the fuck am I going to do with that? You can't give a guard a thousand dorin as a bonus, Highness."

Beau grabbed Elias's forearm and smacked the gold back into his hand. "Says who? *I* didn't fight in that ridiculous outfit; you did. And anyway, now every noble here wants you—let's call that security against someone luring you away with the promise of better pay."

His First rolled his eyes. "There's not enough gold in Granvallée, Highness."

·𝕾𝕼·𝕾𝕼·𝕾𝕼·

B eau was antsy when he walked into the ball. Hungry. After the ridiculous day, he wanted company of exactly the variety Lady Macabrie had described—unmarriageable fun. In the isles, Maisie wouldn't have let him get more than two dances in before she recognized this mood and dragged him into his room at the inn, but the nobles didn't know him well enough to recognize it. Even if they had, the crown prince didn't have the freedom of a quick fuck with nobility. Sleeping with absolutely anyone at this ball would be a political nightmare.

Still, he was drawn to those 'unmarriageable' sons invited for their humor and their dancing, who had no stake in the larger political plays being made at the Macabries' since none of them could ever be queen. They were easy with him, quick to laugh, quick to touch.

At the midpoint of the evening, when musicians took their break and most people drifted into conversations or dined, Beau found himself out in the torchlit gardens with a handful of lords, arguing animatedly about the benefits of sabers versus rapiers versus smallswords, and what it said about the type of men who wore each.

"A true gentleman needs nothing more than a smallsword," said Lord Deirre, so pompously Beau assumed it had to be an act, a character he was playing for laughs. "Anything larger gets in the way on city streets or in palace walls."

"Anything larger makes you seem to be compensating for deficiencies elsewhere," interjected the dark-haired Lord Gandinne with a laugh that showed off pretty dimples. Gandinne looked over to see if Beau laughed, and Beau rewarded him with a wide smile.

Pulling his rondel from its tooled leather sheath at his waist, the prince twirled it in his fingers dexterously. "That's why I only ever carry a knife. Nothing at all to compensate for."

When that drew laughs from most of them and a considering look from Gandinne, Beau nodded toward Lord Harcine, a slightly unpleasant young man from a very unpleasant family—his father's name had shown up on Dubois's list, though Beau was trying not to hold his family's sins against him. "You don't seem to agree, my lord.

Tell me, does some aspect of your person make you feel compelled to wear a greatsword out and about?"

The gathered men's laughter intensified, and Beau fully expected Harcine to retort with something cutting, but the man narrowed his eyes at the prince and said, "Would it please you if it did, Your Highness? We're all trying our damnedest to figure out just what *is* to your taste."

The laughter trailed off, replaced by curious looks all around. Beau studied them back, one face after another. "Sussing me out for your sisters?"

Harcine spread his hands, half welcome, half shrug. "If you prefer." His voice left open other options, other preferences. Beau reassessed the group quickly; maybe they were more open to being unmarriageable fun than he'd assumed. Were all of them options?

Beau gave Gandinne another once-over. He had *such* a weakness for dimples.

But Elias shifted his weight behind Beau, not enough to be an obvious signal, but enough to make a faint crunch in the gravel and remind the prince what he was there for. Beau sighed. "I'm not sure what I prefer really factors in." He tried to twist the bitterness into wry humor with an upturn of his lips.

They variously shrugged and nodded; they all knew perfectly well what was expected of him. He supposed he could marry a man and then father a bastard or two to name as heirs, but that seemed unfair to all involved, and it certainly wasn't a secure way to pass down a crown.

"But out of respect for the information-gathering missions you've all been given, I'm sure, by your dear mothers," he said, "what can I tell you about my taste?"

"Anything," one of the lords burst out, a small man with pale, silvery hair. He blushed when he realized how loudly he'd spoken. "Blonde, brunette, dark skin or light, tall or short?"

Beau made a face. "I don't care about any of those things."

He found certain features more attractive, of course, but it was a stupid thing to choose a wife over. "Honesty. Wit. Kindness. Curiosity. Beauty obviously doesn't hurt, but it's authenticity I'm looking for. Interesting interests, hobbies, intelligence…" *Nose rings. Ink on their hands.*

The noblemen exchanged glances, and the chuckles began again, this time slightly awkward. "Well, my sisters are out then," Harcine said, and they all laughed in earnest.

Back in the candlelit ballroom, the musicians began a rousing group dance to bring everyone back to the floor. Beau gestured toward the open doors. "Shall we?"

As they made their way back, Gandinne slowed to walk beside the prince. He said, "You'd like my elder cousin, I think, but since I'm here and she's not, could I ask you to save a dance for me?" His eyes were intent but sad. It didn't quite fit the words he spoke.

Beau grinned at him, hoping to cheer the man, but for some reason that made him swallow hard and turn away. "I definitely will," Beau said. "But first, please excuse me."

Three glasses of chilled juice had worked their way through him. A servant showed him to the powder room off the main hall.

As the prince washed his hands, he saw Elias in the mirror, shifting his feet uncomfortably as he did when holding back something he wanted to say. No one else was around to hear, which meant whatever he was not saying, he held back because he thought it would upset Beau. The prince's good humor sagged, and he met his reflection's eyes. All the tiny inconsistencies in how the noblemen reacted to him, the disconnect between their eyes and mouths and words began to line up. "Gandinne doesn't want me, does he."

His First winced. "Don't ruin your own good mood."

Beau scowled at him as he toweled off his hands. "Does he?"

Elias hesitated, then shook his head. "I know how much you hate the idea that your position would make someone uncomfortable telling you no, but to be fair, *he* asked *you*."

"But you agree, he doesn't want to be here. Probably none of them do. Someone told them to get close to me. Watchers *fucking* take me." Beau's hope in the potential of the evening evaporated. "Why is it so much easier to spot it when the ladies are manipulating me? Shit, maybe I don't know how to recognize genuine attraction from a man."

Elias's hazel eyes caught the light from the low lamps in the powder room as his chin came up. He studied Beau's face. "What are you trying to do, Highness? You're looking for a wife. Are you *trying* to find genuine interest from a man?"

"No. I—I don't know. I can't, really, can I." He sighed, plucking at lint on his pants leg.

Elias reached out to rap Beau's arm with the back of his hand. "You do still *like* women, don't you? I know you had Maiz and Léontine in the isles, but you haven't shown interest in any of the noblewomen. If you need it to be a man, you could probably make things work if—"

"If I were willing to fuck around and set my bastards up for a fight when I die?" Beau finished dryly. "I'm not going to do that. And yes, of course I like women. I *prefer* women, I think. Or at least I did in the isles. It's just, none of the ladies here will talk to me like a human being except Lady Penamour, and she fucking hates me."

Elias set a hand on the back of Beau's neck and leaned in to drop his voice further. Beau tried very hard not to feel anything at all about the calluses against his skin because this was not a *romantic* touch, it was friendly, it was encouraging, it was a guard touching his prince and nothing, nothing, nothing else. "It's not going to get better if you keep avoiding them, Highness. You *can* find what you're—"

A servant chose that moment to enter the restroom, and Elias took a step back and dropped his hand, alert again.

"Is there anything I can get for you, Your Highness?" the serving man asked in a papery voice. His eyes flicked, bird-like, over every detail of the room. Beau wondered what he was going to report about the scene, and to whom. Other people might not understand the ways Elias touched him, that they didn't mean anything. No doubt he'd soon be hearing gossip about himself and his secret trysts with his own staff.

"The facilities are perfectly well equipped, thanks," he said shortly, brushing past the man and running squarely into the back of the young lords Deirre and Gandinne, who seemed to be waiting for him, chatting together. The perfect targets for his frustration.

"Just the men I wanted to see," he said, pulling Gandinne around to face him. "I've got a room upstairs, bed all ready. If I told you to come with me right now, would you *want* that?"

Beau caught the strain in the man's neck as he drew his head back, swallowed, and then pasted on a grin. "Of co—"

"Stop," Beau said, waving him to silence. "And you?" He pointed to Deirre. "You've been flirting all night. Would you drag me upstairs yourself?"

Deirre shot a quick, startled glance at Gandinne and licked his lips. "Your Highness, if you'd like—"

"*Stop*," Beau repeated, and both men stared at him, baffled. He rubbed his forehead, smoothing away the lines frustration had drawn there. "Stop lying to me. Stop pretending, please. I'm begging you. No, I'm ordering you: speak plainly. Neither of you is actually interested in me. What do you want?"

No two men had ever been so eager to flee, but they held their ground uncomfortably, silently. Beau sighed and shook his head. He wanted to shake them both, to shake all the nobility until their honest thoughts fell out.

He spoke to Deirre. "Fine, if you won't be honest about yourselves, throw each other under the wagon wheels. Why doesn't he want to be here?" He pointed at Gandinne.

Gandinne's eyes narrowed at Deirre, throwing daggers. Deirre hesitated, then looked past Beau at Elias and wilted. "Lord Gandinne is an honorable man. He has a fiancé in Durebord. He feels being here, getting close enough to ask a favor, is a betrayal of—"

"Deirre!" Gandinne called the other man down sharply. Huffing out a sigh, he flicked a glance at Beau and said bitterly, "Since we're speaking *truths*, Lord Deirre here doesn't even like men! He's just a whore for power."

Deirre grabbed Gandinne's shirtfront and reared back to punch him, but Beau seized his hand. Behind him, Elias made a choked sound of irritation as he had to step in and pull Deirre back, now that the prince had included himself in the brimming violence.

"Thank you for your honesty," Beau grated out. One man all but married, the other not even gay, and both willing to do anything, it seemed, if the prince was willing to look past their reluctance. "Let me make something clear: I don't fuck for favors. So whatever you came here hoping to gain by getting close to me, you're much better off *asking* me for it."

Deirre looked mulish, Gandinne scandalized, but the prince pushed on, shaking Deirre's arm, since he still held it. "What under the twelve would make you flirt with a prince when you don't even like men? What do you want?"

Deirre looked surprise by the question. "To be Prince Consort," he said with a shrug.

"Just power, then? As he said?" Beau pressed. "For what? What change are you trying to make in the world?"

"Change?"

A wave of such contempt for the viscount rolled through Beau that touching him disgusted him. He dropped his arm. Of course he wanted power to have power, no further thought than that. His scorn must have shown on his face; Deirre skittered back a step.

With less curiosity and more demand in his voice, Beau asked the other man, "Gandinne, what made you come tonight? What was worth fucking over the love of your life?"

The dark-haired Viscount of Durebord straightened his shoulders, all trace of smile gone, and brushed a curl out of his eyes. "Last year, Paibona torched and salted our fields. They're ruined—we can't grow a thing. And they were thorough. The only place they missed is my mother's personal apple and pear orchard, and we've distributed that fruit as far as it will go."

Beau's ire dissipated as he listened. Gandinne went on, "Our second year without a harvest, we can't support our people anymore. Durebord wasn't a wealthy viscounty to begin, and our coffers are empty from buying grain and produce. Lord Courdur did nothing to help, though I've pleaded with the duke himself and with his son in Piagette. He's taken us for nearly every penny we have, and what's left, we need to pay our soldiers, to keep the Paibons from taking what we've scraped together. We're at wit's end, Your Highness."

"Why haven't you brought this as a formal petition?"

"We have. My uncle asked for aid last year. Your father assured him we're at peace with Paibona and ordered Lord Courdur to sell to us at whatever price he found fair." Bitterness rasped through his voice. Gandinne's pretty blue eyes were intent on Beau's, honest, *angry*, no longer shaded by his lashes in faux-flirtation. "I know Durebord is not important, on the grand scale of the kingdom. But my people are important, and they're starving. And I…I heard you'd spoken to His Grace in court about our struggles, all the viscounties in Suteneir. That's why I came. To talk to *you*."

His people were important enough to trade his own happiness for. Beau's respect for Gandinne grew, and a wave of wistfulness shook him. He gripped the lord's shoulder. "They are important. Bring this to court again next week when we're all back, and I will help you." He could feel the other man's relief in the way he sagged, his shoulder dropping under the prince's hand.

"And you," he said, turning to Lord Deirre, "find someone you're actually attracted to and dance. Stay out of my sight."

Deirre vanished, and Gandinne was close behind, pausing only for a deep bow. Alone in the hallway, Beau let out a deep sigh that started in his toes. Elias put a hand on his back, a reassurance and a reminder that he had things to do yet.

He was too much in his head tonight. Normally, he could ignore the warmth and strength of Elias's hands, but in that moment, all he could think was, *Elias has that dimple in his right cheek.*

Shameful.

"Back to it," Beau said, striding into the ballroom and straight for Haydée Macabrie.

She seized him the moment he was in reach, both hands digging into his sleeve. "There you are! I've been looking for you all evening. When the next song starts, we must dance. Come here, come here! I was just congratulating Lady Penamour on what an excellent idea the fighting ring was. I haven't had a show like that in years."

The duchess, draped in pearls and moonstones this evening, gave Beau a smug, close-mouthed smile. "Oh, that was *your* idea," he said. "And you *do* listen to my stories and how I tell them." Her smile widened, showing sharp canines.

"We all listen to your stories," Macabrie said, not understanding the dynamic between Beau and Penamour. "And now we all have new stories to tell about your great defender."

Her eyes scanned past him to where Elias stood. Then she reached out to touch the guard, her fingers prodding at the muscle of one of his arms like she was examining a horse at auction. El did nothing but watch her, but Beau bristled. "I'll ask you to keep your hands off my guard, Lady Macabrie. He has a job to do, and entertaining noblewomen is no part of it."

She withdrew, pouting, but then brightened again. "Well, when I buy him off you, I'll make it part of his job. He entertained us all exceptionally today. He'll be a delightful toy."

Lady Penamour coughed and bent her head, covering her mouth with her hand. Beau was so shocked by the statement—by Haydée's implication that Elias was *for sale*—he could only stare for a moment before hot, red rage rose. "Are you out of your fucking—"

Elias's knuckles knocked against Beau's back twice, an urgent signal to reel himself in. With a deep breath, Beau recovered. "I'll give you a moment to think," he said coldly, "and figure out what was wrong with what you said. You can apologize once you've got it."

Lady Macabrie's stricken face seemed trapped between disbelief and horror at Beau's outburst. She settled on disbelief, which bubbled out of her in uncomfortable laughter. "Your Highness, I'm sorry if I've—"

"Not to me," Beau said. "To Elias."

She laughed again, more uncertainly, her mouth hanging open as if the thought of apologizing to a guard was as bizarre and inexplicable as wishing a piece of furniture a good day or challenging a goat to a game of cards. "I don't understand. He's just a *guard*. How have I offended you? I *complimented* you on your guard and his—"

Beau turned and left, ignoring her spluttered objections. He'd marry that woman the day the earth split open and swallowed every other person in Granvallée, and maybe not even then.

Elias waited until they were in the hall out of sight of guests before grabbing the prince. "Highness, stop. You can't storm out of the Macabries' ball because she was rude to me."

"Fucking watch me."

"*Highness*, stop, *now*." He half growled the order, and Beau was surprised enough at being commanded by his own guard that he stopped. "Look at me. I *do not care* what unhinged things the people in that room say about me. And you also need to not care because it doesn't matter—you have things to do."

"It matters if they don't think you're a person, Elias," Beau said, and when El began to speak, he overrode him. "Not because it's *you*. I can't trust them to give a shit about people when they don't even *see* people. I will not marry Haydée. I'll find someone else, some*where* else. We're returning to the capital in the morning. I'm done with this fucking place."

7

A HIGH ORDER

Every paper he set on the corner of his desk to be filed away with the seneschal was replaced with three more awaiting review. Four hours into his work, Beau's hand, neck, and shoulders were cramping. The horrendous silence in his rooms weighed so heavily he could feel it pressing down on his back, forcing him slumped against his desk.

It wouldn't have been so bad with Elias beside him, but it was Elias's day off. He *hated* Elias's days off.

For the thousandth time, the urge seized him to simply grab a swath of papers and sign them, unread, and for the thousand-and-first time, he sighed and reminded himself that he was going to do this right. To do it like Char would have done it.

After the disaster of the missing artifacts, he was terrified someone would discover he didn't know what was going on before he could get through these papers and catch up. He'd been unknowingly neglecting so much.

Massaging the back of his neck with one hand, he stood and did a lap around the room. Then he tied the latest stack with a ribbon, sealed it with green wax and his signet, and rang the bell to summon Theodore.

"G'morning, Highness," Theo called, mouth full of pastry he'd shoved in all at once to free his hands. "More for Master Ferrial?"

Beau held onto the papers until the boy had dusted his hands off, then passed them over. "Yes, thank you. No need to run—nothing time sensitive in here."

Theo shrugged and smiled. "I like running." As Beau let his door shut, the heavy, too-fast footsteps of a child growing into long limbs pounded away down the hallway.

The prince sat heavily and picked up a record of payments made to Lord Lamont. He scanned it, eyes catching on the small section at the bottom that recorded historical payments. The same large number, repeated month after month. It tugged at his memory.

Setting the sheet aside, Beau dug through another stack he'd made of inventories and reference lists. He flipped through until he found the minutes from a court session three years prior. It'd been included, he assumed, because it detailed approvals for allowances paid to three lords for taking in wards of the palace, orphans from a conflict at sea with Sharzhakaman that sunk a pleasure ship.

Yanking the paper from the stack, he scanned down until he found Lord Lamont's name—there, next to a number much lower than what appeared on the record of payments. Beau paced with them, searching from one to the other for what he'd missed.

The description line on each was the same: *Ward allwce. ref: Miss Alyna Vernier.* But the payment made by the palace pursekeeper monthly was nearly triple the court-agreed amount.

Setting those aside, he thumbed through to find similar records for the other two lords. Twenty minutes of searching rewarded him with payment stubs for Lord Tirel and Lord Tremblay, the two counts in Lamont's duchy of Estforet, each showing records of payments too large. Why on earth had the leaders of Estforet been compensated so much?

He rang the runner bell again.

"I need Master Ferrial. Is he busy?"

Theodore shrugged. "He's having his midmorning tea, Your Highness. I think he was impressed with your work."

"Why do you say that?"

"When I was leaving, he said, 'That boy's digging like he's looking for buried treasure.' He seemed surprised, is all. Should I run tell him he needs to come up?"

"Yes, please tell him I expect him shortly." The boy fled with the grace of a foal, grinning as he turned the corner.

Master Ferrial made good speed for a man well into his sixties, and he hardly seemed to notice the horrendous state of Beau's study. He bowed at the precisely appropriate angle, but the prince was impatient with niceties. "Have a seat, please," he said, pulling out his chair for the man. He'd laid his papers in a neat array on the desk, shoving the stacks aside.

"I found something interesting," he continued as Ferrial took a seat, reaching past his shoulder to point at the numbers that did not match. "We're paying an absolutely exorbitant amount to these three lords every month. I looked, and we do have wards fostered in other holdings, but there's nothing like this happening on those accounts. I wasn't sure if I was missing something, or…I don't understand what's happening here."

The pursekeeper stared down at the papers for a long time, though there wasn't much to take in. He licked his lips, a deep frown line pinching between his brows. Twice, he cleared his throat, but then stayed silent. Finally, he spoke.

"You're correct. This is an interesting discrepancy."

"Is it a mistake?"

Master Ferrial stood slowly and leaned on the back of the chair with both hands, not turning toward the prince. "Are you asking, Your Highness, if my office is aware of the difference in what was agreed in court and what is being paid?"

"I'm asking if it's a mistake," Beau reiterated, "and if it is, how easily we can rectify it. My father rejected several requests for aid in court in the last two weeks that totaled less than this. If we can recover money paid out in error, we can give more with intent."

Now Master Ferrial did turn fully toward Beau, the crease in his brows deepening. He cleared his throat yet again. "These payments are not being made in error, Your Highness. They were changed to this amount eighteen days after the original request was approved and signed."

"Changed by whom? Was there a reason given?"

Ferrial tilted his head, studying Beau with narrowed eyes. "Court decisions may only be amended by the king or approved agents in which the king has vested authority to do so. The late Prince Charmant, gods rest his soul, and you are the only two provisioned this authority."

"So Char changed it?" Beau asked, plucking at his lip in thought. That didn't make sense; these men had taken on no additional responsibility or risk with these wards. There was no reason to increase the payment, which was already higher than a normal foster allowance because of the urgency of the situation.

"Your Highness," Ferrial said, a faint edge of incredulity in his voice, "by the signature on the order of revision, *you* did."

"My signature?" Beau looked at the papers blankly. "Is it here?"

"No, I keep the original orders of revision in my office, and you requested in your letter that no copies be made."

Beau met the man's eyes, aghast, looking for some indication of a joke. "I didn't sign anything like that. I didn't even know I *had* that authority." He scrubbed a hand through his hair. *Those are things you were managing by correspondence and haven't touched since Char died*, his father had said. And now this.

Who the fuck was sending letters to the palace, pretending to be Beau? Who had known what Beau could do? Who could've signed his signature?

"I think I'd better take a look at what you have in your office with 'my' signature on it," Beau said. "But first, can you help me fix this? Do I need to fill out another—whatsit—order of revision? I can re-propose the requests from Lady Ovanne and the Barbeau brothers tomorrow afternoon and use these funds, if we can get it cleared up today. I know the Barbeaus need to be back on a ship by the end of the week with news, one way or another, and Lady Ovanne will want to let her sister know before the baby is born."

Master Ferrial's mouth fell slightly open. "You…didn't sign this." Hand pressed to his mouth, his eyes went far away, every sheet of paper the man had ever seen flicking past his mind's eye. "Gods," he breathed. "Yes, I'd say we do need to take a look."

In Ferrial's office, they found dozens of forms with Beau's signature on them: undoubtedly, indisputably Beau's signature, and not one on anything the prince had ever seen.

"I don't understand," Beau breathed, touching yet another signature that *had* to be his. He would've staked his life on his own fingers having penned it if he hadn't known for a fact he'd never seen a *Request for Payment: Custom Saddle & Tack, Qty Eight, Payable to Mssrs. Lev & Aleksandr Babanin* before in his life. He'd never even had one custom saddle made—what the hell would he need eight of them for? "And you never questioned these?"

"Each of these arrived in envelopes signed by you and sealed with your signet, via a messenger who claimed to have been sent from you on the isles," Ferrial said, defensive.

"No, I didn't mean to imply you hadn't done your due diligence," Beau clarified. "I meant—these requests are outrageous, and they must've cost the crown a fortune. Even if they were supposedly from me, why didn't anyone say *no*?"

Ferrial shrugged helplessly. "You have authority to draw from the royal purse as you see fit. Your father wanted to cut off your access. A few times." He chuckled slightly at that. "Prince Charmant convinced him you deserved another chance. That you were just as much a royal son, and cutting you off would be unfair to you."

Fondness and grief washed over Beau. Char had never said anything like that to him, but it was nice to know he'd spoken them behind Beau's back. Though he did wish his brother hadn't championed him so uncritically in this particular instance, since any amount of investigation would've turned up these discrepancies sooner.

A nagging, nauseating feeling tugged at Beau's stomach. *Any amount of investigation would've turned up discrepancies.*

Beau didn't write a lot of letters; he'd put his signature on file with Ferrial when he turned thirteen, but until Beau started working through this paperwork, he hadn't really had cause to sign anything.

Except that one letter to Char when Beau was seventeen, right after he left for the isles, that went unanswered.

He rotated his signet ring on his little finger. Char had given him that ring. Had it made for him. Beau had treasured it because his brother *thought* of him.

"Master Ferrial," he said hoarsely, "do you happen to have a receipt of a payment to the jeweler who made my signet ring? It would've been—" He cleared his throat, which had gone froggy. "—ten years ago. Early spring."

The man began to open drawers, humming thoughtfully to himself, and Beau sat back in his chair heavily. Ferrial had nice leather seats in his office, much more comfortable than the one Beau's desk had been equipped with. The low lamps in this room guttered in a constant draft, but it was otherwise extremely cozy, all warm woods and leather, with row after row of meticulously maintained folios of papers on shelves. In the next, larger room, scribes at their desks scribbled furiously, the sound of scratching pen nibs broken only occasionally by a cough or quiet word.

"Here we are," Ferrial said, passing a crisp paper to Beau.

He scanned it, sank deeper into his seat, grew queasy. "That's for a ring and a stamp."

"Yes," Ferrial said, nodding. "It's very common to have them made as a set, since the stamp can be easier to use for seals."

Beau bent, resting his elbows on his knees, afraid he'd be sick on Ferrial's carpet. "Char didn't give me a stamp."

Silence. The scratching of pens. The creak of leather. Beau's own breathing too fast, thready with emotion he couldn't name.

"What are you saying, Your Highness?" Master Ferrial asked carefully, eyes wary and sad and fixed on Beau so he couldn't bear to look up at him.

"I…" He couldn't speak the words. "Nothing. I'm not sure what I'm saying yet. Um, can we…can we focus on the ward allowances for now?"

"Yes, of course," Ferrial said, the small spectacles on the end of his nose catching flares of lamplight. "And I'll spend the evening identifying any other recurring charges in your name, so you can decide whether you want to reverse them."

Beau nodded. "Thank you." He bounced his fist against his mouth, fighting to find the words for the tangle in his head. All he found was another, "Thank you," and then he left.

·§12·§12·§12·

B eau could've cut the tension in the room with the knife at his hip, and the burning hatred directed at him from Lord Lamont made him wish he had the knife in his hand. He didn't let the anxiety bleed into his voice though.

"It's a simple enough question, Your Grace. How did this mistake go uncorrected for so long? It's too significant an amount of money to have skated past your pursemaster unnoticed."

"It's not my responsibility to correct your mistakes, Your Highness," Lamont said, radiating fury.

Beau took a steadying breath, fighting down defensiveness. "Are you a peer of the realm, Lord Lamont? Your *responsibility* is to Granvallée. If you believed you were receiving an unearned share of the kingdom's wealth at the expense of others who have need of it, it absolutely was your responsibility to correct that mistake."

Heading off the explosion from Lord Lamont, the king raised his hand for silence. "It's not like Master Ferrial to allow an oversight of this magnitude. Can you speak to this, Ferrial?"

"No," Beau interrupted, seeing the alarm on Ferrial's face. "It was not Master Ferrial's error. The proper forms were submitted to make the change, but—"

"You called me down in front of the entire court when there wasn't even a mistake?" Lamont shouted, ire purpling his face. "Your Majesty, am I to bear such insults from your son?"

"Lord Lamont, my apologies," the king began.

Beau interrupted a second time, and he saw fury tick up into his father's eyes. "The request was made fraudulently, which we would've discovered had Lord Lamont and his estate immediately noted the overpayment."

"Fraudulently?" Lamont shouted.

The king ignored him, turning narrowed eyes on his son. Barely above a whisper, he hissed, "In whose name was the charge 'fraudulently' made?"

Beau swallowed. "Mine. But—"

"Lord Lamont," King Fortin said, standing and waving the petitioners to their feet, "please accept my formal apologies for the inconvenience and confusion of this session. There is no complaint against Estforet or your person, and this session is now adjourned."

He swept away from the table and through the back door of the hall. Beau followed as quickly as he could disentangle himself from the table's drapery, Elias in his wake.

"Father, I spoke with Ferrial yesterday. There are *dozens* of—"

"How could you embarrass me this way?" Fortin's face was paler than usual, lined so heavily his features were almost lost in the deeply graven creases. "Casually accusing the Duke of Estforet of stealing from the crown, when it is *your* mistake that has been—"

"It wasn't my mistake!" Beau shouted. "Someone has been—"

"—siphoning off funds, not to mention the *egregious*—"

"—using my—no, I have *not* been *siphoning*—"

"—overspending with no thought of—"

"—for *fuck's* sake, *listen* to me, I'm—"

"—anyone but yourself and don't you *dare* use that kind of language with me, I—"

"—I'm trying to fix the—"

"Enough!" Fortin shouted, incandescent with anger. "I am your father and your *king*! You will hold your tongue with me." When Beau opened his mouth to explain himself anyway, the king snapped, "A high order from the crown."

Beau's mouth clacked shut again. A *high order*? Disobeying that meant a prison sentence, at best, and he'd invoked it to shut up his own son? Frustration, disappointment, and outrage at the unfairness of it all warred in Beau.

He raised his hands in helpless claws, then turned without a bow or a dismissal and left. Elias matched his furious pace through the corridors toward the stables.

Beau wanted to explode in outrage, but the *high fucking order* held his tongue. In the sunlight of the yard, grooms and footmen and cook's assistants were everywhere, so he held it in longer. At the stables, the stablewoman, a stocky grouch whose hair leaned more salt than pepper fixed Elias and Beau with a stern stare.

"I hope you're not planning to ask for your horses," she said. "His Majesty's orders—you two are a flight risk. No tacking up Tempest or Pormort unless the king or queen say otherwise."

The low growl in Beau's throat was involuntary, but as soon as he recognized he was doing it, he stopped. This wasn't the stablewoman's fault. "Fine," he snapped. "I'll walk."

He strode into the aspen forest south of the palace, where the pale trunks grew tall before shooting out the first branches and the underbrush was low and scrubby. With visibility so clear, there was no need to stay on the trail; Beau stomped a straight line into the trees and threw back his head for a wordless shout of anger.

"I'm losing my *fucking mind!*"

"You absolutely sure that ship hasn't already sailed, Highness?"

Beau threw a dark look at Elias, in no mood for jokes. His First did not look chastened, but he did at least bob a bow of his head and mutter, "Sorry, Highness."

"I hate this place so much. Nothing ever goes right here. Nothing's ever good enough here." He hurled a stick as far into the shade before him as he could, scattering a burst of chattering birds. "They hate me so much and they won't let me *fucking leave!*" His shout carried forever in the forest.

Elias let him spend his energy on chucking rocks and sticks at nothing for several long moments before speaking again. "Maybe you can visit him this evening and explain things when emotions aren't running so high?"

"Difficult to do without speaking, which I'm currently forbidden from doing in his presence," Beau said bitterly. In the most mocking voice he could muster, he muttered, "*A high order from the crown.* If he thinks so fucking little of me that he won't even listen when I speak, why does he want me to be king? Appoint a different heir, hand the throne off before you die so the transition is peaceful, and be done with it."

"There's no one else—"

"I *know* there's no other option, Elias," Beau snapped. "I know I'm the last fucking choice available. I know."

"You're not—"

"Okay, fine, maybe I'm not the *last* choice, but I'm the last choice that doesn't cause any immediate violence, so I guess I'm one notch better than civil war," he said, his voice rising in volume again as he lost control of it.

"That wasn't what I was saying at—"

"Stop trying to make me feel better!" Beau shouted, sending a squirrel skittering up a tree in a frantic rush.

When its panicked chittering ended, the forest was quiet for a heartbeat or two. Then Elias said, "Is that a high order from the crown prince?"

Beau dropped the stick, stricken. He closed his eyes, took in a deep breath, held it, and then released it again. "I'm sorry. I'm… you're right, I'm not listening. Please, speak your mind."

"What I was saying is there's no one else with the same interest in fixing what's broken that you have," Elias said. He set one hand on Beau's shoulder and tugged Beau's knife out of its sheath with the other. He lined up shoulder-to-shoulder with the prince and threw the blade, sticking it in a tree a few paces away.

As he talked, he retrieved it and handed it back to Beau, gesturing toward the tree. "You already *have* power, and now you want to use it to help the kingdom. The other dukes are the only ones with any chance at the throne, and they're obsessed with gathering power, money, followers, what have you. They're not looking outward. And your efforts to make change *threaten* what they gather."

Beau hucked the blade, and though it didn't spin as prettily as when Elias did it, it did stick point-first and hold, wobbling. Elias continued, "You're pissing them off, and obviously that's not *ideal*, given that you're trying to make connections, but it means you're *doing something*. You're the best choice for king, and you're *doing* it."

The prince exhaled, flexing his fingers as the guard retrieved the blade again. El's argument was logical. It didn't make him feel better, so even if he had issued the 'high order'—meaningless from any mouth but the king's—El wouldn't have been in violation of it.

"Someone's been using my name to leech from the palace for years. Someone's emptied the vault of magical artifacts," Beau said. Elias threw the knife and hit his first mark perfectly. "Paibona is raiding our southern border and Sharzhakaman and Altagna are flirting with an alliance to the north. The nobles are indifferent to me at best and despise me at worst. I *don't* have power. If I'm making any fucking difference, it's to make things *worse*. This entire house of cards collapses on me the moment my father's last breath hits it."

He winced at his phrasing. Angry as he was, the thought of his father's death made his chest ache until it could've cracked in two. "Perhaps I can convince him to live forever."

Elias slapped the handle of the knife into Beau's palm. "I suspect he would if he could."

Beau shook his head, not in denial of Elias's statement, but in refutation of the world, of the way things were. "I'm running out of time, El. My father's getting weaker, and the mess I'll inherit is messier by the day. And at *some* point in the next few weeks, my mother's going to marry me to someone if she has to tie me to the altar and speak the vows by ventriloquism."

"Pick someone, then," Elias said, shrugging. "It will happen whether you control it or not; take control of it."

"If it's that easy, why don't *you* do it? I'll abdicate in favor of you. Have at it."

Elias chuckled. "I'll immediately order you to marry me, make you Prince Consort, and fuck off to the woods. You'll have to rule anyway, you just won't get to wear the *really* fancy crown."

"You're so mean to me, Elias. One of these days it's going to really hurt my feelings. Let's head back. I need to talk to Master Ferrial again, and I'm still allowed to speak to *him*."

"You know what else we could do?" Elias said.

"Hmm?"

"Ask Mistress Dubois for a second list of nobles who are *kind* to their servants. Might give you a good place to start, in terms of picking a wife."

Beau nudged Elias with his shoulder. "That's it, you're in trouble now. You're in violation of my high order."

THE SCARIEST MAN ALIVE

B eau's mother invited him to a state dinner with the two ambassadors recently returned from Paibona. As his father stubbornly refused to lift the high order, it would be a long, awkward meal two seats down from the king where he couldn't say a word.

As soon as they filed into the dining room and Beau saw the place cards, he searched for his mother and found her staring levelly at him. She raised an eyebrow at his scowl. The king, as usual, sat at the head of the table, and Queen Acier at his left. The senior ambassador, Kent, was seated at his right with Beau one seat further down. Across from Beau was the other ambassador, Bhatt. And on Beau's right—Lady Penamour.

It was not at all the logical arrangement of guests for the discussions the king wanted. Lord Courdur and the marquesses of Mont Alban and Rouaneaux should've been close, since they controlled the land bordering Paibona, but they were shoved down the table to make room for Penamour. This was entirely his mother's meddling. Having rejected Haydée, he'd be shoved at the duchess.

"What a *lovely* night this is going to be," he hissed to Elias as his father greeted the line of noble guests on his way to his seat, cutting it fine with the high order.

El gave him a sympathetic look, but he could do nothing more than stand back against the wall alongside all the other guards.

Ambassador Kent spoke to the king as Beauregard settled into his seat, waving for his wine cup to be filled. One glass wouldn't hurt, and he was not making it through this night without wine.

"...she's gathering more support than the queen would like, but Almeida isn't concerned at this point that this upstart will succeed," Kent said as he, too, sat.

Lord Courdur leaned across Ambassador Bhatt to say, "If she'd simply take a strong hand with them, make a few examples—"

"Without a standing army, she's having some difficulty. She's sent two parties to capture Chaban, but the woman is slippery and her followers are devout. Queen Almeida doesn't feel she can spare the resources for a full assault on their pockets of resistance."

"Those 'pockets of resistance' cross our border!" Lord Courdur snapped. "Does she expect us to entertain this ruffian's attacks without complaint? If she can't keep her problems confined to her own borders—"

"It's not entirely *her* problem," said Ambassador Bhatt, a slim woman with deep brown skin who deftly shifted in her seat to get Lord Courdur out of her space. "Chaban's Destiny Riders believe they're entitled to all the lands that were once the republic of Coeurserd, which covered a good portion of Granvallée as well. They're only starting with Paibona. We can and should send resources to help her put this rebellion down."

"I'm sure the queen would be very grateful," Lady Penamour interjected. "We could negotiate better terms with Paibona."

The king waved his hand as though to physically dispel her suggestion. "Almeida has assured me she can take care of this herself. What I want to know is how this ragged girl from the back end of nowhere has gotten as far as she has. She has no noble backing?"

"No, Your Majesty," Ambassador Kent said, but Bhatt set her hand out toward the middle of the table to interrupt.

"None publicly, Your Majesty, but she's too well funded and well equipped to be on her own. I don't know what she could've offered—or threatened—but someone is bankrolling the Destiny Riders. There are rumors, even, that they have Maurilel artifacts."

Beau shivered. Artifacts had the potential to be *so* destructive on the battlefield that Paibona, Granvallée, Sharzhakaman, and Altagna had agreed not to use their greedily hoarded stockpiles in war so they wouldn't fall victim to them in return—mutually assured destruction. If these Destiny Riders broke that seal, and it was revealed that Granvallée was unarmed…

"Unconfirmed and unfounded rumors," Kent said, frowning at his counterpart.

"Dangerous all the same," she insisted. "Even if they're not true, they add to Chaban's mystique and momentum. She's already picking up speed with the common folk everywhere she goes. They hide her, supply her. Queen Almeida is out of her depth when it comes to the kind of guerrilla tactics and messaging war Chaban is waging. She's ill-equipped."

Beau had questions—many—but he couldn't say a word with King Fortin sitting there. He raised his hand to grab the group's attention, locked eyes with his father, and gestured toward his mouth. The king stared back as though he had no clue what Beau was asking for, although the faint tightening of one corner of his mouth said he was ever-so-slightly amused.

Beau sighed, stuck his tongue out, and pinched it between his thumb and forefinger. "Fine," he said, words mangled, "I'll hold my tongue." To Bhatt, he said as clearly as he could, "How long has Chaban been operating? Are all Paibona's attacks her work?"

He felt ridiculous. He sounded ridiculous. His father was gearing up to be angry and his mother hid a laugh behind her hand. Nobles down the table stopped to look at him. But the ambassador he'd addressed answered as if he'd done nothing at all strange.

"We believe so, Your Highness, though it would be easy enough for the queen to disguise a few of her own pokes and prods."

"They burned and salted an entire viscounty," Beau said. He paused, released his tongue to work some moisture back into his mouth, and then reclaimed it to speak again. "I wouldn't call that a poke. What do they gain from ruining land they want to claim? Doesn't make sense."

The ambassador shrugged and began to answer, but the king cut her off. "Beauregard, stop making a fool of yourself. If you're going to mock serious affairs, you can go to the far end of the table and eat with the dogs."

Beau released his tongue again and swallowed with as much dignity as he could muster. Queen Acier tutted and said, "By the Twelve, Fortin, lift the order."

"Fine. Speak." He sounded resigned, like he expected Beau to tell an off-color joke.

"Thank you, Your Majesty," he said formally, keeping all trace of sarcasm out of his voice. Then he ignored his father completely, focusing on the second ambassador. "You were saying, about the Destiny Riders ruining the land?"

"Well, there is a rumor—and this is even more poorly substantiated than the rest, so take it with a grain of salt—but it's rumored they've obtained an artifact to enrich the land, make it more fertile. Some in Paibona are whispering that that's how they've gotten the common folk on their side: making their farms and gardens flourish. Maybe they believe they can repair the ruined land, once they've weakened us enough to take it from us?"

Beau swallowed hard. He didn't like the idea of previously unknown artifacts floating around in the world. What if it was true, and that had once been part of Granvallée's trove? Who the *fuck* had taken all their artifacts? Their wards had seemed impenetrable to Beau, Beau had been the one responsible for it and hadn't been here to lend relics out, and Char had had the keys.

Char had had the keys.

His stomach churned again, confusion blanking out everything except those words: *Char had had the keys.*

"I hardly think we need to entertain every bit of tavern gossip," Kent said. "Your Majesty, perhaps you and I should discuss the queen's letters further. This merits caution."

Fortin nodded, and he and the ambassador spoke quietly, heads together so their conversation had the illusion of privacy. Beau sighed, irritated at being excluded again. He nodded to Bhatt and leaned forward, making his own conspiratorial band across the table. "How urgent do you think the situation is, then? Is it escalating?"

"Queen Almeida is afraid. She's putting on a good face because she doesn't want our intervention—or, rather, the price we'd exact for our intervention. But I believe she'll lose control of parts of Paibona in the next year, and I think the queen believes that, too."

"Would Chaban treat with us?"

Lady Penamour snorted. He hadn't realized she'd leaned into the conversation as well. "Do you want a war with Queen Almeida? Because reaching out and legitimizing her rebels by treating with them directly is a good way to start one."

Beau tilted his head to one side and the other, considering. "The queen has no standing army and the Destiny Riders are, at the very least, causing considerable violence on our borders. If it came down to who I'd prefer to be at war with…"

"Think, too, about who you'd prefer as a neighbor," Bhatt said. "Chaban's people are extremists who believe they're owed half the continent. Not people I'd turn my back on."

"True enough." Beau studied her profile for a moment. She was a handsome woman, strong-featured and tall. "Are you part of a noble line, Ambassador?"

She shot him a wry, knowing look. "I am not. And I'm not in the market for a husband, either, so ply your troth elsewhere. I understand you're up against a deadline." Lady Penamour's arm brushed Beau's; she'd leaned into his space to hear the ambassador. The duchess seemed to realize the proximity at the same time he did and immediately sat back.

"There are a couple of weeks yet left in the season," Beau said. The spot where his arm and hers had touched tingled. He rubbed at it, but the sensation didn't fade.

"The buzz when I stepped off my horse yesterday was that you'd snubbed Lady Macabrie. Who's the leading aspirant now?"

"Um..." Beau's awareness of Lady Penamour next to him grew until it was the only thing he could think about. She said nothing, but he felt her judgment all the same. "I suppose that depends on who you ask."

"What if I asked you?" Ambassador Bhatt said, smirking now.

"I'd hate to single anyone out. They've all been charming."

"Don't bother trying to get more out of him," Lady Penamour said. "Ask more than two questions and you arrive back at nothing but secrets, lies, or pure disdain for other nobility."

"Excuse me? You want to talk about *disdain*, Penamour?" Beau said, stung. "You've been relentlessly cold to me since our first conversation, and I still don't understand why."

She sat up straighter, dark eyes flashing in the candlelight. "You may call me '*Lady* Penamour' or 'Your Grace,' Highness."

"I think you'll find I'm the prince and I can call you whatever I want," Beau said. He crossed his arms over his chest. "Tell me more about these lies you're imagining you hear when I speak. What exactly have I lied about, *Penna?*"

"Lady. Penamour. I think the quicker answer would be what you've told the truth about. You're never the same person from one conversation to the next. With Lady Macabrie, you were by turns saccharine, vicious, or barely in the same room as your body. Your masks are constantly changing. And with me, you pretend to be friendly and interested, when I know—"

"Have you considered, Peppaninny, that maybe I *am* friendly and interested?"

"I have not," she snapped, "because I know that's not true. You keep coming back to needle me, but I don't know why. You've already gotten what you want. You're the next king—congratulations! I have nothing to offer you."

Even in his outrage, Beau knew enough not to address the congratulations on a job he did not want at this table. "*Needle* you? What, thanking you for speaking up in court? Having brunch with you at a brunch event? Of the two of us, Pimento, who has intentionally set up events where the other would be uncomfortable, hmm? Which of us is *needling*? And, while we're on the subject, how the hell did you know I'd be uncomfortable with the fighting ring?"

"*Lady! Penamour!*" The duchess stabbed him hard in the chest with a finger. "I knew because I have eyes. You're hiding something—you wouldn't wear the stupid robes at the picnic and I saw how quickly Elias jumped in to save you from wearing that gladiator monstrosity." Beau recoiled. "Not to mention every time someone turns the subject to violence or fighting, you start scrambling like you're looking for an escape hatch. We all know you're an accomplished fighter. You were good before you ran away from the capital and I'm sure you're better now. So why don't you want anyone to think about you *eliminating your opponents with violence*, hmm?"

"You've clearly got some theory—" He scrambled for another annoying nickname. "—Purloiner. So why don't you just tell me why you think I don't like to talk about some of the worst moments of my life with casual acquaintances?"

"Oho, do you really want me to get into my theories *here*? You want me to spill your secrets in front of your mother and father?"

"What secrets? You don't *know* me!" Beau whisper-shouted.

"Yes, I do," she hissed. "*Yes*, I do. And if it puts me in danger for you to know, fine. I don't care anymore. I can't keep watching you…just…get away with it!"

"Get away with what?!"

Too loud. Beau had said that *much* too loudly.

Conversation stopped; every eye turned to him. He raised a hand in mute apology, embarrassed and irritated. Ambassador Bhatt had rested both elbows on the table and propped her cheeks in her hands, watching them. Beau dared not turn to look at his father.

"I'm sorry, Ambassador," he said, "I believe you asked a question but I have no idea now what it was. Clearly, the lady and I have some disagreements to work through."

"Clearly," Bhatt said dryly.

Lady Penamour's chair scraped back and she said, "Forgive me, Your Majesty, but I'm not feeling well. I'll bid you good night."

Beau scowled up at her. She was leaving? She hadn't answered a single damn question for him. And she was still so *wrong* about him! He wanted to correct her. He wanted to fix it. He wanted her arguments with him to be the smiling, intense things she had with Lord Arshakuni over Maurilel lore, not *this*. He wanted…

Penamour didn't turn back as she left, her regal bearing spoiled only slightly by the constant shaking of her head, as though she were arguing with herself. Beau turned back to his plate, desperate for dinner to be over already.

"Beau. *Beau*." His mother waved to get his attention without speaking more loudly than a whisper. She pointed after Lady Penamour, then jerked her eyebrows up significantly. "Go after her!" she hissed. "Talk to her."

Beau raised his hands helplessly. What could he possibly say? She didn't believe him. But the queen's eyes were insistent, and then King Fortin looked up from his meal with a scowl and nodded toward the door as well, a clear dismissal. Beau tried not to see the way all the diners' eyes followed him as he crossed the room.

By the time he emerged, Lady Penamour was already halfway down the next hall and moving quickly, but she was nearly a foot shorter than him, so his long stride caught up easily. "Slow down," he called. "Don't make me chase you the entire length of the palace."

The duchess swiveled, hands raised as if to fend off a blow. Beau stopped six feet from her. "I'm not going to hurt you, Pandarast. Why are you afraid of me? What did I do to you?"

"It's not what you've done to *me*, as you know perfectly well."
Her eyes went to El and back to him; she was shaking, terrified.
Nilah wasn't with her tonight. Beau edged back another step. "I
know what you've done. And you know that I know. So if you're
going to silence me—"

"Can I also please know what it is that I know you know?"
Beau demanded.

"You killed your brother!"

Silence.

Beau turned the sentence over in his head, trying to examine
it from different angles until it became something with meaning.
"What? What are you talking about?"

She threw her hands up. "More lies! I should've known—"

"My brother died falling off a horse!" Beau said, stepping
closer so she was sure to hear him. "It was an accident. You were
there! I've worn a lot of hats in my time, but I've never been *gravity*.
The only responsibility I have for Char's death is that I'm the one
picking up all the pieces of what he left behind."

The duchess shook her head. Her eyes were glassy with fear or
grief or something entirely beyond his ken. She didn't believe him.
There were few things Beau hated more than not being believed.

"Please help me understand why you could *possibly* believe I
killed him." Beau tried to come closer, to look in her eyes, but she
edged toward escape.

Her face contorted. "Forget it. I will find the truth, and I won't
let you chip away at the things I do know with your lies."

"No, not 'forget it,'" Beau snapped. "You've accused me of
something both horrifying and impossible, and I want to know why!
I want to—I want—I want you to stop hating me!"

"Why?" she demanded.

"Because I need a wife!"

What? Why the fuck had he said that? He wanted her to
stop hating him because he hated to be hated, because it wasn't fair,

because he liked her more than he'd thought he would, not because he… He couldn't *marry* her! Right?

She agreed with the frantic voice in his head, by the way she jerked back from him, horror in every line of her face and body. "Well, it won't be me. And if I do my job right, it won't be any lady of this court. No one deserves to be married to a man who'd murder his brother for a crown."

"But I don't even want the crown!" It was a pointless addition; Lady Penamour was already walking away—practically running, actually. Beau reached back for Elias, needing something steady. "What the fuck is going on, El?"

His First wrapped an arm around his shoulders, but El wasn't looking at him. Face carved in stone, Elias watched Lady Penamour turn the corner. When he didn't speak, Beau shrugged his arm off and nudged him. "What's wrong?"

"Hmm?" Elias emerged from deep in his mind. "I don't like things I don't understand. And I don't understand Lady Penamour. We should head back to the rooms. You need to relax."

"Relax?" Beau asked incredulously, but he let Elias lead him back anyway.

When they passed Jude at the door and went in, both maids were in the study, laughing quietly as they stacked books in front of the shelf so they could dust. Uriel popped his head into view from the bedroom and smiled. "Oh, you're back early!"

"Everybody out," Elias said. "His Highness needs to be alone."

"Of course," Master Uriel said. "Last of the water's over the fire, so you have a hot bath. There's cheese, fruit, and wine on the sideboard, and I've turned down the bed."

"Perfect, thank you, Uriel," Elias said. "Good night, Aloise. Good night, Capu." The guard saw everyone out, locked the door behind them, and marched Beau to the dressing room by the shoulders. "Strip. I'll finish the bath."

Beau dropped his jacket and waistcoat on the floor and unbuttoned his shirt, but the cuffs of his sleeves stymied him. Uriel had used fancy looping cufflinks, and he couldn't get them undone one-handed. He was prying them with his teeth when Elias returned with a smirk.

"The bath is ready, and I already took the food in there, so there's no need to eat your jewelry. Give it here." Elias took one of his arms and unfastened the sleeve neatly, dropping the cufflink on the bench, then did the same with the other arm. He hooked his finger in the back of the collar and pulled the shirt off, and Beau shivered. He *wanted*.

"Go get in the bath if you're cold," Elias said, bending to pick up the other discarded clothes with his back to Beau.

When the prince sank into the steaming tub, he groaned involuntarily: it was precisely the right temperature, heat biting into his skin, soothing the tension in his muscles. Master Uriel was a bath wizard. He settled in, afraid Elias meant to leave him alone with his thoughts while he soaked. But the guard dragged a chair in from the study so he could sit against the wall and talk.

"What do I do with that?" Beau asked. "She earnestly believes I murdered Char. Why?"

Elias shrugged. "You can't reason with crazy people. Did you *mean* to imply that you wanted to propose to her? Because...you said you weren't going to do that."

"She's not insane," Beau said, ignoring the question he had no answer for. "She's too smart and competent to be imagining something like this. It came from *somewhere*. Something happened that made her think Char was murdered and that I could be responsible."

"Highness, her fiancé died," Elias said. "Grief affects everyone differently, and it's rarely rational. Maybe it drove her to need Char's death to be someone's fault. She latched onto you."

Beau shook his head, idly drawing hot water up over his shoulders. That didn't make sense to him. Lady Penamour would've had to be in love with Char to be driven mad with grief, and his mother said they barely knew each other.

"The more important part of that conversation is the threat she made," Elias said. "I want to know how she's planning to make sure none of the noblewomen marry you."

Beau shrugged. "Make sure they won't marry me, or that I won't marry them? She sabotaged Lady Macabrie, but all that did was further highlight Haydée's faults. It doesn't really matter, though. I'm low on options even without her intervention. The only two unmarried duchesses are Lady Penamour—obviously a no—and Lady Andremiere, who's well out of childbearing age. Daughters of dukes are thin on the ground, too. Haydée Macabrie's already out, her younger sister's too young, and Lord Lamont's oldest daughter isn't even six."

"Doesn't Courdur have an unmarried daughter left?"

Beau swiped wet hands over his face to rinse away the salt of the day. "Cecilia Courdur was born with a man's name. She's working with the wrong equipment, unfortunately. One of Penamour's younger sisters is unmarried, but I'm sure she shares the duchess's opinion of me. And also, I'm fairly certain she only likes women."

"Go one rank down."

"Okay. Lady Roben is a marchioness. And she's…fine. Still young enough for children, pretty. She's good friends with Penamour, though, and she's been courted by Lord Blanchet all season. Plus, she's less interesting than paperwork. Lady Ovanne's a countess, but she and her husband had no children before he died—no way to know if that was her fault or his. All the daughters of counts and marquesses are too young, too old, already married, or on Dubois's list of abusive nobles."

"Who else showed up on the *nice* list?"

Beau sighed, rubbing his eyes. "Scores of married women. Of the single ones—Penamour. And about a dozen viscountess and below who I can't seriously consider." He slicked his hair back from his face, blinking drips of water out of his eyes. "Maybe I should marry

Queen Almeida? That would solve the Paibona issue. Strengthen our ties with our neighbors."

"And take an *incredibly* long time to negotiate, possibly delaying your marriage in perpetuity," Elias said, smirking. "But I'm sure that didn't factor into your consideration at all. I was under the impression your brother already tried that and was rebuffed by the queen before he proposed to the duchess?"

Beau rested his hands on the water, letting the surface tension tickle his palms. That was true, but not common knowledge at all. "Is that palace gossip as well?"

"You'd be amazed what servants hear, especially when the crown prince makes several trips back and forth across the border."

"I swear, you're better than Father's spymaster," Beau said, chuckling humorlessly.

"Yes, I'm sure the head of the kingdom's entire intelligence network is quaking in his boots because a guard periodically listens to kitchen chatter."

"Her boots," Beau corrected. "Or slippers, rather. Mistress Isely. Funnily enough, I spied on her on a couple of her visits to my father when I was a kid. Strange woman. Very quiet. But I suppose that's normal if you're in the spy game."

Elias hissed air in between his teeth, squeezing his eyes shut in a sharply pained expression. He tapped his fist against his forehead a couple of times and then said, "Highness...the identity of the king's spymaster is literally the most closely guarded secret in Granvallée. And you...said it out loud."

Beau performatively looked left and right. "There's no one around to hear, for once. And besides, I'm not going to tell anyone."

"You *just* told me. Now I know that, too. The thing even you are not supposed to know."

"Yes, but telling you isn't telling anyone. You're...Elias."

The expression his guard turned on him was so fond, so baffled, so tortured, that Beau didn't know whether the man was going to kiss him or hit him. El did neither, of course; he dropped his head and shook it, hair falling out of the knot he wore it in to hide his face like a curtain. "Maybe you shouldn't trust me *that* much, Your Highness. I'm a guard."

"You can pry my trust for you out of my cold, stiff corpse," Beau said bluntly. "I don't want to talk about marriage anymore. It's depressing. What do you think of the Destiny Riders?"

"Oh, they're *much* less depressing," Elias snarked.

Beau ignored him. "I think Ambassador Bhatt is right: if we can send Almeida what she needs to put down Chaban, we can also negotiate help for those on the border who've had to put up with the Riders' raids. And we could recover any magical relics they might have. I'm not sure what's holding Father back. It'd take coordination, but if Courdur called up the men of Suteneir and I called up mine in Verdmont, we'd have the whole border secured, and we could pull men from duchies farther north to supplement their guards and farmhands in the interim."

"That requires a lot of lords agreeing to call their men to arms," Elias said.

"They've pledged to do so at the crown's order. And this is hardly a whim—they'd have to take up arms once the Destiny Riders started claiming land on our side of the border anyway, and this way we catch them before they've shored up their power and resources in Paibona."

Until the water grew too cold to comfortably sit in, Beau talked through the problem and Elias poked holes in his plans. As Beau dried off and redressed, Elias made tea.

Beau took a sip as he climbed into bed. "Dreamroot?"

"I figured you could use the help sleeping."

"Hmm." Beau grunted in assent. He drained the rest; Elias knew the dosage of dreamroot for him well enough by now that he assumed it wasn't dangerous. While El put the lamps out, Beau settled in.

"I hope all that fighting skill wasn't for show. If any of my problems come to a head, you might have to kill people. You ready?"

Elias chuckled in the darkness. "I'm always ready."

"Don't sound so damn cocky." Beau yawned, feeling the tug of the dreamroot already. "You haven't had to do anything like that for at least seven years. How are you staying keen?"

The silence of the room was broken only by the creak of the chair near the bed as Elias settled into it. Beau blinked his eyes back open. "El?"

"I stay sharp. Don't worry." Elias sounded strange.

"Why do you sound like that?"

The guard sighed. "I…am realizing you think I haven't had to kill anyone the entire time I've been in your service."

The words sank in through the dreamroot haze, and Beau sat up abruptly, blankets sliding off the side of the bed. "Wait, what? *Have* you? You've been *killing* people, and you casually drop this on me when I'm half asleep? What happened? When?"

"Lay back down, Highness." Unseen in the dark room, Elias put his hand on Beau's chest and pushed him back to the mattress. "You hired me to be so good at my job you never had to notice these kinds of things."

His skin tingled in the outline of Elias's hand. He squeezed his eyes shut. Not *now*. Not that there was ever a good time to want his guard's hands on him, but *definitely* not when said guard was telling him about the people he'd murdered. Beau *had* hired him and he *was* good at his job and that made him an employee and off-limits and on the count of three he would stop thinking about Elias's hands. He counted himself off sternly and opened his eyes again.

"Just because I don't notice doesn't mean I don't want to know."

"You *don't* want to know. Stop asking questions—just be confident that I am very capable of keeping you safe."

Beau hauled the blankets back up. "Be serious. You've actually killed people?"

"Yes."

"Recently?"

"Exclusively recently. I've only needed to kill people since we came back to the capital. Most of the powers that be ignored you while you were a non-issue on the isles."

"When? How many?"

Elias sighed, and Beau could picture him pinching the bridge of his nose as he always did when Beau badgered him. "I'm not going to tell you how many. I'll give you an example. A week after you told Courdur not to levy taxes, two men showed up at that croquet game on the lawn, waiting for you to leave. You remember when I excused myself to the trees?"

"I thought you went to piss! You weren't gone ten minutes!"

Elias sounded amused. "Should it have taken longer? It was only two men."

"Longer than a *bathroom break*!"

There was a rustle in the darkness as Elias slid down on the chair, stretching his legs out in front of him. He said only, "Nah."

"You didn't have blood on your hands when you came back!"

"They didn't die bloody. And Courdur hasn't tried again, so—"

"He tried to have me *killed* because I wanted his people to survive the fucking Destiny Riders?" Beau reeled. "Who else—" Despair nearly swallowed him. They didn't just hate him; they wanted him *dead*. His nobles, his kingdom; they wanted him dead.

"No, no no no," Elias said, and his hand found Beau's chest again. "Stop that. Stop spiraling." His thumb rubbed along Beau's collarbone, and because it was dark and El couldn't see, Beau closed his eyes and let himself enjoy it. "It's not you. Everyone's trying to kill someone. Everyone's spying on everyone. We guards are *working*. A couple weeks ago, I put down an assassin waiting for Lady Penamour. I assume it came from Macabrie, but I'm not sure."

"You protected Lady Penamour?"

Elias's hand stilled, lifting slightly away from Beau's skin. "Should I…not have?"

"No, I'm—I'm glad you did. Has she tried to kill me?"

"No. She hasn't. As far as I know, she's not trying to have anyone murdered."

The dreamroot dragged Beau's eyelids down heavily, but his heart was pounding fast enough to keep him thuddingly awake. "This is a lot, El. This is—this—how do I talk to them, when they're sending assassins? How do I…"

"Nothing's changed, Highness," El said, resuming the soothing motion of his thumb. "They'll play whatever games they play. I won't let you marry someone I've had to fight death threats from. And in the meantime, you are *not* in danger. I won't let anything happen to you."

He wanted to reach up and set his hand on Elias's, but he knew better. "What if they send more than you can handle? We don't always bring the rest of the flight. Should I tell Jude and Oria to come along when—"

"Highness." Elias's sternness was faintly amused. "I'm not being cocky when I say I am the best. They *can't* send more than I can handle. They've tried; they didn't come close. You didn't even *notice* me killing them. I've never had so much as a scratch, and neither have you. If you wanted me to, I could take out every enemy you have *tonight* and be perfectly ready to have breakfast with you in the morning and start our day."

A moment of silence stretched into the darkness as Beau considered the easy, confident way Elias delivered the news of his own deadliness. "You are the scariest man alive."

El laughed, a dark rumble of a chuckle that made the skin under his palm *burn*. "Not to you, Highness. But to your enemies? I fucking hope so."

9

A COCKROACH

"I don't have to take the day off, Highness. It's not like I have anything in particular to do. Today's going to be—"

Beau cut his First off. "Today will be fine. It's your leave; take it." He shoved Elias toward the door, and though he and the guard were of a height, El was remarkably difficult to move. "Go send your sappy love letters to whoever it is you're always writing to."

Elias paused, and Beau realized the other man had been letting him push him before; when he didn't want to move, he was immovable. "You...know about him?"

Him? Lights sparked up in Beau's brain, unworthy thoughts. Beau had never known if it was a man or woman Elias penned his letters to. The man was secretive about it, as he was about almost everything, so Beau hadn't asked. And he'd forced himself for years not to try to find out who Elias was attracted to because it didn't matter to Beau, obviously.

"You're allowed a life, and it's none of my business. Don't worry about me today. By tonight, I'll be engaged, I guess. To somebody. I'll figure it out. So when you come back you can congratulate me."

Elias turned and raised an eyebrow. "You do not want to be alone today with Jude or Oria. I know you."

No, he didn't want to be alone with them. He wanted El with him like he wanted all four limbs still attached. But Elias was human, and if Beau didn't force him to take a break every two weeks, he'd run himself to collapse.

Still…Beau couldn't shake their conversation about the assassins. Ashamed as he was to admit it, Beau was scared. Reluctantly, he said, "What if you took your break tomorrow?"

Elias beamed at him. "I'll take it tomorrow."

A knock sounded at the door, four quick taps, then a small, dancing sort of rhythm. "Your Highness?" Theodore called. "Got a message for you."

Elias opened the door as Beau prepared himself for Theo's boundless, jubilant energy. "Morning, Theo." The runner fished a thick piece of creamy paper tied with ribbon and sealed with wax out of the pocket of his apron.

Beau took it with a frown; his father's seal. "Thank you. And by the way, you can wear whatever you like in my service," he said absently as he cracked the wax. "If gowns and aprons are more comfortable, fine, but if you'd prefer trousers…" He trailed off as he scanned his father's message:

> *Due to a poor night's rest, I will not be attending court this afternoon. Please convey my regrets to any petitioners and let them know I will next hold court in one week's time. I'm sure you will find something worthwhile to fill your empty afternoon.*

> *—F*

Beau could taste the sarcasm dripping from that last line. A poor night's rest? He didn't like that at all. His father hadn't canceled court once in Beau's memory. For him to do so now spoke of a progression in his illness Beau didn't want to think about.

But then…he hadn't *exactly* said to cancel, had he? Clearly that's what he intended, but since he hadn't explicitly ordered it, there was a bit of room for Beau to finagle a different result.

Beau's mind raced. If he held court alone, he could do something about Paibona and about the troublesome nobles in one fell swoop—something his father wouldn't be able to reverse in the moment. Excited to have a problem before him that he *could* solve, Beau slapped the paper against his hand and grinned. He would indeed find something worthwhile to fill his afternoon. It was an opportunity he couldn't pass up.

"Theo," he said, all urgency, and the boy perked up immediately, "I need you to bring me Mistress Dubois, as quick as you can."

"You've got it, Highness!" Theo gave a quick nod and took off at a dead run, as always.

"Don't run anyone over, please!" Beau called after him before darting into his study and bending over his desk to scribble furiously on the closest piece of paper at hand. "If we send…" he muttered to himself, and later, "…but then who would…?"

Elias came to peer over his shoulder but said nothing, leaving Beau to swirl in his own thoughts. Theo slammed into the room a few minutes later, announcing Mistress Dubois loudly at the same time Oria did. The guard was annoyed. "Hello, thank you for coming," the prince said, and he immediately launched into his plan.

She listened intently, and though her head shook and a frown creased her face, she didn't interrupt. When he'd poured it all out and stood silent, she said, "It's bold. With nothing to connect them, they're not going to understand why they've been singled out. They'll think you're mad, Your Highness."

"When I die, they can put Mad King Beauregard on my tombstone," Beau said with a shrug. "I told you I'd ask for your approval before I moved. But it needs to be today, or it may have to wait for…a while." He wouldn't summon a worsening of his father's condition by speaking it aloud.

Mistress Dubois spread her hands. "I don't see how this would endanger my girls. But," she squinted at him, "at the risk of speaking treason, you know *you* are not unkillable, yes?"

"I'm immortal until proven otherwise," Beau said with a grin that made Dubois's concern visibly deepen.

"He'll be fine," Elias said, setting a hand on Beau's shoulder and staring Mistress Dubois down until she made a small, concerned sound in the back of her throat and spread her hands.

"If your only issue is me, I'll consider it approved. You don't have authority over whether I make people angry with me." He clapped his hands and blew his breath out noisily. "All right. I've got to get ready for a court to remember!"

He prepared, Elias watching him more quietly than normal. Beau suspected the man was mentally preparing for the next wave of attempts on the prince's life. When they stepped out and met Jude and Oria in the hall, Beau said, "Whichever of you is joining us, you should know I'm about to make some people *very* unhappy. In fact it might…well, just be ready."

Oria's eyebrows shot up in alarm, though Jude looked, as always, like a carved block of stone. "Are we going to have to fight our way out of the hall, Your Highness?"

"No," Beau said, shaking his head. He hesitated, then repeated, "No, I don't think so."

"Come on, Jude," Elias said.

In the petitioners' chamber, El and Jude followed him to his usual chair to the right of the throne, flanking him as he sat. A large crowd had gathered today; Beau broke into a sweat. He raised his hands, and those facing him quieted, frowning.

"Welcome, everyone," Beau called. "If you could take your seats, we'll begin."

Confused, they sat, conversations petering out raggedly in a wave that spread from Beau's seat. Some swiveled to find the king, muttering to their neighbors when they saw only the prince.

"King Fortin sends his regrets that he's unable to attend this afternoon," Beau said, "but I will hear your petitions, after I make an announcement of my own."

That stilled the room quickly enough. All eyes were on him, expressions ranging from neutral to baffled to sneering. Lady Penamour sat near the front, and the combination of her bronze silk dress and the steely look in her eyes made her seem armored. Beau tried not to look at her; it only made him more nervous.

"Many of you will have heard that Paibona is plagued by a group called the Destiny Riders, led by the rebel Chaban. While there are many rumors about this group, what is true is that they're causing difficulty for Queen Almeida, and they've also caused no small trouble for our southern border lords. I intend to do something about that."

Murmurs rushed through the group, cutting off abruptly when he swallowed and spoke again. "Every lord and lady in Granvallée is pledged to defend our borders and our way of life when called upon. Some of you are better positioned than others to do so, in this case. I speak now to these families—"

He listed each of the noble Houses on the list, dropping the names into the utter silence of the room like stones in a pond. No one moved, as though drawing his attention would add their names to the list as well.

"These families hold land in all parts of Granvallée. We won't weaken any one part of our kingdom when our northern neighbors speak of allying with each other and could turn their eyes to us.

"The named Houses will have the honor of sending no fewer than one-third of their liegemen to the southern border to aid those marches in protecting their land and their people from the Destiny Riders' attacks. Each of these parties will be led by the patriarchs and matriarchs of the noble families themselves."

Shocked and outraged susurrations swept through the room like an undammed river. "They'll carry with them the supplies needed to cross Granvallée and to protect the border for a period of three months, after which time we'll reassess the situation. No one may strip the lands they pass through on the march, even for coin."

Several nobles spoke out at this point, but since they spoke over one another, it was impossible to know quite what they said.

Beau waved them to silence and continued, "I understand this may be a hardship, and I wouldn't want men on the move burdened by staff who cannot withstand travel. Any servant from these households who wishes to may put in a request with our steward, Mistress Dubois, for assignment here in the capital. A suitable replacement will be provided for servants that exercise this option."

True silence fell again. It was such an unusual thing to include that none of the assemblage knew how to respond. Beau spied a few of the people he'd named seated throughout the hall, their faces darkening with anger. Two, Lord Abadie and Lord Harcine, walked out without being dismissed. Most of the rest appeared stunned. Lady Penamour sat all the way forward, almost spilling out of her chair as she watched his every move and expression with painfully intense attention.

"I'll hear your petitions now," Beau said, waving for the clerk to read the first in queue.

The named woman stood, cleared her throat, and said, "I cede the floor. It's clear there's more pressing business than what I bring today. I'll resubmit at another time, Your Highness."

Beau made a small, exasperated sound, but nodded. "Very well. Who's next?"

They all ceded the floor, and one by one, they trickled away until so few remained that slipping out would make a large, obvious statement. They *did* think he was mad. Or perhaps they didn't trust Beau had the authority to hold court without his father.

In irritation, he waved a dismissive hand. "All right, this session is adjourned. My father will hold court in a week." He stood while most of the room was rising and descended the narrow spiral staircase at the back of the hall to the garden door. He couldn't stand still. He'd expected some argument, some fight; he'd been ready to defend himself. The nobility leaving in silence left him with too much restless, antagonistic energy and nowhere to put it.

"Well, you didn't have to carve a path out for me," he said over his shoulder, glancing back to see if Elias would respond.

To Beau's surprise, Jude spoke. "What did they do to you? Those nobles?"

"To me? Nothing."

"But you're…punishing them," Jude insisted.

"Perhaps they'll see it that way," Beau said carefully. He didn't trust the big guard enough to tell him the truth. "We're all called to do things at times that feel like punishment. Speaking of…" He glanced north but couldn't see the clocktower from where he stood. "I'll have to head back to my rooms soon and let Uriel make me presentable for the grand event."

Elias and Jude followed his winding, circuitous route through the gardens and outer halls of the palace. He wasn't precisely avoiding the corridors likely to hold other highborn, but he certainly didn't take any of the main paths.

"Highness! Your Highness!" Theodore careened breathlessly around the corner, rebounding off walls in his haste. "Thank the gods I found you. Thought I'd have to tell the king you were lost."

"Did he send for me?" That was fast. One of the lords must've run straight to him.

Theo leaned over, hands on knees, and sucked air. "Yes, Highness. He said, uh—well, it wasn't very nice, but he said you were supposed to come right away."

Beau hunched his shoulders and glanced behind him for support. Elias met his eyes steadily, giving him the smallest nod. "Take a break, Theo. You look like you've been running for an hour straight. Jude, head back to my rooms. El can accompany me." He didn't want any more witnesses than he had to have for whatever was waiting for him with his father.

His feet didn't move as quickly as they ought to. The weight of dread made them drag along the floorstones. When he finally stepped into the royal wing, the guards on the door announced him when he was still yards away. Like a poisonous gas, the king's voice seeped into the hall. "*Beauregard.*"

Beau edged into the room, bracing himself. His father was not at his desk; in fact, there was no one in the parlor. He stepped further in and saw his parents' bedroom door was open. He hadn't been in that room since he was barely old enough to walk.

King Fortin sat in the massive bed, blankets piled three-deep atop him. He was grey, his skin chalky, but his eyes flashed bright and furious. His mother sat in a chair to the side, but Beau's eyes were on the almost unrecognizable man lying in that bed. He'd never seen his father look frail. He was the king; he was unimpeachable, unchangeable, unshakeable.

"Father," Beau said, bowing. "You wanted to see me?"

"Yes," Fortin said, bending to cough and then straightening his shoulders again. "I wanted to look on the death of my legacy."

A frisson of pain jolted through his middle. "Excuse me?"

"It was bad enough to have a worthless son when I still had an heir who would build on what I created," Fortin said, voice thin but clear. "But now I have only you. You, who wasted yourself, wasted our fortunes, wasted your name. But like a cockroach, you survive the disasters that kill your betters. Gods, I've tried to imagine you doing this without bringing Granvallée to ruin. I've tried to coach you, tried to teach you. But you can't shape a pile of shit and pretend it's a lump of clay. Every tiny bit of responsibility or trust I've given you has shown that all the kiln's flame will do for you is make you crumble to dust."

Beau's mind was completely blank, the cold cruelty of his father's words echoing inside his skull. He opened his mouth to speak, but nothing fell out.

"Nothing to say now? Nothing else you wish to ruin?" Fortin hissed. "You had plenty to say this afternoon as you destroyed every scrap of goodwill and loyalty the crown has built with its nobles. Plenty to say about our *ally* Paibona, who you cast aspersions against. And now you rally our people to war against them!"

"Not war," Beau croaked out, finally finding a thread of voice. "Protecting our own people, our own lands."

"You dare imagine that sending the best of our leaders out against these chicken-thieving rebels is going to protect—" As a coughing fit seized him and shook him in its jaws, Beau seized the opportunity to speak.

"The ones I named are the *worst* of our leaders. They not only don't care about the people they've been charged to govern and protect, they actively *hurt* them. They abuse their power, and they have to be made to understand—"

"You could teach them a masterclass on abusing power!" The king's voice was hoarse as he tried to shout. "What kind of delusions do you play in your head, that you think you're better than them? After years of draining the treasury to spend on your whores and whiskey and whatever whims struck you?"

"That wasn't me!" Beau said. "It was…I think it was Char. I've been working with Ferrial to try to get it sorted out, but—"

"You *dare* blame your brother for your faults? You stand here and lie to my face? You *conniving little*…" He took a deep, shaking breath, then coughed again painfully.

"Why won't you *listen* to me?" Beau asked, desperation making his voice break.

Fortin shook his head, disgust in every line of his features. "Because I know what you are. Truly, I've shamed myself and this kingdom when the best I can give it is you."

Beau shuddered. Horror made the world foggy, unreal. Was he really standing here, hearing his father say these things to him? He couldn't feel his hands or feet, couldn't feel the ground underneath him. "What is happening?" he whispered. "I'm trying my best. I know I'm not Char, but I'm not a *cockroach*, I'm not—"

"You're going to make a mockery of my throne," Fortin said. "Our best—our only hope is that you marry a better woman than you're worthy of and let her rule through you. Here." The fingers of his right hand took hold of the ring finger on his left, a tremor running through them as he pulled off his wedding ring. "For your proposal. Maybe magic will sweeten the pot enough that whoever she is will accept you."

He flung the ring on the floor in front of Beau's feet, and it rolled a few inches before knocking into Beau's boot. He stared down at it, stunned. "I'm sorry," Beau said. "I just want to help people. I want to be a good king. I'm sorry to have disappointed you."

"Get out of my sight," Fortin said, the words coming out of him like a sigh, rattling in his throat. "Do not let me see you again unless I summon you."

Numbly, Beau bent to pick up the ring and turned, unsteady on his feet. His own blood rushing in his ears made his footsteps inaudible and also blocked out the sound of his mother following him out into the hall. She touched his arm, turning him back to her.

Beau felt a moment of relief as he looked down into her grave, glassy-eyed face. Hopeful, he waited for the gentle, soothing words that would salve the wounds his father had made. She reached for his hand, and he let her take it.

She put another ring in his palm, the matching one she always wore. "For tonight."

He looked down at the ring and then back at her as she released his arm and took a step back. He blinked; he waited. After a brief nod, she swept back toward the bedroom. With a swallow that tore at his throat, Beau said, "That's it?"

She stilled but didn't turn back. Beau felt fragile in the middle, like if he took too deep a breath, he'd crack in half. After a few more shallow breaths, he realized she wasn't going to speak or soothe. His hand tightened on the rings until the metal bit bruisingly into his flesh.

These rings had been a part of his mother and father his whole life. The flickers of understanding and silent communication passing from one to the other as they caught and reflected each other's emotions through the rings were Beau's entire picture of love, of partnership. "You were wearing this," he said, a thin crust of calm barely covering the waver in his voice. "Is he just angry? Or did he mean it?"

He could see only a thin sliver of her face, but it was enough to see her crumple. She inhaled in pieces, ratcheting herself up to speak, her shoulders rising, and Beau knew whatever she said next was going to be a lie.

He fled.

There was a butler's pantry beneath the royal apartments; he and Char had snuck in once when Char was fourteen and Beau was nine and stolen two bottles of wine each. Beau hadn't liked the taste at the time, but he loved when Char included him in his schemes, so he drank along, swig for swig. It wasn't until Beau was throwing up on the carpet that Char, laughing, revealed he'd been spitting his into one of the planters.

Beau found his way down to the pantry, feeling almost as sick as he had at nine with his first bellyful of alcohol. He grabbed two bottles at random out of the racks, ignored the serving men, and walked straight back out.

His feet followed the same track he and Char had taken years before, down the servants' stair and out a small wooden door into a courtyard draped in drying laundry. It was growing dark; laughing women plucked sheets from the line and folded them into baskets.

Beau walked through the courtyard and back into the palace on the other side, a shortcut to the library. Because he expected no one there, he was unsurprised by the dim silence once the door shut behind him. It smelled of ink and binding glue. In the dark, he couldn't find a chair, but the floor suited him fine.

Kneeling, he pulled his knife from his belt and stabbed the tip into the cork of one of the bottles at an angle, twisting and pulling until it was halfway out of the neck. He yanked the knife out and tried to stab the cork through the side to pry it further, but in the darkness, he missed. A sharp line of pain drew itself along his thumb where the blade bit him.

"Ah, fuck," he hissed, dropping the bottle with a thud to clutch his thumb. It bled, but the cut was shallow. He'd never made a habit of cutting his fingers; they hurt too much and got in the way as they healed. People noticed when you cut your fingers.

He ignored the sting as he grabbed the bottle again, working the blade more carefully. The cork popped free and rolled across the floor, and Beau took a long, thirsty gulp from the neck of the bottle and inspected his thumb in the dim light. He'd need a bandage, but he wouldn't lose any meat. He turned his hand so the blood would run into his palm and not drip on the carpet.

Blood pooling in his hand and wine pooling in his stomach. Beau felt a dark twist of amusement; just like old times. This was what he'd been afraid of when he came back to the palace. He'd gotten better in the isles, let go of self-destruction. Five years since he'd hurt himself on purpose. Four since he'd gotten too drunk to stand. Two and a half since he'd needed a drink to get through the day.

And here he fucking was again. A cockroach, outliving all the good things, even his own best efforts.

He hefted his dagger in his palm. Char had given it to him on his thirteenth birthday. It had drawn a lot of Beau's blood. He'd taken it off and put it in a chest in the isles, afraid if he carried it on his hip that he'd use it too much, too quickly—too permanently.

"What are you doing, Highness? You disappeared so fast." Elias's voice in the dark was gentle, quiet; it didn't startle Beau.

The prince raised the bottle in mock-celebration, not sure whether El could see, and downed another mouthful. He paused only long enough to swallow, ignoring the burn in his throat, and drank again.

El lifted the wine out of his hands and knelt down in front of him. "What did he say?"

"Everything he's been holding onto," Beau said. "Let's see... worthless, pile of shit, insect, shame to the crown? Something to that effect. More words, obviously."

Elias took a swig. "You scared him with your announcement. He doesn't mean it."

"He does."

When Elias handed the bottle back, Beau reached across to take it with his uninjured right hand. His guard noticed the motion immediately. "What's wrong with your other arm?" He didn't wait for an answer, grabbing Beau's wrist and inhaling sharply when he touched blood.

"Just an accident with the knife," Beau said lightly. "Corks are slippery buggers."

With a growl, Elias released him and stood. Beau craned his neck to watch him. "What are you doing?"

Under his breath, Elias muttered, "Contemplating treason."

"Sit down. It *was* an accident. I'm fine." Beau sighed and sipped more conservatively. "I just needed to be alone for a minute."

"Alone, bleeding, and on the way to drunk," Elias said, voice low enough that he clearly hadn't meant to be heard, but annoyance dragged up the volume. "I'm sorry I let you get ahead of me."

"S'fine. I move fast when looking for a place to fall apart."

"You don't really have time to fall apart right now, Highness. What say we get you bandaged up and dressed?"

Stalling for the time to take another gulp of wine before his guard hauled him to his feet, Beau asked, "What time is it?"

"I don't know—getting dark?" Elias pulled him up and Beau curled his arm against his belly to keep his palmful of blood from spilling everywhere. Setting the wine on the floor, Elias took hold of Beau's elbow and walked them both toward the pool of light from the lamps in the main corridor that cast warmly through the glass on either side of the library's doors. "Uriel will be losing his mind."

"Ah good," Beau said. He didn't feel tipsy, just warmer and looser. He couldn't remember the last time he'd felt tipsy. "Someone else to disappoint by being the shittiest crown prince today."

Elias stopped, pulling Beau short before they left the library. "Please pull out of this. You're not your brother, Highness. And I know you think that means you're *less* than he was. But you'll do things he couldn't have dreamed. When the day comes that you're king, you may be a reluctant king, but you'll be the *right* king. And I'll be proud that you are my king."

"You're setting your expectations way too high," Beau said with an abysmal laugh. "Now I've got to disappoint *you* too."

"Shut up, Highness."

Beau reeled back, scoffing in his throat. "I'm sorry, *what?*"

"Stop repeating the meaningless trash people say to you," Elias said. "Will you *listen* if I'm cruel? Fine, I'll be cruel. You're too intelligent to be such a trusting moron. Your father is a sick, bitter old man who treated you like shit and justified it in his own head by making up some grand narrative about you *deserving* to be treated that way, and your brother made it worse, constantly. He hates that you're going to change all the worst things he and his ilk brought about. He hates *you.* Why the fuck would you listen to him?"

The warmth and looseness from the wine evaporated, swept away by a cold wind. Beau took a deep breath and then said levelly, "I know he hates me. I know Char and my mother barely tolerated me. But they're my family; they're what I have."

Elias tried to speak, but Beau raised a hand. "You will be quiet now, Elias Batesian. You've said your piece. I ask your counsel because I like to have it and because it's easier to reason things out when we discuss it. But at the end of the day, I'm the crown prince. I see what needs to be done, I do it, and I bear the consequences of it—so if you feel I'm not listening to you, I'll ask you to bear in mind that you're my guard, not my advisor."

Elias's chin rose, but Beau couldn't tell if it was defiance or an acknowledgement. He continued, "I'm not, as you so skillfully put it, a 'trusting moron.' I know people are lying to me. I try to surround myself with people who tell me the truth, but here in the palace, *no one* tells me the truth. Even you. You lie to me constantly; just not about the things I care about. I know you want me to succeed, and I know you'll protect me. That's true and you've proven it, and you can keep whatever other secrets you want.

"My family despises me, the nobles despise me, the majority of my own guards despise me, the staff despise me and have to be won over one at a time. Those who don't hate me still lie to me." Beau shook his head and reached into his pocket, pulling out the two rings. "I'm supposed to go out on that lake tonight and put one of these rings on a lady's finger so I can feel, every second of every day, how much she loathes me. Her contempt for me if I accept her lies; her frustration if I don't. So she can feel a constant feed of my despair."

Beau folded his hands around the rings and fought the desire to launch them into the dark library. Instead, he stuffed them into his pocket. "Several people warned me today that sending nobles to the border would get me killed. And all I could think was what a fucking relief that would be. I can't kill myself, because this kingdom is my godsdamned responsibility and I can't abandon it the coward's way. But if they murder me, it won't be *my* fault I didn't fix every problem in Granvallée alone."

"You're not alone," Elias said.

"No," Beau agreed bitterly, "you're always here to keep me from escaping by any route."

For once, Elias had no response. Beau clenched and un-clenched his hurt thumb inside his fist. It throbbed with his heart-beat. "If you really want to protect *me*, not the future king of Gran-vallée, but *Beauregard*, find some way to get me out of this tonight. Find some way to help me escape the pressure of this fucking marriage so I can figure the rest out."

He pushed out of the library, leading the way to his rooms as El ghosted along behind him. When they were two turns away, Elias said abruptly, "I can't do that."

Beau laughed darkly. "Then this *trusting moron* will just have to trust you to keep me alive while I become a king they all despise."

10

A WEIGHT OF INDECISION LIFTED

Boats. Everyone was loading into stupid little two-person boats, and Beau couldn't get drunk enough fast enough.

Beside him in a small, lantern-lit gazebo. his mother sat wearing a flat expression, nothing belying her nerves but the silk handkerchief she strangled in her lap.

Near the dock from which boats launched, noblemen spoke with heads together and hands stroking mustache stubble—hiding their mouths as they watched Beau with hard, hooded eyes.

In knots like posies of flowers in their white and cream, narrow-skirted dresses, the noblewomen fanned themselves and whispered and let loose bell-peals of laughter, and watched Beau. Their glances were cutting, eyes narrowed, hidden in flutters of eyelashes.

The servants, passing nimbly through the crowd, watched Beau, but they also watched everyone else, feeling out the tide in case it might shift, preparing to lurch for shore.

Everyone watched, but no one had spoken a word to him since he arrived except the servant who brought him a steady supply of champagne flutes. They all knew Beau was supposed to choose someone, clamber into one of those boats, and propose.

Beau's hands were cold, his fingers stiff, but his neck and face were stiflingly hot. He stared out over the water, tried not to fidget. All was fine. He wasn't panicking. His scar wasn't tingling all along his back and arm, reminding him what it felt like to be sliced by a blade intent on killing him. He wasn't treading water in the ocean, watching for any sign of a rescue ship while sharks circled.

The serving woman brought an entire tray of champagne, and Beau grabbed one in each hand, downing them back to back and dropping the empty flutes with muted *tinks* onto the silver. Bending her knees in a suggestion of a curtsy, carefully balancing the tray, the servant waited to see if he'd take another—and he did—before sweeping away.

"I know why *I'm* not in a boat: I've never liked them. But you're a sailor." Lady Penamour strode into the gazebo, the cream of her dress with its gold embroidery making her glow in the lamplight. She cast a scathing look at Beau, then turned to the queen. "Good evening, Your Majesty. I see the king is resting tonight?"

"Good evening, Your Grace. He'll be right as rain tomorrow," Queen Acier said with a small smile. "You look lovely."

"Thank you." As she turned from the queen back to Beau, Penamour's smile slipped off. "Well? Haven't we all gathered to witness your marriage proposal? Where's the lucky lady?"

Beau met her brown eyes, little lamp flames glittering in their depths, and swayed, the champagne fizzing his brain into a gentle fog. "You win." It came out low and quiet. "You're a talented politician, Pellabell. I never stood a chance."

She was the first to break eye contact, blinking out at the water with a strangely dissatisfied expression overtaking her face. After a long few heartbeats of silence, she said, "If you'll excuse us, Your Majesty, His Highness and I need to speak."

His mother nodded, and Lady Penamour drifted a few steps away, glancing back once at Beau to see that he was following. Slightly unsteady on his feet, Beau stood and paced after her into the darkness between the gazebo and the torches near the water. He expected the duchess to stop there in the shadows, since it seemed she wanted to speak privately, but she strode past the pale bouquets of gowns to the dark water, its surface scattered with gold flame flickers and the steady white of moonlight.

Lady Roben and her fresh fiancé, Lord Blanchet, stepped back from the boat they'd been about to enter. "By all means, Your Grace, Your Highness, please take this one," Blanchet said, gesturing magnanimously toward the elegant little rowboat.

"Are we getting in that boat?" Beau asked, surprised.

Penamour arched a brow at him. "I believe we're obliged to." When she spoke quietly like that, her voice had a deep huskiness that settled in his belly and made him regret to his marrow the misunderstanding driving her hate. The rings burned in his pocket.

"Who am I to turn down an obligation," he said as lightly as he could manage. His chest was too tight to speak casually. Taking her hand, he helped her into the boat and then lowered himself in with surprising grace for how inebriated he'd become. As she settled against her seat, spreading her skirts neatly around her, and looked out over the water, Beau paddled them smoothly away from the dock toward a fairly empty spot on the lake.

She waited until no one else was in earshot before speaking. "What under the Twelve were you thinking when you made that announcement this afternoon?"

Beau hadn't expected that. He let go of the oars in their oarlocks and let their boat drift as he rubbed his hands together. "If you wish to file an official complaint about protecting our borders, Pellmell, I'm sure there'll be a line at the next court session. You're welcome to join it. Or you can quietly subvert and sabotage my efforts from the shadows, since that's perhaps more your style."

She made a sharp, annoyed sound. "I have no complaints about sending defenders. It's not *enough* to resolve the problem, but it's a start. I want to know why the Penamours weren't on your list of nobles charged with defense."

"You want to go to the border?" He *really* hadn't expected that.

"Not particularly, but if you're only going to send the most indolent and self-absorbed dregs, you should send someone who actually cares what happens," she snapped, her crisp diction ensuring he understood every word, though her voice was pitched not to carry. *She thinks they're bad nobles, too?*

"You know I have an interest in Suteneir, and they'll bear the brunt of this. Not to mention, you and I shared similar opinions at the ambassadors' dinner—you know I would've supported this. Why did you announce it without discussing it with *any* nobles first?"

"Discussing it?" Beau scoffed. "You and I have such a successful history of *discussing* things. I'm sure that would've gone delightfully well." He took a deep breath. He supposed he could add her to the list, since she was asking for it. But if she did believe more needed to be done, he wouldn't put it past her to send people over the border, and that would cause headaches. He was counting on the chosen parties' disinterest in doing anything to keep them from doing things he didn't want. "As I said, if you want to complain about my changes, get in line."

Penamour reached for one of the oars and drew it with some difficulty until the boat drifted slowly around so Beau's face would be visible in the light from shore. A crescent of her face was warmly, flickeringly lit, the rest cast in deep shadow. "I don't want to complain. You've proven you have no issue with being unpopular, so what would one more complaint do? And also…" She sighed. "They're not *bad* changes, the things you've done."

Beau studied the way she crossed her feet on the burden boards, listening hard.

Penamour shifted. "Will you please look at me when I'm speaking? I know you don't like to, but it's challenging having a conversation with the top of your head or the side of your face."

Beau looked up, met the dark glimmer of her eyes. "I've been told that when I look at people, I'm very intense."

"You are," Penamour agreed, but she didn't look away. "Tell me what's going through your head. I want to understand *why* you've changed what you have. Did you think Charmant wouldn't? That his approach would be so different? Is that why you killed him?"

Beau growled, dropping his chin to his chest and shaking his head. "And we're back to you throwing out the most hateful questions you can imagine."

"You severely underestimate my imagination," she said flatly.

The wine from the library and the champagne from the gazebo and the complete lack of any other food in his stomach combined to make his tongue alarmingly loose. "If you're so certain I'm a murderer, why would you want to be out in the middle of a lake with me? It's dark. You can't possibly swim in that. Neither of our guards are anywhere close. Aren't you scared?"

Her chin rose, her beautiful, full lips shining faintly from whatever gloss she'd painted on. "Are you threatening me?"

"No!" Beau said incredulously, too tipsy to control volume. "For fuck's sake, I wouldn't hurt you for anything, and I don't want you to believe I would. How do I fix this? How do I explain I could never have done what you think when you won't even tell me *why*?"

Penamour tutted. "You want to fix things so you never have to face consequences?"

"That is *not* what I want to fix." The boat rocked as he leaned forward and took one of her bare hands in his, her skin buttery soft under his fingers. "I was wrong to say I wouldn't have you, that it wasn't possible to trust you because of your political bent. And I want to fix that. But you are more wrong. Wronger. More wrong." He frowned, uncertain, drunk. "Whichever. You don't know me, and you're *wrong* about me. I want to fix that. I want...to marry you."

He could feel her pulse fluttering in her wrist, but she didn't pull away from him, and her eyes were steady on his face. "Oh, you *must* be desperate," she said, low and simmering with some emotion he couldn't name. "Is this an attempt to keep your enemies closer, or were you planning to propose to anyone who'd get in a boat with you this evening?"

"Neither." He tightened his grip on her hand and pulled her more into the light so he could try to read her face. "I want to marry *you*. I looked for someone who was interesting and I found you. I looked for someone who was kind to their servants and I found you. I looked for someone who would understand what the fuck I'm trying to do in court and I found you. By any possible measure, you're the only right choice.

"You are beautiful and bright and powerful and well-studied and if the way you've decimated my every plan is any indication, you're unstoppable politically in ways I can't imagine. You already wanted to be queen—you'd already made the arrangements. And I *know* I'm not Char, but...I feel like the only thing standing in the way is your misconception of who I *am*."

Something flickered in her face. He couldn't read it, even desperate as he was to understand, but for a brief, brief moment, her fingers tightened on his hand. Then she squeezed her eyes shut, drew an iron mask of hardness over her features, and yanked her hand back. "Do other people find you charming, Your Highness?"

"No, they don't. You know they don't. My brother was the charming one. His name meant 'charming,' after all."

"And yours means 'beautiful,'" she muttered, sitting back and crossing her arms.

He wasn't sure he was meant to hear that. It shouldn't have cut so deep, but it did. He wasn't as striking as his brother had been—golden curls versus unruly brown waves; bright green eyes versus muddled hazel somewhere between brown and green and grey; towering, broad-shouldered height versus lean, wiry agility—but people had found him handsome before.

Not Penamour, though. Not the person who mattered in this moment. "Did I miss your appointment to the official task of humbling me, Panman?"

She trailed a hand in the water and rolled her eyes. "I'm sure such a position would be a full-time commitment, and I have much more important duties than slicing away at your ego."

Beau studied her for an uncomfortably long time. "You don't understand me very well."

"And you don't understand me at all if you think I'll be thrown off the scent by flattery and broad dismissals. I will see the truth uncovered."

They were going in circles. Beau grabbed the oars and began pulling them back to shore again, too frustrated to sit here in the lapping darkness any longer. As they neared the dock, he said, "Tell me what you're looking for and I'll give you any truth you want."

"I can get what I need without enduring your lies, thank you."

"By, what, following me? Studying my every move? Listening to every word I speak? I have nothing to hide from you and nothing to lie about, Pinafore. You'll find, if you watch long enough, that you would've wasted less time by simply listening when I answer you."

Others at the dock helped hold the boat steady and hand Lady Penamour out. When their hands reached for Beau, too, he waved them away.

"Thank you, as always," he said to Penamour, "for the delightful company and painful conversation." He kicked the dock to send his boat splashing out into the water again and lay back miserably, staring up at the stars. He could hear the couples floating around him, snippets of laughter and murmurs of flirtation bouncing off the water as rippled and fractured as the reflections of lamplight.

What the hell had possessed him to say all those things to her, when it was obvious she despised him to his bones? He'd set himself up for a brutal rejection he *knew* perfectly well would happen. And the knowing didn't make it sting one bit less. He'd thought for a *moment* she was warming to him, that something he said got through, and that glimmer of hope had made the shutdown even worse.

When he tired of his own circular thoughts, Beau rowed back to the dock and let someone take his forearm and help him up, giving Lord and Lady Cellier a chance to float. Elias was at his side before he'd taken two steps, a hand on his back.

Beau was ashamed of how much he needed that small gesture of familiarity and comfort. The day had beaten him to a pulp.

He headed for the gazebo, already bracing for his mother's disappointment in the son with two rings still in his pocket. As he crossed the grass, though, he saw Lady Penamour had taken his seat next to his mother, and they were both listening to a man in the sober black frock coat and red collar of a doctor. Penamour held his mother's hand. Beau's heart dropped, and his pace quickened.

"…a great deal of rest, but we may yet—" the man was saying quietly, but he cut himself off at Beau's approach. "Ah, Your Highness. Good evening to you."

"You have news about my father?"

The man's lips pressed tightly together in an uncomfortable smile. "Ah, no. Or, that is, I've been instructed by His Majesty, um…" He trailed off, fidgeting uneasily.

Beau was confused, and then he was cold with understanding. "He told you not to tell me." He sighed out an almost laugh. "Can you at least—is he—" Beau gritted his teeth, shook his head. "Fuck it. Nevermind. If he doesn't want me to know, I just won't know."

Why did it hurt so much? Why did it hurt *so* much?

Lady Penamour's eyes were on him, examining him, picking him apart. *Does the pain of my father's hatred of me entertain you? Is it an interesting problem to identify?*

Gods, he wanted to fucking leave. He wanted to get on his horse and ride hundreds of miles away and never come back to this godsdamned place.

Lady Penamour cleared her throat politely and said, "Your Majesty, I wonder if you might consider releasing His Highness's horse tomorrow."

Beau blinked. Had he said his thoughts out loud?

The queen also blinked as if she'd emerged from a dim hallway into a room blazing with sunlight. "His horse?"

"Yes. I have urgent personal business at the border of Estforet, which will take me right past the isles. I wondered if His Highness might accompany me, since he knows the area well. I'm sure he's homesick." Lady Penamour delivered this entire speech without acknowledging once that Beau was standing three feet from her.

Queen Acier frowned. "Do you think it wise for Beauregard to leave the capital *now*?" She glanced up at the doctor and then at Beau, her frown deepening, and the prince's dread about his father's failing health ratcheted up.

"Just a quick jaunt, I assure you," Penamour said. "A week there, a week back. And it would give us plenty of time to…talk." She raised her brows, giving the queen a significant look.

Elias shifted behind Beau, nudging him with his knuckles. When the prince glanced at him, he was shaking his head. "You can't leave the capital, Highness," he mouthed.

Beau turned back to the duchess, mind scrabbling for any way to make sense of her request. She thought he was a murderer. She knew his father's health was failing. She didn't *like* him. Why the fuck was she asking his mother's permission to bring him along on a two-week roundtrip to the isles?

Had he gotten through to her? Was she trying to make time to talk and *listen*?

Queen Acier's eyes were sharp on Penamour's and some understanding passed between them that Beau couldn't intercept. "Yes, I'll send a note this evening. It shouldn't be a problem."

"Wonderful." Lady Penamour stood, bowing her head to the queen. "We'll want an early start in the morning, so I'll take my leave. Good evening, Your Majesty."

"Wait," Beau said, confused by how quickly they moved. "You haven't actually asked me if I'm interested in accompanying you to this 'urgent business.' What kind of business requires you to leave first thing in the morning? And Mother, is Father's health—I mean, is it—is he—" Beau couldn't form the words, *If I leave for two weeks, is my father going to die in the interim?*

"You'd miss an opportunity to get away from the palace and see your isles?" Penamour put a hand on her hip and frowned.

His mother strangled the handkerchief, but she straightened her shoulders with a sigh as if she'd made a hard decision and was squaring her resolve. "Two weeks is no problem. You've been missing the isles, haven't you? A brief visit will be good. Help you…refocus."

An opening, an escape, a shaft of light piercing down into the well he'd fallen down. He didn't want to question it; what if they snatched it away again, buried him alive again? Beau had no one to propose to tonight and no one to celebrate when he picked a crown up off his father's corpse on some tomorrow, but he *did* have the isles. He loved the isles, and the isles loved him.

"You want to leave early tomorrow?" Beau asked. Elias fully grabbed the back of Beau's shirt and *shook* him, too familiar and too aggressive. Beau didn't look back; he knew Elias wanted him to stay here and face all the problems in the world, but here was this glorious out. And it'd give him time to talk to Lady Penamour, perhaps convince her at last that he wasn't capable of fratricide. "What time?"

"*No*," Elias whispered. Lady Penamour glanced unreadably at him, and El stepped up beside Beau, arm brushing the prince's. He stared Lady Penamour and Queen Acier down. More firmly and more loudly, he said, "His Highness can't leave the capital when His Majesty's health is so uncertain. You're too smart to be that foolish."

Beau startled. Guards did not talk to nobility—*royalty*—like that. His mother reacted with the same surprise, but where Beau's was morphing into concern over what was going on with Elias, Queen Acier's sharpened into cold fury.

"Leave us please, Dr. Geuris." When the doctor stepped away, she said frostily, "Master Guardsman, whatever unusual privileges you've enjoyed as a result of your inappropriate relationship to my son, they do *not* include speaking to the peerage that way. You may pack your things and find alternative employ—"

Red fury took Beau over. "You do *not* have the authority to dismiss *my* staff," he growled. Beau had never in his life considered pulling rank on his mother. He deferred to her. But while his father could do whatever he wished with Beau, the Queen of Granvallée had no weight to throw around with a crown prince and duke unless granted it explicitly by the king.

He was drunk; he was angry; he was suddenly aware of how buzzingly good it could feel to *have* power when one needed it. She thought she could take Elias away from him on a whim?

He glanced at his First and nodded back toward the palace, and El immediately stepped away, standing at attention out of hearing range where he could watch for threats.

Wine made a slippery decline of Beau's self-control, and words he'd never imagined speaking slid out of his mouth. "I don't know what fucking 'inappropriate relationship' you're envisioning, but you can keep your imagination to yourself. Elias Batesian keeps me *alive*. And he's able to do that because I'm not so godsdamned stupid as to imagine the only good ideas in this world will be birthed from highborn brains. So when he raises genuine concerns, I *listen*."

Far from being chastened, the queen grew colder and calmer, as though a weight of indecision had been lifted from her. "Your father can dismiss him."

"Yes, but my father is not *here*, which is the crux of Elias's concern," Beau snapped. "Would you have pulled this shit on Char?"

"I wouldn't have needed to. Charmant understood where his priorities lay, and would never have insulted his peers for the sake of a common sellsword," Acier said coldly. She exchanged another meaningful, uninterpretable glance with Lady Penamour. "I'll release your horse, as you've begged for since you arrived. What you do from there is none of my concern."

She stood and swept toward the palace without another glance at Beau or Elias. Lady Penamour made no comment, just watched Beau with hooded, suspicious eyes and said, "I'll be waiting by the north gate at first chime." Then she followed the queen.

Beau watched them leave with a growing sense that he'd fucked up somehow, though he wasn't sure what he'd have done differently, had he a sober mind and hindsight's advantage.

He and Elias argued most of the way back to his rooms, and then continued when Beau told Uriel to have him packed for two weeks by first chime.

"I get it," Beau snapped eventually, exhausted and swirling from the wine and crushed by the day. "You think my father's going to die and I'll somehow miss the window on taking my throne. And I'm telling you there's not a fucking *chance* my mother would let me escape that easily. If there were any chance of that, she'd have somebody bar my fucking door from the outside. I want to see home at least *once* more before I'm trapped under that crown."

"I thought you *listened* when I raised a genuine concern?" Elias snapped back, frustrated.

"I'm going. End of discussion."

11

FRUITLESS ENDEAVORS

Uriel, Capucine, and Aloise had packed. Jude and Oria had readied the horses. Elias made his disapproval known with blank faces and short, abrupt answers. And Beau, ferociously hungover and miserable to be awake so early, was impatient to be home already.

A small hand tugged on Beau's sleeve. "Do you have an extra horse, Your Highness? I don't have one," Theodore said, rubbing a finger along the side of his nose. Beau hadn't heard the boy come in amidst the chaos of the morning's scramble.

"Master Moulin," Beau said gently, "you're not going with us."

Theo's chin popped up, consternation plain on his face. "I promise I won't get in the way! I can ride double with someone, if there's no extra. I want to see the isles! I'm already packed!" He was kitted out in trousers and cap, travel bag slung across his shoulders.

"I'm not worried about you getting in the way; you're a useful lad. I'm worried about you getting hurt." Beau winced, seeing that would make Theo dig his heels in harder. "What about your mother? You'd leave her alone for weeks?"

"She's not alone. I've got four other brothers and sisters. She won't miss me. Besides, I'm the oldest; I can strike out on my own. You left your mother and went to the isles!"

Beau laughed. "I was a few years older than you, Theo. But I need you to stay." His mind turned quickly. "I've got an important letter to leave with you. The most important I've ever written in my life. And when the time comes, I need someone I trust to deliver it."

Theo frowned skeptically. "What letter?"

As far as Beau was concerned, there were two potential outcomes to this outing: he successfully persuaded Lady Penamour of his innocence and competence, at which point he'd have a powerful ally and being king might be workable; or he failed, and he'd know the throne wasn't meant for him. If the latter occurred, Beau wanted to be ready. He'd already be in the isles, where a ship could take him anywhere. No reason to return to the palace at all.

"Just a moment." Beau strode past the sacks and packs to his desk, fumbling around for paper to scrawl a letter quickly:

> *I, Beauregard Mylan Adelard Tristain Highput, in the interest of the continued prosperity and progress of this kingdom, formally renounce my claim to the throne of Granvallée, from the moment this letter is presented to the court and thereafter.*

He signed it with a flourish, stamping a seal both on the inside alongside his name and on the outer ribbon. Let no one question the veracity of that one. Maybe it wouldn't be needed, but maybe it would.

When he turned, Theo stood rather too close to him and startled at the sudden movement. "I need you to make two promises," Beau said quietly, holding the letter out but not handing it to the boy. "First, you *cannot* read this letter, under any circumstances. It's to be delivered exactly as I hand it to you, seal unbroken and no tampering. Is that understood?"

When Theo nodded, he continued, "Second, if I send you a pigeon that says it's time, you take this to the king and queen and ask them to present it in court. Make sure it gets to them. Make sure they understand it's from me. Can I trust you with this?"

"I swear, Your Highness, I'll do it just like you said. You can trust me." Disappointment twisted his face, but he gave a solemn nod of acceptance.

"Good." Beau clapped the boy companionably on the shoulder and ushered him out. "Keep it safe, Master Moulin, and watch out for yourself. I'll see you again soon enough."

A line of horses awaited them outside the stables, starting with Oria's and ending with two packhorses loaded with gear. Beau's mare Tempest and Elias's warhorse Pormort awaited their riders, Beau's girl stamping her feet impatiently.

He gave Tempest a scratch under the chin and she butted her nose against him hard enough to knock the air out of him, begging for more. "Are we ready to ride?"

Elias nodded stiffly, hefting himself up astride Pormort as the rest of Beau's party mounted up. Beau swung into the saddle, clicked his tongue, laid the reins across Tempest's neck, and pressed a leg in to bring her around. The day was clear and beautiful, an idyllic scene scored by the chirping of birds and the rumble of occasional carts passing on the road. It felt like the entire world was celebrating Beau's brief freedom.

Lady Penamour waited exactly where she said she'd be, only her guard and two servants riding with her. Beau pulled Tempest up alongside her. "Where's the rest of your retinue? There's only one waypoint with an inn—we'll be sleeping rough."

"I know the route, Your Highness. Are you ready?"

They rode.

The road was quiet, lightly trafficked this early, and Lady Penamour was silent.

Beau looked for Elias, hoping for conversation, but El had dropped back next to one of Penamour's servants, a broad-shoul-dered man in his mid-thirties with an unpleasant twist to his mouth. They quietly conversed, leaving the prince stranded with a duchess who seemed perfectly content never to speak again.

After hours of unrelenting boredom, Beau said, "So what's your business in Estforet?"

Her hair was braided back severely today. Beau wondered how long it had taken her to untangle her curls, arms aching. "Lord Tremblay has a Maurilel artifact too fragile to be moved, and he asked me to take a look. I have a knack for identifying their uses."

"Laccombes has an artifact? A recent addition, or…?"

"I'm not sure."

"How is that urgent?"

Her dark eyes were amused. "Some prince ordered his entire household to the Paibon border. Perhaps he's hoping this artifact can change that outcome."

Beau snorted. "So he tempted you out with the promise of getting to play with magic, and you tempted me out with the promise of good stew and isles air. Ah, to be known."

From the corner of his eye, Beau caught the flash of her nose ring, rose-gold, and the dark sweep of her eyelashes as she looked him up and down. "Tell me something true, Highness."

Beau chuckled humorlessly. "As I always do, Penn." Tempest frisked, and Beau calmed her with his knees. He let the birdsong soothe him. "Ask me anything you like, so long as you're answering my questions in return."

"Are you ever going to call me by my actual name?"

Beau smirked. "Remind me of your actual name, Participle?"

"Victoire Penamour," she said, glaring holes through Beau's forehead. "I'll even bend on the 'lady' and 'Your Grace'—you can call me Victoire if you *must*. But the nicknames—"

Beau wrinkled his nose. "Victoire? That's terrible. Doesn't sound anything like you. You have a question or not, Perpendicular?"

She sighed, irritation flattening her lips into a line, then rolled her eyes and summoned a question. "You told me once that you didn't want the throne. What did you mean by that?"

The prince laughed, surprised into amusement by Penamour's insistence on imagining deeper levels to even his most obvious statements. "I'm not sure how much clearer that can be. I don't want to be king. I know I will be. I'm prepared for it. I'm sure there are *some* advantages to it. But I'd rather be elsewhere. I despise politics."

"You can't despise politics," Penamour said incredulously. "It's just knowing what people want and giving it to them. What's there to hate about that?"

"No one *tells* you what they want. They tell you what they think you want them to want, and then tell the next person what *they* think they want them to want, and the two of them imagine things *you* must want that you've never said, and no one will take a straight fucking answer when you tell them what you *do* want."

"This sounds like a skill issue."

"It's *absolutely* a skill issue, Pishposh," Beau agreed. "I have no skill in navigating dishonesty, and everyone else seems to lack the basic skills of making their faces match their words match their godsdamned actions."

"That's rich, coming from an accomplished liar." The wind teased a few strands of her dark hair out of her braid, and Beau watched them dance around her face. Her hair looked so glossy, like it would run under his hands like silk.

"I would genuinely *love* to hear where I gave that impression."

"You have the court convinced you're some drunk, bumbling idiot, not a murderer with a calculated plan to reshape Granvallée."

Tempest frisked again, bored with their pace, and Beau bent to pat her neck. "I could be both. Minus the murderer bit."

"You *could* be a lot of things." Lady Penamour chewed her lower lip, frowning toward two oncoming wagons taking up most of the road. "What you are is a mystery."

"I'm really, *really* not," Beau said with a laugh.

"All right, then, solve some mysteries for me. What did you do with the money?" She jabbed a finger at his boots. "Charmant complained constantly about you draining the treasury, but I've seen better equipped merchants. Did you spend it *all* on Elias?"

"On Elias?" Beau was baffled.

"I know that training didn't come cheap, and he has good quality armor, good weapons, a hell of a horse, but even all of that together doesn't add up to—"

"What training? I haven't paid for any training *or* for his equipment, although now that you mention it, I probably should've. Elias came to me fully equipped."

"From where?"

Beau scratched at the back of his neck. "Altagna, originally? He speaks another language, but I don't remember if it's Altagnan or Alzhaki. I'm pretty sure he's lived in Granvallée most of his life."

"No, not where—" Penamour gave him the strangest look, brows creased. "What do you mean, 'pretty sure'? Do you two not even talk after?" She gave an unladylike snort and shook her head. "I meant from what organization? Who taught him to fight like that?"

Talk after what? "Um, another...guard...position? I suppose?"

"By the fucking Twelve," Penamour muttered, and he was surprised to hear the curse from her mouth. "You can't even be honest with me about *this*? Why all the damned secrecy?"

Beau scratched Tempest's withers, more to reassure him than the horse. "Penderast, why ask me questions if you won't believe a word I say? You answer one. I heard you blackmailed your family into supporting your claim for the title of duchess. Is that true?"

She seemed to wrestle with the urge to demand more from him, but eventually she nodded. "Yes," she said, no trace of contrition on her face, "although, some context. I'm not a villain stealing a seat." She shot him a significant look at this. "I was and am the best person for it; some people just needed to be made to understand that. My father died when I was twelve, and my mother fought all four of his brothers to hold onto the estate and title. She *won*."

The pride that lit her face made her glow, breathtaking. "Quite a feat," he said.

"Yes. Yes, it was." Her eyes flashed, and she looked ferocious as a hunting bird. "When she died three years ago, I did the same. My sisters and I held onto Veritelutte and I held the title of duchess by pulling every trick I had at my disposal. My two living uncles on Father's side are in poor health, but they wanted to claim it for their own lines. One of their firstborn sons is a good friend. He knew I'd handle the family name better than he could. His is the strongest claim behind mine; his support carried a lot of weight.

"The other was not as easily convinced. But he has a second family he doesn't want his wife to find out about. So I was able to go to the king with both of their support, and I got dispensation to hold what's mine. All it cost was my hand."

"In marriage, you mean? Your betrothal to Char was part of the negotiation?"

She smiled, and it was a vicious thing. "Your brother had the same problem you do—not enough available, powerful women, although he didn't scorn them *personally* as you have. He simply refused to consider anyone with less than a duchy at their disposal."

"He could've married Haydée, couldn't he? Except, no, she'd have been, what, ten years younger than him? Was she even of age when you two got engaged?"

"Eleven years younger, and no, she wasn't, although I don't think that would've deterred Charmant. I wasn't interested in seeing the Macabries grow more powerful. So I pulled a few strings to make Haydée less of an option for him, as I did for you."

"Ah." Beau nodded. "You showcased how cruel she always is?"

Frowning at him, Penamour said, "No. I reminded Charmant that Lord Macabrie has always been critical of the crown—and him—and that Haydée has a large, active group of friends. Charmant liked his girls dependent on his attention, and he *despised* being criticized. You're harder to read, but I knew if she said to your face what she'd said behind your back about Elias, you'd snap."

With a quick glance at Elias—still riding next to Penamour's man—Beau cleared his throat, "I don't like that she thinks people are for sale, fair enough. You don't sound…forgive me if this is a rude question, but you don't sound like you *liked* Char much."

"That's not a question," she said dryly. "It's a statement of fact. He had me fooled for a while. He was charming. Good at everything. Loved the finer things and lavished the people around him with them. He insisted on only spending time with *special* people, which had a way of making people feel special. But there were cracks. He was cruel, as most noblemen are at times. That *doesn't* mean he deserved to die. Murdering one's political rivals is the behavior of low, unintelligent cretins who lack the social skills and common sense to outmaneuver them."

Beau could tell she meant these things to sting him, but since he had not, in fact, murdered any political rivals, they washed over him harmlessly. "Yes, Elias told me you were one of the nobles who hasn't tried to have me assassinated. Thanks for that. We're aligned in that philosophy, Primrose. I would never—*never*—kill someone to steal more power. I certainly wouldn't have harmed my brother. I'd have done anything for him."

"Are you going to pretend you two were thick as thieves?" Penamour's voice dripped disdain. But her eyes were rabidly attentive, and he wanted to hold that attention, so he was more honest than he meant to be.

"No. We weren't particularly close. I wasn't close to *anyone* in the palace. Growing up there was about as you'd expect: formal, cold. Didn't lend itself to affection. I saw my parents once a week and Char every couple of days, if I could convince him to let me hang around. He was older, though; he had other friends, other responsibilities. So I spent most of my time alone, reading or exploring, talking to the staff, playing with the dogs, that sort of thing."

"So you resented him."

"No," Beau said with a laugh, shaking his head. "He could barely shake me loose. I was always begging him to ride with me, spar with me, play games. I drove him out of his mind. He'd set missions—things to steal from the kitchens or pranks to play on the servants—and wouldn't speak to me until I'd done them. Just wanted peace and quiet, I'm sure."

Gods, it was hard, talking about Char, all his grief compounded by his confusion over what it meant that Char might've been the one defrauding the crown in Beau's name, and he'd "constantly complained" about Beau doing it, according to Penamour. Why had he needed the money? And why use Beau's name instead of his own?

"Why on earth did you see your mother and father so rarely?"

Beau looked up, surprised, and then shrugged. "They're the king and queen. They were busy. They saw Char more often, of course, because of his duties as crown prince. But they didn't have much need to talk to me. Even when I got in trouble, it was with Dubois or my nurse. They didn't escalate it to my parents often."

"What sorts of things did you get in trouble for?"

"Char's missions, mostly," Beau said with a laugh. "But with my father...he has very high standards. I'm not good at meeting them, and never have been."

Penamour's hands fiddled with her reins idly, as if her mind was elsewhere. "Why?"

Beau shrugged again. "I'm a half-wit. Lazy, unfocused, abnormal, disrespectful. He had Char first, and then me. Hell of a downgrade." He grinned wryly to take some of the harshness out of the words, but Lady Penamour had turned her head and shoulders fully to stare at him.

"I don't understand you," she said at length.

Beau sighed. "Well, ask more questions then, Pomegranate."

So their day went, alternatively confrontational and overly honest. It was...strange.

It was uncomfortable, but Beau could've bowed out of the conversation at any time and found he didn't want to. He liked talking to her, and it felt like she perpetually *almost* enjoyed talking to him, always on the edge of laughter before she shoved it back behind her suspicion.

When they camped the first night, Master Uriel proved the efficiency of his packing and staff by assembling Beau's tent and getting dinner over a fire in less time than it took Beau to picket, untack, and curry Tempest. Beau sat on a stump by the fire and watched the duchess, her guard, and her two servants arrange their own campsite a few paces away.

Elias squatted next to Beau, sitting on his heels and propping his arms on his knees. His eyes stayed fixed on the other campsite—on the serving man he'd spent a good portion of the day riding next to, Beau realized.

"Do you know him?"

El shook his head, bending his mouth down at the corners in a frown. "No. No one does. Her usual footman woke up ill, and Gerard replaced him." Elias's eyes followed Gerard as the man hefted saddlebags over a shoulder and carried them toward Lady Penamour's tent. He was well built and craggily handsome in a broken-nose, scar-over-the-eye kind of way, only a couple of years older than Elias. Perhaps El liked his men blond and taller than him. A prickle of jealousy jabbed at Beau and he stamped on it hard.

"I imagine no one would notice much if the two of you disappeared for a while after dinner," Beau said companionably. "Jude and Oria can keep an eye on things here."

"The duchess is bound to notice if her footman doesn't come back," Elias said dismissively, shaking his head.

Beau's mouth popped open in confusion. "What?"

He glanced back at Gerard, then at Elias, recalculating. "Wait, did you think I was suggesting you *kill* him? Why on earth would I tell you to kill a random footman?"

"I was surprised," El said. "What were you suggesting?"

Beau's face flamed with heat. "I…well…sorry, I thought you were attracted to men. Nevermind. I shouldn't have, um, assumed."

Elias's eyes and mouth both opened wide, then tightened in incredulity. He stared at Beau for a horrendously uncomfortable number of seconds. Then he laughed, a single exhalation of humor. "Highness—" he began, then shook his head, rubbed a hand over his mouth, and laughed. "I thought you were being self-deprecating at the Macabries', but you are *clueless* aren't you?"

He stood as Beau tried to remember what he was referring to; the Macabries' retreat was a blur of unpleasantness and boredom. Elias chuckled again, a disbelieving sound. Quietly enough not to be overheard, El said, "I'm not attracted to *Gerard.*"

Then he left to help Jude with the firewood, and Beau furthered his embarrassment by helplessly watching the way he swung an axe and the dimple that appeared when he smirked at something Jude said and the almost-too-pretty face turning back Beau's way, quirking into a bemused expression. He tried not to be disappointed that he was wrong; what did it *matter?* Elias was off-limits, and Beau had a mistrustful, hostile duchess to win over.

The next two days were more of the same: rising early, riding steadily, conversing exhaustingly, and settling around two separate fires and two camps in the evenings. As the palace grew more distant and the isles grew closer, Beau began to despair of convincing Penamour of his innocence, but his excitement to be home again outweighed the disappointment.

On the third night, Gerard crossed the space between the fires as they burned low, carrying a bottle of wine like a peace offering. He settled across from El and Beau, the only two who remained at the fire as the rest of Beau's staff readied the camp for sleep. "May I sit here, Your Highness?" he asked, though he was already sitting. He gave Beau a grin that put the prince in mind of a shark. "I hear you don't mind having a drink with commoners now and then."

Beau frowned at Gerard. He didn't like him but couldn't put a finger on why. "Where'd you hear that?"

"Oh, Elias has been telling me all about you," Gerard said, his grin widening as he pointed the neck of the bottle at Beau's guard.

He pulled the cork and took a swig straight from the bottle before offering it across the fire to Beau.

Beau took it but didn't drink. "Has he? Strange. He's never been much for gossip."

"Ah. You like men who keep their mouth shut."

The prince recoiled at the tone. It was suggestive, he thought, but so far from *flirting* that it felt more like a bizarre threat or accusation. Beau could make neither heads nor tails of it. "I like a guard who knows his job."

Gerard's sharklike smile widened, showing too many teeth. "Yeah, Elias is such a pretty *guard*, so versatile, isn't he? I'm sure you put him to all *sorts* of uses."

It struck Beau all at once that this man thought Elias was decorative. Incensed, he opened his mouth to invite the man to find out just how versatile El could be while kicking someone's ass, but El set a hand on his arm. After a brief pause, Elias's hand stroked along the inside of Beau's forearm to his wrist, a teasing, featherlight tickle that seemed to confirm every sly comment of 'inappropriate relationship.' It wiped the prince's mind completely blank.

Beau shuddered visibly, but El's grip tightened before he could pull his arm back in surprise. "No need to worry about Gerard's opinion of it," Elias said, voice low, but he turned his face far enough that the blond footman wouldn't be able to see his prompting expression. *Ah*, Beau thought. *He's pretending to be decorative. To be underestimated, or...?*

"Quite right," Gerard said with a smug laugh. "Who could begrudge a future king his lap candy? Though I can't imagine it's doing you many favors with Her Grace. Not having much luck with her, are you? And the way I hear it, she's your last shot at a decent queen." Beau saw why El jumped immediately to the assumption of killing him, not fucking him.

"Elias," Beau said, standing with an uncontainable look of disgust for Gerard, "would you like to go—anywhere else?"

"Sounds good."

El followed Beau to the tent, where Uriel was brewing an evening herbal tea and the cots were made. "You all right, Highness?" Aloise asked, brown eyes concerned. "You look a bit—"

"Who pissed on your boots?" Capucine asked bluntly. Uriel shot her an exasperated look.

Beau laughed and lifted a shoulder in a shrug. "I'm fine. We were just making delightful conversation with Gerard out there."

Aloise's typically sunny expression briefly curled into a grimace of revulsion, but she said only, "Elias, I was going to clean and oil the tack this evening. If you'd like, I can do your armor?"

For some reason, Elias gave her a warning look. "No thank you, Aloise, *again*." She nodded, glancing at Beau, and he got the sense she was trying to assess if he'd noticed something.

About Elias? Beau did a quick sweep of El with his eyes as they ducked past the canvas flap dividing Beau's sleeping space from the rest. His guard was as alert as he had been since they left, his usual partial leather armor in place, his sword and knife buckled on. As Beau studied him, Elias raised his eyebrows, clearly waiting for an explanation for the scrutiny. His eye sockets had grown bruise-dark in the last few days, and there was something about the way he held his shoulders that gave Beau the impression of exhaustion.

"You're wearing your armor to sleep, aren't you?" Beau asked, and the slight, defensive raise of El's shoulders was enough answer.

"I'm doing my job," El said shortly.

"You have to *rest*, El. You can't half-ass doze all the way to the isles. Is it Gerard that's got your back up? I think you can take a footman," Beau said with a chuckle.

"If that's what he is," El muttered.

Beau sat down on his cot, plucking at his bootlaces. "What else would he be?"

With a shrug, Elias paced the small space. "He thinks he can take the prince's 'lap candy' in a fight. Not many footmen believe that, even if they think you gave me a guard position as an excuse to keep me close."

"Do a lot of people think that?" Beau asked, face growing warm. *Is it that obvious that I want this man? Is it obvious to* Elias?

El's hand on his shoulder was so welcome but also made his face go pinker. "It's nothing to do with you, Highness. My face has been misleading people for a long time."

"Well, if you wanted to be the scariest man alive, you should've thought of that before being born so godsdamn pretty," Beau said, chuckling and turning away so he didn't have the temptation to look at El, and hopefully the blush would drain from his cheeks. "Are you trying to bait him into attacking? Why the performance out there about being"—Beau had to force the words out with a tongue numb from embarrassment—"lap candy?"

Elias's fingers tightened for a second, then let the prince go. "Please don't call me that."

"Oh, no!" Beau looked up at him again, shook his head. "I wasn't *calling* you that, I was repeating—I'm sorry, I didn't mean—"

El shook his head and waved a dismissive hand. He looked so *tired*, lines between his brows and around his mouth, dark purple under-eyes making his hazel eyes look brighter and greener. "I know you weren't. Forget it. Please."

"Are you sleeping at all?"

Elias scowled. "I'm doing my job. Leave it."

"Is that why Aloise wanted me to know you weren't taking your armor off? She's worried about you not sleeping? You *have* to sleep, El, even if it means—"

"*Leave it,*" Elias said too sharply. "What I *have* to do is keep you safe while you win over a duchess so we can get the fuck back to the palace. How *is* that going, by the way? Because I notice there's still a distinctly frosty wall between the campfires."

Beau began to think Elias hadn't slept once in the three days they'd been traveling. His guard didn't talk to him like that. *Ever.*

"She keeps toying with the idea of liking me, and then deciding she doesn't trust me again. It's—"

"This isn't a fucking game," El said, not looking at Beau, pacing. His fingers checked his weapons, clenched into fists, tapped against his thighs, and then began the process again.

Do you think I don't know that? rose to Beau's tongue, but he didn't speak it. Elias wasn't trying to pick a fight. He was nervous. Something had him so spooked he was sitting up all night in armor, getting more exhausted and jumpier by the day. And the only thing the prince knew had changed was Gerard. "Who is he? Gerard? You know something about him I don't."

El shook his head jerkily. "No. All I know is he's *lying.*"

So are you, Beau thought. Without his usual polished serenity, Elias's lies were more obvious. The prince lined his boots up next to the bed, pulled off his shirt, and considered. He was almost certain Elias and Gerard knew each other from before, and what El knew of him made the guard nervous for Beau's safety.

Perhaps they'd served the same noble before? If Gerard's sly digs at El and Elias's sharp reaction to being called 'lap candy' were any indication, maybe El…hadn't been a guard. Beau could understand lying about that, if the memories were bad.

"Hey," Beau said, waiting until Elias met his eyes before saying, "I don't care what you were before you came to me. You're the best guard alive and I trust you. If…if you say you don't know him, I'll believe you, El. But when you're this nervous, I'd really prefer at least a little of the truth so I can understand what's at stake too."

Elias looked devastated. But he didn't speak again, and he didn't take his armor off, and though Beau eventually drifted into unconsciousness, Elias didn't sleep.

12

THE TASTE OF DREAMROOT

They were so close to the isles Beau could practically smell the salt off the sea and the scent on the air of Ma Corlia's stew. One more night camped, and then they'd see the distant glitter of the ocean by midday tomorrow. If Elias hadn't been visibly exhausted, Beau would've tried to ride straight through the night so he could be there by the break of dawn.

But Elias was worn thin by his own constant alert. Beau wasn't the only one who noticed. As Uriel directed the setup of camp and readied dinner's cookfire, Oria said, "I'll make tea. At least one of us is going to have a long night." She cast a viciously annoyed look at El, who merely watched her walk to the supplies. Beau wondered whether she was irritated by what she saw as over-vigilance or by Elias's clear distrust of her and Jude to spell him.

"How long until whatever smells so good is done?" Beau asked, and Uriel smiled.

"Not for a while yet, I'm afraid. But there's bread and cheese."

Beau dragged two camp stools out of the crates and set them next to the fire, grabbing El by the shoulders and forcing him onto one. "You *cannot* go on like this," he muttered. "But for tonight, I'll stay up with you. Then we'll be in the isles and you can relax a little."

Once it was steeped, Oria brought them each a mug of tea. Beau breathed in the floral steam with pleasure. He wasn't sure what Oria had put in there, but it smelled divine.

El sniffed it, tasted it, and then drained the whole mug in one long swallow. "I'll need another cup or two to make it through the night," he admitted quietly.

"You can't stay awake forever, no matter how fast you drink your tea," Beau said, taking a healthy swig from his own mug. It was the perfect temperature, but much too sweet, like someone had coated the inside of the pot with honey. He took another gulp before the aftertaste caught up with him and he coughed on the bitterness. "Oria, what did you—"

He cut the question off because he didn't need to ask. He knew that taste: dreamroot. Buried under honey and hibiscus and something spicy, but he'd drunk the bitter herb almost every night since he was fifteen. Its flavor was usually much more subtle, which meant even under all that extra flavoring, it was *strong*.

He dropped his mug on the ground to split neatly into two pieces and snatched El's out of his hand. Empty. Totally empty.

"Elias," he said quickly, "have you ever had dreamroot before?"

"What? No." El's face lit with concern. "Wh—"

"Then get away from the fire because you're about to fall over," Beau said, pulling El to his feet and around the fire ring toward the tent. "Oria! Jude! Help, Elias is about to—"

Oria stood across the fire, watching. No surprise on her face. No concern. Jude came to stand behind her, holding his sword.

Everything slowed down.

Someone had brewed them tea with dreamroot strong enough to knock a man out on smell alone. Someone knew Elias had no tolerance. Someone wanted them out of the city, away from the palace. Someone wanted them unconscious, or at least incapacitated.

And Jude and Oria were watching, waiting.

Behind Beau, Master Uriel demanded to know what was going on and called for Aloise and Capucine, who both expressed concern for the wavering Elias. It wasn't them; it was Jude and Oria. It was…Beau's head swung. Lady Penamour stood next to her fire, hugging herself, eyes wide but mouth set grimly as Nilah hovered next to her, watching him and Elias. Behind them, Gerard watched too, sharklike smile vanished from his blank face.

"*You.*" Elias pointed a blade at Oria. His hand wavered. "Highness, you have to go."

Years of tolerance built up or not, Beau could already feel the impending wave of sleep coming. "I'm not going to be running anywhere." He didn't draw his knife; he was as likely to stab himself when the dreamroot threw him to the ground as to hit anyone else.

"No, no no no," El whispered under his breath. "This can't be happening. What's the antidote for dreamroot? Gods, I'm not this fucking stupid." He jerked a knife from his belt and threw it at Oria, who would've taken it in the throat if Jude hadn't whipped his sword across to deflect. It sliced along the top of her shoulder before whirling into the grass behind.

Oria hissed and pulled her sword, but Jude held her still. They'd wait until Elias fell, and he would any moment. Beau's mind raced. If they could get to Tempest—

He dragged El backward, away from the fire and the rest of the party, noting how heavy his First's steps had grown. Beau could've been wearing falconry gloves for how thick and clumsy his fingers felt as he tried to untie his horse. She huffed and pressed her face against him, making it even harder to move.

Master Uriel shouted behind him. "What is this? What've you done to the prince? Oria? Jude? What *honor* do you have?"

Elias threw two more knives, each more poorly targeted than the last. He growled when the second throw took him off balance and he fell to one knee. "*No,* get *up.*" He stood shakily and stumbled up back-to-back with Beau. The prince shook Tempest's line free.

"Get on," Beau said. "Get on the horse, we can—"

"You get on the fucking horse," Elias said, words half slurred. "*Run.*" He was standing through sheer will, weaving and wavering, the hand on his sword white-knuckled with how hard he gripped.

Internally screaming at his muscles as they slackened and slumped, Beau hefted his upper body onto Tempest's back and dragged his leg over. It was painfully slow. By the time he sat up, Oria had a bow unslung and an arrow nocked, ignoring the raised hands and raised voices of everyone else in the campsite.

"Shit." He tried to duck down Tempest's other side and rolled off as she shied, unused to being ridden bareback. Hitting the ground knocked the breath out of his lungs.

Elias dropped to both knees as his legs buckled, and Oria and Jude closed in. Nilah followed close behind. *Fuck.* "El, you have to get up," Beau said desperately. He couldn't lift Elias. He wasn't sure he could lift himself. He felt half paralyzed, limbs barely responding.

Teeth gritted, Elias bullied himself back to his feet, but he'd dropped his sword. The other two of Beau's flight stopped a few feet away, healthy fear of El on both of their faces. He lunged, taking Oria to the ground with a tackle around the waist.

They rolled, Elias striking ferociously but slowly, each hit weaker than the last. Jude grabbed one of El's arms, letting Oria get the upper hand and pin him to the ground, grip tight around his throat. For only a few seconds, El clawed at her face before his arms dropped, his eyes rolled back, and he lost consciousness.

Beau, groaning, rolled over and crawled to El's sword. It had to weigh fifty pounds at least. He couldn't get off his knees; he could barely lift the blade. If it hadn't been so fucking dire, it might've been funny: Crown Prince Beauregard on his knees in the dirt, weak as a kitten.

"If you want to kill me, you've got me," Beau said. "Leave Elias and my servants alone. They merely have the bad luck of being in my service." Jude started dragging El into the trees and Beau found more strength in his voice. "I said *leave Elias alone.*" To Beau's immense surprise, Jude did drop Elias and turn back.

Lady Penamour approached at last, eyes cautious but smug around the mouth. "I'm afraid I need you *and* your guard. I have some questions."

"Unconscious people are famously good at answering questions," Beau said. His tongue felt thick, and his words blurred.

"The dreamroot was for everyone's safety. Elias is not the kind to stand aside and let me get my answers without interference. A dangerous man." Behind her, Gerard snorted softly.

He'll kill you the moment he wakes up, Beau thought but didn't say. If they hadn't already thought it, he wouldn't plant the idea to slit his throat now. Sudden anxiety gripped Beau—*if* he wakes up. Dreamroot wasn't some harmless sleep aid; it needed careful dosing. Elias had no resistance at all, and that had been an enormous measure of the stuff.

"Is he breathing?" he asked, nodding toward Elias.

Oria plucked the sword out of Beau's hands effortlessly, tossing it aside. "You're awfully concerned about someone else for a man with a blade at his throat." He realized her sword point was under his chin, and also that his head was very, very heavy.

Dizzy with effort, Beau raised it again. "Cut me, then. See what answers you get."

She knocked him hard over the ear and he hit the ground with first shoulder, then skull. Lying on his side, Beau wavered on the edge of consciousness, swimming in and out of reality.

·§12·§12·§12·

"Pick up his feet and we can tie them both to...no, he's not all the way out of...must absolutely abuse the stuff if he's still... not my fault, is it?"

The voices were indistinguishable, untethered to the world he could periodically open his eyes to see. Beau was carried, dropped, sat up against a tree. Bark scraped his arms as someone pulled his hands around the trunk behind him and bound him. His head lolled, straining his neck.

He could hear people moving in and out, more scraping and dragging, and then the footsteps and voices quieted, and he drifted more solidly into sleep. The prince jerked awake what felt like a moment later, adrenaline pumping through his body.

It was dark, though campfires cast enough light to see. His feet, stretched before him, were unbound, but his shoulders screamed from the way his arms had been tied. He lifted his head. Elias slumped against a second tree across from him.

"Elias," he said thickly, nudging the other man's hip with his foot. He kicked more roughly when the guard didn't stir. "Elias, wake up. Please wake up."

In the dark, he whispered urgently, over and over, "Elias, I need you. Please wake up. Wake *up*, El, *please*." In the flickering shadows, he couldn't see if the man was breathing and couldn't hear over the wind through the underbrush and his own pounding heart.

Elias didn't wake, and footsteps thumped closer again. Beau tried to push to his feet, but the rope must've caught on something because he couldn't drag it up the tree, so he succeeded only in nearly dislocating his shoulder. Beau's knife was gone, not that he'd have been able to draw it, and Elias had no weapons left either.

"Please, El, I *need* you." Elias made the first sound Beau had heard, a quiet groan. He wasn't awake, but he wasn't dead, which was enough to put Beau's heart in his throat.

With fresh urgency, Beau dragged the rope between his wrists back and forth against the bark, trying to wear through it. A cold, sharp point pressed against his jaw, and then hot breath struck his ear as someone whispered, "Should've known a sot like you could sponge up dreamroot like it was nothing."

"Nice of you to rejoin us, Oria," Beau said as lightly as he could manage. "I don't suppose you're here to free the man you're charged with protecting?"

"You're not the man I was charged with protecting," she said, stepping around the tree and lifting Elias's head by the hair to peer into his face before dropping it again.

"I beg to differ." Beau chafed rope against bark again, though he knew there was little hope of effecting an escape that way. "Where are my servants? And what are you doing to El?"

Oria uncapped a small, pungent-smelling canister and held it under El's nose. "Your servants are fine, though I did have to fight Aloise for her frying pan. As for this lout, I'm waking him up. Lady Penamour wants this over with."

When El jerked his head up, gagging on the smell of whatever Oria held in front of him, and flexed his arms to find them bound; when he looked up into Oria's smugly smiling face; and when he met Beau's eyes across from him to see him trussed up in the same way, Elias's eyes widened, the skin around them tightening as he hissed in a breath.

Beau nudged him with a foot. "Are you all right?"

Pressing his leg to Beau's foot, El asked hoarsely, "Are you?" When Beau nodded, El turned to Oria. "I have a question for you."

"What's that?" Oria's face and tone dripped with arrogance.

Elias leaned toward her, dropping his voice, and she leaned in. "Do you have family? Someone you send letters home to?"

She scowled. "Why?"

He dropped his voice further, and Oria, frowning, crouched closer. "I want to know where to send your remains." He headbutted Oria so hard and fast Beau barely had time to hear the crack before she reeled back, nose bleeding. With one leg, El snagged the back of hers while her head was back, and Oria landed hard in the dirt.

Elias's heel came down on her stomach, driving air and sound out of her in a violent yawp, and then he was working her sword out of its scabbard with booted feet.

Oria scrambled back, unsheathing her blade and pointing it at the bound guard. "I'm going to gut you from nutsack to nose," she growled, blood pouring freely over her mouth and chin from her broken nose.

"Oria!" Jude grabbed her shoulder, pulled her back. "We're not here to hurt them. The duchess wants them alive."

"I don't give a *fuck* what she wants," Oria snarled, and Elias replied with a guttural, predator noise that sent shivers of instinctive terror up Beau's spine.

Lady Penamour appeared between the trees on the other side of Beau and Elias from the treacherous guards, staying carefully out of range of Elias's legs. "Mistress Oria, hold," she said, all calm command. "We're too close to what we've wanted to ruin it now. Sheathe your sword."

Gerard appeared behind her, a smudge against the darkness, his watching eyes glimmering in the dark. Elias dropped his weight onto his shoulders to gain reach as he swiped again at Oria's legs, almost catching her foot before Jude stomped hard on his ankle. The First howled in pain, breathing through gritted teeth as he tried to kick Jude instead.

"El, stop," Beau burst out. "Stop before you get killed. *Stop.* If they wanted us dead, they could've slit our throats when we were out. Let's hear what they want."

Panting, Elias looked at Beau, white visible all around the irises of his eyes, a cornered animal, teeth bared in threat as he strained at the limits of his bindings. Something flared in his eyes—not peace, not the calm Beau called for. Desperation. Anguish.

Then he swallowed it, going blank as stone. He hefted himself back up and reset against the tree. Every muscle in his body remained so tight it was painful to look at, but he no longer snarled and slavered like a trapped beast.

Only once he'd visibly calmed did Oria sheathe her sword, and her hand hovered, ready to grab it again. Penamour drew up a stool out of Elias's reach, spreading her skirts neatly around her with an unbothered air. Beau caught the hitch in her breath, though, and the shake of her fingers as she tucked a loose hair behind her ear.

"Is this where you explain why you've committed treason?" Beau asked.

Her dark eyes flashed, hard and glittering. "You're one to talk, Your Highness."

"Contrary to what the peerage seems to believe, pissing off a bunch of nobles is not, in fact, treason," Beau said. He was numb, adrenaline making it hard to feel or think.

She unrolled a cloth bundle across her lap to reveal several small items cast in shadow by her body. "We searched you for weapons and found the most incredible trove. I expected to find some Maurilel artifacts on you, Your Highness, and of course I did, but I do believe Elias was the most magical person on the continent until an hour or so ago."

Penamour lifted one—a butterfly, glittering in the firelight. In her other hand, she held up a glass ball wrapped in wire. Beau knew them both from the vault but went entirely fuzzy imagining how they'd gotten here. *Elias was the most magical person on the continent.*

El had these artifacts. He took them from the vault.

Beau remembered clearly, then, leaving the vault ahead of Elias. He never went back to check the items, never ducked in on his guard because he trusted him completely. He always had.

"This is an interesting collection. An Orb of Tethering?" She examined the glass ball in the firelight. "Strange thing to carry around, given the conditions required for it to work. The feather is, I assume, a sort of weapon? And what does this hideous necklace do?"

Every artifact left in the vaults sat now in Penamour's lap. And there, beside them, the spoon-shaped Useful Thing and two simple rings—Beau's artifacts. Essentially all the magic Beau had ever seen was in the duchess's possession. "We don't know."

She didn't pick it up. "So you carried it around? You're more foolish than I thought. It's corrupted. But *this*—" The duchess picked up a flat, oblong amethyst the length of her little finger and narrow. "This is incredible. No wonder Elias is such a force of nature."

Beau frowned at the stone. That hadn't been in the vault. "It's an artifact?"

"Yes, and powerful. If I had to guess, I'd say it's a Perception Stone. There weren't many made, but well-kept stones can last a long time; they don't degrade like some of the relics have."

"And Elias was carrying it?" When Beau snuck a glance at him, Elias was glaring determinedly at Gerard. Where the hell had Elias gotten another artifact? He wished then that he'd cared more about making Elias tell him the truth. Beau was missing something, and he suspected it was about to get him killed.

Lady Penamour was too perceptive by half. She smiled wolfishly. "Oh, you didn't know he had this? Now that has to be an interesting story. Guards don't just happen upon Maurilel magic. Did you steal this from the palace vault right out from under the prince's nose?"

Elias turned his glare on Penamour but said nothing. She kept the stone and the rings in her hand but rolled the other artifacts back into their bundle and tucked it into a pocket of her skirt. "Now I'm the most magical person on the continent," she murmured. At a normal volume, she said, "The question is, which is a better tool for getting the truth out of you? It's not a good idea to use more than one at a time."

"You don't need any of them," Beau said, flexing his shoulders fruitlessly, trying to gain any relief. "Here's the truth: my brother fell off a horse. It was an accident. He died. My life was ruined. Your plans were ruined. Everyone lost."

"Your brother died from a paralytic *you* had shot into him. And before you get any ideas of doing it to me, I had an antidote made. Did you think no one knew? We found the dart."

Beau sat up straighter. "The what? The *dart*? Hold on, someone shot Char with a poisoned dart?" He pictured his brother, strong and statuesque, slipping sideways out of the saddle, slumped like a sack. Such a freak accident. But if he'd been hit with poison... "The fucking Twelve, he *was* murdered?"

"Enough of the lies!" Penamour snapped. "Gods, I've never met someone so good at acting and so over the top with his lies. You *had* to know you were overselling it. 'Oh, my brother was a saint, I'd do *anything* for him.' As if I didn't know what you two were to each other. But then you paint on that innocent face and get all teary-eyed, like you've never been hurt deeper in your life. Like you're *capable* of being hurt like that." Her scowl sliced through Beau.

Beau retreated into his skull, shrinking until he was so distant from the world he peered out through the holes of his eye sockets like windows in a far wall. Her words ricocheted, echoing through the cavernous expanse of his head. They made no impact at all.

Char was murdered. Someone had murdered his brother, shot him with a paralytic poison. It wasn't an unforeseeable accident, a horrible twist of fate. It was planned. It was intentional.

"Who would do that?" he muttered, barely summoning air for the words to float on. "Why would—he was—" Then it became hard to speak; puppeting his mouth took too much.

"*Look at me*," Penamour demanded, grabbing Beau's chin and jerking his face up toward her. She blazed with fury; he must've been ignoring her for some time. "I want to know *why*."

"So do I," Beau shot back.

Snarling in frustration, Penamour stuck the Perception Stone in her pocket and shoved a Ring of Thrones onto Beau's pointer, then slipped the second over her middle finger. Dread filled Beau as he waited for a maelstrom of emotions to slam into him.

But instead, when the rings connected, he felt...curious. Cautious. Surprised. Guilty. Wondering. Overwhelmed. Each emotion lapped over the last, soaking into his head like tea leaves leaching into hot water. Beau reeled; the emotions didn't even feel alien. They felt like an extension of his own, like someone had parted his brain in two and only emotions could pass between the lobes.

Fascinated, horrified, Beau summoned all his anger at the invasion of his mind and *pushed*. Lady Penamour stumbled back a step, crying out. A rush of her anger slapped back at him, and this *did* slam, filling his mouth with the coppery taste of blood. The shock of it shook Beau's concentration. He couldn't hold onto anger when there were so many other things to feel. Penamour, too, seemed only to have had the one blast in her.

They stared for a long moment, her eyes scanning his face in excruciating, painstaking detail as her mind sifted through his. Whatever she saw, it didn't satisfy her.

"This—" Her voice came out hoarse, shaky. "This will help me get the measure of you. But *this* is how I get the truth." She drew a small glass vial out of her pocket and held it up in the moonlight so everyone could see the faintly glowing blue petals of a fragile-stemmed flower floating suspended within it. "Do you know what this is, Prince Beauregard?"

Beau was barely conscious of the question with her eagerness, triumph, and nervousness so present. He still reeled at the revelation: his brother had been *murdered*. He shook his head.

"Your brother didn't know either, when he gave it to me as an engagement present. 'A beautiful flower for a beautiful woman.' But the Maurilel created nothing for beauty alone. I spent months researching these flowers: the *sihhafleur*. Their council would brew the petals into tea to facilitate open discussion. And on occasion, when they needed to question a criminal—"

She gingerly opened the vial, reached in, and plucked a petal from the flower, leaving it bedraggled with only three. "—they had them eat a petal directly. For a few minutes, that person was magically compelled to answer any question with absolute honesty. They cannot lie or stop themselves from speaking."

She held the petal reverently, and its faint blue glow pulsed, casting her face in eerie light. He tasted her wonder like spun sugar.

"It doesn't hurt? Just makes you tell the truth?" Beau's mouth was numb enough that it felt like someone else's. He was empty, a vessel for the sea of strange ebbs and flows in his head. "Give it to me. I've got nothing to hide." That wasn't strictly true; he had a few state secrets that shouldn't be revealed, but those didn't occur to him until the words were out of his mouth. If it would clear this up so they could discuss what happened to Char, he'd take the risk.

Lady Penamour's face went blank as she 'listened' through the ring, then pursed in confusion. "So eager? You can't defeat it, you know. It's a magical artifact—there's no way to prevent it from forcing the truth out of you."

Beau looked up at her from deep within his own skull, summoned his voice from its burial in his chest. "I understand. My shoulders are killing me. Let's get this over with." The insanity of the situation struck him again, and it sparked a flurry of words. "If you want to hear me say I didn't shoot my brother from horseback through an entire column of riders in some way no one else noticed, give me the fucking petal, and I'll say it where you believe me."

Penamour's anger reacted, washed another blood taste into his mouth. "I know *you* didn't shoot him. There were half a dozen eyes on you at the time. But your guard here—he was out of sight, and he *can* make that shot, I have no doubt."

Beau turned his head to gape at Elias, who looked poleaxed, then swiveled back to the duchess. "Have you been drinking? El was by my side the entire time!"

"Except for a few minutes where he rode into the woods alongside the column, out of sight, which happened to coincide with the exact time of Char's death."

Elias's voice was strangled. "Are you talking about when I went to help Lady Abadie? That was one minute—two at the most."

Certainty tasted like stone dust, and it was heavy on Beau's tongue from the ring. "Time enough, if you're good," Lady Penamour said. Elias was good—very good—but this was ridiculous. Beau's mind moved slowly, gummily. "Open up, Elias. I want to hear this straight from your mouth. No way to weasel out of it."

In a swift, sharp movement, El shoved up the tree to stand, dragging deep scrapes along his arms from the bark. The other guards stepped back, and Penamour lurched to her feet, dumping the stool on its side, but Gerard pressed forward. His eyes were fixed on Elias, face grim, and El stared back at him.

Holding the petal tightly between thumb and forefinger, Penamour watched El like a wolf stalking through camp. "If you're not willing to do this nicely, Jude and Oria can always help."

"If Oria puts her hands near me she's going to lose a few fingers. To start." El's teeth snapped together audibly on the final syllable. "Fine. Give me the fucking truth plant."

In a surprising show of bravery, Lady Penamour carried the petal to him herself. Her skirts dragged across Beau's legs as she stepped over him to the tree-bound guard. Elias sharpened. Every cell and fiber of his body focused on Penamour in a stillness so infused with potential energy Beau feared an explosion. And he knew, he *knew* Elias was going to hurt her. Kill her, take her hostage, *something* to get himself and Beau out of this.

"El, no," he said quietly, certainly.

A tremor, a flicker of violence jolted through Elias, and then he sighed. He stared at Penamour for a long few seconds as her shaking hand held the blue glow to his lips. After swallowing hard, he let his mouth fall open.

The moment the petal touched his tongue, it dissolved, flooding the inside of his mouth with blue glow that spilled over his lips. Elias choked, gasping for air and gagging.

"El?!" Beau's chest was going to crack open.

"He's fine," Penamour said. "It takes some getting used to." She retreated out of Elias's reach and righted her stool, but remained standing. Hugging herself, she rocked from foot to foot.

The buzz in Beau's body intensified as Elias took a ragged, wheezing breath in, blue-painted mouth working soundlessly. The guard shook his head and spoke in a low, authoritative voice made gravelly with strain. It was not the voice he used with Beau; he sounded like a completely different man. "I know why you're doing this, Your Grace." He made the title sound like an insult. "It makes perfect sense—a power-hungry younger brother ordering fratricide to seize the throne *is* the most likely theory, if you pay no attention to the people involved."

Everyone was silent. Even the wind seemed to whisper. Beau held his breath, watching his best friend force words through a pinched-closed throat. Gerard advanced to just beyond the duchess's shoulder, eyes intent on Elias.

"But you're looking in the wrong place. Prince Beauregard didn't do this. He would never, *never* have hurt his brother. He would never have ordered his death. If he'd thought there was a plot against Char, he would've done everything in his power to stop it. He'd have taken that poison dart himself. He'd have thrown me in front of it."

That's not true, Beau thought, then felt guilty, both because he'd never have traded Elias for his brother and because El must believe he would, since he couldn't lie. The guilt was so strong it took him a moment to realize it was being fed by Penamour through the ring, borne across on waves of sour grapes and pungent rosemary—horrified, stunned.

Coughing, Elias continued, "You've been watching the prince, so you've seen he's *good*. He's a good man. And things have come out after Charmant's death that made you question whether he was the man you thought he was. I can see you trying to fit the pieces together. You're so obsessed with the idea that Prince Beauregard is lying about his brother, but the thing is, he's not a good actor. He can't keep his thoughts off his face for shit. He's not lying about Char—he's just *wrong*. He truly believes his brother was a good man who deserved the throne."

Beau didn't recognize the contempt that dripped from Elias's voice when he talked about Char. He wished he was standing; from this angle, El looked like a stranger with the odd shadows cast by the fire and by his faintly glowing tongue and lips.

"You want to know whether I would've killed Char if His Highness had ordered it? In a *heartbeat*." His intensity shook through Beau, and goosebumps sprang up all over his body. "Forget orders—I'd have done it if he'd halfway implied it would please him for Char to be dead." Beau's heart thumped queasily. "But he didn't. He'd never have done that."

Penamour's head shook as though rejecting Elias's testimony, but the pulses of acidic horror and bewilderment said she believed him. "You truly didn't have him killed?" she asked Beau, disbelief and miserable guilt chasing across her face and through the ring.

"I fucking told you I didn't," Beau snapped. "I didn't even believe he'd *been* killed until you told us about the poison. I thought it was an accident."

She pressed her hands tight against her face, bending at the waist. "Oh gods."

Beau gagged on the bitter seaweed and citrus peel, the horrible salt and sour yogurt. He had to squeeze his eyes shut, close out everything else to focus on pushing back the flood of emotions from her. "Enough, enough, *end* this. You know the truth now—"

"Yes," Elias gasped, though his eyes were on Gerard, not the duchess. "End this. Untie me. *Please.*" Gerard stalked forward by inches, something predatory on his face. There was nothing in his hands, but Beau nevertheless felt the threat of a weapon. What was he doing? What did he want? Why was Elias watching *him*, afraid?

"Who is he? El. Who is Gerard?"

Elias's eyes widened as they met Beau's. He opened his mouth but nothing came out. His eyes bulged. Veins stood out along his throat. He jerked against the ropes with sudden urgency.

"No—forget it, I take it back," Beau spat hastily as Elias writhed. "I'm sorry, I didn't mean—don't answer that! It's all right!"

Lady Penamour stood straight again, looking between Beau and Elias in confusion, and then turning to her footman, who'd gone still as stone, eyes the dead black of murderous intent. "Who is *Gerard*?" she asked, confused.

El's grimacing mouth showed all his teeth, the blue brightening until it must be burning his tongue, his gums, his lips. He panted, but his chest didn't rise or fall. The air circulated uselessly in his mouth, stopped from supplying his lungs by the Maurilel magic.

"Elias, you have to answer or it's not going to let you breathe," Beau said, alarmed. "Penamour—call it off!"

Nilah edged into the space between Gerard and everyone else, pulling Lady Penamour aside. As if by magic, Gerard's fingers twitched and a knife appeared. He hurled it at Elias, but Nilah was quick—she knocked it off course and cursed as the blade bit the base of her thumb.

Jude jumped into the mix, grunting in surprise and pain as a second thrown knife drew a burning line across his shoulder. Kicking Lady Penamour hard, Elias knocked her flat on her back as another knife whistled past where she had been.

Beau barely had time to draw his knees up to his chest before Gerard's large figure barreled into the space between him and Elias, blade flashing. El whispered something fiercely to himself—the answer to the duchess's question, since he took a full, greedy breath after—as Gerard tripped over Penamour's prone body.

Taking advantage of the momentary stumble, El slammed a knee into Gerard's stomach and then hooked his legs, knocking him off balance. Then there was a horrific, gritted-teeth howl of effort and pain. A breath later, Elias's hands were free, though his sword hand still trailed rope. His left hand he cradled against his stomach.

"You've never been good enough to fight *me*, lap candy," Gerard said with a low laugh. He stabbed at Elias, and El grabbed his wrist, twisting it, stripping the knife from his grip. He flipped it in his own hand and stabbed once, twice, three times in rapid succession, too fast to track. But Gerard moved just as quickly to dodge.

Many people were shouting. Nilah pulled Lady Penamour away from the fighting and tried to find an opening, Jude held Oria back from the fight, and Beau, numb, could only watch, tied and useless. He could only trust Elias.

El and Gerard both had blades, and Gerard had something else Beau couldn't make out in his off hand. They fought like Beau had *never* seen two people fight, skill and speed Elias had never hinted at, even when showing off. He hadn't known it was possible to be as deadly as these two men were. He understood, now, why Penamour had wanted to know where Elias got his training. This wasn't normal. This didn't even seem *human*.

But Gerard had the reach and two functional arms and no one had poisoned him tonight. He slammed his off hand under El's shoulder blade, and Elias dropped, motionless.

He lay on the ground and didn't move at all.

"Elias? El!" Beau tried not to be frantic. "Someone fucking cut me loose! Elias?!"

Gerard stood over El for a moment, squaliform smirk vicious in the firelight. "Consider this your warning, Lexi, to get clear." Then he turned and vanished into the trees.

Nilah knelt behind Beau, grunting quietly as she cut through the ropes. As soon as Beau was free, he dove for Elias. "El? El?"

Lady Penamour crawled over. "A dart," she said, breathless. "It was a dart, just like..." She trailed off as Beau rolled Elias over, barely listening. He knew his hands were too tight on the guard but he couldn't stop clutching at him.

El's eyes were open, and his chest caved with each breath. He *was* breathing, then. But he wasn't moving, and if that dart was the same—hadn't she said it was paralytic?

"What do I do, El? How do I help you?"

The unnatural blue of the Maurilel flower flared, and Elias's throat constricted with a wet wheezing sound. His eyes widened and watered, locking onto Beau's desperately.

"He can't answer if he's paralyzed!" Penamour said. "It'll kill him if—"

"I take it back! I take back the question, don't answer it!"

The relief on El's face was immediate, and a shaky breath whistled into him. To make sure the air made it to El's lungs, Beau set his hand on Elias's chest. His fingers shook ferociously.

"Antidote," Beau said. "You said you had an antidote! Where?"

"I only have..." she began hesitantly, eyes scanning the trees around them as she reached into the pocket of her skirt to remove a small, padded leather pouch. From inside, she produced a tiny ampule of pale, milky liquid. "There was only enough poison on the dart to make one dose from. I needed the Bounty Flask to make more in case other people got hit, but—"

"He only *needs* one dose." Beau tried to snatch it from her hands, but she pulled it away. "Give it to him!" Probably best he didn't grab it anyway; his fingers weren't steady, and he was afraid he'd drop it. Every time El fought another breath in, Beau's own chest tightened.

Elias grunted and slowly, barely shook his head. He met the duchess's eyes and then cut a glance toward Beau, twice in rapid succession. "You want me to save it for the prince, in case there are more shots coming," Lady Penamour guessed. She carefully avoided making it a question, but Elias slow-blinked in affirmation.

"Fuck that," Beau said. "Give it to him. *Now*, Penamour."

With a mint waft of fear, she nodded, uncapped the vial, and dripped its contents between Elias's blue lips. They sat perfectly still for several heartbeats. Beau held his breath and chewed his lower lip.

Elias gasped. He sat halfway up, but then collapsed on his side and vomited violently into the grass. When he expelled everything and flopped onto his back, the forest had gone silent. The prince set his hand on El's chest again, feeling the breath move in and out, trying to stop shaking.

"Please tell me you killed him," Elias spoke into the darkness.

"No," Nilah said.

"Gods damn it." Unsteady, Elias rolled to his feet.

"What are you going to do?" Beau asked. He snatched the blade Elias had been using before the other man could bend for it. "You've been poisoned not once, not twice, but three times, not to mention whatever you've done to your hand. Sit down."

"He cannot get away. He *cannot* get away." Elias's voice was froggy and ragged. He extended a hand for the knife, but Beau held it out behind himself. El rotated so he was between Beau and the rest of the guards. "Give me the *fucking knife*, Highness."

Not liking the way Oria eyed his First, Beau put the hilt of the knife in Elias's palm.

"No one follows us," Elias said, pointing the blade at each person in turn. "None of you are half as hard to kill as Gerard; I *will* kill you if you chase."

Guess we're leaving, Beau thought, backing up as Elias did, then turning to find their horses. He could only see Pormort, who'd been unsaddled. Fuck. As adrenaline drained out of him, it was replaced with rage.

How *fucking dare* they do this to him? To Elias?

"Po's fine bareback," Elias muttered, eyes darting. "Climb on. He can bear both of us."

"Wait, please," Lady Penamour said. She followed like she hadn't heard a word of Elias's warning or her own guard's exasperated calls to stop. "Please, you're not in danger. I was wrong, but no one's going to hurt you, and we have to talk about what just happened. Your Highness, Elias, stop! You can't ride out in the middle of the night without—"

"Get back," Beau snapped, planting himself squarely between her and Elias. The rage took over, filling every corner of his head. "You almost got him killed. You wouldn't *fucking listen* to me, and you almost got Elias killed!"

"I'm so sorry." She was grey, stricken. "Is he—are you all right now, Elias? I'm sorry."

"What the fuck do you think an apology is going to do?" Beau advanced a step and the duchess flinched back. "Unbreak his hand? Unpoison him?"

"Highness. The horse. Now," Elias said firmly.

Beau ignored him, too angry to think. The shaking of his

hands climbed into his body, rattling him in his bones. "Was it worth it? Your answers? Did you get everything you wanted? Look at him! Do you even know what all those poisons will do?"

"*Highness!*" With an arm around Beau's shoulders, El yanked him toward Po. "Get on the godsdamned horse! We're leaving."

"Give me the artifacts," Beau demanded, half choked by El's arm. "Now."

Penamour fumbled the cloth-wrapped relics out of her pocket and handed them over. "Please, I didn't mean for any of this to—"

Beau turned away from her and swung himself up with effort onto Po's back. Elias tried to set his hands on Po, but the glancing touch of his wrist against the shifting warhorse made the guard hiss and explode with, "*Fuck!*"

He yanked his arm back against his body. "It's fine," he cut off Beau's unspoken concerns. "I broke it getting loose. It'll be fine." One-handed, he swung his leg and hefted himself onto Po's back, nearly unseating Beau. "Let's go."

Elias against his back, night-dark forest ahead, and the duchess calling after them, Beau squeezed his legs and urged Po toward anywhere safer than here.

13

HOME AGAIN, HOME AGAIN

Hours of riding an unfamiliar horse were hard on Beau and grew harder as Elias lost consciousness and collapsed against him. Beau kept El's arms wrapped around his waist so he didn't slide off, maintaining balance for both of them. His core muscles ached.

His thoughts were disjointed on the ride toward the cries of gulls and briny ocean air, eyes searching the horizon for the shadow of Leaurepit. Three separate nightmares had happened in that clearing in the woods, and he wasn't sure what to make of any of them.

First, the duchess and his guards had betrayed him, but that was the easiest to understand. They'd believed him a murderer and they'd behaved accordingly.

Second, they'd been attacked by Gerard, who was certainly not a footman, but Beau had no idea what he *was*. Why travel with them? Why choose that moment to strike? Why did he have the same sort of dart that had killed Char, and why use it on *Elias* instead of Beau?

Which led him to the third nightmare: Elias had not just lied about not knowing Gerard, he'd been willing to *die* lying about not knowing Gerard. Whatever that not-a-footman bastard was, they both were. And that was the hardest thing to understand.

Beau held onto Elias's arms around him, careful of the broken hand, felt the silken slide of Elias's hair against his neck as the guard slumped semi-conscious against him, and tried to find the limits of his trust for his First. How many secrets and lies could he put up with for the best guard who ever lived? For his only friend? For his…his…for Elias?

As dawn broke, Pormort crested a rise and Beau soaked in the sight of his beautiful isles with warm relief, longing so strong in his chest he could barely breathe. They rode through the village that had grown up around the ferry, and Beau found the ferryman, bleary-eyed and yawning, to make arrangements. He closed his eyes and inhaled the salt spray as they were ferried onto Leaurepit.

The knots in Beau's shoulders loosened as he set foot on island soil, and he felt Elias stir, groaning. The wind only whistled that particular way through the eaves of Leau's houses and the rigging of her ships. It carried the teasing lemon-sweet scent of Mistress Danica's winter honeysuckle, which she coaxed into flowering regardless of weather like a green witch.

Leau was just waking, so few people noticed two riders on a lone horse making their way through the winding streets to The Powdered Hops, Ma Corlia's inn and Beau's home for nearly eight years. He could hear Ma singing to her pastries as Po got close.

"Ma," Beau called hoarsely. "Ma! I need Hugo and Viv!"

Mistress Corlia's warm, round face appeared in the open kitchen window, and she gasped. "Oh! *Oh*! Is that my boy? Is that my boy!" She darted past the second window and then out the common room, barreling through the inn's front doors. "My Lamb! My boy! What's—"

She pulled up short, delight fading as she realized he and Elias shared an unsaddled horse and Elias was very, very unwell. "Oh gods, what's happened to Ellie? Viv! *Viv!*" Bellowing loudly enough for half the island to hear, she called for Leau's healer. "Hugo, come here! Ellie's hurt. Help me get him down."

With the stableman's help, Beau and Ma were able to get Elias off Pormort's back without injuring him further. Elias tried to wake and fight when so many hands grabbed him, but the dream-root, the paralytic, the antidote, and the *sihhafleur* stacked on top of his exhaustion to make him clumsy and semiconscious at best. Beau kept tight hold of his forearm to ensure he wouldn't hit his hand.

Vivienne emerged from her workshop across the way, stomping on an untied boot. Her other leg ended not in a flesh-and-blood foot but a cleverly hinged length of wood that she always left bare, pant leg tied up to show the detailed carvings in it. The leather bag slung over her shoulder was so heavy it made her lean wildly the other way to counterbalance.

"You said it's Ellie that's hurt?" She nodded an acknowledgement of Beau and peered into Elias's face where he hung in Beau's and Hugo's arms. "You *would* vanish for months and come back with broken pieces, you big lump," she said affectionately, though El wasn't awake enough to hear it. "Bring him inside, let's lay him down in his and Lamb's room."

They carried El through the achingly familiar inn to the room he and Beau had shared for years, and the prince was surprised to find it exactly as he'd left it, untouched. "You didn't rent it out?" Beau asked Ma as he hefted El in. "It's been vacant all these months? You didn't need to do that. Don't hurt the Hops on my account."

She gave him a stormy warning look that meant he wasn't to offer her a single cent. "My inn and I do just fine without me turning over yours and Ellie's room. Help me get his boots off, Lamb. No boots on my clean sheets."

Beau fretted helplessly as Viv looked Elias over, poking and prodding until he opened his eyes with enough cognizance to say, "Hey, Viv." Viv looked the same as she had when they'd left nearly a year ago except that she'd shaved the sides of her grey-streaked hair, leaving only the braid she always wore on top. An eccentric woman in her forties, her bedside manner left much to be desired, but she had a talent for keeping folks whole and hale.

She gently but efficiently ran her fingers along El's arm and hand, searching for the broken pieces. The process looked brutally painful. When she loosened the straps of his vambrace and tried to slide the splinted leather over his wrist, the guttural, half-gasped sound El made burrowed into Beau's gut. "Why'd you keep this on, you damn fool?" Viv muttered. "Have to cut the straps."

She grunted in annoyance, grabbed two flasks from her bag, and hefted Elias's shoulders up until he sat reclined against her arm. She poured one into his mouth, and he choked and spluttered before swallowing. When she let him take a breath, she watched the rise and fall of his chest with focused eyes, then popped the other flask in and poured that down his throat too.

"What are you—" Beau began, but Viv cut him off.

"He eat dreamroot straight? You mix it in his salad as a prank or something?"

"No," Beau said, "not a prank. Someone dosed us both and tried to kill us on the road."

She gave Beau a quick once-over. "I'd tell you to lay off the stuff, but if you're reacting this lightly to a dose that did this to him, you're in way too deep. Quitting would kill ya."

"He was poisoned with more than dreamroot." Beau laid out the relevant details of what happened to Elias, leaving out explanations for things he didn't understand, and Viv's face grew stormier by the word. Behind him, Ma was on the edge of combusting.

All Mistress Corlia said, though, was, "Thank the twelve you had the sense to come straight home." She pulled Beau into a powerful hug, crushing him affectionately. He wrapped her up tightly, breathing in her warm-bread-baking-and-stew-on-the-fire scent.

"I missed you, Ma. Been too long away." He relaxed into the soft strength of her.

"Sit down; you're dead on your feet. You ride all night?"

Beau nodded and let her guide him to El's cot and sit him down. Her hands stayed on him. He'd always liked Ma Corlia's hands. Her plump forearms narrowed into delicate wrists and small, graceful hands perfectly attuned to cooking and comforting, hospitality and haggling and hauling recalcitrant boys over the coals.

"When El's well enough to travel, we may need to catch a ship," Beau said. He felt dazed by the horrors of the previous day, the long empty anxiety of the ride, the sudden warmth of being home. "I don't…really know. I'm not sure what to expect. But we're not safe."

Ma's round face and grey eyes were ferocious beneath her steel-grey hair. "You're safe enough to get some rest and a few good meals in you. Won't nobody touch you or Ellie on *my* island." She kissed his hair and pulled him into another hug, hurting him with how tightly she held him. "There'll be a ship out overmorrow or the day after if you need it, but you rest up in the meantime, Lamb, hear me? We'll look after you, so don't you worry your head for a tick."

"Thank you, Ma," Beau said. He choked up, grief and homesickness and the relief from hours and hours of fear sneaking up on him all at once.

"He's good as I can make him tonight," Viv said abruptly, standing with a thump of her wooden foot. "I'll plaster his hand when he's up and about. For now, he needs sleep."

Ma and Viv swept out with exhortations that they rest and reassurances that they wouldn't be bothered, and Beau wearily dropped his boots next to El's. He tucked the blankets in around Elias, who slept fitfully in Beau's bed, and claimed El's cot for himself.

As soon as he closed his eyes, he heard El muttering. "High… Highness? Highness?" The guard shifted, eyes closed but hands searching. When he found nothing but sheets, El tried to sit up, half awake and visibly disoriented. "High…where are…"

Beau stood and set a hand on El's shoulder, which calmed his First immediately. "Shh, go to sleep. I'm fine. I'm right here. Rest."

El collapsed back on the bed like his muscles had been disconnected from the rest of him, solidly asleep.

Beau straightened the blanket over him again, sat down on the cot, made to lay down, and heard Elias start to mutter anew.

They repeated the cycle twice more before Beau said in laughing frustration, "El, for fuck's sake, I'm *fine!*" He sighed. "We'll share, if it'll make you actually sleep."

He climbed into his bed from the foot, crawling up the space between El and the wall so he wouldn't have to shove his First out of the way. Fully dressed, he wasn't particularly comfortable, but he already dreaded what El would say when he woke to find himself sharing a bed with the prince, and Beau didn't want to add any amount of nudity to that.

He slid under the blanket, sank into the familiar softness of the mattress, and tried not to think about the way his shoulder touched El's back or the million answers he wanted to demand from the man or the many, many times he'd imagined sharing this bed with Elias and how few of those fantasies had included actual sleep.

The guard shifted, rolled, readjusted. He turned over to face Beau, grumbling in his sleep. Planting his unbroken hand squarely in the middle of Beau's chest, he tucked his chin against the top of Beau's shoulder and breathed warm, ticklish breath against the prince's neck.

Beau froze.

He's going to kill me. When he wakes up and finds me sleeping like this with him, he'll stab me. I need to go back to the cot. He can be restless.

Elias's fingers tightened and loosened on Beau's chest spasmodically as he slept, eyes darting rapidly under his eyelids. When Beau tried to shift out from under his grip and slip free of the bed, the guard pressed closer and sighed out a word: "Beau…"

The prince went still again.

My name. He said my name. Not Highness—Beau.

The fingers against his chest twitched, and Beau gently reached up to lay his palm atop them, pressing them down flat. *Stop touching him. Don't move,* his mind scolded firmly enough to keep him from craning his neck far enough to breathe against those full lips, parted in sleep, just enough to press his own—

Abruptly, Beau became aware of the pool of emotions in the back of his head. He'd been ignoring it alongside all his own emotions since he climbed on Pormort's back, and the sudden recognition of pomegranate curiosity tempered with the cheap-wine taste of uncertain concern flooded Beau with a shock of embarrassment. He was airing his panic to the duchess. Oh *gods*.

If he moved enough to pull his ring off, he'd wake Elias, or at the very least upset this delicious, terrifying equilibrium. But if he spent another second blasting Lady Penamour with how much he wanted the man next to him he'd die of humiliation.

There was a brief flash of contrition, and then Beau dropped into the cold emptiness of his own stale thoughts. The duchess had taken her ring off. And the prince was stunned by how vacant and unpleasant his head felt without the pool.

Maybe it was selfish. Maybe it was inappropriate. Maybe he should've followed his first instinct and gotten out of bed. But under El's hand, straining to hear his name again, Beau slept.

He woke too warm, lying on his side. It took a moment to orient, to understand why he felt so safe. It wasn't the dying sunlight outside the window over his bed or the comfortable chatter of an inn common room on the other side of his wall.

It was the arm wrapped around him, pulling him tight against Elias, the forehead pressed to the back of his neck, the way his guard was tangled up with him and exhaling in perfect sync with Beau.

Fuck it, I abdicate, Beau thought. Whatever it took to stay right here, no changes, no moving. No isle folk on the other side of the wall growing more impatient to see him by the minute; no traitors in the woods somewhere south of him withholding their complex, confusing, wonderful emotions; no secrets threatening this bubble of peace and comfort.

Beau tried to remind himself of the secrets and the lies, the ways he *shouldn't* trust Elias, but the tip of Elias's nose traced the nape of his neck lightly, and he exhaled too sharply and forgot everything but wanting and trusting and wanting and depending on and *wanting*. El shifted, sighed. His hand clutched Beau tighter, and his last two fingers curled under the edge of Beau's shirt, sending electric sparks through him where they touched bare skin.

Don't wake up, don't wake up, please don't wake up, I want to stay here forever—

"'Bout time for you to get on up, Lamb, and have something to eat," Ma said, rapping sharply on the door. "You slept a whole day away! I made your favorites, and half-a Leau's here to see you."

Beau went entirely still, waiting for Elias to wake, to realize, to question. But El didn't jerk or startle. He smoothed Beau's shirt back down and rolled easily out of bed, stretching his neck side to side with his back to Beau. The prince watched the sliver of his face he could see as Elias examined the splint immobilizing his hand.

"Good morning—or, evening, rather," El rumbled, voice pure gravel. "I'm sorry."

"Sorry?" Beau sat up, swiping his waves out of his eyes. "For..."

"For failing? For lying? For—" Elias turned at last, and the terrified contrition on his face made Beau's stomach flip uncomfortably. "—stealing your pillow, apparently?"

Beau gave him a half smile, an invitation to laugh about this. "I didn't mind the pillow so much. You don't drool."

El didn't laugh. The bruised lividity of his eye sockets had abated, but lines of worry and dread were drawn around his pretty, pretty hazel eyes. "Highness, I know you must have a lot of questions, but—"

"Oh, don't quit calling me by my name *now*," Beau said, dropping his eyes to the blanket and picking at the quilting so he wouldn't have to deal with the desperation on El's face.

"What?" When Beau risked a glance up, Elias was baffled.

"Nothing." He swallowed his disappointment. "Never mind." Beau stood, padding around barefoot to see what clothes they'd left behind when they left for the capital. He dug up a plain white shirt he'd deemed unsuitable for the capital because his tattoos showed through and trousers of rough fabric meant for labor, not court, and quickly changed. "You'll need to see Viv about your hand today. She needs to plaster it up."

"Highness, you're avoiding being angry with me."

"I'm not avoiding it. I'm just not angry with you," Beau said, shrugging as he buttoned.

"*Highness*, I—"

"Don't have a say in whether I'm angry with you or not." He didn't turn to his guard, though he knew that's what Elias was looking for when he repeatedly interjected with 'Highness.' He hated the dread on El's face.

"For fuck's sake, Highness, I almost got you killed. You're—"

"Alive because you broke your hand and got your ass poisoned getting me right back out of trouble again."

"*Beau*." El grabbed him, turned him around by force, and Beau's thoughts stuttered and jumped. "Ask your fucking questions. I can't live with them hanging over my head, waiting to find out you've stopped trusting me. Just—just—*say* it, please."

His hand burned against Beau's shoulder; the pad of his thumb pressed to the muscle of Beau's neck. He was so close and Beau's entire mind had evacuated his skull. "I trust you. That hasn't changed. I trust you."

Elias's expression broke, and something bubbled up from beneath, too intense to be witnessed. Beau shut his eyes. "But you want questions? Fine. Gerard is some sort of trained assassin, I assume. You knew him. He called you 'Lexi.' Should I...be calling you something besides Elias?"

"*No*." El's voice was ferocious, too intense. "Elias is my name."

Beau nodded without opening his eyes. "I'm guessing you trained together before you met me. You left. You became my guard, the best who ever lived. And I—" He hesitated, stomach churning, vertigo shaking him. He made a decision. "I don't need to know any more. I've never made your life before we met my business, and I'm not going to start now. If you hadn't been whatever you are, Gerard would've killed me. None of the other guards came close to matching him. So I'll be grateful and I'll trust you and that's the end of it."

And I'll die someday still wishing I'd been allowed to touch you.

At least Elias could touch him. And did. Often.

Hmm. Elias did touch him…often. All the time, really. Shoulders and arms and neck and back and chest, and no one else touched him that much or in half so many places. Even Maisie kept her hands to herself more often, although that wasn't a fair comparison because Maisie was a lover and Elias was a guard. A friend. An enigma wearing secrets like a shroud. A beautiful, beautiful man. Untouchable. Off-limits. Calling him *Beau* exactly like a guard didn't.

Beau took a step back, then another, letting Elias's hand fall off him, and opened his eyes once they were a safe distance apart. "*Can* you tell me what Gerard is?"

"No," Elias said hoarsely.

"Figured as much. Can you tell me what he meant when he said, 'this is your warning to stay clear' once you were paralyzed?"

"No."

Beau puffed his cheeks up with air, then blew them out noisily. "Okay. Can you tell me why you protected Lady Penamour last night after she'd already betrayed us?" Elias looked cagey, so Beau pressed, "You kicked her flat so she wouldn't eat a knife, El, I saw it."

Elias nodded slowly. "Because you're completely in love with her, and now that she knows you're not a killer, she's at least halfway in love with you, too. For you to be king, you need a queen; she's it."

Am I completely in love with her? He wasn't good at identifying such things in himself, but it would explain why he felt this incessant need to throw himself at her walls of hostility and *make* her understand he wasn't what she thought.

Right, Beau thought. "Right," he said. *Right*, the joined voices of his parents and every noble and the weight of his line of royal blood said. *I'm going to be king. Which means I need a queen. Not...*

Beau's eyes traced the sharp edge of Elias's jaw and he thought of that letter he'd left with Theo. "If something happened to me," he said abruptly, and El's eyes sharpened, hazel going dark, "and I wasn't able to be king for whatever reason, who do you think would claim it?"

Elias stared at him for a long time, seeing more than Beau liked. At length, he said, "Courdur. Almost certainly."

"Courdur?" Beau scowled. "Why *him*? He's an idiot."

"He is *not* an idiot. He's an asshole," Elias corrected. "A very rich, very well-connected asshole who controls the border the other nobles are nervous about."

"*I* control half that border as Duke of Verdmont."

"Yes, and if 'something happens' to you, who will claim Verdmont? He already has soldiers nearby on your orders. And who'd fight him for it? He's well connected with almost every other major house—including your duchess's. The only person who truly stands in opposition to him is Macabrie, and you pissed Macabrie off by snubbing his daughter. Which is why his wife tried to have your duchess killed, by the way, since she'd stolen your attention."

Elias delivered this with a matter-of-fact certainty with which he never commented on politics. El was a master of delivering snide comments, pestering jokes, and leading questions, and Beau realized all at once how often El knew the answer long before he did.

"You weren't trained *just* to fight," Beau said, combing El's face with his eyes, looking for unfamiliar things.

Elias's lips pulled tight, flat, and then he shook his head. "No."

Who are you? Who are you? Who are you?

"Can I trust you, Elias?" he asked quietly.

"To protect you? Yes. To put you on the throne? *Yes.* To make your life as happy as I can possibly make it? Yes. To tell you the truth?" He gritted his teeth. "As often as I'm able. As often as it doesn't endanger you or your throne or your happiness."

"Okay, forget my happiness for a second," Beau said, scrubbing a hand over his eyes. "Answer honestly. Please. Courdur's a good politician; he's built a network of people in Granvallée and in Paibona who answer to him, who listen to him; my father's trusted him for years; he knows the ins and outs of how to be properly noble—" Beau chewed on his lower lip for a second, then blurted out, "Would he be a better king than me?"

Elias was silent.

Beau sighed explosively, letting it drift into a laugh, and shook his head, staring fixedly at the floor. "Yeah, I guess when I say it all out loud like that, of course he would. Stupid. And I've galvanized the nobles against me as a common enemy, so he wouldn't even need a civil war. It might even be less conflict than me ascending. So I should...I should name him and abdicate. Get on the ship. It's the least damaging way, the best for the most people."

Oh gods, Beau thought, realization making him feel ill. *I don't want to abdicate. I don't want to see my kingdom led by Courdur, who doesn't care about any of the people in his duchy at all unless they have a title next to their name. I want to do a better job than he would. But... I'm not capable. I just want to.*

I want to be king, but only if I could be a good one. And I can't.

Elias grabbed Beau's jaw, tilted his face up, glared down at him. He leaned down until they were eye to eye. "You're rushing to answer for me, and you're getting it wrong. I was trying to figure out how to say this so you'd believe me, despite everything."

Beau stared up at him silently, waiting for the blow to fall. El licked his lips and said, "You are the most compassionate, brilliant, hard-working, thoughtful, impulsive, easily distracted, *hungry* man I've ever met. You are *magic*, Highness. No one thinks like you do. You're something different. Courdur is better than you at the performance of being a noble. *You* are a better man and a better leader. And you *deserve the crown*. You deserve it. You don't have to earn it.

It's yours and you'll do great things with it. Fuck Courdur. Fuck your parents and anyone else who thinks you're not the best man for it."

Beau floundered for a way to respond to *that*, to a belief in him that he couldn't possibly merit. At length, he laughed and said in a thick voice, "Were you also trained to recognize good kings?"

"Yes," Elias said with a shrug and a grin. "I was, actually."

The soft slam of Ma's fist on the door rattled it again. "Lamb, bring Ellie out here. Viv's here to see to his hand and both of you need to eat before you keel over."

El's grin softened into a fond smile. To Beau, he said, "In the morning, we'll scrape together enough of a guard to get you back to the palace in one piece. I don't fancy protecting you alone with my hand broken. But tonight, enjoy yourself a little." He pulled the door open, said, "Hi, Ma," wrapped her up in a one-armed hug, and planted a kiss on her temple.

The soft, grey-haired woman beamed until her eyes disappeared in her smile lines as she squeezed El's arm affectionately in both hands. "Ellie, love, you've been looking after our boy right enough, but not yourself, eh? What'd you do?"

"Don't give him a hard time about saving my life or he might not do it next time," Beau said, ushering Mistress Corlia out of their doorway toward the common room.

As Beau appeared, a cry rose up from the sun-beaten faces and chapped smiles of many friends. They pounced on him to hug and ruffle his hair and pluck at his clothing and kiss his cheeks, and Beau felt both a deep sense of peace and a growing, living buzz in his veins, like being gradually filled with bees in a bizarrely pleasurable way. He felt *right* in ways he never did in the palace. He felt fully alive. To be loved by so many people he cared about made him feel immortal and thirty feet tall and strangely powerful.

Vivienne claimed Elias, dragging him to a table in the corner where her massive bag already lay open, and Beau was snagged by a dozen other people, each with scores of questions for him and their own news to report.

"Took you long enough to find your way back, Barfly," Malachi, a leatherworker and frequent drinking companion of Beau's said as he wiped his hands on the handkerchief stuffed through his belt before giving Beau a fierce, back-clapping hug.

"How've you been, Mallet? Did Jojo take pity on you yet and drag you to the well?"

"Aye, she did," he said, holding up his ringed left hand with a smile that glowed with pride. "And more news yet—we'll be three in a coupla months."

"Pregnant? Congratulations!" Beau grinned at the man. Malachi was normally less expressive than stone, so for the man to be smiling ear-to-ear that way, his joy must have been damn near irrepressible. "Where's Jojo? I need to congratulate her—and commiserate about her marriage to the grumpiest sot the isles ever made."

"Ah ha," Malachi said, laughing as he grabbed Beau by the shoulders and shook him. "You got a ring on your finger, too. You and Ellie finally get hitched? Now *there's* a grumpy marriage and make no mistake, though no one's calling Ellie a sot."

"No," Beau said, neck going pink. "No no, I'm not—we're not—I'm a prince, Mal. If I marry, it'll be a queen."

Malachi sucked his teeth but said nothing, nodding toward the next people trying to catch Beau's attention. The blacksmith Delphine and her brother Alain came to hug him and kiss his cheeks. While Delphine went to embrace Elias, Alain held out a crooked knife with a snaggle-toothed edge to its blade.

"Can you tell me what the hell I did wrong?" Alain and Beau had both apprenticed under Delphine for a while, but Alain was hopelessly bad at blacksmithing. "Delly won't teach me more 'til I know what happened with this thing, and everything I guessed s'been wrong. You gotta help me, Fine-eye!"

Behind them came Nicolas, Marc, and Adrien, who'd sailed with Beau on the *Siren's Lament* and decided when he did that life on the high seas was not for them. They had a fishing boat now, and stuck close to shore. "Nicky!" Beau called, ignoring the man's attempt to shake his hand and hugging him instead, to Nicolas's great annoyance. The other two piled on their own hugs, laughing when Nicolas shouted about being crushed.

"Why do you look like you've all been in a fight this week? Skid, you're supposed to keep them in line."

"Yeah, well, Limerick and Horndog wanted an ass beating," Marc said, "and we were happy to oblige. Shame you weren't here— you on their side might've made it a fair fight."

"Nah nah, can't fight Crowregard without getting Ellie in the mix, and ain't nobody having a fair fight then," Adrien said, eyes on Elias. "Speaking of, what the *fuck*'d you do to Ellie? Thought he was indestructible?"

Beau clicked his tongue. "Closer you get to the crown, tougher the fucks they send to kill you when you piss them off."

All three nodded sagely. "Well, I hope Ellie put 'em in the ground," Marc said. "We don't stand for nobody trying to kill our Crow but us, and we do it the old-fashioned way with liquor." He gave Beau an exaggerated, overly loud kiss on the forehead, clutched the prince to his chest dramatically, and then said, "He's all *mine*, Maiz, don't even *think* about it."

From the crowd, Maisie appeared, her bobbed curls bouncing around her face as she showed Beau the depths of her dimples and the breadth of her smile. Her wide, pale eyes sparkled as she shoved Marc aside and leaped, fully expecting Beau to catch her. "What, His High-Highness doesn't even swing by to say hello before he hides himself away in Ma's inn?" she called before peppering his cheeks with kisses. "I brought Ollie and Laurent to play. I knew you'd want dancing. Why didn't we know you were coming back? And what on the gods' green earth did you do to poor Ellie?"

"He broke his hand," Beau said, unable to set Maisie down with her clinging to his neck.

"Shame. Won't be able to ride those fingers this visit," Maisie said with a mischief-sparkle lighting her freckled face.

Beau rolled his eyes. "Have you ever?"

"Wouldn't you like to know, fancy-pants," Maisie said, sticking her tongue out, dropping to the floor, and clapping. She shouted to the room, "Clear the floor! Barfly got better looking in his absence and I'm hankering for a dance. Ollie, give us a tune!" The room cheered as people shuffled to give dancers room to press in.

Ollie, the lanky fiddler, hopped onto the corner ledge that served as a stage alongside his short, blond turkey of a flautist, Laurent, and played the opening strains of *The Lady's Secret*, an outrageously raunchy song Mistress Corlia would never let him get away with. Ma's glare could've scorched a line through every body between her and Ollie and still been hot enough to melt his teeth.

He let his bow drone across all four strings and melted the song into *Fairies' Fancy* instead, grinning knowingly at Ma all the while. Beau led his curly-haired girl onto the floor as she glinted and glittered. Dancing with Maiz was warm and familiar and easy. She had a cadence to the way she liked to be led that was so predictable he could make her glow with delight without a moment's thought or questioning. She wanted to be shown off for the first verse, tilting her head back to expose her pale, pretty neck and swinging her curls in eye-catching arcs.

Then, as Ollie bore down on the bow and trotted them all into the chorus, Beau pulled her in closer, letting her mold her curves to him, taking smaller steps so they didn't have to part. Maisie smiled at him like they'd last danced this way just the evening before, not nearly a year ago. She rolled her body, pressing each part of it against him in turn, and he grinned back.

Second verse, she wanted to spin. Muscle memory took over, and Beau spun her easily before him, between his hands, around his back. When she was dazed and flushed and dizzy, she stepped up onto his boots to dance closer, like she used to do back when she was his first and he was her only. It put her at the perfect height to tuck her head under his chin, and he remembered every time she'd ever done it before.

When he finally ended the dance with a dramatic dip that made her hair pool briefly on the floor before he brought her back up. She kissed him, hot and hungry. "I missed you."

For months, he'd been hopelessly yearning for people he couldn't dream of touching; being kissed freely surprised him. He was out of the practice of being casually liked. Beau found himself glancing up, searching the crowd, finding Elias drinking something caramel-colored from a low glass and watching him as Viv finished with his hand.

When he glanced back at Maisie, he'd hesitated too long. Her sparkle flickered, dimmed, and her quicksilver face flashed into a frown. "Missed you too," he said belatedly.

She took a step back, flicking a look over him that caught on his ringed left hand. "What'd you get up to at the palace, Barfly? They never let you marry Ellie, surely?"

"Why do people keep saying—"

The music began again, and Beau danced another with Maisie. "Lift me!" she cried, beaming. "Gods, these muscles—when'd you get so strong? Must've been working out with Ellie. No excuses for not flipping me at least once. Let's show off a little."

So they showed off. He *had* gotten stronger; she was easy to swing around, and he liked doing it for her.

Ollie and Laurent poured their souls into rollicking music. Maisie radiated joy. Beau smiled and tried to keep up with her enthusiasm as the room clapped along to the beat.

When the music crashed to its conclusion, she shot him an impish grin and kissed him again, tracing her tongue along the inside of his lip. "You been practicing on noblewomen or did I forget how good you are at that?"

"There's a notable lack of interest in this kind of thing among noblewomen," Beau said dryly. "You'd better leave my ego alone or I won't be able to carry it for another dance."

"Ollie's spinning up a stomp, anyway," she said, tapping his hands so he'd release her to find a seat at the tables. "Have fun!"

"Oh, I think I'll sit this one out." Typically, he liked the stomps, when most of the men and a few women like Viv and Delphine lined up to dance together while the rest of the crowd watched and whistled and picked their next partner. But tonight, it felt like too many stares, especially when people kept eyeing his ring and asking where El was tonight.

Elias caught him as he tried to escape. His hand on Beau's chest walked him backward, and Marc and Adrien looped their own arms around his shoulders and neck, drawing him out to dance as they whooped and hollered. The music started low and droning as the crowd found the beat. The stomping began, rattling the rafters as bootheels slammed the floorboards in rhythm.

The core dance was simple—standing in a line, the dancers rocked to the beat, every fourth step a quicker shuffle turning them slowly in place. Some kept it simple, others made it fancier, but as the music got faster, someone would step in front of the line and show off until they were challenged and replaced with someone else. Elias slid in next to Beau, but with the row of men too long to fit shoulder-to-shoulder, he stood a little behind the prince.

He leaned over Beau's shoulder and set his hand on the prince's hip to mutter, "How many times have you been asked if we got married in the capital? I've fielded at least ten irritated questions about why we didn't have a well-and-bell ceremony and whether I lost my ring when I broke my hand."

"Don't they understand," Beau said stiffly, hyperaware of each fingerprint on his hip as he danced, "that you're my employee? That that would be—" Nicolas elbowed Beau back a step on one of his shuffling turns, and Beau stepped on Elias's foot, half-stumbling into him. El's hand slid around to press him back against a very sturdy chest, and held him so their feet were staggered and wouldn't tangle.

"Inappropriate?" Elias prompted, a hint of laughter in his voice, when Beau didn't finish his sentence. El hadn't shaved for days as they traveled, and the stubble scraped roughly against the side of Beau's neck as he leaned in close to speak quietly.

Between the rasp against his neck and the warm, flat hand against his stomach, Beau didn't process the word at all. He closed his eyes and swallowed hard. He'd danced with Elias before without losing his mind. But waking up in the same bed had damaged some load-bearing part of his wall of self-control, and the closeness as the music pulsed and the stomping beat picked up drove him mad.

"Let me go, El. I have to sit this one out."

Elias's hand tightened on his shirt, and the guard chuckled. The sound was ticklish against Beau's neck. Maddening. "Why? There are no duchesses to impress, and everyone here has seen you dance with me."

Someone leapt out to dance a feature, a fisherman Beau didn't know well. Elias continued, "Are you enjoying the dance?"

"Yes, of course I am," Beau said. Adrien stepped out of line to challenge the first dancer and the stomping grew louder, the crowd calling encouragement. "But it's…I'm…"

He couldn't stand Elias's hand sliding across his stomach another second without igniting. Beau turned, facing the guard instead. "I'm trying to be good, El. You're my only friend and you are my *employee*, and this—if I'm completely honest, this—this is more than I can…"

Elias grinned and tugged one of the laces of Beau's shirt. Oh, facing him was so much worse. "I had fun giving you these," he said, running a knuckle lightly along the loop of one of Beau's tattoos. "Maybe we should do more."

Think of something else. Talk about something else. Oh my gods, he has to stop touching me or I'm going to tackle him to the floor right here.

"Did you sleep with Maiz?" Beau blurted.

El blinked as though surprised, then squinted and scrunched his mouth to one side. "I don't know if 'slept with her' is the best description. A couple weeks before we left for the capital, she came by wanting you, but you were with Jean. She settled for what I could do for her quietly without Ma finding out I was profaning her common room." A smile flitted over his face at the memory, but then he tilted his head curiously. "Why, was she off-limits? She was with that captain by then—I thought you'd mostly given up on each other."

"No, she wasn't off-limits. You do whatever you want," Beau said. "I just didn't...I didn't know you..." *For fuck's sake, this isn't taking me any further away from how close Elias is and all the unkingly things I want to do to him.*

Elias leaned in close again, too close, his breath on Beau's ear when he said, "I am *begging* you, Highness, to get a fucking clue. Ask. *Ask* me. Please."

"You...like women and men, like me?" Beau guessed, heart pounding hard enough to burst through the thin skin of his neck.

El tipped his head back, closing his eyes as he danced for a minute, a faint smile on his lips. "Yes, Highness. I like women." He paused. "And men like you."

Beau's face heated. "No, I didn't mean *men like me*, I meant—"

"I know what you meant," El said. "And I know what I said. You don't have to marry me; just turn around and dance with me."

Beau's mind scrambled. He had to escape before he did something insane. In the center, Nicolas jumped in to challenge Adrien, both of them goofy and cackling as each tried to move in ways they weren't flexible enough to move. Beau could do it, though.

As Adrien raised his hands, defeated, and returned to the line, the prince slipped out and squared up with Nicolas. Nicky grinned, reached forward to poke Beau in the chest, and Beau flowed out of the way so he never touched him, rolling his body back in a wave. The inn went wild when he took a step toward Nicky and did the same thing in reverse, making the sailor retreat. The spectators called for Nicky's signature move, dropping low to the floor and kicking his legs out in a way only someone with iron knees and impeccable balance could pull off.

Nicolas put his hands up and summoned more shouts from the gathered ladies before he obliged, sinking into a deep squat and swinging his legs out to the beat. It wasn't graceful, but it was skillful, and Beau couldn't match it.

Instead, he said, "Oh, are we flaunting what our knees can do?" He dropped backwards like he was falling until his knees were folded completely and his back was horizontal, then hauled himself smoothly back to standing without touching the ground. Even Nicolas whistled in approval as Beau danced a grinning circle around him. *Do not think of Elias. Do not wonder if he's watching. Do not think of him at all.* With an exaggerated bow, Nicolas conceded.

As Nicky returned to the line, clapping and spinning, an arm came over Beau's shoulder and a hand closed around his throat. It could only be Elias; El would've never let anyone else that close to the prince with even an implied threat. But that could *not* be Elias's voice in his ear saying, "What else can you do on your knees?" because Elias didn't talk to him like that.

Or he never had before.

The hand on his throat led, pulling Beau back, rounding the back of his neck to spin him, yanking him closer until he found himself eye-to-eye and chest-to-chest with El. Every cell in his body was melting as the temperature of the entire room ticked up.

Elias's thumb pressed under his jaw, lifting his chin. "I know I'm not as good of a dancer as you are," El said, "but you're supposed to surrender anyway so someone else can challenge."

"I surrender," Beau said, or tried to. It didn't make noise. Elias read it on his lips.

Something dark and wild lit up in Elias's eyes. A desperate face, an edge of hunger that scared Beau. It was the face of someone who wanted something so bad he'd kill for it—or die for it. El swallowed and shook it away immediately, but it was so jarring Beau stopped dancing.

They were out in front of everyone, the feature. People cheered, jeered, made lewd jokes, called for someone else to challenge them both. But Beau was frozen. "Kiss him or I'm gonna!" Maisie called from where she sat back, elbows leaned against a table. Other women picked up the cry. "Kiss him already! Kiss! Kiss! Kiss!"

Elias smirked. "That's less of a 'clue' and more of a brightly lit directional sign."

I want him I want him I want him I want him, Beau's brain chanted, but beneath the mind-deafening mantra, he tried to form coherent thoughts. *What changes if I kiss him?*

He could feel two choices looming before him. If he kissed Elias, if he answered the chanting with the enthusiasm this situation warranted, he wouldn't be king. He'd get on the ship. He'd abdicate. He'd let Granvallée be ruled by the victor of whatever came after and he'd escape to somewhere else and be some*one* else, someone who got to love El.

Or he could do what he was supposed to do. He could be completely in love with Penamour; she'd *wanted* to like him even before she knew he wasn't a killer, and it wouldn't be that hard, he knew, to make himself forgive her. He could marry a queen. He could be the king Elias believed he was going to be. And El would be his guard, as he always had been.

That could be enough. It could be.

It *should* be. A wife he loved and respected, a loyal guard, a *crown*, for fuck's sake.

But Penamour was in the woods, or maybe headed back to the capital to destroy more of his plans, or maybe crossing into Estforet to forget about him entirely as she focused on the more interesting problem of a magical artifact. And Elias was right here, a foot away.

Six inches away.

Two.

Elias was breathing against his mouth.

Elias's lips were so, so soft.

The inn filled with cheering, and Beau hovered a foot off the ground, he flew, he left the atmosphere entirely. Elias's hand on his waist was so strong and his mouth moved against Beau's like they'd been made to kiss each other. Then cheers died off in a wave from the front door in. The music tapered to a stop with a last screech from Ollie's strings.

Beau blinked his eyes open, took a step back, turned to look at what everyone else saw.

Amidst the simple, sturdy clothes, roughened hands, wind-blown hair of sailors and fishermen and crafters and housewives, a green silk gown, and the flash of gold jewelry, and the glowing softness of clean fawn skin: Lady Penamour was in his inn. Face completely unreadable, she stepped past the first row of tables, glanced around the still room, and then turned to Beau.

"I think we should talk, Your Highness."

14

ONE NIGHT

Elias slid in front of Beau immediately, blocking his view of the duchess and the front door. "What the fuck were you thinking, bringing them here?"

Beau peeked past and saw, behind Nilah and his staff, Oria's scowling face and Jude's stony, indifferent one. His stomach tightened until he could've vomited. *Here*, in the Hops?

"Get out of the inn," Beau said, pointing firmly toward the door. "You're not coming in here and endangering these people—"

"*Endangering*?" Ma interjected, elbowing through the crowd. "Who's this then?" Ma never used a tone that unwelcoming, so she must've been mirroring Elias's tension.

"The reason my hand is broken," El growled.

"Please, I didn't come to start trouble, Your High—" Penamour began, stepping forward.

Everyone moved at once.

Beau blinked, and isle folk had hold of every person who'd walked in with Lady Penamour, including the duchess herself. They were stripped of weapons, wrestled to their knees, all three guards forced into chokes or pinned to the floor by a mass of Beau's friends.

"Hold, *hold*, everyone hold on," Beau said hurriedly, lifting Maisie and Ma off Aloise, who fought like an alley cat to get free of them. "Nobody hurt anyone, *please*." He pulled Aloise to her feet, sent her toward the far corner of the common room, and waved for Nicky to release Uriel. He didn't see Capucine. "Whoever's holding the redhead, send her over here, too. They're my staff—they didn't do anything wrong."

Elias twitched, watching the red-faced guards as they fought the people holding them down, and Beau set a hand on his back. "Let's take this outside. This doesn't need to involve—"

"You *would* find dumb brute allies in a bar, you pigeon-livered drunk," Oria choked out, sneering, as she twisted Adrien's arm. "Prince Charmant wouldn't have been caught *dead* in a place like—"

"Charmant *was* caught dead," Elias cut her off viciously. "Which wasn't Highness's fault—it was *yours*."

Oria elbowed Marc hard in the throat. Nilah and Jude had gone quiet, but Oria fought harder, *furious*. "I hope that worthless scut fucks you well enough to forget you're a milksop's lapdog," she hissed at Elias.

"And *I* hope," Elias continued, picking up a knife from one of the tables as he wove closer to her, "that you got to look Char in the eyes and see him lose faith in you as he died."

"El—" Beau called, trying to slow things down. Everyone in the inn seemed to hold their breath. Heart in his throat, Beau couldn't think fast enough to calm the room.

He met Penamour's wide eyes. Obviously she hadn't come here to fight. Beau and El had both been distracted; she could've had Nilah and Oria shoot them from the doorway and end this immediately. Beau didn't like seeing a sailor's hand over her mouth, the rough hold of her shoulders, though she wasn't struggling. He was angry with her, but he didn't want *this*.

"I'm—I'm pardoning you," Beau choked out, and Penamour's eyes went wider. Raising his voice slightly, he said, "She's pardoned, and the others can swear—*Elias!* Stop!"

El punched the table knife under Oria's ribs hard enough to drive the handle in too. "No pardons for traitor guards," he growled. He jerked the knife sideways until it *schlucked* out her side with a lurid spray of blood. Guttural gasps choked out of Oria's throat into the uproar of noise in the inn. Shaking, Oria tried to hold herself together with the arm she'd worked free.

It was sickening to watch. "*No*, I don't want—Viv, help her before she—" Beau swiveled toward Vivienne, but she had her arms crossed and a hardness to her face he'd never seen.

"She the one who hurt Ellie?" Viv asked. "The guard who betrayed you?"

She'd asked Beau, but it was Elias who said, "Yes, her and the big one."

Vivienne was not the only one of the isle folk to growl at that. She made no move whatsoever to help Oria, who shuddered and gulped out animal, desperate sounds. Elias stood, head swiveling toward Jude.

Jude didn't move or try to fight at all; he bowed his head. "I'm sorry," he said. "I didn't—they said no one was going to get hurt. I didn't mean for what happened."

But the isle folk drew in closer, faces clouded with the same anger distorting Elias's face, clutching makeshift weapons or the ones they'd pulled off the guards. El advanced on Jude with furious, focused intent. Dark mutters filled the inn, and through it all threaded the awful whimpering of Oria as she died.

"*Stop*." Beau barked the command in the deep, humorless voice of authority he never used. Everyone stopped. The inn went completely still.

Pushing past Nicky, Delphine, and Marc, Beau knelt next to Oria, whose mouth opened and closed wetly, eyes watery and terrified. Elias had killed her—there was no question of her surviving this—but she'd take a long time dying. Letting out a short, sharp sigh, Beau snatched her belt knife out of Marc's hands and slit her throat with it, a quick, sure swipe.

His hands twitched at the feel of flesh and tendon under blade, hideously familiar. He dropped the knife with a clatter on the floorboards.

At last, Oria went still and quiet.

"*No one else dies tonight*," he said in that same tone, and the isle folk nodded. Elias, his back to Beau, was tensely stiff. "Elias, Lady Penamour, come with me. Everyone else—*do not* hurt anyone. When I come back, I want everyone in the same state I left them." Again, most of the inn nodded along, though Beau saw murderous glances thrown Jude's way.

The prince pulled restraining hands off Penamour, dragging her to his room without glancing back to see if his guard followed.

He did. As soon as they were both inside, Beau slammed the door and repeated Elias's first question: "What the fuck were you *thinking*, bringing them here?"

Lady Penamour looked calmer now, even with Beau shouting and El prowling like he wanted to tear a throat out with his teeth, even with blood on both their hands.

She spoke quickly. "After Gerard, it seemed prudent not to travel unguarded, or to leave you with only one injured guard. Jude came to swear to you again, and Nilah was prepared to do for Oria what Elias did, if she proved unwilling to do the same. I'm sorry, Your Highness. I could see you were having a pleasant, um, evening. I didn't mean to…"

Beau flushed abruptly pink, remembering what he'd been doing when she walked in, but the embarrassment and queasy anxiety over what that might have ruined was distant; in the forefront of his mind was Elias's vicious disemboweling of his former flight-mate. "And *you*," he said, turning on the guard, "gut-cutting her and leaving her? What kind of *cruel*—"

"I'm sorry you had to get your hands dirty," Elias interrupted, eyes on Beau's bloody wrist. Beau realized he'd been tapping his blood-tacky fingers together and stopped. "She *had* to die, Highness. You know that. Even if she'd pretended remorse, Oria was too smart and too skilled by half to leave her alive. I'd never have trusted you with her again."

"Do you decide that?" Beau asked, feeling himself slip into that unfamiliar voice of command again, standing straighter.

Elias's eyes narrowed. "I've never waited on an order from you to take care of a threat."

"Speaking of threats," Penamour interjected, "Gerard? Have you seen him? Where is he? *What* is he? And thank you, by the way, Elias. I didn't miss that you protected me in the forest, too."

Elias bent his head to her, the slightest bow, but he didn't answer her questions. Instead, he said, "You don't think Jude's a threat?"

"I don't," Penamour said, shaking her head firmly. "*I* was the one who made him believe His Highness was a usurper, and he never wanted him hurt. It was Jude's idea to use dreamroot to avoid violence. But there are three *sihhafleur* petals left. Ask him yourself."

"And you?" Elias asked, stepping closer to the duchess so he towered over her. She swallowed hard. "Will you eat a petal too? Answer Highness's questions and mine?"

"Yes."

"Are you quite done negotiating *my* pardons?" Beau asked, irritated when they turned with identical expressions—a thin skin of apology over fond exasperation—and more irritated still when he realized they'd worked out together exactly what he would've asked for next anyway. "Call Jude and Nilah in. They can *both* swear."

Penamour raised an eyebrow. "Is that my punishment? You're stealing my guard?"

"We can *share*," Beau said with a vicious, unamused grin. "Since it seems you've been borrowing two of mine for a while, and the third had to split his attention to protect you from the threat you brought with you."

Thoroughly chastened, Penamour nodded. "Fair enough. Oh, before I forget—" She reached into the pocket of her dress and held out the Ring of Thrones on her palm.

Beau stared at it for a few seconds too long, considering. This felt like a turning point, too, just as the kiss on the dance floor had. He couldn't square the choice he wanted to make with Penamour against the choice he'd made with Elias. He couldn't think at all, and when he made no move to take it, her fingers curled, hiding the ring.

At length, he said, "Put it on. I want to be forewarned if you're planning something dangerously stupid again." *I want to taste your emotions again. I want. I want.*

"I assure you, Highness, my days of daring plans are over," she said dryly, but she slipped the ring onto her right hand.

Beau braced himself for fear or worry or desperation—the things he'd felt when she'd last worn it—but what washed into him was relief like sugared almonds. It was so intense it felt like fingers scratching at his scalp, drawing out his worries, soothing his anxieties. His breath wobbled, vacillating toward a laugh.

"What?" El and Penamour stared at him. "What are you so relieved about?"

Penamour's pupils had grown huge, and he tasted spun sugar. "You're speaking to me. You want to share guards. You want to monitor my feelings. I *hope* that means there's a chance you'll forgive me, at some point in the future."

Beau's eyes went to El's broken hand, and the half of his brain that had demanded he kiss the man revolted at the idea. But the other half, the half that had imagined taking the throne with Penamour by his side, preened. "We'll see."

·§12·§12·§12·

Nilah's blue-lipped answers were simple and expected. She'd done as she was told, she'd been afraid of Elias, and at the end of the day, she hadn't wanted Beau hurt, only brought to justice. When it was clear they were wrong about him, she'd wanted to make things right.

Jude took his petal eagerly, no gagging or wheezing, and immediately said, "I swear to serve you until you no longer need me. I'll obey your orders and guard you as well as I can."

Elias seemed about to ask him a question, but Beau jumped in first. "Did you know you could've killed Elias, dosing him with that much dreamroot?"

Jude's eyes widened. "I don't think anything can kill Elias."

Beau blinked. He'd said that with mouth blue, unable to lie. The man firmly believed Elias was unkillable. El smirked. "Why do you want to swear to me? Just to be pardoned?"

Shaking his head, Jude said, "No, I wasn't happy with what happened. We put you in harm's way and you weren't even what they said you were. I don't know any way to make up for that except to be better at my job. Also, if I don't, Elias will cut my skin at the ankles and peel it off me like he's field dressing a rabbit."

"That's...specific," Beau said, throwing a curious look at Elias's innocently blank face.

"Well, that's what he said he'd do. And I believe him."

Beau grimaced. "Anything else I should know, while you're magically truthful?"

Jude considered. "I like you, Highness. I think you'll probably get me killed, though. You make powerful people really angry. I mean, I guess you're a powerful person, too, you just don't know how to use it yet. Maybe the duchess can help you. Or..." He laughed self-consciously. "I'm not a very smart man, Highness. I don't think there's anything else I can tell you."

Last, the duchess held the vial out to Beau so he could see the scruffy stem with its single blue petal. "Do you want to do it? So you know I didn't tamper with it or anything."

Beau took the vial, fished out the flower, and held the petal on the tip of his middle finger. He could *feel* the magic in it. It buzzed down his hand, powerful and alive in a way that tugged at him and made him strangely...homesick. When he looked back at the duchess, she opened her mouth, and he pressed the petal down on her tongue.

His finger caught her lower lip as he pulled it away, and a frisson of unexpected pleasure jolted through him. A moment later, the pool of emotions began to heat, and spice like peppers built on the back of his tongue. *What is* that *taste about? What is* wrong *with me tonight? Focus.*

"Was there ever really a magic relic in Laccombes?"

"No," Penamour said. She pressed her palms together nervously, rotating them with the faint *schiff* of friction. "I contrived to be heading near the isles because I didn't think you could resist coming back here, and I needed you away from the palace."

"What if I *had* ordered Char killed? You'd have executed me?"

Her mouth formed a frown, but her brows were upturned, almost pleading, like she'd been hurt by the question. "No. Your mother and father knew of my concerns. If you'd done it, your father would've disinherited you. Jude and Oria were to put you on a ship."

"*Ha*," Elias said, quietly disbelieving.

"Yes," Penamour said, agreeing with him immediately. "I see now that Oria would've tried to kill him, but I didn't understand her...vehemence...when the plan was made. And none of us could plan for how difficult you'd be to manage, Elias. You wouldn't have let us ship him off without a crown, would you?"

El smirked again, dark light in his eyes. "Not a chance."

"What else did you lie about?" Beau asked, drawing her attention back. "Our conversation on the ride—how much of it was lies?"

"None of it," she said, frown deepening. From the ring, he tasted faint embarrassment. "I didn't lie to you except about why I was traveling. I very much enjoyed talking to you, actually, and constantly told you more than I meant to. It was infuriating."

He studied her dark, curious eyes, the eager tilt of her chin as she awaited his next question, the slight parting of her full, blue-glowing lips. "I've never lied to you, either. So you know the kind of man I am, the kind of things I want. Knowing that—can I trust you?"

Before she spoke, her tongue darted out along her lips, and Beau was suddenly very aware that she could feel what he felt, too, including perhaps the draw he felt toward those pretty, soft-looking lips. He glanced away, and Lady Penamour chuckled, quiet and low. "Yes, Your Highness. You can trust me."

Because he frowned down at the floor in silence, she spoke again. "I'm a little surprised you set no conditions on my pardon. You still could, I suppose. But there's a lot you could ask of me, and you haven't demanded any of it."

"I stole your guard," Beau said with a shrug.

She shook her head, meeting his eyes levelly. "I have political power you need. I'm on better terms with the king and queen than you are. And, as you said on the lake, by any measure, I'm your best choice for a wife that supports the way you want to be king."

It was his turn to frown as though he were hurt by the question. "You're *surprised* I didn't set you an ultimatum—marry me or be executed?" His stomach flipped at the idea, and he couldn't keep the disgust off his face, let alone what she must feel through the ring.

"No, I suppose not," she said with a little laugh. "That's not your style, is it?"

Elias nudged Beau lightly. "May I ask a few before the petal fades?" When the prince nodded and sat down heavily on his bed, El asked, "Why was Gerard in your party?"

"When my footman, Philippe, woke up sick to his stomach, I asked Mistress Dubois if she had another who could replace him on short notice for risky travel. She sent me Gerard. I've never had any issue with a recommendation from Mistress Dubois before." She tucked the corners of her mouth down. "Although I suppose he was a good footman, until he decided to attack. If you're asking whether I knew he was a danger to His Highness, *no*, certainly not."

"Do you know of anyone who *is* a danger to His Highness?"

"Anyone?" She laughed incredulously. "Yes, dozens of nobles I primed against him, thinking him a murderer. Not a danger to his person, necessarily, but certainly to his claim to the throne. But among the party I brought, no. In fact, the person I'm most uncertain of is *you*, Elias, but it's clear His Highness trusts you even with whatever secrets you're keeping—and perhaps you've shared them with him. You're certainly devoted, so I can't think you're a danger."

Something about the tone of *certainly devoted* made Beau blush again, thinking of that kiss on the dance floor. *I shouldn't have kissed him. That was insane. What was I thinking?*

What was I choosing?

"And what will you do now, in regards to His Highness's claim to the throne?" Elias asked, a note of sharpness in his voice.

She took a deep breath, looking down at her hands. No ink on them today; not much time to write on the road. Lady Penamour toyed with the ring, and Beau tasted her uncertainty. "Whatever he wants me to do, I suppose. I can shift the tide back, given time."

"But do you want to?" Beau asked.

Penamour met his eyes, and he tasted confusion. "Want to…?"

"To shift the tide. I assume you mean make them support me again? Instead of Courdur."

"You're asking if I would prefer you as king or my uncle?" She laughed and the bubble of bitter amusement was burnt and citrusy on his tongue. "Your Highness, I'd *much* prefer you. Even if you weren't the rightful king—which obviously you are—I like the way you reason, the things you see as problems, the solutions you find. You're unpolished, and you'll have to find *some* courtiers you're willing to trust, or you'll never get anything done, but *gods*, to have a king who gives a shit about his people?" She laughed again. She was so pretty when she laughed.

And she thought he'd be a good king.

Beau shivered. He'd never heard anything like that from a noble. It made it feel possible and tangible in ways he hadn't been willing to entertain. It made him *want*. He was a cyclone of want this evening, wasn't he?

When he glanced at Elias, El was staring at him fixedly, some of that strange desperation on his face that Beau had seen on the dance floor. But then the guard took a deep breath, smiled, and inclined his head toward the duchess. "Back on track," he muttered. "Better than before."

He turned to speak quietly to Jude and Nilah, leaving Beau staring. *What does that mean?*

"Are you all right, Your Highness?" Penamour asked, stepping close enough to set fingertips on his arm. He was surprised; she hadn't touched him unprompted before.

"Yes." Realizing his hand was still spattered with blood near where Penamour touched him, he withdrew, self-conscious. "I should go take care of Oria's...um...I should—"

"Thank you for ending it quickly." Penamour's expression was so open, so kind. She'd never looked at him like that, with no suspicion or anger. It was disorienting. "I know you have an aversion to violence. So that was as kind as could be in that situation, I guess."

Beau exhaled a laugh. "An aversion?" he repeated queasily.

Her fingers found his arm again. "I'm sorry, Your Highness. I truly am. I kept trying to lump your discomfort in with some sort of guilt over what you'd done or attempts to cover your tracks because I...well, I didn't know what to believe about you. But I see things more clearly now." Her eagerness was tart and sweet on his tongue. "I certainly wouldn't plan a sword-fighting exhibition for you now. Or expect you to wear a gladiator outfit and show off—" She nodded toward his chest, and Beau remembered El had unlaced his shirt; his tattoos were visible.

Beau flushed nearly purple and pressed his hand to the slice of bare skin. "Um."

She glanced away primly, a smile lifting her cheek. "Sorry. I thought you were showing them on purpose. They're very pretty."

In the back of his head, the burn of ginger and chili flared, tinged with sweet and salty. He didn't know what it meant, except that it called up a similar heat in his belly. He risked a glance at her and saw pink staining her cheeks. *Oh*. She…thought they were pretty. She liked the look of them. She *wanted*, too.

And she hadn't asked what they meant or why he had them, so maybe it was okay that they showed. She'd already seen a bit of them. Actually—he glanced down at the way the tattoos showed dark through his shirt—she'd seen all of them. "Well, no sense hiding them now."

Lady Penamour squeezed his arm, gave his chest another quick, eyelash-sweeping glance, and went to the door. "I'll talk to Master Uriel and take care of Oria, don't worry. Maybe you could introduce me to some of your friends in the inn?"

"Yes," Beau said, though the thought of managing the way the isle folk talked to a duchess exhausted him before he even began. "Let me wash up, and I'll be right out."

Elias glanced at him and frowned at something on Beau's face, and Penamour caught the motion. She glanced back at the prince, a quick, evaluating look. "No," she said, "not tonight; I can see you're tired. I'll see if I can get a room, and we can make introductions tomorrow? You could show me around the island, if you'd like."

Beau nodded gratefully, and Elias ushered the other two guards and the duchess out, following them. The prince heard El's voice raised over the hubbub, explaining the situation to Ma and the others who peppered him with questions, so Beau knew it was handled. He took his boots off, washed his hands, and tried to process.

He waited for Elias to come back. And waited. And *waited*. The inn quieted as the common room slowly emptied, and then went silent except for the muffled noises of someone cleaning up for the night and the squeak of stairs as the remainder found their beds.

Though he'd slept most of the day, Beau was exhausted. He readied himself for sleep, lay down, and tried to drift off, but Elias's absence bothered him.

Eventually, grumbling, he climbed out of bed, fumbling for his dressing gown in the dark. When he jerked the door open, a hulking form that had been leaning against it stumbled into the room—Jude. "What are you doing? Where's El?"

Jude recovered his balance. "He put me on watch. Went upstairs. Said if anything happened to you, he'd pull out every vein in my body, braid a rope, and hang me with it."

"*Gods*," Beau said, both horrified and impressed by the creativity of the threat. "Okay. I'm going up. Make sure no one else comes up the stairs, all right?"

"I should stay with you. He left me in charge of you."

"I'll be with Elias, Jude." Beau padded past the big man to thump up the stairs in his bare feet. The main hall of rooms was quiet and empty, the occasional snore the only sound. Beau went straight for the narrow stairs to the roof.

"El?" he whispered as he lifted the door at the top of the stairs, peeking out at the moonlit rooftop. Seated on the edge of the roof with his back to the door, Elias didn't turn at the sound of Beau's approach or the whispered call. He did, however, lift a half-empty bottle of whiskey to his mouth and take a long swig.

Beau stole quietly across the roof and crouched next to Elias. "What are you doing?"

El lifted the bottle, eyes fixed on the town spread out before the inn. "Drinking."

"All right then." Beau dropped down next to him, letting his feet dangle over the edge. When he tried to pluck the bottle out of El's fingers to share, the guard snatched it back.

"That's mine."

Beau peered more carefully at Elias, looking for blown-out pupils or a sway, but his guard was, as ever, an inscrutable mystery. "Are you drunk?"

Tilting his head back, Elias sighed. "Can't get drunk, however much I might want to." He took another swig. He opened his mouth, made a sound like the start of a word, then snapped his teeth shut again. When Beau set a hand on his arm, Elias jerked away and swigged a massive drink. "You should go to bed and leave me alone, Highness. You've got to wake up and show the duchess around the island. I've got to get up and audition some guards, if I can find any."

"Just ask for one from the same place that birthed you and Gerard," Beau said dryly. When Elias made a pained sound in the back of his throat, the prince said. "I'm *joking*. Obviously, if you're going to ask, ask for two so we can have a full—"

"I cannot explain to you how not funny that is." Elias took another long swig, and Beau was certain the man was on his way to drunk no matter what he said.

"Is that why you're drinking? I know you have a secret?"

"Yes," Elias answered too quickly, lying.

Turning fully to face Elias and sitting cross-legged, the prince stared until El was visibly uncomfortable. Still, El said nothing, so Beau leaned onto his folded hands, putting his face irritatingly close. "Stop," El said flatly, refusing to turn Beau's direction. "*Stop*."

"I slept all day; I've got hours of staring left in me."

Elias sighed, and when he finally met Beau's eyes, that desperate expression crept back into his face, the horrible *need*. Their faces were too close. "It was nothing, Highness. It changed nothing. Forget about it. The duchess followed you here; we go back to the way things were."

With a dry laugh, Beau said, "'It didn't bother me at all,' says the man drinking alone on the roof when he should be sleeping off his poisons." Plucking the bottle out of Elias's grip at last, Beau drained a mouthful. "I'm sorry. I shouldn't have kissed you."

El shrugged. "It didn't dissuade her. She was practically begging you to propose again. So there's nothing to regret."

"Then why are you drinking?"

Elias snagged the bottle back. "I'm celebrating. Here's to things working out. You and the duchess—you're going to work out."

"El. I regret it if *you* are upset. I'm not worried about the duchess right now."

"I'm—" The guard laughed, a helpless sort of chuckle. "I'm not upset. What would I be upset about? Everything's going according to plan: you're on your way to a royal wedding and a coronation, and I haven't gotten either of us killed yet, so I'm at least reasonably doing my job. Anything else, we can *forget about*."

"Is that really what you want me to do?"

"Don't," Elias said, the last consonant clicking sharply between his teeth, "ask me what I want." He drank again.

Beau studied the clean, sharp lines of his profile, the stubble along his jaw. "Why not?"

"*Beau*," Elias said, and even the exasperation in El's voice wasn't enough to draw the thrill out of hearing his name spoken from that mouth again. El licked his lips, set the bottle down, turned his hazel eyes back to meet Beau's. "Because I don't know."

The guard's hand lifting to Beau's face, knuckles running over the prince's cheek, seemed to surprise them both. "I want you to be king and marry a woman you love. I want to be your faithful guard for the rest of my life. I want to protect you and her and your children and I want to make godsdamn sure you get to the throne and stay there. Because that's my job."

Beau couldn't move. Elias's hand flattened against his face, thumb running along his cheekbone. "And I want…to fuck all that up immensely." His fingers slid back into Beau's hair, pulled him closer. "Because I'm an idiot."

Though his words said *I know better than this*, Elias's body moved closer. Every sound in the isles went silent when his breath played over Beau's lips. There was never a doubt Beau would cross that tiny gap of night air. He was helpless against the offer.

Elias tasted like whiskey. An idle thought wondered what emotion that would equate to, if El were wearing the ring. And then every thought in Beau's brain was dedicated to *more, closer, yes.* His hands found all the parts of El's body he'd stopped himself from touching for seven long fucking years. Elias bit his lower lip, and Beau growled low in his throat, and El dragged him away from the edge of the roof and kissed him so ferociously and so desperately that Beau couldn't breathe.

"Wait," Beau said, pushing El back. His fingers marveled at the feeling of Elias's chest even while he tried to bring his mind back into order. "What does this mean? What does it…"

"Change?" Elias was breathless. "Nothing. It can't change anything."

Beau struggled to sit up straight, keeping his hands on El's chest to hold him where he could see him, could talk to him. "Changes *nothing*?" He shook his head. "I don't fucking think so. You can't do that to me."

"I'm not doing anything *to* you."

"Yes, you are!" Beau half laughed, though he wasn't amused at all. "You *have* to know, El. You *must* know I love you. That's why everyone in the godsdamn Hops asked if I'd married you while we were gone. You've said before that I can't keep anything off my face, so I *know* you know I can't kiss you like that and go back to pretending things are normal."

El's good hand slid along Beau's jaw. "*You* are not the reason they're asking if we got married," he said, gruff amusement in his voice. "Before we left, I overheard Ma talking to Nicky and Skid. They were joking that I'd find another job in the capital, and Ma said—" He hesitated, then let himself smile a sad, devastatingly gorgeous smile. He bent to kiss Beau again, and the prince let him because he had to, because he needed Elias like he needed air.

He pulled back far enough to whisper, "She said, 'There ain't a single part of Ellie that don't belong to his prince. Heart included. He ain't going nowhere.' And she was right."

Beau couldn't bring in a breath, couldn't blink or think.

Elias loved him.

Elias wanted him.

And there was not a fucking thing a *king* could do with that information.

"I left a letter," he blurted. "That said I was abdicating. One pigeon, and the crown is Courdur's by the end of tomorrow."

El jerked back, sitting down hard. "You what?"

Hefting himself up, Beau reached out to grab his good wrist. "I don't get to be king and have you. But if I give up the throne, we can go anywhere. I've got some money. We can get new names, get a place, a job. We can go to Altagna—that's where you said you're from, right? I don't speak the language, but if you do…" He trailed off as Elias lurched to his feet, pacing.

"Fuck, *fuck*, this is exactly—no, you can't *abdicate*. I can't steal the fucking king."

"I promise you can."

El dropped to his knees in front of Beau and grabbed his face with both hands, the splint pressing painfully into Beau's right cheek. "You have to be king. You have to marry the duchess and make her a queen and rule this country. You have to. I am *not* fucking things up this badly."

"Why?" Beau demanded. He waved away the first answer he could see Elias forming. "I know why I want to be king, and I know why Penamour wants me to be king, but if *you* want me, why are you fighting so hard to put me on the throne?"

Elias swallowed hard, then grabbed Beau's jaw and kissed him like he wanted to consume him completely. When he broke away, he pressed his forehead to Beau's so Beau couldn't see his eyes clearly. "I've told you why you deserve the throne."

"That's not answering the same question."

"I can't tell you more than that."

Beau shook his head, pulled away, stood. "No. I'm afraid that's where I draw the line. You don't get to tell me you love me *and* tell me to forget that and go on and be king if you won't tell me *why*." Elias on his knees, hair falling out of his half-up bun, eyes fever-bright, was a beautiful thing. But he was a mystery. He was a *liar*. "Who am I in love with, El?"

"An idiot," Elias said viciously, clearly furious with himself. "A moron who *really* thought he could steal a fucking taste and not— *fucking Twelve*, I'm so godsdamn stupid."

"El—"

"No, no no no, I'm going to bed. I'm—fuck. Forget it, Your Highness, please," he said in as formal a tone as he ever used. "Please chalk this evening up to temporary insanity from all the many, *many* poisons I enjoyed yesterday and ignore anything I've said. It was all lies and hallucinations. I'm not in love with you. I'm not even attracted to you, actually, so let's just put that right behind us." Elias snatched the bottle up, hurled it off the roof to shatter against the cobbles far below, and went to the roof hatch.

"*Wait*, Elias, please, for fuck's sake," Beau said. He'd never seen El so upset. He caught the door before El could open it all the way and slammed it shut again. "Sit your lying ass back down. You're not going to unfuck this situation by pretending it never happened."

"I actually don't think there's any other way to unfuck this, Your Highness," Elias said, but he sat, looking lost. Elias never looked lost; the expression made Beau want to hold him, reassure him, kiss him again. Everything made him want to kiss Elias again.

Beau tilted his head, trying to sort through what could possibly be going through his mad guard's head. "You're upset that I said I was willing to abdicate."

El scoffed. "Obviously."

"So you *don't* want to run away with me."

"I...don't, no." That was, at best, only partially true, but Beau let it slide.

He sighed. "That was all you had to say, then. Don't start ordering me around, telling me I *can't*. It's my life. But obviously I'm not running away with you if you don't *want* to run away with me."

Beau rubbed a hand over his chest, which ached. "If you don't want me, tell me *that*."

Elias was silent; he sank slowly until he lay flat along the roof, staring up into the starry sky. "If I don't want you?" he said quietly.

He said nothing more, nothing to clarify, no answers, and Beau rolled his eyes, irritated. "You know I don't understand these things at the best of times. Don't be cruel; talk to me. What is going on with you?"

"I don't know," Elias muttered.

"Yes, you do! You must've felt this way at least since before we left for the capital, if Ma commented on it."

"Ha," El laughed quietly. "At least."

"But you were the consummate professional all that time."

Elias tilted his head back, fixing Beau with a wryly amused look. "I absolutely was not. Surely you're aware the entire palace thinks we're fucking."

Beau sighed. "You do touch me a lot." His gaze traced Elias's hands, then met his eyes again. Such pretty hazel eyes, so soft and so tortured right now.

"And you look at me like that a lot."

"Do I?" Beau plucked at his robe to give his hands something to do. "Still, we were doing all right not acknowledging it. So what changed?" When Elias went blank, Beau's voice grew harder. "*You* changed it, El. You were the one acting different tonight on the dance floor. Why?"

Elias lifted his shoulders almost to his ears, held them there, then sighed explosively and released them. "Because I was very much *not* doing okay not acknowledging it." He stared fixedly up at the moon. "And I thought there was a perfect little window where everything aligned. You were in love with the *right* person, so I thought it was safe—you wouldn't get thrown off track. And you weren't actually with her yet. I knew you wouldn't be disloyal, and once you married her, I'd never have the chance again, so…"

He trailed off as though he expected Beau to say something, but the prince only watched and listened, transfixed by Elias actually revealing his thought process for once. El continued, "But I forgot you're an all-or-nothing kind of man. You don't have the shades of grey necessary to have a taste, enjoy it, and then move on and let things be the way they're supposed to be."

"Hey! I'm capable of nuance," Beau said, stung.

"Highness."

"I am! I'm not an idiot."

El smirked at him. "I didn't say you were an idiot; I said you're all or nothing."

"Enlighten me about these shades of grey, then. I wasn't supposed to admit I'd give up the throne for you. What was I *supposed* to do with your declaration of love? What was this supposed to look like in your dream scenario?"

El's smirk turned bitter as a nightjar trilled its rapid, thrumming call. "To start, it didn't include the duchess walking directly into our first kiss."

"That was a surprise," Beau muttered mildly.

"I don't know, Highness. Tomorrow you're going to make a duchess fall in love with you and probably propose to her. So I guess I just imagined…one night."

A breeze whistled over the roof; Beau shivered. "One night?"

Elias tilted his head back again, meeting Beau's eyes with that desperate, aching look of insatiable hunger. "Yeah. One night where we get whatever we want. And then…tomorrow, we make the right choices again. I go back to being your guard and you go back to being the crown prince and we get back to the business of marrying you off to somebody else."

"And you're *fine* with that? With *one* night?" Beau tried to keep his incredulity out of his voice. He knew in his bones it would kill him to have Elias and give him up again. But he also thought… it was already too late. Going back to bed alone, trying to sleep knowing Elias was somewhere else *loving* him, was unthinkable. He was already drowning; giving in to El's impossible proposal was taking a big, deep breath underwater.

"That's all I want," Elias said, convincing no one at all, but resolute nonetheless.

This is a terrible idea. "Just tonight," Beau said slowly anyway.

Elias's eyes lit with hope as he realized Beau was agreeing. He leaned forward, eyes scanning the prince, waiting for a rebuttal that didn't come. "Just one night," he whispered, barely audible, as he reached out, brushed Beau's waves aside, and kissed him again.

The prince expected El to be rough, urgent, but he moved with slow, focused intent, almost reverence. While his mouth formed itself to Beau's, his fingers dragged down the prince's throat, down the strip of his chest his robe parted to reveal, down to the tie at his waist, which Elias untied with one smooth pull. Then his hand was on Beau again, and Beau moaned into his mouth when El drew the backs of his fingers down his hard length, blunt fingernails scratching deliciously sensitive lines through Beau's linen drawers.

"We're doing this," Elias murmured, sounding awed and surprised. He kissed Beau's shoulder, bit him. Then, so quietly Beau almost couldn't make it out, "I get to kiss my prince. Mine." Beau tugged El's hair out of its tie. He'd always wanted to know if it was as soft as it looked. It slipped through his fingers like cool water.

He chuckled breathlessly as lips and tongue traced the shapes of his tattoos. "Yours. I think once you rescue someone enough times you probably do own them, with all the life debt."

Elias's low laugh was absolutely menacing as he nipped the prince's abs. "How many saves would you say that takes? I'd like to know if I'm getting close to owning a duchess as well." He winced as he shifted to put his weight on his forearm, dealing gingerly with his broken hand. Under his breath he said, "One night, and I've got to do everything one-handed."

"Here," Beau said, sitting up and pushing El onto his back. "I've got two perfectly good hands, and they're shamefully idle."

Hastily, he unlaced El's shirt and pulled it off. Elias was beautiful, sculpted to perfection, hair splayed loose around him and every muscle shaped with an artist's loving attention. For a long time, Beau stared, a heartbeat longer for every time he'd ever made himself look away from this man. Elias watched him silently, smiling.

"I know you've made a habit of not touching me," El said, "but I promise you can."

"Shh, I'm enjoying myself. And anyway, I've had a mantra of *don't touch him* running in my head nonstop for years. It takes a minute to get over." He set his hand flat against El's breastbone and felt his heart pounding against it. Elias's breathing was uneven, hitched, the same heartbeat that pulsed against Beau's palm also visible in his throat. "Are you nervous?"

Elias closed his eyes. "Yes."

The prince almost teased his fearless protector about being afraid of *him*, of all things, but when he leaned in to press a kiss to Elias's lips, the tremor in the guard's exhale was too raw, too honest. So he said only, "Me too." Though he wasn't, really. He'd imagined this a thousand times. It felt as natural and inevitable as gravity.

He took a deep breath and set his hands on Elias's chest, dragging his thumbs across the muscle. El exhaled sharply, eyes slitting open. "You're so tense," Beau said with a laugh. "Come here. I'll give you a massage, loosen you up."

He didn't wait for Elias to move, just dragged him along as he propped himself against a chimney and sprawled his legs out in front of him. El lay between them, back against his stomach and head propped on Beau's shoulder. The wind caught their hair, blew it in their eyes, teased their bare skin. "Now," Beau said, "the only job you have is to relax. So *relax* for me." He reached over El to massage his shoulders, his chest, his arms. Smooth and warm and traced lightly with scars, Elias's skin was pure pleasure to touch.

Until he loosened the strain in Elias's muscles, he didn't realize how tight they actually were. As each muscle slackened under Beau's massaging fingers, he started to understand that he'd *never* seen Elias relax, not even for a moment. He reached further down, massaging along El's abs, and rested his cheek against the top of the guard's head.

"Do you have any idea how much I've wanted to touch you?" Beau asked quietly.

Elias's *hmm* fell between acknowledgement and laughter. "I may have an inkling."

How long had Elias been holding back interest behind blank faces and professionalism? Had the thousand small touches on Beau's shoulders and neck and arms been intentional choices or desire breaking out of containment? He wasn't sure he'd ever know. Elias kept so many secrets. "Tell me something true about yourself, El. Something I don't know. Please."

Elias took a deep breath, belly shifting under Beau's hands. Lines on his face Beau had assumed were permanent vanished as he calmed under the prince's touch. It made him look years younger and soft in ways Beau barely recognized. Beau couldn't stop staring at his face.

"You're fishing for secrets that'll put your life in danger," Elias said. "Stop it."

"Nothing *dangerous*. Just *something* about you. How about some incentive?" Beau shifted Elias slightly to one side so he could reach over El's hip and slide his hand under the fabric of his pants. "You keep talking, I keep touching." El was as hard as he was, and when he brushed his fingers over the tip, El's whole body went tight again, then dropped more heavily against him as the guard panted.

"You really going to stop touching me?" Elias asked, eyes closed but strain in his voice.

Beau grabbed him firmly, loving the shudder it drew. "Please don't call my bluff."

El chuckled, ran his good hand up the inside of Beau's calf. "Fine. I...what can I tell you? You were right, I'm from Altagna originally, close to the border with Sharzhakaman. So I speak Altagnan and Alzhaki—it's a border pidgin. But I came to Granvallée a long time ago." Beau's hand worked up and down El's length, and El groaned from somewhere deep in his chest.

Fuck thrones and crowns—this was the power Beau craved: knowing exactly how to please someone he loved, being able to do it, watching them succumb to it.

When he slowed his hand, moving teasingly as if he'd pull away, Elias grabbed his arm to hold him in place and said, "I'm talking, I'm still talking. I came to Granvallée by ship when I was nine. I was alone. I had to learn the language, learn to make a living. It was hard." He panted, eyes closed, hips lifting to slide himself through Beau's hand. "Didn't...love the work I found."

"What kind of work?" Beau asked, and Elias gritted his teeth for a moment before tilting his head back to look up at the prince from the corner of his eyes.

"The type that earns you nicknames you still can't shake twenty years later," El muttered, dry amusement coloring his voice. *Lap candy.* "You *have* to already have guessed. Didn't take you for the sort to get off on digging out your partner's shameful secrets."

Beau hesitated, then said, "You know every secret I've ever had. We're beyond embarrassment. But I didn't ask for anything specific; this doesn't have to be the one you tell me, if you don't want to."

He replayed what Elias had said in his head. "Wait—" *Twenty years later? We celebrated his thirtieth birthday last year.*

"Don't do the math. You'll only upset yourself," Elias said, exhaling a humorless laugh. Beau's hand paused, but Elias wrapped his own around it, tightening their grip and pressing his head back hard against the prince's shoulder.

"*Who* did you work for?" Beau asked, more insistent, anger leaking into his voice.

"I can't tell you."

"Because I'll kill them?" Beau's voice broke up an octave.

Elias chuckled, genuinely delighted by Beau's reaction. "Unfortunately, you can't kill them. Neither can I. Most of them are as deadly as Gerard."

"But you got free of them."

The tension returned to Elias's face, and his teeth ground against each other. His abs rolled as he pushed up against Beau's hand faster. "Yes. I found a strange, handsome, plain-spoken prince with a gnarly sword wound sitting on a rooftop and I offered to be his guard. He was crazy enough to accept, and the rest is history."

Beau's left arm snaked around Elias's neck to grab his chest as he drew more groans from Elias with his right. He pressed his face to El's hair. Gods, he loved this man. "Very boring history, until the last week or so," Beau said jokingly. "Guarding the most peace-loving prince who ever lived on the most peaceful islands while I tried ten thousand hobbies and abandoned them a week later."

"I loved—" Elias caught his breath, struggling to speak. His eyes squeezed shut tight, a flush rising in his skin until he nearly caught fire. "I loved every second of it. I've never been happier in my life, Highness." Another ragged breath in that came back out as a moan. "I would do anything. Anything. Anything at all for you." He crushed Beau's hand around him with his own, each moan so desperate it was almost a sob.

"*Anything*? And you're mad I'd give up a throne nobody even wants me to have? For fuck's sake, let me repay the loyalty."

Elias laughed breathlessly. "Repay? I'm trying desperately to meet my debt. Not going to do that by losing you your birthright and the partner you *deserve*."

"Penamour?"

"Yes, Penamour." Elias's breaths were coming too fast, each sound cutting off the next. "I know she's perfect for you. I'm just coming to terms with you not needing me anymore."

"I have never needed anyone or anything as much as I need you, Elias."

"As a guard," El said, his voice breaking. The wind picked up again, making his hair tickle Beau's chest, his throat. It chilled the sweat on both of their bodies, and they shivered in unison. "You'll always have me for that. It's the other things."

Elias's grip on Beau's hand was merciless, and so was Beau's grip on El's chest, like the moment would be ripped out of their hands if their fingers uncurled. "What things?"

"I'm the first person you look for when you open your eyes in the morning. The last words you say before you fall asleep are for me. When you're—*ah fuck*—when you're nervous or upset and I touch you, you calm down. When you don't know *how* you feel, you ask me." He cried out too loud for the quiet night, and Beau let go of his chest to cover his mouth.

Beau ached. He couldn't lose those things. He couldn't bear it. Lady Penamour was beautiful and charming and intelligent, and Beau was going to find a way to convince her to marry him. But if marrying for love meant never getting to look at Elias and feel the peace of his absolute, cocky-ass certainty in his own capabilities, Beau would find some way not to fall in love.

"Those are my favorite things," Beau said. "And I *will* be the kind of king who protects the good things. So be there in the mornings when I open my eyes, okay?"

A shudder ran through Elias; his face crumpled in what looked like pain. He went still, every muscle taut, and then he groaned into the hand Beau kept over his mouth and spent himself into the hand that had brought him to the peak. He panted and shook against the prince, and Beau held him as close as he could, pressing his forehead to El's hair.

"*Ah lur oo,*" Elias said, muffled in Beau's hand. Beau peeled his fingers away and the guard repeated himself. "I love you."

Beau absorbed it like a flower soaking in sunlight. But everything had gotten so heavy, so intense, he couldn't resist lightening the mood. "Yeah, yeah," he teased in a low voice. "You already said that and took it back once tonight. I think it's the orgasm talking."

With a breathless laugh, Elias sat up enough to look at Beau. "Give me a minute, I'll see if I still feel that way."

Beau drew his hand away and licked it clean, filled with smug satisfaction at the way El's laughter evaporated and his eyes went dark and feral again. He offered his sticky hand to Elias and smirked. "Sorry, did you want some?"

El's hand closed on Beau's throat before he realized El had moved. He leaned close to say, "No—I want to give you more."

"So aggressive," Beau said lightly, though he could barely breathe. "Anyone would think you were a trained assassin. Is this what you've been holding back all this time? I've been trying not to lick the sweat off your abs and you've been fighting the urge to choke the life out of me?"

The way Elias tilted his head to the side felt more dangerous than the hand on Beau's throat. "You wanted to lick my abs?" he asked quietly. He leaned back, letting go of Beau so he could support himself with his good arm. "No one's stopping you now."

Beau didn't waste a second. His tongue traced a path from Elias's neck along his collarbone, down his chest, and over each rise of muscle in his abdomen. He sucked gently on the skin as goose-bumps pebbled its surface. When he tried to pull Elias's pants out of the way so he could keep going lower, Elias dropped flat on the ground and slid his hand into the hair at the base of Beau's neck, tightening until it hurt. He dragged the prince up to his mouth and kissed him hungrily. "I've already had a round," El said. "Your turn."

"Maybe I like making you break," Beau said, smiling against Elias's mouth.

Elias hummed in his throat, almost a growl. "Good. Earn it."

Absolutely nothing could've prepared Beau for his reaction to those words. Some part of his brain switched off, and instead of words or logic or reason, his mind flooded with irrational, animal need. He scratched and tore at Elias, trying to get closer, and El had his mouth on every part of Beau he could reach. They were a whirl-wind of limbs and flesh and heat. In a brief window of lucidity, he was aware of Elias putting weight on his hurt wrist so he could pull Beau's hips to his.

"You're going to hurt yourself," he gasped.

"I don't care," Elias said. Then his slick fingers were slipping inside Beau and all arguments were driven from his mind.

Every touch was flawless, sublime satisfaction and made him ten thousand times hungrier. Both keening, neither with a spare hand to muffle the other, they gave voice to need around the mouth or neck or shoulder under their lips. Elias rolled so Beau could sit atop him and grabbed Beau's hips to align them—he was definitely not supposed to use that hand—and the press of guard into prince was exactly as painful and as perfect as Beau had expected it to be.

"El, El," Beau said, strangled, frantic.

Elias snarled, thrust himself in deeper, deeper. "*Yes*, Beau. Yes. Yes. Fuck, you feel so good. That's it. That's it. Fuck, yes, ride me—"

Anything. He'd do anything for that man, anything to make him keep making those crazed sounds, anything to hear another *yes* like that. Beau jerked himself with one hand and planted the other on Elias's chest for leverage to roll his body down harder, one gasping, moaning inch at a time. His fingers clawed into El's skin until they drew blood, but the guard never stopped his litany of, "That's my Beau, that's it, keep going, just like that."

The feeling of settling all the way down on Elias's hips, his body reshaped to match El exactly, brought Beau to the brink. "I'm so—close—"

El groaned.

"Good boy, Highness. Come around me. I want to feel it."

Who was he to deny a command like that? He shook with the force of an orgasm so intense it almost hurt, waves of nearly unbearable pleasure that painted Elias's chest and stomach. El cupped his cheek, whispered kindnesses and cruelties and proclamations of love. Coming down off the high was like falling, turning him inside-out.

He wanted to lay his head on Elias's chest, to catch his breath, but El was already moving him.

"Lay down," El said. "I'm not done with you." He curled up behind Beau, an almost-perfect mirror of waking up together, except now Beau wasn't begging the gods for any scrap of physical affection, he was taking El inside him again and wrapped up tight against the guard with every available limb. El buried his face in the place where Beau's neck met his shoulder and rocked them together and said, "I love you, I love you, I love you," until he found his release again.

They stayed that way, as the wind tried to freeze their over-heated bodies and the silence of the night settled on them. Neither was willing to pull free from the other, and they'd emptied themselves of all their words.

A sense of unreality swathed Beau; he was untethered from the earth. It wasn't possible that he'd had the best sex of his life with the man he'd been in love with and unable to touch for his entire adult life. It wasn't possible that he was going to be unable to touch him again tomorrow, unable to hear him whisper *I love you* while they were the closest two people could possibly be. So reality simply couldn't be true. This was a dream.

Elias ran his nose up the back of Beau's neck, and the prince shivered. "You do that in your sleep."

El laughed, low and smoky. "No, I don't, Highness. I do that when I'm trying to decide how much I can get away with when I've got a prince pretending to be asleep in my arms."

Surprised, Beau sent his own laugh into the night as he watched a light flare on in a window on the other side of the island. "I really don't have a single secret, do I?"

Biting lightly at the nape of Beau's neck, Elias said, "Not one."

The wind blew again, sneaking into every tiny space between them. Their sticky skin chilled. "We could go inside, you know. I've got a very comfortable bed in there."

"No," El said, squeezing Beau tighter. "If we leave the roof—"

He didn't finish his sentence, but Beau understood. It'd be different if they left this place. There was something magical here, something suspending time and reality. Inside, there'd be people and shared walls and reminders of responsibilities that returned at sunrise. The spell would be broken.

Beau closed his eyes, tried to absorb the feeling of Elias holding him with no pretenses. Behind him, El whispered, *"Phelya idif ajiki mandistrasi fina ea'istia."* In Alzhaki, his voice was softer, silvery.

"What does it mean?"

Elias bit him again, slid his hand over Beau's stomach. "It means, 'Every mistake I've made was worth it for this'."

Beau exhaled slowly, letting the sentiment flow over him like warm water. "How would I say, 'This is my husband, Elias, and we need a place to stay while we find work. Do you know of anything?'"

The laugh-sob that came out of Elias cut Beau to the quick. El's forehead crushed against the back of Beau's skull. *"Rei kyriv."*

"Seems a bit short," Beau said lightly, a catch in his throat.

"One night, Highness. *Rei kyriv.* You agreed."

Beau let himself deflate with a sigh. "So I don't get to kiss and touch you every day forever; I can still *imagine.* Imagine with me, Elias. Close your eyes. Picture our house. Maybe a little hammock in the front yard? Somewhere we can read on quiet mornings?"

"Stop. *Please.*" Elias turned Beau in his arms, kissed him. "I can't imagine that. It'll break me."

Pressing a finger to El's lip, Beau said, "You're unbreakable."

Elias's hazel eyes glittered too brightly in the starlight as he shook his head. "Everyone has a weakness. Even…whatever I am."

He cleared his throat, smiled wryly. "Speaking of weaknesses, if yours is licking me clean, there's no better time. I'm a mess."

"Careful," Beau said, even as he slid down to press his mouth to El's sticky body, "this has been known to cause further messes."

"Oh, I'm counting on it," Elias growled.

15

A PEARL FOR PENNY

The problem with packing every moment one has ever wanted to experience with someone into a single night is that it is exhausting. And when one is exhausted and curled up perfectly safe against the warm, bare skin of a beautiful man, one might fall asleep on the roof of an inn and be woken late the next morning by one's adoptive mother banging a pot with a spoon and grumbling irritatedly about leaving noble guests rattling around her common room.

As Beau and Elias hastily, blushingly reassembled their clothing to the chorus of wolf-whistles and jeers from the street below, Ma Corlia continued her harangue.

"—has been perfectly polite, of course, and we've all been taking turns telling her stories about you, but I can't imagine a highborn lady who followed you this far is too pleased to think you're having your hurrahs on the roof with Ellie when you said you'd show her round the—"

"Please, Ma," Beau interrupted hoarsely, tying his dressing gown, "it's too early."

"—island and introduce her to—eh? Ain't early at all, Lamb, that's the problem. Ellie, you're putting that shirt on backwards, boyo. Let me—"

They finally struggled down the stairs, Elias tying his hair back and Beau fighting the scorching red out of his cheeks, and spotted Lady Penamour surrounded by half a dozen Leau residents, each competing to tell their story first and more loudly. Elias shoved Beau into their bedroom before she could glance up and slammed the door after him. When the prince scrambled to dress and slow his heart from its panic, he found himself reliving the night.

It was perfect. Every single moment of it, perfect.

And he'd never have it again.

"That's His Highness's doing. He helped me design the whole thing when we rebuilt, and built damn near half of it with his own hands!" Ma's voice rose easily over the others in the common room, and Beau swallowed a sigh. He was proud of his work on this inn and its cheery, cozy atmosphere, but he found being talked about cripplingly embarrassing. "Kept Samuel and his cousin from leaving any corners cut. They're good carpenters, but they'll leave a job unfinished if they can. Paid for it all too, every last cent. And still thinks after all that I'm gonna let him pay for a room, the daft boy."

Beau heard the faint, melodic sound of a question in Lady Penamour's voice, and then Ma said, "Well, it burned down, didn't it? That fool boy Cedric tried to start a fight with His Highness when Miss Solene took a shine to him, nevermind my Lamb had never looked at her twice, and he found out quick that Ellie wouldn't stand for that sort of nonsense. Ellie knocked him right through a wall! Took a lamp or two down, and the whole thing went up like a torch. Old wood, you know. We got everyone out, but that would've been the end of me and mine, out on the streets for good, if my boy hadn't stepped in."

Beau, dressed now, slipped out of his room, burning with a blush he couldn't shake. "Well, I had to. It was my fault," he muttered as he dropped an arm around Ma's shoulders and kissed her hair. "Morning, Ma."

"No, it weren't, it was Cedric's fault and he knows it. Hasn't put so much as a toe on Leau since 'cause he knows I'd tan his hide.

Sit down, Lamb, and put something in your belly. That rich castle food's been doing you good, and the practice with Ellie, but you're still too skinny. You should've seen him when he showed up on my doorstep, Lady, soaking wet, bleeding through grungy bandages, one little bag of clothes on his back and a big ol' sack of coins in his pocket. Scrawny thing, all he'd say was his name was Beau and he needed a place to stay."

Beau grimaced. "Ma, please, can we not—"

"He didn't tell you he was a prince?" Penamour asked, eyes sparkling. She flicked her eyes to Beau, grinned, and then turned her attention back to the innkeeper as the plump woman stacked honey cakes, sausage buns, and raspberry muffins onto a plate.

"Not a word about it. Asked if anyone had work that needed done on the island." Ma laughed. "Had a thousand dorin in a sack and wanted work. Ha! Tried to give me the whole thing, too, when I gave him that room." She jerked her head toward Beau's door.

"So you took him in?" The duchess had an empty plate in front of her, only the sticky remnants of honey and raspberry crumble to evidence the breakfast she'd eaten.

"My son, Garrett, died ten years ago, and I... Well, the way I saw it, I needed someone to take care of and he needed someone looking after him. We found each other at the right time." Ma pressed a kiss down on top of Beau's waves, set the plate in front of him, and sat heavily on the bench beside him. "Everybody knew he had to be noble—too proper, too rich, and didn't know a damn thing about anything. But I never saw a soul work half as hard as him, and he learned everything 'bout as quick as we could teach him. Kept expecting somebody to come looking for him, but nobody ever did."

"Ma," Beau said gently, trying to slow her, "Lady Penamour and I should probably—"

"Maybe I shouldn't speak ill of royalty in front of a duchess," Ma rolled on unstoppably, "but if I ever stood in front of the king or queen, I'd be hard pressed not to wring their necks. The things this boy would say about himself when he was drunk—"

"*Ma*, please—"

"—and nevermind all the times Viv had to patch him up for the cuts he gave himself."

Beau's stomach dropped as Penamour asked, "Cuts?"

"*Ma!*" He said it sharply enough to get through, and both women, along with the other Leau folk lingering around, turned to him. "Please. Stop."

Slightly chastened, Mistress Corlia leaned against his shoulder for a moment, pointed at the plate of food, and sighed. "Never understood you getting shy over other people hurting *you*," she said.

She waited until he'd filled his mouth with honey bun before continuing, "'Course, he never liked hurting other people neither. Thought he'd never speak again after the ship. You know about it? Pirates gutted him like a fish, but he managed to kill a half dozen or so to get out alive. He's got a gentle soul, Lady. He ain't a killer. We pieced him back together, but all he'd do was sit on the roof and drink. Couldn't even get a proper meal in him."

As he struggled in vain to swallow so he could stop the woman's tirade, Beau was surprised to feel Lady Penamour's fingers on his wrist, the slightest squeeze, like a plea not to interrupt.

Ma barreled on. "It was Ellie brought him out of it. At first, he'd just sit next to him and they'd stare at the island and didn't say a word. Days like that. Then they started talking. His Highness couldn't move much while he was healing, so he'd watch Ellie practice with his sword or they'd talk for days and days."

Beau glanced up at Elias, who stood against the far wall of the inn, staring out the window and pretending not to have ears. He remembered that period of his life very well, unfortunately. He'd been dangling his feet off the roof of the inn, enjoying his first mug of wine of the day and lamenting that the sword wound hadn't *quite* killed him when Elias sat down beside him and said, "I think you're in need of me."

And he was.

Barely two days had passed since he'd admitted to Mistress Corlia that he needed a guard when Elias showed up. He hadn't even considered what he needed in a guard, and certainly didn't know how to evaluate fighting skill. El had looked fit, so Beau told him he could have the job if he'd scratch the itch in the middle of his back that had been plaguing him for days.

"When he started getting stronger, they did everything together. A lot of dancing, a lot of drinking, and a lot more work around the isles. But mostly they talked. Never seen any two people take to each other like those two did."

Beau forced a wad of sticky-sweet pastry down his throat. "Ma," he choked out, "this isn't really...I'm sure the duchess doesn't want to hear—"

"I want to hear it," Penamour said eagerly. "I can hardly credit all the stories I've heard this morning. Is it true you fought off a woman's abusive husband and then delivered her baby?"

"Well..." Beau might catch flame. "To be fair, he nearly killed me, and I ripped open all my stitches in the process, so I was more of a bloody nuisance—literally—than any help, but I was *there*, technically, so—"

"And you hauled in Mouthy's—"

"Toothy's," Ma corrected.

"Sorry, *Toothy's* nets when he was sick for weeks and shredded your hands?"

"I had soft-ass noble hands," Beau said uncomfortably. "I was a laughingstock."

"And you taught Mallet how to—"

"I'm sure it's all true, to some degree," Beau said quickly, trying to forestall the litany that made him want to curl up and hide. "Although everybody here exaggerates when they tell stories, so assume they're half true. I'm sorry I left you to be harangued by everyone on the isles. I forget how rabid they get when somebody who hasn't heard every tale turns up."

"I think it's sweet," Lady Penamour said. She looked stunning this morning, hair braided back simply with little curls falling around her face, fresh face free of makeup except for something shiny on her lips. He found himself staring, and his stomach flipped when she stared right back. "They all wanted to tell me how much they love you and why."

There was no way to respond to that, so Beau shrugged a shoulder and let the corner of his mouth pull up in a smile. "So you can see why I missed home."

"Yes," she said simply. Her fingers were still against his wrist, and they traced slightly along his arm as she pulled away. "Lots of nicknames on Leau. I don't think I've heard a single person called by their actual name."

Beau quickly chewed and swallowed a sausage roll, brushing his hands clean. "Oh, please tell me they've called you Your Grace like they *know* they're supposed to."

She laughed, a bright, happy sound. "I got 'Your Grace' and 'Duchess' at first, then someone called me 'Gracious' and another called me 'Gracie,' which seemed to have morphed into 'Grey' and then 'Grey Lady,' and then someone said '*Gold* Lady, actually,' which became 'Goldie' and just 'Lady.'"

"Oh gods," Beau muttered.

"Well nobody's angry with you, Lady," Ma said, unperturbed. "Round here, you only use given names or titles if you can't stand somebody or you're fightin' mad."

"She fought very hard for her title, Ma," Beau explained. "She deserves—"

"I don't mind," Lady Penamour said.

Beau raised an eyebrow at her. "You very much *do* mind nicknames. You scolded me every time I gave you one."

"I didn't understand the spirit in which they were meant," she said, folding her hands on the table primly. "Now that I see how affectionately they're used on Leau, I don't mind at all. And in fact

I'd prefer you didn't address me the way you isle folk only do when you're cross."

Beau studied her warm, teasing dark eyes, and his stomach did another strange flip.

"All right, Penny," he said quietly, shuddery fingers of happiness spreading along his scalp at her teasing him, calling him 'isle folk,' acknowledging that he'd been affectionate all along.

A pure-sugar shot of pleasure radiated over from her, so sweet and sudden it made him breathe out an involuntary laugh. He'd kill for more of the syrupy taste of her happiness. It was the most incredible feeling. *Penny* it was, then.

Overfed by Ma Corlia, Beau eventually extricated himself from the storytelling isle folk, made sure his staff were settled in, and escaped the inn with Penny beside him and Jude and Nilah trailing behind, leaving Elias in the yard with a handful of aspiring guards.

As they walked the waterline, greeting friends and acquaintances who hadn't made their way to the Hops, Beau plucked a dog-rose from a shrub devouring a garden fence and offered it to the duchess. She sniffed it, then arched a brow at him. "Should I read into your giving me a flower that means 'second choice'?"

"What?" Beau asked in alarm. "That's not what it means on Leau—dog-rose is for beauty. Simple pleasures."

"Hmm," she said, tucking the pale pink blossom behind her ear. "Different flower language in different places, I suppose. What about daffodils?" She nodded toward a row of yellow flowers along the road ahead. "Do those mean friendship here, too?"

He shook his head. "Daffodils are for happiness. Bluebells or tulips for friendship."

"Ah, tulips are for familial love, unconditional," she said. Her pomegranate curiosity was tempered with a light nuttiness he associated with eagerness. "What about violets?"

"Violets don't grow well on Leau," Beau said, "but violets and lavender are both for…peace, I guess? But the healing kind. Building quiet strength. You'd bring them to someone's bedside while they recover." His room at the inn had smelled like lavender for months; even after the place burned down and was rebuilt, he still caught a whiff every now and then.

"Hmm. That's lovely." Someone waved to them from a boat, and they both lifted hands to return the greeting, though Beau couldn't identify them, squinting into the late morning sun. "I've seen quite a lot of people growing hollyhock. Does that mean chastity here as well?"

Beau was too surprised to suppress his snort. "You're messing with me. Hollyhock does *not* mean chastity, surely?" He was overtaken with giggles.

"Why?" Her mouth shaped a smile, ready to join his laughter. "What does it mean here?"

He laughed harder. "People who throw hollyhock in the well are looking for a *lively* bedroom. As I've heard it said in vows, 'We want lots of children and lots of fun making them.'"

"Well," she said, a blush heating her face as she chuckled, "who doesn't want that?" A tinge of spicy-sweet bled over from the ring. "Into the well?"

"Ah, it's the marriage tradition on Leau. There's a bell hung over an old dry well. Couples find flowers that say their wish for their life and toss it in the well. Then they say their vows on the steps and ring the bell."

Beau laughed again. "And then the whole island gets the happy couple drunk and dances until their feet fall off."

"It sounds lovely."

Beau shot her a knowing look. "I know, it's not the big to-do we get in the capital, with months of planning and every detail accounted for, but it *is* nice. I love the tradition."

Penny's face and ring-wash were both slightly exasperated. "I *said* it sounds lovely, and I meant it. I like simple, beautiful things. I like showy, well-planned things, too. They all have their place."

"Sorry," Beau said. "Didn't mean to imply you don't mean what you say."

"Hmm. You don't think much of nobles, do you, Beauregard? Oh!" She looked slightly alarmed for a moment. "*Can* I call you Beauregard?"

The pink in her cheeks made her look angelic; Beau stared for a half second longer than he ought to have before saying, "Call me Beauregard, call me Beau, call me Barfly or Fine-eye or Crowregard or something else entirely. Just not Lamb—that's Ma's." He remembered she'd asked a question. "And no, I don't think much of nobles. I don't think much of liars in general."

"Do you find me to be a liar?"

Beau raised an brow. "You? Who conspired and deceived me out of the palace so you could poison me and El and accuse us of murder? *No.*" He laughed. "To be fair, you're the most honest of the bunch. You're not very much like a noblewoman, really."

She snorted. "You're being an ass." As Beau coughed out a surprised laugh, she continued, "You are! I'm *just* like a noblewoman because I am a noblewoman. Anything I do or am is, therefore, what a noblewoman would do or be. I'm not unique. I'm not unlike all other nobility. You've been exceedingly unfair to your peers since you came back from the isles. You came in determined to despise them all. I watched you: you started every conversation hostile."

"They all tried to manipulate something out of me! Or were so hateful to their people I couldn't stand to be around them."

"The latter I'll give you because Haydée Macabrie is a nightmare," she said dryly. "But the rest is categorically untrue. You interpreted every harmless attempt to get the measure of you as some sort of dishonest attack. They don't *know* you! And you were so miserable all the time. They were trying to find some way to cheer you up so you'd speak. The only people you were remotely kind to or interested in were a handful of young men who can't do anything for you, politically, and me. And I was about as hateful as possible!"

Beau's shoulders drew up. "You were interesting. Authentic."

"I was consistently cruel," she insisted.

Stung, the prince tried to summon a response and came up short. Penny softened. "I understand why things were difficult. You'd lost your brother; you were navigating waters you'd never had to sail before. And may I speak frankly?"

"Have you *not* been?"

She set her hand on his arm again, a warm and bracing gesture. "Your introduction to nobility was honestly barbaric. What you described about growing up in the palace—that's not normal. Parents seeing a child once a week? Denying affection, giving only criticism? That's not 'noble' behavior. That's cruelty." She inhaled sharply. "Which I suppose is why my cruelty felt like authenticity, but that's not who I am, or—it's not who I *want* to be. I was spiteful because I believed something about you that wasn't true. It wasn't interesting. It was hateful."

Beau absorbed all of that, not sure how to take it. His eyes traveled—as they always, always did when he was uncertain—to where Elias usually stood behind him. *When you don't know how you feel, you ask me.* Except El wasn't here.

He turned back to Penny, who smiled uncertainly at him, and felt her warmth in his bones. "That's not what I found interesting about you. Maybe, if we've gotten off that far on the wrong foot, we should start over? Reintroduce ourselves."

"Gods, no! Don't you dare," Penny said with a laugh. "We've spent *months* figuring each other out and only just gotten to any level of understanding. Don't make me start again as a stranger, I beg. You're terrible with strangers. Let's do the *opposite* of starting over."

"What, start at lovers, work our way backward?" Beau snarked without thinking, then immediately colored. One didn't joke about such things with a duchess. "I mean—"

Lady Penamour was also pink, but the ring sent across only heat and sweetness, no outrage. "That seems a bit complicated, given our respective positions," she said lightly. "Although I'm not entirely opposed to—oh!"

A small, human-shaped cannonball slammed into Beau's waist, knocking him back a step and surprising the duchess into a quiet exclamation.

"Angel!" A beaming, snaggle-toothed face looked up at Beau.

Grinning, the prince crouched down eye-to-eye with Nathan. "Well, hello there, sir," Beau said. "Tell me, I wonder if such a tall young man as yourself has seen a little boy called Nate? He'd be about half your size, just six years old—"

"It's me! I'm Nate! I'm *seven* now! And look, I lost *two* teeth!" Nathan vibrated with energy, hands on Beau's shoulders as he tried to climb the prince and shout at the same time.

"You?" Beau exclaimed in mock-confusion. "No, it couldn't be! You're much too big!"

Bernadette, Nathan's mother, leaned against the wall nearby and smiled fondly down at Beau and her boy. "Aye, he's getting far too big. I keep putting rocks on his head to hold him down, but he grows to spite me."

Beau let the boy climb onto his shoulders and stood, balancing him so he could give Bernadette a hug. "Good to see you, Bunny," he said, kissing her cheek before grabbing Nate's ankles and doing quick squats until the boy shrieked with exhilaration.

"You too, Angel. You brought a highborn lady to us?" She had a narrowed-eye smile, too knowing. "Come for the well and bell?"

"Um," Beau said, cheeks burning, "Lady Penamour, Duchess of Veritelutte, this is Bernadette, a friend of mine, and this little heathen on my shoulders is Nathan. Bunny, Nate, this is Lady Penamour. We call duchesses 'Your Grace,' Nate."

"Hullo, Grace," Nate said sweetly, and Penny beamed up at him. A fond wash of warm-bread tenderness came through the ring.

"Hello, Nate. And it's lovely to make your acquaintance, Bunny. You can call me whatever you like, I suppose. No need to be formal." The cries of the fish market floated across to them on the breeze, carrying the faint smell of the catch of the day with it. "Is this 'little heathen' the baby I heard about you delivering?"

"Oh aye, he is," Bunny said. "Nate was coming to invite you to the blue hole, Angel. Fancy a swim?"

"Uh—" Beau threw a quick glance at the duchess's fine dress. "I don't know that we—"

"We'd love to," Lady Penamour said with a wide smile. When Beau looked hesitant, she asked quietly, "Is a duchess not permitted to like swimming as much as the next person?"

"It's just…that's a nice dress, and it's public. It's not really the sort of thing nobles do."

"Have *you* been swimming at the blue hole?" she asked dryly.

"Well, yes, but—"

"Mum has extra swimming clothes, if Grace needs to borrow any," Nate said. He wiggled and kicked until Beau let him down, dancing on the cobbles of the street.

"There you are, his mum has extra swimming clothes," Penny said briskly. "So it's all taken care of. Lead the way, young man."

Nate took off like a shot, darting over fences and hedges to take the straightest line home. Beau led Penny the long way around with Bunny, up and down the sloping hills of cobbled street, guards trailing behind. Every few feet the boy popped up atop a fence post or tree, waving and calling to be chased. Penny said, "If I weren't here, would you follow him through all those yards and gardens?"

Beau grinned sheepishly. "Yes, probably."

She set her hand on his arm, drawing him to a stop. "I asked you to show me around the isles because I want to see *your* isles. The way they are, not the way you expect me to want to see it."

Beau shifted his feet and shoved his curls back from his face, but Penny didn't let him turn away from her. "You're nervous that I won't like Leau. I understand. You love it. But if you keep spending all your time trying to make it 'proper' for a noblewoman, you'll never know if I actually do like it or not. And everything you've shown me so far has been wonderful."

"Be gentle with him, Lady," Bunny said. "We've never made him be a noble here."

"Yeah," Nate popped up, bouncing out of a hedge, "he's not a noble, he's mum's guardian angel! 'Cept he's real. And a king!"

"I'm not an ang—" Bunny smacked Beau hard enough to cut him off, and Beau sighed. "Fine, I'm not a *king*. I'm a prince."

Nathan's brow furrowed as he scratched an arm. "But you're going to be king, right?"

"Well, sure, if I live that long," Beau said with a hollow laugh.

"What?" Bunny said, just as Penny said, "*Beau.*"

"You're dying?" Nate shrieked.

"No—oh, no no no," Beau said, backpedaling furiously. "I just meant, you know, sometimes princes die and then their younger brothers have to—" Nate's face contorted in horror on the edge of tears. "*No*, no, no, I'm sorry. It was a bad joke! Dark humor. I'm not dying. I'm not going to die, Nate, please don't cry. I'm going to be king, and I'll wear a big silly crown, and sit on the throne next to the queen, and I'll rule the whole kingdom. Okay?"

Nate sniffed dubiously, watching Beau with wary yes. After a consideration, he pointed at the duchess. "Is this the queen?"

"Oh—um." Beau tilted his head to the side, struggling with how to answer that. "Not…yet?" Penny turned to Beau, eyebrows high. "I just—I—" He bent close to Nate and stage-whispered. "I haven't asked her yet. It's a secret." He pressed his finger to his lips, and Nate grinned, following suit.

"Do you have a ring?" Nate whispered loudly. "I found Uncle Mallet a piece of sea glass and he made a ring for Auntie Jojo and *she* said yes. I could find you something for a ring, if you wanted."

Beau had a sudden, overwhelming urge to squeeze Nate and had to grit his teeth to avoid crushing the boy. Instead, he smiled. "Yeah, I'd love something pretty for a ring."

"Okay!" Nate said, then promptly shushed himself and Beau with his finger pressed to his lips. He skipped away, and Penny sidled up to Beau's other side, all warm syrup on fresh bread through the ring with the ever-present burst of pomegranate curiosity.

"Yet?" she said quietly.

Beau scratched at the back of his neck. "Not that I'm making any sort of assumptions."

She stopped him before the turn into Bunny's yard, and Bunny, after a quick glance at them, went into the house to give them privacy. Penny said, "So you've forgiven me, then?"

Beau had the sudden urge to touch her silken dark hair, and because she was looking at him with such open happiness, he let himself, tugging gently on her braid. "If I'd thought someone murdered my brother, I'd have done worse." His fingers dislodged the dog-rose, and he caught it as it fluttered down, handing it back.

Penny stared down at it, twirling it in her fingers, and when she met his eyes again, she looked pained. "I understand the message you've been trying to send, and I...well, I understand."

"Message?"

"The second-choice flower?" She gestured with the dog-rose.

"But that's not what it—"

"And leaving the ring on last night? Leaving me waiting while you got 'caught' this morning? I *understand* what he means to you, Beau, and what that means for—"

"Wait, *wait*," Beau said sharply, "oh, fuck, I left the—" His stomach dropped, a deep swoop of embarrassment, and he groaned. "None of that was intentional. It wasn't a *message*. And it wasn't what you think it—oh *gods*."

Penamour laughed, a bright trill of surprise.

"All right, your *unintentional* message, then," she said. "Still—"

"No, 'still' nothing." Beau waved his hands as if he could smooth over the misunderstanding physically. "He doesn't even want—I mean, it's not—" He blew all his breath out at once, lifting his curls off his face. Humiliating as it was, he'd have to tell her at least some of his and Elias's business, since he'd accidentally made it her business.

"I know everyone in the capital—and on Leau—thinks El and I are together. We're not. Last night was the first and *last* time we…" He swallowed down the thick, painful lump in his throat.

Penny's fingers rose to touch her own throat. "*He* doesn't want…" she muttered.

"I mean, it's mutual. I don't want anything he doesn't want. And it doesn't matter anyway because I'm going to be *king*, you know, so—so I have to—" He gestured toward her, then paused, horrified. Words rolled out too fast, half stuttered. "No, I don't mean *have to*—I—*fuck*, I can't even explain myself without sounding like a complete fucking asshole."

"What on *earth* is going on out here?" Bunny said, reappearing with a baffled grin and a stack of towels in her arms.

"Angel's being a complete fucking asshole," Nate repeated in a near-perfect recreation of Beau's intonation, scrambling over the rocks. Beau slapped a hand over his face, digging thumb and forefinger into his eyes as he tried to process all the mortification at once.

"Nathan Dane, *language*," Bunny said sharply. "Though why I even try—the boy's got a dozen sailor uncles and fishwife aunties all trying their best to teach him every swear word in the isles. He doesn't need it from you, too, *Highborn*."

With a deeply apologetic look at Bunny, Beau scooped up the boy, swung him around, and all but sprinted the distance to the blue hole. He flung the shrieking boy into the water, and then pulled off his boots and shirt as Nate bobbed up, giggling and splashing. Beau dove past and swam beneath him so Nate sat on his shoulders when he resurfaced. Bernadette and the duchess, in deep conversation, lingered at the shore while the duchess changed behind the shelter of Bunny's towel, and Beau played with Nate.

When at last Penny swam smoothly over, Beau threw Nate backwards, waiting for the splash and the squealing laughter. He took a deep breath to calm himself, but Penny didn't try to pick up the conversation where they'd left it. Her eyelashes beaded together with water and a few loose curls plastered themselves to her graceful neck. Beau had never wanted to kiss her more, and never been more mortified to know she knew that from the ring.

"Shall we race?" she said, a grin chasing playfully over her lips.

Beau smiled back. "On the count of three..."

They raced. They floated. They played with Nate and splashed one another and had the kind of time Beau hadn't thought nobles *could* have, without pretending to be common for a while. But Penny was right; they were noble. What they did was what nobles did.

"Should we head back to the inn?" she asked eventually, soaked and bright-eyed and beautiful. "I'd like to see what recruits Elias found." Beau nodded.

They bid Bunny and Nate farewell as they dried and dressed, and the boy pressed something tiny into Beau's hand: a shimmering, uneven pearl, its pale surface shading toward pink.

"That's beautiful, Nate," he said, hugging the boy to his side. An idea sparked. "Do you want to see some magic before we go?"

"Yeah!"

Beau reached into his pocket and pulled out a spoon. "Prepare yourself. This will boggle the mind. I have only to speak the magic word—d'you know the one? *Please*. Could you be a toy horse, please?" He cupped his hand around a miniature metal horse.

"You can change spoons into toys?!" Nate shrieked. Penny laughed, and Beau winked at her, a grin spreading across his face.

He held the Useful Thing higher so Nate couldn't snatch it from his hand. "Not just toys. Let's try something else. Could you be a small cup, please?" Into the now-cup, he dropped the pearl. "And now, for something that may not be possible. The grand finale. Nate, could you give us a drumroll?" As the boy pounded on the ground in a loose imitation of a drum, Beau said, "Could you be a beautiful ring incorporating that pearl, please?"

There was a pause this time, and Beau worried for a moment

it wouldn't work. The Useful Thing grew hot in his palm, a faint glow lighting his skin. Penny made a small, choked gasp. And then, in his palm, a stunning ring lay. It looked like it'd been grown, not made, its intricate, organic whorls wrapping the pearl elegantly. Beau had never seen anything like it. He examined it, ignoring Nate's exclamations because he was getting saccharine, delicious pulses of emotion from Penny. He felt his body relax in reaction, his lips curve up, his heart speed. It was incredible: she felt this much joy naturally?

Feeling it with her was like stealing something from her, though he knew the ring didn't diminish one's own emotions as it broadcast them. But something so good couldn't be freely available; it had to be stolen, surely.

"Are you all right?" Penny touching his arm, and he met her eyes as her joy tinged with concern and amusement.

"How are you so happy?"

She laughed. "Why wouldn't I be happy?"

"This ring is for you!" Nate screeched, trying to grab it.

"Well—hold on, there's a proper way to do things," Beau said, settling the boy down with a hand on his shoulder. "You don't hand someone a ring sopping wet on the edge of a swimming hole if you want to marry them. You plan something special, think about things they like, create some romantic atmosphere. You have to—"

"No, you don't," Penny interrupted. "Nate, the only thing you *have* to do is form the words of a question and *ask* the person if they'll marry you. Everything else is optional."

Beau stared at her, surprised. That had sounded, despite the horrific bungling he'd made of everything that morning, like an invitation to ask. As Beau studied the light in her eyes, her amusement spiked, fresh orange in his mind.

"That does leave one open to a particularly painful brand of rejection," he said, and found his voice quite hoarse.

She winced. "Not if the person you're asking has any sense at all," she said, and the treacly taste of apology slicked his tongue.

That seemed obvious enough. It was exactly what he'd wanted, what he'd hoped for, and still he hesitated. He cleared his throat. He rolled the pearl ring in his fingers. "Victoire Augusta Bridgette Penamour," he said quietly, "Duchess of Veritelutte by cunning and force of will…"

He licked his lips, and Leau went still. Penny's eyes were wide and luminous and expectant. Beau swallowed and continued, "Formerly my most formidable opponent and currently—" He laughed hollowly. "—the keeper of my sanity. Would you marry me?"

He held out the ring, and Penny plucked it gently from his fingers, studying it with a warm, delighted smile and a warm, delighted syrup of emotions in his head. Beau's dread began to dissipate, though not completely; she hadn't answered yet.

"You know, you already gave me a ring. I'm not sure a second was strictly necessary."

"The first wasn't an engagement ring. It was a threat. Something new was warranted."

Penny's smile broadened, grew wicked. "Are you going to want the 'threat' back, then?" She made as if to pull off the Ring of Thrones, and Beau jerked toward her.

"What? No, of course not." The thought of losing her constant, cool pool of emotions in his head was repellent. "How else will I get my dose of joy—and curiosity?"

"You've got your own fair share of the latter."

Nate tugged Beau's shirt. "Did she say yes?"

"I don't think she's decided yet, Nate," Beau said, watching Penny spin the ring between her fingers, heart pulsing in his throat.

Penny's face creased with incredulity as she slipped the pearl-adorned Useful Thing onto the ring finger of her left hand. "Of course I've decided, silly man. Yes. I'll marry you."

When Beau took her hand, intending to kiss the back, and she pressed closer to kiss him on the lips instead, the rush of joy through Beau's head was all his own.

16

THE HONEYCOMB

News of their engagement spread mouth to ear across Leau faster than the prince and duchess could walk, so it was no surprise Elias already knew by the time they'd reached the inn yard.

"Congratulations," El said, not looking at either of them. "We've got our newest guard—" He nodded at Aloise, rosy-cheeked and proud with her bow in hand. "—so we can be on the road to the capital first thing tomorrow. In the meanwhile, I recommend you both go see Herb and send news of the engagement to as many Houses as he has pigeons."

Penny frowned at Elias, pomegranate curiosity sharpening into something more acidic, closer to suspicion, as she studied him. Beau was too busy trying to bury the hollow ache in his belly at how unaffected El seemed to piece together why. "Oh, well done, Aloise. I didn't know you were the guarding sort." He smiled at her, and she grinned back. "I think we can wait to bring the news back with us, El, if we're heading to the palace first thing—"

"No," Penny interrupted, eyes on the guard, "he's right. Things could move quickly while we're gone, and I left a very different impression of you than I'll return with. Better if we spread the news now. In fact—Beau, I know this is sudden, but would you mind terribly if we had a bell-and-well ceremony here? Tonight? And sent news of a marriage, not just an engagement?"

Beau saw Elias's slight eye-widening of alarm and felt a shadow of it, though he didn't understand it. "*Tonight?* That's, um…I'm not opposed, but is there a reason for the haste?"

"Engagements can be made and broken. I'd like there to be no doubt the Penamours are behind the rightful king, should…anything…happen before we get back."

"Should my father die," Beau clarified flatly.

She gave him a pained nod. "Yes. I'm afraid, given the state we left things in, that others might proceed differently if I communicate anything less permanent than marriage."

Beau scrubbed at his forehead with one hand. "Is there a plan in motion to unseat me?"

"Not necessarily in *motion*, but—" Penny began, just as Elias said, "Almost certainly." They exchanged a glance, and each seemed to get a great deal more out of the glance than Beau did, watching.

"Well, fuck. I guess we get married tonight, then." Beau turned to inform Ma, who'd rally Leau into action, but then paused. "Wait—*will* your marrying me be enough to stop whatever's cooking? Because if not, if whoever's planning to—"

"Courdur," Penny and Elias said simultaneously.

Beau stared at them a moment before continuing, "If Courdur moves forward with, I assume, killing me and taking the throne, he'll kill you, too. You'd be tying yourself into my fate. Seems risky."

The duchess frowned. "Are you saying we *shouldn't* marry?"

"I'm saying you should think about whether it's worth it for you to take on that risk," Beau said, frowning.

"Oh, you—" Her hand pressed to her chest and she tilted her head to the side, eyes flicking over Beau. The fondness that came through the ring nearly choked him with its warm bread taste. "You are actually as sweet as you seem, aren't you?"

"What?" Beau asked.

"Yes, he is," Elias said sharply, "and *don't* listen to him. You made this problem, Duchess. You fix it."

Penny crossed her arms, raising a wry eyebrow at Elias. "Not even pretending you're just a guard anymore, hmm?"

Glancing at Aloise, Jude, and Nilah, the only other people in the yard, El shrugged. "No idiots here, and we're short on time."

"Yes." She nodded. "If you'll point me toward the pigeon-keeper, I'll send the announcements. Beau, come by once you've talked to Mistress Corlia and Uriel, and you can see them before I send them." The duchess squeezed his arm gently, and he had a sudden rush of realization that she was his *fiancée*. So strange, so exciting, so overwhelmingly *fast*.

He was watching her walk away when Elias poked him hard in the side. "Go talk to Ma. I've got to get your flight in order and tell Uriel what to expect."

Beau caught El's wrist before he could escape. "El…"

"*Rei kyriv*," Elias warned. "That was it. No more discussion."

The prince's mouth closed with a click of teeth. He inhaled sharply through his nose, then nodded, trying not to look like that was the most devastating thing Elias could've said. "Right."

Stiffly, Elias said, "I wish you'd taken the ring off, but you said exactly what you should've said this morning when Duchess asked you about it, so…good job."

Beau's head came up, surprised. "How the fuck do you know?"

Scrunching his mouth to one side, the guard bent and pulled the Perception Stone from a clever pocket in the side of his boot, cut open on the inside so the stone could touch his skin. He lifted it between his first two fingers. "Bunny's house isn't *quite* far enough away to keep me from hearing, with this."

Beau's mouth fell open. He watched the flash of the stone in the sunlight and blinked stupidly, thinking of all the many, *many* times Elias had seemed to know things long before they happened. He'd heard them coming. "Where the hell did you get that?"

"Oh, not you accusing me of theft too," Elias joked quietly.

"To be fair…" Beau drawled, and Elias nodded, glancing away.

"Yes, I earned that. It seemed prudent to keep them safe, when we didn't know why all the others disappeared. I'm sorry I didn't tell you."

Beau watched the other guards chat on the far side of the yard, relaxed and smiling now that they were all trusted again. He drummed his fingers against his hollow belly. "Were you ever going to tell me, if Penny hadn't forced your hand?"

"Yes," Elias said, then winced. "If…we ever had need of the artifacts."

"So no." Beau traced the line of Elias's profile with his eyes, then turned back to other guards. "Why don't you trust me, El?"

"I *do* trust you!"

"Just not with the truth. About anything." He raised his hand to forestall whatever non-answer Elias was about to give. "But *rei kyriv*, right? The time for asking questions and getting any sort of honest answers has passed."

·⸱𝔖𝔩𝔢·𝔖𝔩𝔢·𝔖𝔩𝔢·

Ma screamed in excitement for three minutes straight before enlisting all of Leau to prepare for the evening's festivities, though Beau told her repeatedly they needed nothing beyond the well that had stood on Leau for generations and the inn's usual fare.

While a flustered Uriel, who couldn't imagine a wedding with little enough pomp that a few hours' notice would suffice, tried to secure worthy clothing, Penny was swept away to learn the wedding customs of Leau, and the rest of the island abandoned work to string up flower garlands, put candles and lanterns on doorsteps, and heap food onto Ma's prep counters.

Herb, the pigeon-keeper, a tiny, ancient man who seemed in awe of the duchess, brought an armload of wafer-thin scraps of paper for Beau to look over as Uriel combed his hair. The prince picked through them, scribbling a signature across any written by "him" and dropping the rest into a pile as he scanned them. They were all close to the same, and he trusted Penny to speak to nobles more than he trusted himself.

"Looks good, Herb," he said, handing the heap off.

Penny's ring pulsed with excitement and rosemary nerves.

Elias came in only once, meeting Beau's eyes in the mirror as he plucked the Perception Stone out of his boot and tucked it into the drawer of Beau's bedside table. Then he nodded at Beau and disappeared. *I'm giving you your privacy*, the gesture said. Beau ached.

He wanted to be just happy, but how could he be *just* anything? He was engaged and he'd be king, or maybe not because maybe Courdur was already moving against him, and maybe Penamour marrying him would stop that and maybe it wouldn't and she'd die too. He was in love with Elias and Elias loved him back, only maybe not because how could anyone who loved anyone be happy with just one night and moving on?

He was a tangle, unsortable, and instead of dealing with any of it, Beau dissociated as Uriel primped and prodded him, letting the emotions swirl around him to be viewed through frosted glass.

Laughter and cheers rocked the inn when Penny emerged, as people encouraged her and called out suggestions of flowers to find. Once she was out of sight, Ma opened Beau's door.

"Are you ready?" she asked, the apples of her cheeks red from smiling. Beau nodded and kissed her temple, letting her wrap her arms around him. "Know what flowers you'll pick? Something beautiful, I'm sure. Graceful. Queenly."

"I have some ideas." He looped his arm through Ma's and led a small, informal procession out of the inn. People chatted and speculated as some raced ahead toward the well and others gathered neighbors coming in on boats who hadn't heard the news. Isle folk surrounded him, but except for the occasional congratulations, no one spoke to him.

Ma kept a comforting grip on his arm as he searched for his flower. Typically, they were everywhere, invasive and pervasive, but he reached the circle of cobbles around the well without finding one.

He spotted what he was looking for as Ma gave him a kiss and melted into the crowd, and Penny reached the well's small courtyard. In the setting sun, she was radiant, glowing golden like a goddess, hair pinned up in curls around a flower crown in pinks and oranges and yellows and creams. She held a bundle of heather in her hands. Unbidden, Beau's fingers ran over her shoulders, left bare by the gown she'd worn. "You look beautiful," he breathed.

Her smile lit the courtyard. "Oh," she laughed breathily, "let's walk away and do that again; that felt good." He felt his own delight bounced back from her along the ring.

Penny reached up and brushed her fingertips against his cheekbone, her thumb against the corner of his mouth like she was teasing out a smile. Her eyes softened when they met his. "You don't always have to borrow happiness, do you?" she muttered. Delicious emotions flooded him, so many and so strong he had to close his eyes and turn his face up to the sky to absorb them. His reaction sparked fresh joy from her, and he chuckled.

"Careful. People are going to think I'm drunk," he teased. He *felt* drunk, tipsy and giddy from the continuous feed of orange and lemon and strawberry, all soaked in syrupy happiness. Seizing her hand, he spun her around, letting her skirt swirl out around her as she laughed, and they made their way to the well.

"Where are your flowers?" she asked, waving her heather.

Beau held up a finger, then bent to the base of the well, where a spiky milk thistle grew up from a crack in the stone, its starburst purple head a bright spot of color. Reaching carefully through the prickly leaves, he grabbed the stem, hissing when a thorn cut into his thumb, and snapped it off. He held it up, grinning at Penny, and she raised a skeptical eyebrow.

"Did you just wait to see what flowering weed was growing at the well?" she asked.

Beau shook his head, slightly affronted. "No. This was the only place I saw any thistles."

Her mouth shaped a question, but Ma loudly called for all the gathered isle folk to be quiet, and he and Penny looked up to find hundreds of people had circled the well's courtyard to witness. Beau called out, "I intend to marry this woman. Does anyone object?"

"Aye, if you take that beautiful lady away from here, I'll be heartbroken," Adrien shouted, and he and Nicolas elbowed each other as everyone laughed.

Beau chuckled too, but he drew his knife and pointed it steadily at Adrien. "You want to challenge me about it?"

Adrien raised his hands, then bowed in acquiescence and said, "I wouldn't know how to keep a lady so fine, Crowregard. Congratulations to you both."

Resheathing, Beau called, "Anyone else?" When the crowd answered with cries of congratulations—and impatient requests that they get on with it so the dancing could begin—Beau met the duchess's eyes and gestured toward the well. "Ladies first."

Penny nodded, a thin thread of nervousness feeding through the ring. She held her heather out over the lip of the well and said, "I'm not sure what they mean out here, but where I come from, heather is for peace and protection. I don't expect our lives will be easy, Beauregard, but I know we both want peace. We want to protect our people. And I think we can, together."

Beau was so enamored with her in that moment. That was exactly what he wanted. He nodded, and she smiled, releasing the flowers into the murky depths of the well. Then her smile sharpened, grew secretive. "I also…" She reached into her pocket and pulled out a single hollyhock flower, its thin petals somewhat crumpled. "…perhaps more selfishly, want this."

The prince laughed, and he wasn't sure whether the surge of spicy-sweet started with her or with him. As the gathered crowd chuckled appreciatively, she flicked it into the well and folded her hands at her waist, looking deceptively prim for how heated their bond through the ring was growing. Beau cleared his throat and tightened his grip on the thistle, the sharp shock of pain clearing his mind so he didn't start panting in front of all these people.

"I…" He held up the flower. "People don't usually choose thistle for this. In fact, not many people will mess with thistle at all, because it hurts. It asks a lot."

A bead of blood welled up from the spine that had stabbed through the pad of his thumb. "But if you're willing to do the hard things and risk a few cuts, thistle rewards you with sustenance. Healing. A relief from pain. I want our marriage to be that: not always easy, as you said, but something we can draw from to heal whatever wounds the world gives us.

"And thistle, it's a hardy son-of-a-bitch, as anyone who's ever tried to get rid of the stuff can attest." The gathered folk laughed. "May we be as stubborn about thriving where we choose to make our home, and as difficult to unseat."

Penny breathed out a laugh of acknowledgement, bittersweet, and watched him toss the thistle into the well, standing on her tiptoes to peer down after it. Beau reached for her hands, then realized he was bleeding and fished a handkerchief out of his pocket.

"Sorry," he mumbled, "didn't think about what the damn flower would do to the hand-holding part." He pressed hard on his thumb until it stopped, then wiped his hands clean and pocketed the cloth again. "All right, where were we?"

"The vows, I believe," she said, her mouth curving slightly, though he could feel her jubilance dancing across the ring. He liked that she didn't show it all on her face, that some of her emotions were for only the two of them to know.

Dropping her voice, the duchess whispered, "I'm not sure I remember them all. I know I'm supposed to go first, but—?"

"We'll say them together." Gods, she was so exquisitely beautiful. He could stare at her for days. Her hands were small in his, but it seemed like the right fit. "Ready?" When she nodded, he spoke the vows, and she met him in unison.

"You cannot possess me, for I belong to myself. But while we both wish it, I give you all that is mine to give. You cannot command me, for I am free. But I shall serve you in those ways you require, and the honeycomb will taste sweeter from my hand. Do not walk in front of me; I may not follow. Do not walk behind me; I may not lead. We'll walk beside one another, my love, heart to heart and hand in hand, faithful friends, and each a comfort to the other's soul."

And such a comfort she was right then. Her warm-bread tenderness soothed every worry, banished any anxiety or doubt. He pushed across his gratitude as gently as he could, but Penny gasped anyway, tears springing up in her eyes, and he pulled back. He didn't want to shout at her, he only wanted her to understand.

Maybe she did. Penny pulled him down until she could stand on her toes and kiss him as cheers and applause broke out from the witnesses. The moment their lips touched, he felt her 'shout' back at him: warmth and possessiveness and joy and impatience and *lust*. He couldn't hold back the growl, could barely control his hands enough to make them grab her face and hold her to him instead of hoisting her up by the waist and wrapping her around himself.

"I don't think they needed the hollyhock," Maisie said dryly, and the assemblage laughed. "Ring the damn bell! My dancing feet are itching."

Without pulling away from the duchess, Beau reached blindly, found the pull cord and yanked it, sending the bell clanging painfully loud. He and Penny both flinched and then laughed, but the spell wasn't broken and the spicy-sweet onslaught didn't slow. Beau clutched her tightly to him, one hand buried in her hair, the other spread over her back.

It was such a strange, unfamiliar delight to touch her, to kiss her. No one got to kiss a duchess; no one got to hold her waist in his hands; no one got to feel the slope of her neck in his palm. She felt almost fragile, though he knew she wasn't. It felt like stealing, even though—and he shivered at the thought—she was *his* now. And he was hers.

Vaguely, he heard the crowd start to dissipate, heading to the Hops for the dancing or returning home. Traditionally, the couple led, but Beau didn't mind giving them a head start.

Penny's mouth on his was soft and sweet and eager, but inexpert. Which made sense, of course. She was a duchess—she hadn't had his luxury of playing at romance. Beau reeled himself in as he recognized the herbal, anxious taste heavy on his tongue.

Panting, Penny backed out of reach. "You're...intense," she said with a breathless laugh.

Beau looked away from the swollen redness of her lips and the flush of her cheeks and the perfect curve of her neck and tried to catch his own breath. "Sorry. We can slow down. I didn't mean to overwhelm you. I know you haven't, um... Why don't we go dance?"

Hand in hand, they were welcomed in the inn with cheers and music and food. Drinks were pressed into their hands, kisses pressed to their cheeks. Celebration rolled out of the common room, flowing into the yard beyond, lit by candlelight and stars.

He danced with his wife—his *wife*. She was a dream to lead, anticipating his movements, shifting at his slightest pressure. Penny danced with her whole body, silky hair to the tips of her toes, and he was continually fascinated by the flash of her nose ring or the curve of a curl along her shoulder or the pressure of her hand on his chest before she whirled away from him again.

Cheeks flushed, eyes bright, she got used to being touched by him. She drew closer. She kissed him, and after five dances and two drinks, there was no acid burn of anxiety, no herbal nervousness. She nearly climbed him in her eagerness to reach his mouth, and when the room cheered her on, she grinned and bit his lip.

The sound Beau made was entirely sinful. He picked her up, shoving her skirt higher up her thighs so she could wrap her legs around his waist, and she obliged with a laugh. He kissed her like he needed her lips to live. Every movement of her body against his lit fires under his skin and sent him further into madness.

If he hadn't torn open the thorn-stab on his thumb and left a bright streak of blood on her cheek, he might've had her there in the common room. But the dark, wet mark against her perfect skin was enough to slip a sliver of sanity into his head.

With a monumental effort, he released her, letting her slide down his body to settle on the ground. Bending to press his mouth to her ear, he whispered, "Do you want to come to my room?" When her back stiffened, he said, "You don't have to. We can stay and dance. Or you can go to your own room. *You* tell *me*, Pen."

Penny clutched his shoulders, panting like she'd just run a mile. "Yours, please." She beamed at him, squeezing.

"Okay." He brushed a kiss to her temple and called, "My wife and I will see you in the morning. Good night! Enjoy the party."

Everyone raised a glass or hand and shouted, and Beau scooped Penny up in his arms, holding her against his chest. Laughing, she clung to him as he let them into his room and gently set her back down on her feet.

He grinned crookedly, foolishly at her, marveling at the unbelievable good luck that had brought him here. "You're my *wife*."

She smiled, too. "And you're my husband. How strange. The ceremony's a little too short. No time to get accustomed to the idea."

Shrugging, he laughed and bent close enough that she could kiss him if she wanted to. She did. "I suspect most people get used to it over an engagement longer than a couple hours."

The duchess—his *wife*—glanced at the bed and the spicy-sweet of the ring-wash tinged with rosemary and acid again, nervous, bordering on fear. She spoke before he could.

"Please don't borrow from me. Don't lose your enthusiasm." She laughed nervously. "I'm fine, I just haven't done this before, and I know it always hurts the first time, and I've never been very good with pain. But I do *want*—"

"Shh," Beau said, feeling her working herself up higher, acid building in the back of his throat from her. He ran his thumbs over her cheeks comfortingly. "Hold on. Who told you it always hurts? It doesn't have to. We *do not* have to do anything at all tonight, Pen, or for the foreseeable future. But if you *want* to, I promise you, I can take my time so I don't hurt you."

Her eyes searched his, pomegranate spiking. "Can you?"

"Yes," Beau said, nodding. He pulled her closer with gentle hands, reassuring motions. "I'm not going to hurt you. I'll make you feel good." He kissed her slowly, teasingly, feeling the ginger-mango heat rise. A smirk teased his lips up. "In fact, with this ring I've got powers beyond mortal ken to make you melt for me."

She swallowed hard, eyes on his, but the herbal nervousness had almost vanished, replaced with melting want and a syrupy sort of happiness. Beau set his hands on her hips, drew them closer to him, and kissed her again. "Do you want this?"

"Yes."

"Then trust me, and 'I will serve you in the ways you require,'" She smiled at the vow repeated. "I'll tell you what to do. All you need to do is tell me how much you enjoy it."

She nodded, but when he lifted her against him, he felt her anxiety in her body, muscles stiff. That wouldn't do at all. Mind racing, he guided her to the bed and sat her down, then stuck his head out the door. As soon as he was spotted, the common room lit with cheers and bawdy jokes, but he ignored that, meeting Nilah's eyes. "Can you bring me Lady Penamour's comb?"

A frown of confusion on her face, Nilah said, "Of course, Your Highness." When she reappeared to put it in his hand, she said, "Her Grace doesn't like other people to—"

"—to brush her hair because she has a sensitive scalp, I know," Beau said. "Thank you."

He shut the door again and saw a similar light of confusion and suspicion on his wife's face, though the ring gave mostly amusement and curiosity. "You must be tired of all those pins," he said. "I'm going to comb your hair out, and I will not hurt you. When I'm done, if you want me, I will touch you and kiss you and lick you until you beg me to make you mine in every possible way. And I *will not* hurt you."

There—there it was. The rush of syrupy sweet and burning spice, the way her pupils ate up the warm brown of her eyes, the parting of her lips to take in a shallow breath. Exactly what he wanted. He sat beside her and gently teased out one pin and flower at a time, drawing them from her curls without pulling her hair. Painstaking work, but between each pin, he got the shivery joy of pressing a kiss to the back of her neck or drawing his tongue along the edge of her ear. And Penny's spicy-sweet anticipation grew. Beau ached with want but didn't hurry.

When a pile of pins and flowers lay on his bedside table and her hair hung loose around her shoulders, he slid his fingers along her scalp, gently massaging it until Penny slumped against him. "You are powerful and beautiful and brilliant and sexy," he murmured. "And you have the future king of Granvallée wrapped around your little finger." She hummed happily.

Beau picked up the comb, parted one lock out of the rest, and slowly detangled it from the end up. Intensely focused on the feel of her hair under his hands and the pool of emotions in his head, he paused at any catch, worked it out gently with his fingers, teased tangles free until a lock was perfectly smooth, then went to the next. Penny tilted her head back to watch his face.

"I always heard you had no patience," she said. Pure pleasure danced over the ring, juicy pear dripping down his throat.

Beau smirked, not taking his eyes from his work. "I'm extremely patient, when I need to be. Meaningless court arguments? No. Paperwork? Not a chance. But to pleasure my wife—patient as a stone." He finished a section of hair and gently carved out another.

The duchess's hand reached behind her, slid up his thigh, and Beau held his breath. When her fingertips found his hardness, he paused his hands' work and laughed heatedly. "Now, if you start that, I'm going to get less careful."

More insistently, she ran her fingers along his length, finger-nails scratching lightly against the fabric of his pants. With a shaky exhale, Beau resumed his task, frowning at her hair in concentra-tion. It took ages to work his way through it all and run the comb through her hair smoothly, and Penny clearly felt the wait as well. As soon as he set the comb down, she spun and leapt onto his lap, kissing him until he could feel that joy-and-lust drunkenness rising.

Mouths hungry, hands fumbling at clothes, hearts pound-ing, they scrabbled and fought to undress each other. As soon as Beau's shirt was gone, the spicy-sweet intensified painfully. Penny's hands traced the lines of his tattoos, fingers dragging over the scars they only partially disguised. When her mouth found his neck, he clenched his fists on her dress until his knuckles creaked and the fabric strained; he had to keep control.

"Lay back." He stripped her of her gown so her body was teasingly visible through the thin, soft fabric of the silk chemise, and he ran his hand down it from her throat to her belly button, watch-ing it pull tight against every curve. "I want you. I want all of you."

He took his time. He eased the chemise off her shoulder and kissed her there, bit her. He did the same on the other side. His fingers slid up under the bottom, reveling in the taut skin of her legs. A line of kisses traced down the column of her throat, along her collarbone. He hooked a finger in the neck of her chemise and drew it down until it revealed the swell of her breasts, the perfect peaks. When his tongue flicked over one, Penny let out a gratifyingly desperate moan.

"Beau, *please*."

"Yes. Beg." He returned to her breast, circling it with his tongue, sucking it into his mouth. Her hands tangled his hair, strain-ing between drawing him away and pulling him closer.

Gentle. Slow. Intense. Unrelenting. His mouth and hands could not be hurried and could not be slowed and Penny writhed and mewled under him. Lower he went, lower, stripping her naked and moaning at the view. "I'm going to eat you alive, Penny. You're too fucking delicious." Hungrily, he licked up her thighs, met her lower lips with lips and teeth and tongue.

He had never, never felt anything like what she gave him through the ring: pleasure so pure and so searing it threatened to melt his bones, and he wasn't even being touched. She was wet and sweet, and Beau ate ravenously.

"Open up for me, lovely," Beau whispered, sliding a finger along her slit, gathering the slickness, tracing her opening. He moved slowly, coaxing, while his mouth found her clit and sucked gently. He closed his eyes to focus on the ring, searching for any sign of pain as he eased his finger in further. She whimpered, *need* pouring into his head, and his answering call rumbled in his throat. "That's right. Let me in."

"Beau, *Beau*—" Her hands were so tight on his hair, pulling him harder against her, desperate. He was happy to oblige, lashing his tongue against her harder, more steadily, while his finger gently pressed against every side of her, stretching her. Twice, he heard her sharp inhale at the same time a warning pulsed through the ring, and he eased back. He was in no rush; he'd happily grow old and die here between her legs.

When he could swirl his finger in her with no hint of warning pain, he sucked harder until she wailed, "*Beau*," but eased off again before he brought her to the brink. Her desperate hands clawed into his scalp, his neck, his shoulders, but he also felt her drowning in a sea of pleasure and he wouldn't cut it short.

"Another finger, you think?" he murmured. Her incoherent moan could've meant anything, but the ginger-chili-pepper rush said *yes, yes, yes*. She was so tight around his fingers, so hot, so drippingly wet. The pleasure reflected back from her brought him to the verge himself. "You're doing so well, taking my fingers. You're so close to taking what you really want."

"*Now*," Penny said through gritted teeth. "I want it now."

Beau chuckled darkly, closed his mouth over her clit again, drove her incoherent once more. When he sat up, face and fingers dripping, he said, "I said you'd beg me to make you mine. That didn't sound like begging."

"Please," she said with no hesitation, "*please*, Beau."

Normally, he'd take a partner to the finish before he entered, but he thought it'd be easier with her this hungry and willing. And besides, he couldn't bear another moment of teasing. Wiping his face on his forearm, he stripped off his pants hastily and then slid his fingers back inside her while his other hand stroked over his length. "Are you sure? It's going to stretch you much further than a couple of fingers. We can go to three first, before…"

Her eyes widened at the sight of him unclothed, and he felt, distantly, a thread of nervousness return. He pressed his thumb against her clit and she jerked, nerves vanishing. "How many times must I beg?" she growled.

His patience, strained to its limit, snapped. "That'll suffice." Crawling up her body, he kissed her as he aligned them. When his hand slid under her lower back to lift her to him, she moaned into his mouth in happy surprise. "Slow and easy. Open up for me."

When the first inch of him slipped into her, their rings burned physically hot from the explosion between them, ricocheting, multiplying. He couldn't hear over the ringing in his ears but he could feel himself cry out, could feel the same from Penny in the vibration of her chest, the heat of her breath against his neck. If pain came through the ring, he never felt it in the torrent, and she never voiced it. Nothing, nothing had ever felt this good. Nothing could. He was losing his mind. He was losing control. He was losing his grip on the face of the earth, coming untethered, floating away.

Her teeth sank into his chest, sharp enough to ground him in his body, and he moved. It was the slightest movement, half an inch out, another inch in, but they gasped like they'd been struck, and his head crackled with blue-white lightning. Beau's shudder carried him deeper into her, and he felt a catch that *could've* been pain, but Penny didn't flinch and the ring didn't pulse and then he was all the way inside her and pleasure had a new definition.

"Yes, Penny, *yes*. Gods, fuck, yes. You're so perfect. You fit me so perfectly, *fuck, yes*—"

She climbed; she peaked. Head thrown back and eyes squeezed shut, face flushed and fingernails clawing at his back, Penny had never looked so beautiful. The rolling crush of her body around his drew a whimper of need from him. The white-hot maelstrom in his head, impossible to think through, was blindingly pleasurable. He was losing control again.

He scooped his hips, grinding inside her, and Penny's cries reached a new pitch.

"Beau," she sobbed, "It's so—it's so—"

"Yes." He could barely form words, barely process what was happening, but he knew he wanted words from her. "Say my name. Tell me how it feels."

"Like—" She moaned again, her body trembling around him. "Like I was made for you."

Beau shuddered, feral longing seizing him, grinding him into her harder, faster. "I'm so close. You're going to make me come. Your perfect, perfect body is going to—" He groaned. He could barely breathe. "Penny—"

She didn't answer with words, and he hadn't really asked the question, but he was so close, and speaking was so hard. He quaked under the waves of pleasure from her, from the ring, from his own body, from everywhere, all at once.

He gasped out, "May I…please…fill you?"

Her legs wrapped around his waist and her hands pressed against his lower back, urging him deeper. "*Yes*, Beau."

Everything crashed into him at once, all the bliss and spice and joy and everything physical and everything mental and he was *crushed* by how good it was and he wanted to howl and a guttural, animal sound poured out him. And he finished, flooding his wife and shouting through the ring because nothing could possibly feel this good, but it did.

It took everything in him not to collapse on top of her, but he managed to ease himself out of her gently before he crumpled onto his side, the bed creaking under his slamming weight. For a minute at least, they gasped, their pleasure spiraling slowly down, giving them respite, at last, from the unbearable waves of satisfaction.

Penny set a hand on his chest, rolled onto her side, and kissed him. "Correct me if I'm wrong," she said breathlessly, "but that seemed…better than average."

Beau laughed, shakily at first, and gradually with more volume. He wrapped her up, snuggling her against his chest, pressing kisses to her hair between laughs. "Yes, Penny," he said eventually, "that was better than average. That was…" He gasped out another laugh. "Understatement of a lifetime. You fit me perfectly. And the rings—I had no idea what a difference the rings would make. That was life-alteringly good. If I hadn't already married you—hell, if I *hated* you, I'd be dragging you to the well right now."

She blushed, but her smile was smug. When she shifted, a faint grimace flickered over her face. Beau looked her over quickly. "How are you feeling? I didn't hurt you, did I? I know toward the end I sort of lost the plot."

"Just a little sore. Beau, I…" She stared, mouth open, but didn't finish the sentence.

"What?" Beau prompted, tapping the tip of his nose against hers. A wave of tenderness swept across to him through the ring.

"You're so sweet. You're kind. You're just…good. How the hell did that happen?"

Beau laughed, incredulous. "What? I mean, thank you, but what do you mean?"

She said nothing, only cupped his cheek and kissed him, but the ring-wash swelled with protectiveness, worry, tenderness. He shifted to slide his arm under her head and hold her closer to his chest, and she tucked in against him, curling up under his chin. Her fingers traced one of the tattoo lines where it passed over a rib.

"Can I finally ask about these? Or are you still cagey about it? I don't understand why you'd hide them when they're so beautiful."

Gentle waves lapped over his mind, cooling, reassuring. Curiosity in full force, of course, but also warmth and a lingering tendril of want. "It's an *extremely* attractive story," he said, dripping sarcasm. "I'm afraid telling it may plunge us into mindless lust again."

"Tell me anything," she said seriously, and Beau felt the protectiveness in it.

He sighed. "Short story: I wasn't a happy kid, which you know. I don't remember what started it, but I developed a bad habit of…cutting myself." The protectiveness surged in a wave, a strange feeling coming so strong from someone half his size. "Started with my arms, but that got hard to hide, so I moved to my legs, and when that became inconvenient, my chest."

Her finger ran lightly over one of the scars, a faint vertical line. Though everything about the situation was different, a hand discovering his scars by touch struck him with a memory of his brother punching him in the chest and being shocked and alarmed by the bleeding, not realizing he'd opened up rows of barely healed cuts. Of Char dragging him before their parents to tell them what he was doing, despite Beau's pleading to keep it a secret. Of their father's words—the last words he'd spoken before Beau ran to the isles the first time: *Enough of this pathetic play for attention. Either put your blade away and stop this nonsense or cut deep enough to end it once and for all. I won't have you embarrassing this family further.*

Queasy pain rose up in his chest, tightness under his left collarbone. "It was nothing," he said abruptly, shifting her hand away. "I don't know why we're talking about this. It was a stupid, attention-seeking habit for a dumbass kid too fragile to deal with the world."

"Oh, no no no, we're not going to talk about my husband that way," Penny said, burrowing in tighter, pressing her hand flat against the largest stretch of scars. She kissed them lightly and began to push emotions through the ring: soothing, calming, cooling.

"How are you doing that?"

"I'm just pushing over what you usually reach through and dig for," she said.

"I'm reaching through? I didn't realize I could do that."

She chuckled lightly. "Magic is always strange, but I think you have more Maurilel blood in you than most. This is the second artifact I've seen you bend beyond its prescribed use."

"Does it bother you when I reach through? I can try to stop."

"No," she said, stroking his chest lightly, fingers bumping over the rows of scars. "It's a relief most of the time. Your emotions are *strong*. Hard to manage. And I don't know how you experience mine, but for me, it's a very physical sensation. When you reach through and pull my calm or my happiness up to borrow it, you soothe both of us." She hummed lightly under her breath, then said, "You told me about the scars, not the tattoos."

"Ah. Well." He cleared his throat. "El didn't like me hurting myself, for obvious reasons." An understatement: when Beau had healed enough from his near-death on the ship to pick up the habit again, Elias had been relatively new to his service. That hadn't stopped the man from shouting at him and making every edged thing Beau owned disappear.

"The tattoos were something of a compromise. Tattoos hurt. They did the same thing for me that a knife would do, but with less chance of accidentally cutting too deep. They covered up the scars, and it sort of weaned me off the habit. But as you can imagine, that's not something I want to explain to just anyone. So, I hide them."

"Who did them?"

"There's an artist on the next island over who did most of them. But, um…" A blush rose in Beau's neck and cheeks. "…Elias did a few of them. This one here, and these." The blush deepened as he realized she could feel the strange mix of hollow sadness and arousal and longing and dark pleasure from remembering El's hands on him, the burning scratch of the needle—

"Oh," Penny gasped, going red herself. "I didn't realize you... you *like* pain."

"Only in very, uh, specific, um—" Beau set his hand against his burning cheeks, mortified.

"I suppose I won't apologize for biting you, then," she said, smirking, and the heat in his face morphed into a different heat at the vicious gleam in her eye. "Can I ask you something?"

Beau chuckled, rubbing at his red face. "Is there any chance at all of stopping you?"

With a quick eye roll, she asked, "Where did you learn to do what you did? With me, I mean. You knew exactly what to do."

"I've had a lot of sex. Do you really want to hear about it?" She shrugged delicately, but pomegranate raged through the ring. He laughed. "All right. Um, did you meet Maisie? She and I started sleeping together after the ship, when I healed up enough to dance. She was my first. Taught me a lot. When Léontine wanted someone to show her the ropes, as it were, she told Maiz, and Maiz came to me. She taught me how to make it easier, the first time."

"She brought her friend for you to deflower?"

Beau cringed at the wording. "Ugh. Um, I guess. She said I was 'eminently coachable' and that Léontine deserved a 'proper introduction,' whatever that means. Maiz did almost the same for me, but in reverse when I told her I'm attracted to men but I'd never been with one. She found Jean and insisted we dance together until we decided we were attracted to each other."

"You don't sound as fond of him."

"I don't know him as well as I do Maiz and Leo. And I wasn't particularly *myself* with him, either. He sails, so he's in and out of Leau. We didn't see each other more than three or four times a year." He shrugged. "Plus, he and Elias never got along."

Penny laughed. "I can't imagine why not."

"What, you think Jean was jealous of El?"

"I imagine they gave each other plenty to bristle about like a couple of toms."

Beau sighed, eyes flicking over the empty room. "Elias doesn't share." He shook his head. "Not that—not that I wanted—he doesn't want—he only wanted one night anyway—"

Penny chuckled low in her throat. "You don't have to explain anything about it, Beau." She pressed her lips against his chest and ran her hands down his body with slow, ticklish movements. Her spicy-sweet taste was mild but coming through loud, so he suspected she was pushing it at him to keep him from sinking into maudlin thoughts. "Would you tell me how to use my mouth on you, like you did on me?"

He immediately rose to the occasion. "I know what you're doing, you minx. And yes, of course I'll let you distract me and manipulate my emotions. Come here. Open your mouth."

17

QUITE REAL

B eau woke to a faint sound and blinked blearily. The bed was empty beside him, though still warm where Penamour had fallen asleep curled in the curve of his body. He rubbed at his eyes and stretched, enjoying the delicious soreness of back-to-back nights of increasingly athletic sex.

He assumed Penny had decided to sleep in her own room, or wanted a drink, or any of a million things. Beau could hear a handful of celebrants still in the common room singing; maybe she was dancing. But then he heard Elias's voice outside, raised and irritated.

Beau inhaled sharply. *Tell me she didn't go looking for Elias to ask about last night.*

His thoughts went straight to the drawer where the Perception Stone sat innocently. He shouldn't eavesdrop on Elias. That would be extremely rude, an invasion of privacy.

But then…El always had it on him, and presumably had for a long time. Beau had no secrets from him; was it *truly* fair for Elias to have so many from him?

Beau's fingers were feeling around in the drawer for the cool, smooth stone before he'd consciously decided to reach for it. As soon as he touched it, Penny's voice whispered directly into his ear.

"—can pretend, just for the course of this conversation, that I'm not an idiot, Elias."

"It's not my place to comment on the intelligence of a duchess, Your Grace."

"Gods, you *are* in a mood, aren't you? *Stop* trying to run away. You're not going to avoid this conversation. What, you think you're going to stand ten feet from me for the rest of our lives and we're never going to discuss this?"

"A man can hope."

"*Elias.* Why did you tell him you didn't want more than one night? You've confused him to hell. He's been trying to convince himself all day that *he's* the asshole for giving in to you."

El sighed, and Beau sat up as quietly as he could. "This has nothing to do with you."

Penny's noise of incredulity was so descriptive Beau could picture the face that went with it. "You don't think I might have some interest in how deeply in love my husband is with his *guard*? And don't lie, it's obvious you're in love. You've been each other's everything for years. You trust each other implicitly. And you finally gave in—so *why* are you being so cruel to him?"

"Cruel?" El *chk*ed annoyance in the back of his throat. "I'm *trying* to put him on his throne with a wife he loves, as he deserves, and not get in the fucking way! How is that cruel?"

"So you *are* trying to get out of my way? That's what this is about?" She exhaled sharply. "Did you think I didn't know about the two of you when he proposed?" After a pause, "Then why assume you were in the way? The road to Beau's heart isn't so narrow that only one person can walk on it. I didn't agree to this marriage to carve you out of his life. I thought it was understood that anyone marrying him would be joining a relationship that already exists?"

Beau's heart jumped, racing at the thought of what she proposed. Was that possible? A relationship with both of them?

"There is no relationship. It was one night, and it's over. He and I already agreed." At the finality in Elias's voice, Beau's heart thumped harder, aching.

"And you're both *so* happy with that arrangement, clearly," she said dryly.

"It's not my job to be happy. It's my job to protect him."

"And his happiness?"

"*You're* responsible for his happiness now." Elias's tone was viciously acidic. "You're his wife. You'll be his queen, the rightful owner of the seat next to his. I'm his *guard*. One fight, one bad day, and all he has to do is fire me. Hell, not even that. All he has to do is put me outside, like he did with Jude and Oria."

"Beau would never do that to you."

No, I wouldn't, Beau silently agreed.

"Maybe not before. But now? You poisoned an entire court against him without breaking a sweat. It'd be nothing for you to poison him against me."

"So it's me you don't trust. Even though I'm the one asking you what it would take to make this work. Do you think I'm designing some elaborate trick to hurt you both?"

"It's not—" Elias went silent, and the sounds of Ma in the kitchen, deep in her cups and laughing uproariously at a joke from Viv filled Beau's ears. "I actually do trust you. I like you. I believe you're good for him and for Granvallée, and I even believe you mean it when you say you want me to be part of Beau's life—"

"—and mine."

"And yours. But I also know what it's like to love him. It's all-consuming, Duchess. You'll want more of him. You'll want everything, every second, every day. You'll start coming up with more things he *could* need you for so he'll want you around more often. You'll learn new skills just so you can teach him when he asks. You will *beg* for new ways to be useful in his life. And—why are you looking at me like that?"

"I'm sorry, I can't decide if that's the most romantic thing I've ever heard or the most demented."

The most romantic, Beau thought. *Gods, if Elias had said that on the roof, I'd have given up the throne no matter what else he said.*

"You need him that much? Need to be *needed* that much?" A pause. "Then why fight having him? You're putting *yourself* outside. I'm saying you don't have to give him up. You're putting yourself on the path to lose him completely."

"I expected that! I prepared for that. I knew it was coming; I braced for it. What I can't do is *hope*. If I believe for even a second that I can have him and then I lose him anyway—"

"It'll kill you?"

"Yes, Duchess. It will kill me. Call me demented for that if you like."

"You're not demented. But you can starve to death on a lack of hope and die just the same. At least the hope route, you get joy in the middle. I *do* think you're being overdramatic."

"No. I don't think I am. He's *magic*. There's something…I think I might actually die. Have you seen his eyes do the thing, when he's particularly happy?"

My eyes? Beau's heart picked up again, knuckles aching as he clenched the stone tightly.

"The gold light? You're saying that's *real* magic? Maurilel magic? I was just telling him earlier, I think he has more Maurilel blood than the average person."

"He does. I don't know if he just has more-magical-than-average blood or what, but it's changed me. Genuine change. I don't think I can survive without him now."

"Then it's decided," Penny said firmly. "You need him. Beau needs you *and* me. We mean different things to him. I know we're all at different places with each other, but we can work it out, the three of us. Don't be distant to make space for me. Stay with Beau. Be who you are to him."

"And you think that would work?"

She sounded hesitant. "If you and I make an effort to trust each other, yes. We'll need to need each other, too, not only Beau."

After a long pause, Elias said, "Does he even want this?"

"Yes, obviously. Desperately. Don't be stupid."

"I'm not being stupid. I'm asking him. Beau's a light sleeper. I assume you're listening, Highness? Since you have my stone."

Heart pounding, Beau leapt out of bed, dropped the Perception Stone on the bedside table, and eschewed his dressing gown to open the door stark naked. "Get in here. Both of you."

Penny and El stared with almost identical open-mouthed gawking. Beau glanced past them at the figures chatting and laughing in the common room, but no one was paying attention to the prince's door. A steady, pulsing spice built through the ring. Elias moved first, shouldering his way inside with one hand on Penny's wrist to draw her with him. He slammed into Beau hard enough to stagger him, kissing him like they'd been separated for months.

The duchess muttered, "Oh my gods," under her breath, and Beau and Elias laughed against each other's lips.

"Let's continue," Beau said between kisses, "the conversation from the hallway."

"If you wanted to keep discussing it you should've put your clothes on. I've done enough talking," El said, all but lifting Beau off his feet as he hauled them one-armed toward the bed.

The ring burned with spice and syrup, but a wash of uncertainty overrode it as Penny stood at the door, watching. "Hold on, hold on," Beau said, laughing and fighting to hold his ground. He felt Penny brace and gather herself to pretend she wasn't hesitant. Beau spoke first. "No one's getting laid right now. We need to *talk*."

With a silent sigh, Elias stopped half-carrying him, but he did claim another searing kiss. The prince held his hand out toward Penny. "Come here. Why are you shy all of the sudden?"

"You were having a moment." Penny lay her fingers in his palm and let him draw her up against his side. "And having seen the man break his own hand to get loose of a rope, the last thing I want is to be standing between Elias and what he wants." Nervous, heated, her eyes watched Elias for any twitch of movement.

She's afraid of him. The thought made Beau queasy, but he understood. She didn't have years of trust built up with Elias, and Elias was *dangerous*. He was a liar, and she knew that.

"Sit down," Beau said, pointing imperiously at the bed. After a moment, Elias obeyed, somewhat sulkily. Beau pulled on his dressing gown, to the low grumbles of both companions. "I'm very fond of any idea that lets me be in love with both of you. But it doesn't work unless you trust each other. And Penny doesn't trust you, El."

"I don't think that's—" she began, frowning, but Beau shook his head.

"You don't trust him. You proposed this for my sake, but you're terrified; I can taste it." To El, "It's one thing to let you have your secrets and lies when it's just me. But that time is over. I can't trust a man I don't know with my wife, my family. It's time."

Elias shook his head, and when Beau stared him down insistently, he shook it harder. "You don't know what you're asking."

"I'm asking who you are."

"Don't do this. Please." Elias looked from the prince to the duchess and back, and despair cracked over his face, dripping like egg. "Fuck. I don't want to lie to you. Please drop it."

"Then don't lie," Beau said. "I thought you'd do *anything* for me? You were willing to die, and you won't even *talk*?"

Elias growled. "Knowing the answers to your questions is a death sentence."

With an unconcerned grin, Beau said, "You'll protect me. I trust you."

This seemed to be the most disarming, devastating thing he could've said. Elias folded in half with a sound like a sob. When he sat upright again, a miserable laugh shook out of his throat. "How long did I have hope of having you? Two minutes? Maybe less?"

He got up as if to leave, but Beau planted himself solidly in the guard's way.

"Do I have to hunt down Gerard and ask *him* what you are?"

El's eyes went large, fear spasming over his face. "Don't—" He grabbed Beau's arm, hauled him to the Perception Stone, and slammed his palm atop it. Then he pulled Penny over and arranged their hands so all three could touch it. When he spoke, it was so quietly the sound didn't seem to leave his throat. "Don't even fucking joke about it. He'd slice you to pieces."

"Why?" Beau mimicked El's barely-more-than-air speech.

Elias's eyes went wild, and then resignation crept into them. He opened his mouth, hesitated, and at last said, "Because that's what Watchers do when their secrets are threatened."

Understanding skipped, stuttered, swayed to evade Beau's grasp. *Watchers? Like Char's imaginary Watchers, from when we were kids?* "Watchers are made up. They're not real."

"Are we not?" Something changed in Elias's face, some muscle tightening, some twitch of connective tissue reshaping his expression, and El could've been a stranger. "I feel quite real."

"What are Watchers?" Penny asked. She'd seen the shift, too. Her shoulder pressed against Beau's, opening up a few inches of space between herself and Elias. El glanced down at it, and his face was briefly pained before he hammered it flat again.

"A very secret, very *old* organization. Dates back..." He breathed in slowly, let it out sharply. "To the Maurilel. The *end* of the Maurilel, to be exact. Because we ended them."

Penny's eyes flicked to Beau, who could taste the acid of her sudden alarm but felt none of his own. "You don't, by chance, hunt down people with more-than-average Maurilel blood?" he said, amusement in his voice because what else could something this unreal be but funny?

Elias's face softened into its familiar shape again. "No, Beau. The Watcher council monitors magic relics and sends agents to keep them from being misused or disappearing from our control. We pull a lot of political strings, especially when it comes to…rulers with access to large stores of magic."

Reality seemed to click into place all at once, and Beau felt the alarm that had been threatening, just out of reach. "Oh fuck. I'm in a lot of trouble, aren't I?"

"No." Elias shook his head, and his eyes had gone glassy. It was the closest Beau had ever seen the man to tears, and it shook him to his core. Even with the Perception Stone, El was barely audible as he said, "Because I didn't tell them the vault is empty."

"The vault is *empty*?" Penny's voice felt too loud, though it was barely a whisper.

Beau ignored the question, eyes on his guard. "Why would you have told anyone anything? You're not one of them anymore. Right? You left. You became my guard. *Right*?" Glassiness became brimming lids and beaded lashes on hazel eyes that refused to meet Beau's. "Because you were *lap candy* before. And you were never that for me. So you're not—you're—"

"I was never that for you." Elias nodded, not looking at him. "Because that wasn't what you wanted. You wanted a guard, so I was a guard. That's what we do."

Beau tried to step back, but El scooped the Perception Stone up in his palm and followed, grabbing Beau's wrist so the stone still touched both of them, Penny's fingers sandwiched between. "You wanted to know, Beau, so you're going to know. Watchers do a lot of things, but mostly we get close to targets and gather information. Which means being a lot of different things to a lot of different people—for that, there's the chameleons, the liars, called Faces. When we need someone dead, we send the Fighters: assassins, quick, deadly. The rest have skills for particular jobs: lockbreakers or accountants or forgers. They're the Fixers."

"And you're a Fighter?" Beau guessed.

Elias laughed, a miserable bray of a thing. "I'm a Face."

Beau couldn't sort through his own emotions, but they must've been tumultuous because Penny pressed a hand to her belly and groaned, "Oh, *Beau*, it's all right, it's—"

She exhaled sharply and said, "You needed to get close to Beau because of the vault?"

"Among other things, yes."

"What other things?" Beau demanded.

At last, Elias met his eyes, and it was devastating. El looked like he was watching the world cave in before him. "Can't have someone so close to the throne without a Watcher in arm's reach. You ran from the palace and left your staff behind. So they sent another to the isles; he died on the *Siren's Lament*. So they sent me."

"Why you?"

Elias's mouth tightened like he'd eaten something sour as he shrugged. "Because you were lonely and nobles had a habit of wanting to fuck me." Beau would've choked on the bile in his throat if he were breathing. El saw his expression and tightened his grip, pulling Beau a half step closer. "That's why they *sent* me. That's not what *happened*."

It was Beau's turn to rasp out a miserable laugh. "Isn't it? I wanted you at first sight."

"You were attracted to me. Everyone's attracted to me." He glanced at Penny, who nodded. "But you were decent enough not to fuck me, or I'd have fucked you. And I'd have hated you. And eventually, once I'd extracted all your value, I'd have killed you, like I did the others."

Penny inhaled sharply, but Beau's eyes stayed fixed on Elias. "You killed—"

"Every noble or rich bastard who ever touched me." Elias's face was flat, expressionless in that way that said he was hiding a storm. "Partially a practical consideration: Granvallée's circles of wealth and nobility are relatively small. Hard to change your name and become something new when you might run into the last mark. But mostly because they deserved to die."

Because Beau was spiraling beyond being able to speak, Penny took over. "And Gerard?"

"Fighter. A threat. Highness was supposed to stay at the palace, get married, and ascend to the throne. Instead, he ran for the isles and pissed off a duchess. Gerard came to move things along."

"To take me back?" Beau felt numb, like he was floating adrift. El shook his head. "To kill you."

An absurd laugh bubbled out of the prince. "One Watcher assigned to protect me and another to kill me? Not very efficient."

"I wasn't assigned to protect you; I was assigned to get close. *I* decided to protect you. You have no idea how much I'm protecting you." He looked momentarily queasy, face paling.

"That's why he warned you to get clear," Penny said. "He went to report back, and now they're coming for Beau."

"They...*shouldn't*. I wrote when you came to the isles for him. And now that you're married and Highness is headed back to the capital..." He nodded like he was convincing himself. "They like order, like to proceed as expected. They shouldn't come after him now."

"Why." Beau struggled to find the intonation that would make that a question. When Elias and Penny looked at him, waiting for him to clarify, Beau dredged up more words. "Why fight your own ally to protect me? Why protect me at all? Why fuck me if it was just going to make you hate me? Why say all that shit in the hall about dying without me? *Why?*"

He was shutting down one organ at a time. Nothing made sense. Everything he thought he'd known and trusted was a lie. A Face. Beau buzzed, chaos, a maelstrom in his body.

El had let go of his wrist. Beau sat. Voices whispered. Talked. Talked *loudly*. When a warm, callused hand brushed along his cheek, Beau finally looked up into anxious hazel eyes. "Beau," El said, clearly repeating himself, "I'm sorry. I'm *so* sorry. Beau, please, listen."

He could've pulled away, could've put distance between himself and the apparent stranger who'd been living with him and joking with him and protecting him for seven years. But he didn't want to. He leaned into Elias's hand and looked up at him and listened.

"I love you. And I have for a *long* time. For about two weeks, I sent faithful reports back to my superiors about you. Then I started leaving little things out because I liked you, and it didn't seem fair to you. And then a few weeks later I was leaving much *bigger* things out. By the time I'd known you two months, I was *lying* to protect your secrets, your privacy. I used to be good at this job, Beau."

He exhaled a humorless almost-laugh. "But you didn't want a Watcher to be your pretend friend and shit-ass guard, you wanted *the best guard who ever lived*, someone you could trust. So I became *that* instead of what I was supposed to be."

He swallowed, pausing as if waiting for Beau to speak, but Beau simply blinked up at him and drew the same comfort from El's warm hand that he always had.

Elias continued, "I protect you because I love you and I want you alive and thriving and wielding the power you were born to. I fucked you because it was *never* going to make me hate you. Because I wanted to. I wanted you. And I said I'd die without you because somewhere along the way, when I was deciding to let what you wanted change what I was, I *changed*. Magically."

"How did your superiors feel about *that*?" Beau croaked.

El laughed that same breathy, mirthless laugh. "I've kept that to myself. Gerard was *very* surprised by my fighting in the forest. They made me a Face, not a Fighter, for a reason."

"Your job is to win trust," Penny said quietly. "So where does that leave us? Trusting?"

Elias raised his broken hand in a helpless gesture. "Being in love isn't provable. Wanting someone genuinely isn't provable. Magical change isn't provable, unless you knew me before, but you didn't. You trust me or you don't."

He released Beau to push his hair back out of his face nervously, angrily. "I'll leave if you want. Send me away or kill me, but they'll send someone else to replace me, and the replacement won't lie for you. They won't protect you."

"Is that a threat?" Penny asked.

"No," Beau said before Elias could speak. "He's explaining the risks." He gently pushed El back a step so he could stand and look the Watcher eye to eye.

Taking a long breath in, Beau held it and studied Elias's earnest face, his shoulders, his forearms, his hands, every part of him that had ever made Beau feel safe. Beau leaned forward until his forehead clunked against Elias's, and the Watcher went still.

"I believe you," Beau whispered. "I trust you."

El staggered like Beau had kicked his knees out from under him. He kissed the prince hungrily, gratefully, desperately, breaking away every few breaths to whisper, "Thank you." It took several long minutes to sate them both, to feel like they were still…themselves.

Eventually, Elias stepped back again and turned to Penny. "We started this line of questioning because *you* didn't trust me."

Penny frowned. She studied Beau's face with nearly as much scrutiny as Beau had studied Elias's, and whatever she saw there, she slowly nodded to herself.

"Strange as it is," she said, "I trust Elias the Watcher more than I ever trusted Elias the guard. I told you to be what you are to him. *Don't* disappoint me."

18

THE PRICE

The singing at breakfast was quieter than normal, perhaps out of respect for the newlyweds, but it woke Beau nonetheless. Perfect comfort, the pile of bodies and blankets he lay in. His exhaustion threatened to drag him back under into sleep, but he didn't want to miss a moment of this.

He closed his eyes and luxuriated in the softness of Penny's hair against his chest, the faint sound on some of El's sleeping exhales like a whimper, the sweet smell of baking bread.

Small footsteps pounded eagerly across the common room floorboards, and Nate shrieked something before Ma could shush him. She was almost as loud when she said, "*Get* that mud out of my inn, boyo, I won't ask you again. His Highness will be about later, and then you can…"

The noise subsided, and Elias must've woken, too, because he stretched his back, his body pressing interestingly against Beau. "Good morning, Highness," he rumbled. "How are you feeling?"

"Comfortable," Beau whispered. It was strange, still being this comfortable with Elias. He should've been afraid of him, maybe. But he'd always known Elias was something special; now he had a name for it: *My Watcher*.

El chuckled and pulled Beau closer, making space for his hand to slide down the prince's chest, along his stomach, lower still to the morning's hardness. "You opposed to an energetic wake-up?"

"Nope," Beau said quickly, heart picking up its pace.

"If you promise to come quietly," Elias said as his fingers wrapped around Beau, worked along his length, "maybe we can let your tired wife sleep a while longer."

"She's incredible, isn't she?" Beau stared fondly at the duchess, her hair a wild tangle of loose ringlets around her head, her lips parted in her sleep.

El's hand tightened and began to move faster. "She really is."

With a groan, Beau settled against El. "I want you both."

"You have us," El breathed. "All yours."

With a tinge of bitterness, Beau laughed as he pressed his head back hard against Elias. "The wife I picked, the husband she picked; the guard I picked, and the...target he was assigned."

Elias bit down hard on Beau's shoulder and sped his hand, and Beau had to grit his teeth to keep his groans quiet. "I *picked* you, Beauregard. I marked you." El's hand slid up Beau to the left of his chest, tracing the tattoos inked there. He ran his finger over them again and again, two tattoos, side by side and intricately linked with whorls that matched the rest. He moved slowly, like he wanted Beau to follow the shape as he traced it.

One curling shape with three long arms running parallel to each other. A second that made a corner, one curving line up, and then a swoop across perpendicular. *Almost like an 'L.'*

Beau jerked, sat up to look down at himself. His fingers pushed Elias's aside. From Beau's vantage, the one on the left looked like 'E'. It was El, but made abstract and positioned so only Beau— or someone looking down at his chest over his shoulder—could read it properly.

"Did you tattoo your name on me?"

Elias laughed, dark and full of promise.

The surge of lust from Beau woke Penny like cold water, gasping and flushed. "What—ah." She settled back. "Warn a woman before you throw that kind of horniness around, I beg."

"Here's your warning," Beau said, as Elias's injured arm wrapped him tighter, squeezed around his neck, and the jerking hand moved faster. "Care to join?"

Penny's eyes flashed and her ring pulsed ginger. Before she could touch him, though, someone knocked on the door. Beau was preparing to tell them not to move or acknowledge the outside world until everyone had come at *least* once, when the door opened.

"S'all right, innkeep, Elias would want me to walk *right* in," said a tall, blond man as he shoved Ma out of his path and shouldered into the room, grinning at the three surprised faces on the bed: Gerard. "Morning, lap candy! Pulling double duty these days?"

El rolled out of bed and already had a knife in his hand; Beau was suddenly grateful he hadn't been able to persuade the man to take his armor off for bed. "Get out."

"Oh *that's* no way to greet someone who came to get you out of harm's way. Bid the pretty princeling and his lovely wife the usual farewell, and we can be done here. But you look like you might've gotten a little attached this time." He laughed, bright flash of teeth in his craggy face, and knives appeared in his hands, disappeared, appeared again, too fast to follow. "I'll take care of it for you."

"Get the fuck out, Carver."

"Oho, *you're* breaking character before your mark's dead?" Gerard—or Carver, perhaps—laughed again, eyebrows high. "Never thought I'd see the day. Must've *really* pissed you off when I used your name last time. Sorry 'bout that.

"Speaking of last time, we already flexed, didn't we? And you ended up paralyzed face down. So maybe we don't need to go another round, yeah? Just scoot, let me clean up your mess, and we'll send the rest of His Majesty's men back off the island."

The blond leaned far enough to meet Beau's eyes. "Sorry 'bout your Pops, by the way. Don't worry, King Alphonse'll do your job credibly enough."

Beau yanked his trousers on, watching Elias's stiff back as his guard shifted to stay in Gerard's way. "My father's dead?"

His father had died, and his last words to Beau had been bitter disappointment and hatred. There was no correcting that now. Because he was dead.

The king was dead.

And Beau...was king. *King*.

"Snuffed it days ago," Gerard said. "Lex, move. This is boring."

"*King Beauregard* didn't invite any guests," El snarled, and Beau barely heard it, wrapped in cotton and stuffed in a barrel as his mind was. "Out the window, royals."

Then he whirled into motion, and he and Gerard locked into a fight faster than the one in the forest, blades whistling, hard strikes drawing sharp exhales.

Numbly, Beau grabbed Penny, threw the window up, and hurled her out, following immediately. A few people made their way from homes to boats this early, but the inn's yard should've been empty. It was, instead, populated by two armed and armored men.

"Is that him? That's the prince, isn't it?"

Everything crystallized, clearing into discrete, understandable realizations: His father was dead. He was king. His crown was being stolen. These men had come to kill him. Elias couldn't help him, locked in his fight with Gerard. His wife—the *queen*—would die if he did nothing.

Beau had to fight them. He had to kill them. He had to *move*.

Beau's eyes darted around the yard as the pair approached, searching for a weapon. "Did you say prince? Afraid not," he said flatly, and one actually paused as if he believed Beau. "I'm not a prince. Common misconception."

There—the woodchopping axe, still embedded in the stump. Beau snatched it up, swung it experimentally once. Not a sword, but it'd do in a pinch.

He gave the soldiers a gallows grin. "I'm actually the fucking king. Feel free to kneel."

They didn't fight like Watchers, thank the Twelve, and they mustn't have been expecting a shirtless, barefoot man to be particularly skillful with a woodaxe. He caught the first across the throat with a vicious slash that half decapitated him, then let momentum spin him into a second strike at the other, who barely dodged.

"We found—!" he shouted, but the brief attempt to communicate was enough distraction for Beau to lop his sword hand off at the wrist, and the man's words jolted into incoherent noise before the king's next blow took him in the chest.

Panting, Beau tossed the axe in Penny's direction and snatched the man's sword and belt knife instead. He briefly contemplated their armor, but he didn't want to be picking it off the bodies when reinforcements arrived. "You all right?" he asked his wife, throwing her a quick glance.

Her cream chemise stuck to her where Beau had spattered her with blood, and she looked half wild with her hair in a loose halo and a gory axe in her hands, but she nodded.

From the ring, a steady pulse of determination forcefully tamped down terror. She tried to push confidence and calm to him, but Beau didn't need it; the adrenaline pumping through him slowed things down and made every move progress logically one to the next.

Four more soldiers rounded the hedges. "Over there!" *Four.* Too many. With a sword, he'd fare better than with the axe, but not well enough to fight four men at once.

"Run!" Beau said. He stepped forward in time to block one blow and parry a second before he could dance out of range. Thank fuck for the knife; with it, he turned a jab from a soldier trying to flank him that just missed separating his ribs.

Barely too slow, he hissed as he *almost* dodged a sword point, catching a glancing blow under his collarbone. His knife took a chunk of the man's quad and sent him to his knees, where he tripped up a second. They were bunched up; Beau's sword slice caught one in the eyes, the second in the belly. He stumbled back, trying to maintain space to fight, hoping Penny had gotten out of sight.

Another stab, another soldier dropped, but even the gut-cut one kept fighting, teeth bared in a rictus of determined hate that nearly flooded Beau with despair. They'd keep coming. He wasn't fast enough or practiced enough.

He dodged further and further back until he was pinned against the wall of the inn; they were relentless. One stabbed a burning hole through his left shoulder. Another raked a cold-fire line across his thigh. He was only going to get slower.

Beau heard the *whoosh* of something in the air just before it impacted, and he jerked out of its path too late to have dodged, had it been coming for him. It wasn't; it struck one of the soldiers fighting him in the throat—the axe. Beau glanced over his shoulder: Penny had thrown it.

A soldier took advantage of his distraction to hammer down on Beau's wrist, knocking his sword from numb fingers. Beau barely got the knife up in time to deflect a stab for the heart. Blindly, he backed up toward Penny, cold with terror.

Two on one, and he had only a belt-knife.

A man-shaped blur hurtled out of the inn window, and then a bloody blade-point sprouted from the chest of one of his pursuers; a spray of red foamed from his mouth as his eyes went wide. The second squawked in surprise, and Beau slammed his knife up under his chin. The man's weight, as he fell, nearly pulled the blade from Beau's hand, and he staggered.

Elias caught him. "More?"

"That was the last I saw. Thank you. Penny?" He fought for breath as the queen appeared, bloody and beautiful and terrified.

"Are you all right? Your shoulder looks—"

"You did amazing," Beau said, cutting her off, trying not to feel the injuries she'd brought to the forefront of his mind. "I'd have died if you hadn't thrown that axe."

Elias's hands slid efficiently along Beau's body, checking each of his wounds, assessing the threat. El had a couple slices himself, though none as bad as the king's. "Let's get inside, rally the other guards," he said. "I didn't manage to kill Carver, and he's not the only one here." He met the royals' eyes briefly to ensure they both under-stood he meant other Watchers.

"So Gerard is actually Carver?" Beau clarified, wincing as Elias picked up his pace, rounding the inn to enter through the front door and catch a good view of Leau on the way.

"Carver's the name I knew him by in training," El said ab-sently. "I need you to magic me up, Highness. Tell me I'm the best fighter alive, tell me I'm unkillable. *Believe* it. I think there are four of them altogether, and that's…" He let out a shaky breath, then said more resolutely. "I can fight them. Tell me I can."

I don't know the first thing about magic. I'm not convinced I have magic, whatever you and Penny seem to think, Beau thought, but he could see Elias believed it and *needed* to believe it.

So he pulled El to a stop, set his forehead against El's and his hand on the back of El's neck, and said, "You are the best fighter who's ever lived. You could kill four of them one handed without a scratch." He willed that thought through his guard like he could make it true on hope alone. "You *will*, in fact."

When he pulled away, Elias's pupils were huge, but instead of black pits, they glowed gold. Beau took a startled step back as the Watcher inhaled deeply, smile tipping up, then exhaled a sigh. "That felt good." He cracked his neck once, then resumed his jog.

He pulled up again almost immediately. "Oh *fuck*."

Penny and Beau came to his side, seeing what he saw. *Every-where,* in groups of three or four, soldiers walked the streets, milled among the houses, called to each other, but they were starting to assemble at one end around a tall, blond man and drift toward the inn. Beau realized they'd been spread to search for him.

The bell in the center of Leau began to jangle a wild alarm and shouts rose. Beau spotted a small form bouncing away from it, scrambling up the wall on the other side with two soldiers in pursuit: *Nate.*

"Nate!" Beau darted down the hill, shaking off Elias's attempt to snatch him back.

Climbing was hard, given his injuries, but he scaled the side of Viv's house, tripped across her roof to Jordy's, and dropped down to run along the wall until he could make the short leap up onto the angled roof over Delphine's forge. Nate, tiny legs pumping, face red, darted between hedges. The soldiers were close.

"Come here, you little fucker," one of them called, and Beau's vision went red.

With a growl, he leapt down onto one with a painful impact, though not as painful as the crack of the man's skull against a stone planter. The other spun, and Beau had a knife to his throat, ready to slit it, when he caught sight of Nate's wide eyes.

"What's that?" Beau said urgently, looking past the boy so he'd turn. As soon as his head swiveled away, Beau cut the soldier's throat and dropped him, ignoring his dying gurgles, by the broken-necked corpse of his compatriot.

"Angel!" Nate wailed when Beau picked him up, throwing his little arms around the king. "You're all bloody. They get you? Gramma Corlia said it looked like they were going in every house looking for you. They didn't think you'd stay with her."

"Why aren't you hiding with your Mum?" Beau panted, sliding between houses, glancing both ways up the street, and darting across into the next alley toward Bunny's.

"Gramma Corlia said somebody needed to ring the bell so Leau would wake up and fight."

"She sent *you*?"

"No," Nate said, unperturbed by Beau's alarm. "You're not gonna tell her I went, are you? I don't wanna be in trouble."

So Leau would wake up and fight. These weren't trained fighters. Most didn't even have *weapons*, and Beau had brought danger to them. He felt sick. He was back on the fucking ship, everyone he cared about dying around him because *he* was a prince, because *he* was a king. Beau's hands shook where they held onto Nate.

"S'okay, Angel," Nate said, burrowing his cold little nose against the side of Beau's neck. "We're not gonna let them hurt you." Something like a sob came out of Beau's mouth.

Then they were in Bunny's yard, scattering chickens, and Bunny made a similar sound, hauling Nate out of Beau's arms with tears pouring down her cheeks, almost incoherent with terror. "Thank you for bringing—don't *scare* me like—" She was too busy clutching Nate closer, trying to kiss him and check whether the blood all over him was his, to finish a sentence.

"He's not hurt," Beau said. "That's all mine. Get out of sight, Bun, please."

She seemed to realize for the first time who had been carrying her son. "*You* get out of sight!" she said. "They're here for—"

"I know. I'm going. *Hide*, please. Don't fight them: *tell them where I am*. Please, please don't get hurt on my account."

"I'll tell them exactly where you are," she said fiercely, shoving Nate inside. "In my back bedroom asleep, and if they want you, they can eat a few of my kitchen knives first. Just like everybody else is telling them. You get out of here, Angel, you and your lady wife, and get patched up. Our boy will be a hell of a king, but he's gotta *be* king, first. *Go*."

"Bun—" She'd already disappeared inside after Nate, and Beau was standing in the open, chickens pecking unbothered around his bare feet. Quickly, he reversed course, going high again to scramble over rooftops. He hadn't seen any bows yet, and if the soldiers saw him and chased him instead of harassing Leau, that wouldn't be a bad thing.

Viv was waiting for him when he dropped into the street in front of her house. "You've gotta let me look at—"

"Where's Elias?" Beau demanded, shoving aside her attempts to bandage him.

She jerked her chin toward the ferry side of the island, where Beau had seen the soldiers gathering. "Carving a path off Leau for you. Now hold still so—"

Beau took off, ignoring her angry demands, and picked up another sword off a dead man. Shouts to his left drew Beau's eyes toward fighting: Nicky's voice. Beau easily spotted the man in the flurry—and felt a cold spike of horror as he saw Nicky hit the ground in two pieces.

"No," he choked out. Adrien was fighting, too, and he was about to be overwhelmed. Beau slid down the short grade to them, killed two soldiers, and yanked Adrien, who wielded a pair of fileting knives that had no business in a fight against swords, out of range.

Beau caught two overhead strikes along his sword, kicking at the inside of a soldier's knee. A slice across his hip made him grunt, stagger. He barely brought his hands around to sweep aside another jab. The two cuts in his right leg meant it was no longer trustworthy, shaking under him when he tried to put weight on it. His shoulder, too, screamed when he moved his left arm too quickly.

"For Lord Courdur!" one of them shouted, lunging forward over-ambitiously. Beau side-stepped him, slashed backward with his sword and missed. He had no time to pursue; the other two were much more competent, and each nearly skewered him a half-dozen times as he threw everything he had into defending. They pressed him back, each dodge and sidestep turning him until his back was to a hedge, hampering his movements.

One swung for his head. The king hurled himself forward, getting inside the blade but taking a crushing slam of the pommel to the temple.

All went white; Beau dropped, scrambling blindly back and to the side.

When he lurched to his feet again, he spared a fraction-of-a-second's glance over his shoulder. In disbelief, he saw Adrien on his knees, clutching his guts with both arms, knives abandoned. The soldier raised his sword to stab down into Beau's old friend.

No, Beau thought and shouted and *willed*, but magic didn't work the way he wished it did. From eight feet away, Beau's shout did nothing but make noise, and then Adrien was dead too. Beau barely kept the two swords harrying him from taking pieces.

On a dodge, Beau leaned too far into his right hip, and it dropped him. He rolled out of the path of a stab that drove the soldier's sword half its length into the earth. The second sword he kicked at, managing to disarm the soldier at the cost of a long, shallow cut down his shin.

As the first soldier pulled his mud-streaked blade from the ground, Beau stabbed at him, but Courdur's man seized his wrist, twisted, and the knife fell out of his grasp.

Another twist, and Beau fell to his knees in agony, fingers wrenched back like the man wanted to fold them into his arm.

He fought harder, half feral. The second man had retrieved his lost sword, and easily blocked Beau's attempts to stab up at him from where he knelt.

Fuck. I'm going to die. And then…and then…and then Penny and Elias and everyone else I've ever loved.

Something changed in the air. The pressure dropped, like a storm front moving in. Cold wind swept through the yard.

The men before Beau came apart.

The whirlwind of blood and steel that dismantled them was barely recognizable as a man, much less as Elias, but Beau knew him.

Relief rushed through him, so overpowering it sapped the last strength from his limbs. He sagged, fingers loosening so his sword hit the grass.

Then Elias groaned, and *his* knees hit the ground, and tension snapped back into Beau's body. Relief fled, replaced with fear as the strongest man he knew collapsed. "El?"

"How much of that blood is yours?" Elias asked with an unsettling slur, like his tongue was too large for his mouth. The guard was soaked head-to-toe, hazel peeking out from a mask of red pouring from a cut on his scalp. Beneath the red, he was pale as a sheet.

"How much of *that* is yours?" Beau asked, reaching out to touch a particularly dark spot on El's torso and grimacing as Elias gasped in agony.

"A lot." His eyes flicked up past Beau, and the king turned to see Penny and Viv running toward them, Viv's limp made more pronounced by her heavy leather bag. "Back to the inn! It's not safe."

"Oh aye, we'll leave our king and Ellie to bleed out in the street," Viv said dryly as El stabbed through each of the bodies on the ground, ensuring they were dead. He'd managed to get one leg propped up but couldn't lift himself out of his kneel. "Fine fight you'd put up, when you can't even stand."

Beau took one of Elias's arms cautiously, looking for injuries, and pulled it up across his shoulders. "You're heavy as hell," he said as his right leg trembled under the added weight. "Can you get your feet under you, or…?"

"Yeah," El said breathlessly, "just…give me…a second."

"Are there more?"

"Yeah, but scattered." Elias gritted his teeth, then stood straight, summoning energy from some deeper well than Beau had access to. He put a heavily bleeding arm out toward Viv. "Slap a bandage on…and let me…get back to it."

Penny ducked under El's other side to help, but he shook his head. "Stay clear, Duchess. We're not done."

Viv made a rude sound and pressed fiercely on the gash in his scalp with a rag, trying to stop the bleeding so El's eyes would be clear. Elias staggered and gasped in pain.

"You're not doing any more fighting," Beau said, stating the obvious, and both women nodded resolutely once. Viv's face slowly drained of color as she took in Elias's injuries.

"I'll do what I have to do." Elias's voice was flat, and he had to suck in wet, harsh gasps between phrases. "Can you get the neck-lace…out of my pocket? I need to…put it on."

"The necklace? The artifact?" Penny's voice grew sharper. "You know what it does?"

"I know enough. Get it out for me." He grew heavier, putting more and more weight on Beau, who faltered. Beau's eyes raked over Elias's body, counting slashes in the fabric that revealed broken flesh beneath. So many. Too many. Fuck, *so* many. Viv met Beau's eyes and swallowed hard. She put the rag away, picked up her bag, and gestured toward the inn.

Why wasn't she helping? Why wasn't she taking care of the worst injuries? Beau's heart beat in his throat, cutting off his air with each swell.

Penny reached into Elias's pocket and fished out the hideous amulet they'd found no description for. The Watchers must know more of what it did. Had Elias tried it on? It was insane to play with mysterious artifacts, especially something Penny had described as corrupted. Her fingers curled around the thing, then peeled away as if in disgust. "Elias, tell me what this does."

"Just put it on me," El gasped. "*Hurry*. It'll keep me on my feet. In fighting shape."

Penny stopped short on the path. "Elias. Tell me this is not a Revenant Chain."

El's jaw flexed, and he nudged Beau away from him as two soldiers emerged from between the houses ahead. He swayed. How the fuck was he standing?

"All right. It's not a Revenant Chain." The dryness of his voice came through even in his breathless state. "Give it to me." When he lifted his sword, it shook terribly.

"I'll fight them," Beau said. "You don't have to do anything. You've done enough. I will fight them. Don't do whatever it is that artifact does." He didn't like the horror in Penny's face, didn't like the way the amulet glinted in her hands.

"*Elias*," Penny said sharply as El tried to snatch it and stumbled. "Don't lie to me."

"Make up your mind," El muttered. The soldiers trotted their direction, shouting, pointing. "Every minute you delay...more die. I can hear them."

Far from convincing her, this made Penny balk, and she held the amulet farther from him, eyes narrowing. "You know what will happen when you put this—"

"*I'm already dead, Duchess*," Elias hissed, hand stretched urgently out toward her, palm up. "Do you want the same for him? There is no *time!*"

"What?" Beau demanded, but El didn't answer. Viv made a small, choked sound, and she wouldn't meet Beau's eyes. "You're not going to die, Elias. I won't let you."

Penny's eyes flooded with tears, and her horror and sadness poured across the ring as she slowly, hesitantly handed the amulet over. El's eyes flicked to the soldiers, nearly on them, and he awkwardly lifted the chain with his broken hand.

Numb, shaking, Beau turned away to step between his family and the soldiers, silently inventorying his injuries, forcing all thoughts of Elias away. If he could keep attackers from rounding his weakened right side, he'd do all right. He readied himself to block and eyed the men. One was shorter; Beau had the advantage of reach. The other held his sword awkwardly, like he'd never fought with it or his grip had been injured. Either way, a good sign.

Both men stopped well short of him. Their eyes widened, looking past Beau. They stumbled back a step, then another.

Behind him, Elias made a sound. Not a human sound.

Every hair on Beau's body stood.

A jolt fired through Beau at the way his guard stood, like something had pulled him straight with invisible strings; at the way his wounds poured wisps of green light now instead of blood; at the way the amulet pulsed magic that felt like pure death in the air and made it hard to breathe and made Elias make that unholy sound, a growl and a groan and a demon's condemned scream all at once.

No. No, this is wrong. Something is wrong.

With a jerk, Elias's eyes fixed on the two soldiers. He sprinted past Beau, nothing but a green-lit blur. The men didn't have time to turn and run; they were already in so many pieces Beau couldn't make sense of them as bodies when they hit the ground. A twitch running through him, Elias made the sound again.

Penny grabbed Beau's arm tightly. Hand pressed over her mouth, she watched Elias like nothing so abhorrent had ever walked the earth. Her horror was his horror was hers—they stared after Elias together, spiraling. She hauled Beau toward the guard.

"Elias," she breathed, "take it off. You have to take it off."

El's eyes were not hazel anymore. When they flicked to Beau's, then back to Penny, they left a ghostly trail of green after-image between. "Too late, Duchess." Something was wrong with Elias's voice, making it echo like words thrown down a well or whispered in a cold cave. Behind them, Viv began to whisper a prayer.

Beau wanted to be glad Elias was on his feet, standing straight and moving like he'd never been injured. But El's skin writhed with the verdant energy beneath it. Beau could smell it, like an ancient tree gone up in flames or a temple ravaged and smashed to powder. It smelled like the destruction of something sacred.

"What's wrong with Ellie?" Viv's voice came out shrill and strangled. She stopped short of Beau with her eyes on Elias, visibly afraid to go closer to the guard.

"Nothing's wrong with Ellie now," Elias said, too flat, voice echoing up from some dark place. "Stay close. They're converging on the inn."

Beau tried to catch up to him, but Elias's glare made him drop back. Something was so deeply *wrong* in the way the amulet's magic twitched and juddered through the guard, and Beau was shamefully scared to get too close. Instead, he caught Penny's fingers and brushed the back of her hand against his lips. "Are you all right? Have you fought? Your knuckles are torn up."

"They'll heal fine," she said quietly. Her eyes followed Elias. "I'm not hurt at all, love. You? You're bleeding everywhere. Here, lean on me if you need to."

"Can't. We've got to hurry. If they're at the inn—"

Dread swelled up in his throat, cutting off his words, and Penny nodded. "Whatever happens, Beau—" She shook her head like she wanted to recall the words, then pressed forward anyway. "This is not your fault. This is Courdur's fault, and the…the people who support him. You're the rightful king, and we're all fighting for that. It is worth it."

Why are you saying this? But he knew why. Once the adrenaline drained away, once he looked at the wreckage of his isles, once he saw the bodies—gods, Adrien and Nicky had died for him. How many more? Once the fight left, he'd have nothing but the horrible guilt for what he'd brought here.

For the moment, though, there were sword clangs and distant screams and green-edged wounds on the person he trusted most in the world.

19

OZONE AND SACRILEGE

A t least a dozen soldiers stood in and around the inn, the last of those who'd invaded Leau, and the two on the roof saw Beau's party coming. A handful spread across the road, smirking, holding blades almost lazily. Beau searched past them for Ma or any of the faces he knew.

"Lexi, baby," Gerard called, tone mockingly friendly but shark's smile viciously sharp, "I'll admit, I didn't expect to see you still on your feet. I didn't even think you'd live long enough to bleed out, pretty boy. You've gotten better, but not good enough."

El's gait slowed and dragged again. The king had a moment of realization—*he's pretending, so they'll let him in close*—before Elias exploded into motion, green light tracing after his limbs in the air. He killed so many so quickly. Two, three, four fell in as many breaths. The blond Watcher danced back, laughing in apparent surprise.

"Oh, what did you *do*, lap candy? Break into your boyfriend's magic stash? How long do you think that can help you?" Two bolts fired down from the roof, one going wide of Elias and the other hitting his shoulder and punching out to the left of his spine.

Elias didn't slow for a moment.

Though Beau held his sword, there was nowhere to insert himself into the fight. Three more died. Five. Everyone in front of the inn except Gerard, who'd backed into the doorway, amusement evaporated now that the crossbow bolts and sword slashes had had no effect on Elias.

What the fuck is that amulet? Dread, nauseating, in his belly.

Elias hurtled into the inn, and Beau followed, dodging another bolt from the roof. Inside, all was chaos. There were bodies on the floor—fishermen, unlucky bastards who'd just been enjoying the breakfast at the inn; Gabi the serving girl; and several invading soldiers—but the rest of the inn's occupants trembled at sword point, bruised and bleeding, but alive.

"Ma!" Beau called as soon as he saw her, bound but glaring holes in the soldier that held her. Relief broke over her face, then concern as her eyes swept his body. The concern melted into absolute revulsion when Elias's murder spree took him into her line of sight. Even at a glance, the wrongness was apparent.

Gerard darted to Mistress Corlia and pressed the tip of his blade to her throat. "Slow down, pretty boy. Your little kingling won't be too happy if you get his 'Ma' killed, will he?"

Elias did not slow down. Whether he hadn't heard or simply hadn't cared, he swept like an angel of death through the room. The two soldiers nearest him fell neatly in half as Beau managed to choke out his, "*No, El.*" Elias had to stop, he *had* to stop, or they were going to kill Ma, and Beau couldn't bear—

The blond Watcher tightened his grip on Ma's hair, lifted his blade—and then howled as someone leaped onto his back, snarling and stabbing at him with a tiny knife.

Maisie.

Maisie was attacking a Watcher, a thousand tiny bites with a paring knife as she hung from his throat with one hand, feet scrabbling for purchase on his hip and leg. Ferocious, she clawed and hacked at him, a steady stream of curse words barely intelligible among her growls.

Beau lunged for Gerard, one hand out to grab Maisie and pull her away, but the assassin flipped his sword, deftly grabbed the handle with the blade facing in, and slammed it back along his side.

Maisie dropped. Beau's reach to pull her away became a fumbling catch instead. With a horrible, wet sound, she slid off the sword. Her body was so light, but his arms, his hands, his shoulders were weak. He slid across the inn's floor, trying to soften her landing as much as he could, trying to minimize the damage.

Gerard grinned down at Beau. One hand holding Maisie's head up, the other barely remembering to grip his own weapon, the king knelt before him. "Perfect position, kingling," the Watcher said. "You have quite the talent for being executed." Maisie's blood sprayed off in an arc as the sword lifted.

Elias tackled the blond Watcher to the ground. Weapon gone, he glowed with a sickly, pulsing green that sucked oxygen out of the air. His hands tightened around Gerard's head, thumbs pressing hard against eyes.

Gerard screamed. Elias made that unholy sound again.

The skull cracked like a cannon shot, like a chicken egg. Elias's hands slammed together in the gore. Beau shook.

Perhaps enemies still surrounded him, though by the sounds, Beau thought the fighting was finally, finally over. Perhaps Ma needed help, gasping and calling out as she was. Perhaps Penny needed him; her voice rang out, authoritative, hurried. Perhaps Elias was becoming something other than a man. The ozone-and-sacrilege scent of the amulet's magic congealed so thick in the air Beau struggled to breathe.

But all Beau could see was Maisie, eyes wide and fixed on him, pale face slick with sweat. Her fingernails clawed into his hand where it pressed against the hole through her abdomen. It was messy and open; his hands slipped and slid horribly.

"Hey, Maiz, that was pretty badass," he said hoarsely. He thought he might've smiled, but who the fuck knew what his face was doing. "Just hold on for me, okay? Viv is going to patch you up, and you'll be fine. I know it hurts, but we'll get you sorted. Every-thing's going to be all right. You're going to be all right."

Maisie blinked, and tears rolled down along her temples. "Like fuck I am," she said, fire undimmed. "I'm not stupid. I'm gut-cut. I'm dead." She laughed, a mirthless, hollow sound. "You better be the best fucking king anybody's ever seen, hear me?"

"You're not going to die," Beau insisted. Over his shoulder, he shouted, "Viv! Maiz needs help! She needs you!"

Unclenching one bloody hand from Beau's, Maisie grabbed the king by the hair. "Don't you *dare* make this longer than it has to be. Love you, Barfly. Give me a kiss and make it quick like you did for that guard." Beau dragged in a ragged, sobbing breath. He pressed a kiss to her forehead, then to her temple, then to her lips. She blinked up past him, grimacing in pain as she inhaled. "Ellie."

Elias knelt next to Beau. Though his hands were on Beau's body, cataloguing his cuts and punctures, he spared a glance for Maiz. He said, quietly, in that chill, distant voice, "I'll make it quick."

She smiled, blood pinking her teeth. "Show me what those—" A gurgling, pained inhale. "—hands are good for."

Elias didn't hesitate. He palmed her head, lifting her slightly off the ground, and drove a knife into the back of her skull. Instant-ly, everything that was *Maisie* fled her face, and Elias dropped her limply. It was so sudden, so smooth, Beau didn't even feel the loss; he just went numb. He was shaking again.

El hauled Beau to his feet, dragging him away from Maisie's body, away from Ma, who held Gabi's corpse and sobbed, away from the people carrying in more bodies, some alive and howling in pain, some still. Elias scooped supplies from Viv's bag on the floor.

In the second he let go of Beau, the king's legs abandoned him. He was weak from blood loss and shock and the sight of Capu-cine pressing both hands to Nilah's face and speaking softly to her so she couldn't look down at her mangled leg, of Penny sharing half of Delphine's weight as the blacksmith dangled, unconscious or dead, from her brother's arms.

Without so much as a grunt of exertion, Elias picked Beau up and carried him into his room, which had been tossed.

El set him on the mattress and began threading a needle. "You've lost more blood than I'd like," he said, voice an approximation of gentle despite the menacing green energy jolting under his skin. His fingers twitched, making the precision needed to spear the eye of the needle impossible.

Beau took his hands. His eyesight blurred, and when he blinked, he realized he was crying. "I think you should take the amulet off now, Elias." He barely recognized his own voice, hoarse and thin. "I don't like this. The threat has passed. Take it off."

El stared at him, and for the first time since he'd put the artifact on, the warmth of his hazel eyes shone through. They were desperately, hopelessly sad. "Too late for that, Highness." He looked up as the door opened and Penny slipped in. "Ah, good. My hands aren't steady. You sew, Duchess."

"I've never—"

"I'll talk you through it. This one first. It's worst."

Beau lay silent, buzzing with guilt and terror and grief, as Penny's inexpert hands gently sewed his hewn bits of skin back together, cleaned the wounds, bandaged. He didn't feel like a king, crying in his bed while all around him, people died and screamed and bled for him. He tallied the dead, the injured, weighing them against his own life, and found himself wanting in the extreme.

The physical pain set in, too. It was almost unbearable, but it paled in comparison to the crushing, crippling weight of his thoughts. How could he ever make this right? How could he possibly make this up to the people of Leau?

You better be the best fucking king anybody's ever seen, hear me?

It settled around his neck, an iron noose, a command stronger than any his father had issued. He would be king. He *had* to be, or their deaths were worth nothing. And he'd be the greatest king to sit the sun throne. He owed them that.

"That's the last of the real injuries," Elias said as he walked toward the door. "Get him on his feet. We have to get to the docks."

Beau sat up with a groan. He breathed through the black spots eating at his vision. "I'm not getting on a ship, El."

A massive shudder ran through El's body, hands clenching. He didn't turn toward Beau. "They're not done. They'll send more. Do you want to take the rest of Leau to hell with you?"

"I'm not done either," Beau said. "I'm going back to the palace. I'm claiming my throne. And I'm going to make such an example of Alphonse Courdur that no one ever dreams of trying to take what's mine from me again. No ships. No running. I'll take the road."

Now Elias turned to face him, incredulity creasing his brow. "They'll see you on the road. They'll come down on you in force."

"They'll know I'm not on Leau anymore," Beau countered. "So there'll be no need to come back here and hurt anyone else."

Elias's glowing eyes bored into him, unearthly. The voice that came out of his mouth was not his. "My business here will not be complete until you're king, then." He jerked again, twitching so hard it looked painful, and opened the door. "I'll get the horses."

Beau allowed himself a moment to pull Penny to him and hold her. Beneath the sweat and metallic blood, her hair smelled of honeyed flowers. She was soft against him, holding him gently in the places he wasn't hurt. Desperately, he breathed in the sweet, floral air and the easy, undemanding pressure, an oasis of peace.

He should be outside helping Viv take care of the wounded. Except he was only halfway passable with stitches; medicine had never been one of his miscellaneous hobbies, and if he had to watch another islander die, he'd break down sobbing like a child. That wasn't what a king did, and they died to make him king.

So Beau hid in his room and held onto his wife and dug for buried happiness or calm for both of them through the rings. He could find numbness; he settled for numb. He spoke so the silence wouldn't crush him to death.

"Courdur *and* the Watchers. *Can* I fight them?"

Penny nodded against his chest. She had to clear her throat to speak, and it was clear she warded off despair with words, too. "His forces are sizable, but you could match it with time. With your father's death, you're Duke of Chudeau now as well as Verdmont, so you have a lot of men in and around the capital."

Pressing his face into her hair, he inhaled the sweet, calming scent of her and ignored *with your father's death* as hard as he could. "Verdmont won't do me any good. Chudeau's men are accessible, but Verdmont couldn't muster men and get them to the capital in time to make a difference. I'll be dead."

"Don't forget," she said, turning her face up to him with the faintest ghost of a smile, "you married the Duchess of Veritelutte. We *are* close enough, and my sister's been calling my men up already in my absence, hoping to send them to the Paibon front."

Beau's thumbs traced her cheeks. She was so beautiful when she talked strategy. The light in her eyes made him want to wish on her like a star. "You have less than half of what Courdur does."

"Yes."

"If I can't scrape together my men in time, it'd cripple your House. You'd be wiped out."

Her lashes fanned out over her cheeks as she dropped her eyes and smirked. "Well, you're not counting Elias. He's worth at least half of Courdur's forces."

"Be serious, Pen."

Her eyes flicked back up, deep, lustrous brown. "I am serious. My men are yours. And it's not so hopeless as you think—I have allies. Lady Roben and Lady Andremiere will stand with me, and Roben's men would be carved straight out of Courdur's forces. You've been a friend to several of the smaller houses. Call on them."

She hesitated, tapping her teeth together.

"And you could write to Haydée. She has a soft spot for you, and her father can't be pleased to see the Courdurs ascend over the

Macabries. It would be a shaky alliance, and an expensive one, but maybe worth…"

"Andremiere and Macabrie have the same problem I do," Beau said, frowning. "They're too far from the capital to make the difference. I'd be more afraid Macabrie would sweep down after Courdur and I have gutted each other's forces and install himself."

"He may do that anyway," Penny muttered. "But as long as the Macabries stay neutral, we might be able to pull it out with what we've got. You've got the legitimacy of your claim on your side, which should sway some of the other nobles toward you, if it looks like you can meet Courdur for sheer numbers. But they'll never be seen supporting a lost cause."

Exhaustion swept over Beau in a wave, and he pulled Penny in close again. Sweet flowers, honeyed resolve. From the ring, the stone-dust taste of her certainty. She was determined to defeat his enemies, to support him to the bitter end. "I don't deserve you."

"You deserve more allies than me and mine, Beauregard, but that will come with time and power." The door opened, and Aloise walked in, blood to her elbows and curls stuck to her with sweat.

"Elias and Uriel are getting the horses ready, Your Majesties," she said, "and Elias and I will be riding out with you. Nilah can't travel and Jude is dead—" Beau's eyes went wide. "—which leaves the two of us. I wanted to be sure you knew Elias is…um…"

"We're aware he's a revenant," Penny said. "It's all right."

Aloise swallowed. "Very good. Should I grab anything from your room?"

"The bag by the door, please, and the two pouches in the bed-side drawer," Penny said, smiling as Aloise nodded and disappeared.

"I don't like bringing her," Beau muttered. "It's not safe."

Penny's hands on his chest stilled him. "You're in no place to turn down offers of aid or alliance, Beauregard. When things are this uncertain, every person you 'protect' by not involving them endangers the life of someone who's already committed to you. If you're concerned about Aloise's safety, make her safer by gathering more allies, not by turning her away." She kissed him. "If it helps, don't think of it as fighting for *you*, think of it as fighting for us. You and I, our lives are intertwined now. If you die, I die."

Yes, she was queen now, albeit uncrowned, tied to a king with a price on his head. Any family of his was under threat until he sat solidly on the throne. A horrible thought lurched into Beau's head. "You don't think—my mother?"

Penny raised an uneasy shoulder, and, of all things, guilt rose up in the pool. "She's a powerful political player. If she supported your claim…" Penny took a deep breath. "…she's most likely dead. But she could've come out in support of Courdur instead of you. It'd be a significant blow to your claim, but…Courdur would've left her alive if she played it that way."

They stared at each other for a moment, uncertainty plain on their faces. Beau had no idea if his mother would forswear him to save herself. As much as it hurt to consider, it was logical, given how he'd left things with his parents. "She never had a great deal of faith in me. I hope she did what was necessary to protect herself."

Something flickered over Penny's face: a downturn of her lips, a narrowing of her eyes, a flare of her nostrils. But from the ring came a torrent of anger and dismissal and protectiveness.

And he *knew*, he knew with absolute certainty that for her child—for *his* child—she'd burn the kingdom down before she'd let someone steal their birthright.

He cupped her cheeks in his hands and pressed his mouth to hers, a hungry, aching kiss. "I love you," he said against her lips.

"I know." She smiled, but the anger and sadness only strengthened. "And I love you. Let's go say our goodbyes so we can take back what belongs to us."

When Beau and Penny emerged into the packed common room, silence fell in ripples. Beau bore the weight of the stares, though it threatened to collapse his legs. He cleared his throat.

"I want to thank you all. I know that sounds thin, in the wake of what's happened. But I couldn't be more grateful to have been your Barfly, and your Angel, and your Crow, and your Lamb for all these years. It's only because you invited me to be those things that I can call myself—" He took a deep breath. "—King of Granvallée. But I am the king. And I promise you, I will never forget what Leaurepit has done for me. I would give you—"

His voice broke as he saw Maisie's body, swaddled in a blanket like she was sleeping, laid alongside Gabi. Someone had braided her curls back from her face. "I would give you back those Lord Courdur stole from us if I could," he said, voice strangled. "But whatever I *can* give you, it's yours. You only have to ask."

Ma crossed the room to him in silence, tearful eyes on him. She took his hands in both of hers. "What we want, Lamb, is you on the throne and safe. We want you to kill the bastard that did this. And we want you to come home every now and again."

She wrapped him in a hug, and though she squeezed his injuries until he wanted to gasp from the pain, he said only, "That I can do, Ma."

More friends lined up to hug him, to mutter goodbyes and encouragements, and to echo Ma's requests. It was a solemn procession. When the living had made their rounds, Beau walked the line of the dead, touching hands and faces, whispering sorrows and benedictions. Someone had brought Jude to the end of the line, setting his sword on his chest. Beau pressed a hand to his forehead and muttered, "Thank you for being loyal, Jude. You made it right."

Penny sat at one of the tables now pressed against the back wall of the common room and furiously scribbled on pigeon paper. "It's everyone we could reasonably call on," she said when Beau drifted close. "Hurry and read. Sign if you're happy with them."

Beau signed them unread; he trusted her. Handing the pile to Herb, he offered his wife a hand up and they each received more hugs and kisses and hand squeezes and claps on the back.

Elias stepped in through the front door, and everyone within fifteen feet stepped back.

Magic ran in loops and drips down his body from dozens of wounds that did not bleed. Though it made no sound, it pressed strangely on the ear, a pulsing so unpleasant Beau found himself gritting his teeth as he approached. Nearer, the smell of unholy burning blood made Beau's eyes water. He eyed the chain where it disappeared beneath Elias's shirt with distaste.

No one tried to say farewells to Elias. No one called to him. The common room held its breath, like breathing in the awful magic he radiated would taint them as well. As he waved Beau toward the horses, the guard twitched like his body couldn't bear to stand still.

"We ride." He didn't even glance at the people in the inn.

While Beau and Penny mounted up, the king watched Elias' unnaturally stiff back, the way he sat Po like he'd never seen him before. What was happening to him? And how could Beau fix it? If he *did* have magic, and Elias firmly believed he did, then maybe...

Elias's shudder almost shook him off his horse. He swayed a moment, then yanked himself straight in the saddle again. He heeled Po into a full gallop, and Beau, bewildered, urged Tempest to match Pormort's speed. Penny and Aloise wasted no time in catching up, though it meant the four of them tearing through the narrow streets of Leau too fast for comfort.

El barely slowed for the ferry, leaping Po over the narrow gap between dock and deck. Beau was too careful with Tempest for that; he slowed ten yards short and walked his mare across, ignoring the guard's jittering, jerking impatience.

"Take us across. Now," Elias demanded of the ferryman, and Penny, who'd halfway dismounted, instead kneed her horse onto the deck, calling for Aloise to hurry. She didn't allow herself or her mare near the guard, pressing against the far rail as far from him as possible. She studied him, though, eyes narrowed and a searing mix of pomegranate and horseradish spiking through the ring.

"Are you still there, Elias?" she asked quietly as the ferry began its trek across the water.

Staring out at the land on the opposite side, El ignored her. The twitching became so frequent and so intense that his body continually shuddered. Hateful magic darkened the air around him. Whatever the amulet was doing to him, it obviously made him stronger, faster, impervious to the damage weapons could inflict. But the shaking made him look so...vulnerable. Beau couldn't bear it; he reached out and took one of Elias's hands.

"Does it hurt?" He only mouthed it, barely giving the words enough air to leave his lips.

Elias's fingers didn't curl around his in return, but the jerks and twitches softened into a pervasive tremor. The guard looked at him, and hazel swam up into the bottom of his irises. He looked at Beau like if he blinked, the king would cease to exist. He stared and stared and stared, silent and shaking.

Then the ferry hit land again, and Elias moved instantly, leaping onto Po's back and kicking his warhorse into a flying leap onto the dock. He rode hard, gaining yards of distance before Beau and the others had even remounted. The sun, high overhead, beat down on their party as they all rode to catch him, Beau occasionally shouting after his guard to no response.

A mile outside the town, Beau began to worry for the horses. At the second mile, Tempest was breathing hard, gait slowing.

Cursing, the king drew her up into a walk and let El pull away. "You're going to kill Po!" he shouted. When that didn't stop Elias, he added, "It'll be much slower getting to the palace if you have to ride double with me."

Elias's head jerked to the side, and with a yank of the reins that made Pormort dance uncomfortably, he slowed to a trot. The king kept his eyes on him as Penny and Aloise walked their huffing horses beside Tempest.

"Is he going to be all right?" Aloise asked quietly. "I've never seen him treat Pormort so hard."

Because that's not him, Beau thought, but he was afraid to speak it aloud. He was surer by the moment that the amulet was possessing him somehow. El wouldn't have risked Ma's life with a sword at her throat. El wouldn't have put Maisie down without so much as a soft word. El wouldn't have ridden out without saying goodbye, and he wouldn't be picking up his pace again now, driving Po into a canter while the horse's sides still heaved. After a minute of silence from Beau and Penny, Aloise nodded as if they'd answered.

For miles, they chased the cursed guard, Beau shouting him to a walk whenever his pace threatened the horses again. There were no pauses, no rests. Injuries burning, Beau sweated through his coat while he held himself straight in the saddle. As the day wore on, stitches pulled loose, and the bandages darkened.

"Fuck," he muttered. The saddle was slick with blood from his hip. The sun had slipped low in the sky, melting across the horizon. "Elias! I have to stop—some of us still bleed like human beings."

Without slowing, El turned sharply into the woods, so single-minded he seemed likely to run straight through trees instead of around. Beau cursed and followed; they couldn't camp on the road. Branches whipped thin, stinging cuts across his face, but he squinted into the shaded gloom and kept pace with his guard as Penny and Aloise picked a more careful path behind him.

By the time he reached the tiny clearing where Elias had dismounted, the Watcher paced the perimeter, peering into the trees with restless, dark energy. The shaking grew violent again.

Beau quickly untacked Tempest, then did the same for Po, scratching and soothing both horses. Pormort followed him reluctantly at first, but by the time Beau was done, the warhorse leaned against him and nuzzled against his chest. Elias moved nonstop, more jerkily by the moment, sword in hand.

"El," Beau said calmingly. "Do you hear anything threatening us right now?"

"No." Elias didn't pause in his restless pacing.

"Good. Then put the sword away so we can talk."

Shuddering, green loops of magic pulsing around him, El paced on. His fingers tightened on the sword until they blanched of color. Beau stepped closer, and El spun on him, the glow of his eyes sucking light out of the air instead of radiating it. Aloise moved to stand between them, but Beau waved her back.

"No, no—Aloise, please stay back. He won't hurt me." *Gods, I hope he won't hurt me. I hope he's not that far gone.*

Beau crept closer until the point of El's sword butted up against his sternum. The guard's shaking and jerking drew the tip of the blade in ticklish lines across his chest, snagging on the bandage across his collarbones. "Put it down, Elias."

Elias's hands unhinged mechanically, letting the sword fall to the ground. Beau edged closer still, raising a hand like he approached a spooked horse. Where he touched Elias's shoulder, the shuddering grew less violent.

Carefully, trying not to alarm Elias—or whatever had hold of him—he slid his fingers inward along El's chest until they touched the amulet through his shirt. Beau's hand went cold as numbing, awful vibrations spread up through his fingertips. He didn't try to pull it away. Instead, he pushed into it, forcing his request against it like he did with the Useful Thing.

"Give me my Elias, please," he said. He kept his voice quiet, though he was positively screaming it in his head.

The amulet squirmed. It jerked beneath his fingers like a living thing, and Elias made the unholy sound, more pain than anger in it. He gasped, and tension climbed his throat and face, writhing under his skin. His eyes were hazel, though, and his mouth worked like he was trying to speak for several seconds before he said, "Beau?"

It was his voice, his *real* voice, no echoes or coldness. Relief poured into the king like cold water. "El," he breathed. "What's going on? How do I get this fucker off you?"

Elias pressed his hand to Beau's against his chest, sighed, and then pulled Beau's fingers away. "Don't touch it, Highness. I don't want…it's dangerous. Don't touch it. Or me. I love—" He cut himself off, head jerking hard to the side as he squeezed his eyes shut. "No, no, that's not what I…I should be honest with you now, shouldn't I? I won't get another chance."

"What do you mean? I'm getting this *off* you, and you can be honest with me forever."

An enormous shudder shook Elias, who gritted his teeth. "I…I never loved you. It was all a lie to get close enough to get information, and then I was trying to put you on the throne because you're the horse I backed. I just wanted to win."

Beau hugged his cold hand against his stomach, buzzing with the amulet's magic. "I thought you were a good liar, El? That was pathetically transparent. Quit trying to protect me. I'm *getting* this magic off you. I have magic. I can do it."

"I am a good liar," Elias insisted. He forced his words out through gritted teeth. "But I didn't have to be with you. You're so easy to lie to. So eager to trust. So hungry for a friend."

"*Bullshit.* You *are* my friend, you *do* love me, and you fought for me because you believe in me. So fucking *believe* I'll fix this."

Elias swayed and breathed out a sharp, shuddering breath, then slammed his fist into his own side, where a deep wound spilled green. He staggered, but his eyes cleared. "Would a friend who loved you have killed your brother, Beauregard?"

Beau frowned. "I said, 'Give me *my Elias.*' El didn't kill my brother, and he knows perfectly well he told us all as much when he *couldn't* lie. So what the fuck are you?"

Elias didn't answer. His eyes were squeezed shut, teeth bared as he crushed his fists against his gut. The magic lapped over and around him, trying to drown him. Despite the cold anger swallowing Beau whole, he took a step forward, hand reaching out automatically toward the creature before him in such obvious torment.

El staggered back, falling to a knee. "Don't touch me. Stop. Please stop. You can't—" The green washed over him, climbing his throat. He choked and jerked upright, scratching at his throat, his face. Then the loops overwhelmed him completely, leaking back into his eyes until they were cold and alien. He went slack except for the awful, inhuman convulsions.

A wicked, spine-flaying laugh tumbled out of Elias's mouth, though his vocal cords didn't make it. "You're so *godsdamned easy,* Beau. All I've ever had to do to win your trust is exactly what I wanted. You little broken fucking thing—you made me everything."

It wasn't Elias's voice. It wasn't his eyes. But his mouth was saying the words, laughing and twitching and tracing his tongue along the edge of his teeth like he was contemplating tearing someone's throat out.

"I could tell you to your face *not to trust me,* and it only ever made you trust me more. You're a fool. Was it my face that made you so weak to me? My skill? Or were you so fucking lonely that it didn't matter which Watcher they sent to you?" Elias's body took a step toward Beau, radiating hate. "Allow me to repeat what I said when I couldn't lie, Beauregard, and try to listen more closely this time."

He tilted his head back, and a laugh boiled out that chilled Beau's blood and raised the hair on his neck. "*Beau would never order his brother's death,* I said. *You're looking in the wrong place, Your Grace. The prince is a good man. He believes his brother deserved the throne. Would I have killed Char if His Highness had ordered it? In a fucking heartbeat.* Where in there, dear Beauregard, do you hear me say I didn't kill him?"

Beau's heart beat loudly enough to deafen. The world was suddenly so loud, too loud, smells too sharp, tastes too bitter. He couldn't think, couldn't breathe normally. Because, of course, Elias had *not* said he didn't kill Char. He'd quite emphatically said he *would've,* given the chance. He hadn't lied. He couldn't lie. But Penny had never asked outright, *did you kill Charmant,* so Elias had never answered that question.

"No," he whispered.

"No," Elias's mouth said mockingly. He moved unnaturally, profanely. "*No*—is that all you can muster?" He chuckled darkly.

"I murdered your brother. I rode out of line and I shot him with a poison dart. He was supposed to fall to his right, into the canyon, and no one would've ever found the dart. But he shifted his weight at the last second and fell left instead."

Beau couldn't breathe, couldn't speak. Next to him, Penny said, "Why?" Her voice was clear and steady, like nothing insane was happening at all.

"Watchers didn't like what he was doing with all those artifacts," Elias said. "It wasn't my assignment. I didn't have to kill him. I'm a Face, not a Fighter. But I *wanted* to. Because I *hated* your brother, Beauregard. I fucking hated him and he deserved to die."

"Why did he deserve to die?" Penny demanded.

El was losing control of his hands, his legs, twitching too hard to stand. "Beau doesn't care why I killed him, do you, Beauregard? What's important is that you had a big brother you hero-worshipped, and *I murdered him*. I killed him, and I made you step into his shoes. You could've lived happily on the isles, but instead, you got a dead brother and a crown you didn't want. You had to hear every hateful thing you father really thought of you because of me. You lost people you love on Leau because I set you up for a fight."

There was an audible crack in the back of Beau's head as the threads of his trust in Elias snapped. He boiled alive in anger, in hurt, in confusion.

"Beau," Penny said calmingly, hand on his arm, "he's making you angry on purpose."

"He's fucking good at it," Beau choked out. "Is this monster what you've always been Elias? Is this just your final form?"

"*Yes.*" Five, ten, a hundred voices whispered it at once from El's throat.

"Stop," Penny said, more urgently. "Elias, explain. Tell us why."

"Just let me be a monster, Duchess," the many, many voices said. Elias hulked taller, the dark, verdant magic growing around him. He moved toward Pormort. "I have business left unfinished, and I'm running out of time. Keep them alive, Aloise. I'm clearing a path to the capital."

He reached into his pockets as he walked and dropped artifacts in the grass before he swung onto Po's bare back, ignoring the heap of tack. All he kept was the Revenant Chain, which pulsed beneath his shirt.

"Goodbye, Your Majesty. You'll sit the throne soon enough."

"Stop." Beau's voice had never been so cold. He knew with absolute certainty that Elias would obey, and he did. "Who will you kill in the capital? Courdur's men?"

"Yes."

His mind raced; it was Elias and it was not. It was a beast and it was a brutal killing force that could turn the tide. Some part of him rebelled, calling for him to demand explanations from Elias, to rip the amulet off, to kiss the man until he admitted everything in a way that could be forgiven. But the cold, furious part, the part in charge at the moment, wanted to squeeze the usefulness out of this inexplicably loyal monster.

"They're not at fault for this; Courdur is. The *Watchers* are. And you're the only one who can punish them. If you want to clear the path for me to sit on the throne, you'll ride straight to wherever the Watchers make their headquarters and you'll kill *every Watcher there*." Rage bubbled up in his throat as he pictured Char falling, the months of mourning where this man, who'd killed him, had pretended to comfort and commiserate. What but a monster could do that?

"Consider them dead." The bleeding cloak of magic burned as Elias stared at him, and the forest grew still and quiet. "Goodbye, Beau." And then Elias rode off at a reckless speed, weaving through the trees so he was invisible to Beau four steps in.

The king was left with burning rage and no one to vent it on. He shouted after Elias, a wordless, furious scream, but it only wound him tighter, made his breath harder to pull in. Penny's hand on his back was too much, an immediate sensory overload.

"What's happening to him?" Aloise asked, staring after Elias. "It looks…horrible."

"Aloise, please," Penny said, and the other woman grimaced, then went to the packs and began to set up camp.

"Do you know?" Beau asked as Penny tried again to touch him and send soothing, calming waves through the ring. "What it's doing to him? Do you know what the amulet does?"

His wife swallowed, and each blink sent a slow tear down her cheek. "Not exactly. But I know he was right to make you send him away without trying to get it off."

She left to help Aloise, and Beau slowly sat on the forest floor, replaying every word of the last few minutes. He choked on the realization that even at his cruelest, even saying things he knew would break Beau's heart completely, Elias was still protecting him.

Beau stayed awake the entire night, listening for the crack of a stick or rustle of leaves that would mean Elias had returned or Courdur's men with their Watcher agents had found them.

It never came, so he had hours and hours of remembering the exact faces the people of Leau had made when they died, the shape of Char's body as it fell out of the saddle, the frailness of his father lying in bed the last time Beau saw him, the twitching, broken monster Elias had become.

His fault. All his fault. Lying in the dark, he dug his fingernails under the edges of his stitches and stared out into the trees and let their faces haunt him until dawn broke.

20

A TULIP FAMILY

No one spoke for most of the three days of hard riding it took to cross Chudeau's northern width except to discuss travel logistics, politely offer tea, or point out obvious features of the terrain before them. Beau had nothing to say, Penny seemed afraid to broach the wall of Beau's despair, and Aloise took her cue from the royals.

When they clipped across the far west corner of Estforet and passed into southeastern Veritelutte on the fourth day, the queen finally broke. "We have to talk about your brother."

Beau blinked at the space between Tempest's ears and summoned his conscious mind from the mire of maudlin thoughts it had been floating in. "Do we?"

"What did Elias mean about what he was doing with artifacts? Did he get rid of them? Sell them? Is the vault really empty?"

With immense effort, Beau turned his head far enough to see Aloise on his other side, riding a speedy-looking roan gelding he recognized as Nilah's horse.

He wondered if they could catch him, if he rode away from this conversation. Tempest was quick, but he suspected Penny's Nightbird could outpace her, and the guard's roan had the long legs and bright eyes of a fast horse, too.

"It's empty. I don't know why and I don't know what El meant," Beau said flatly. "My brother was the one with the keys, even though it was theoretically in my name. Just like all the money requests 'I' made while I lived in the isles were signed and sealed, most likely by the one other person who had access to my seal and had a signed letter from me."

Penny absorbed this. "So…it's possible he was telling the truth. That your brother *did*…"

"Deserve to die?" Beau couldn't modulate his voice; first it was too flat, now too sharp. "For making me look wasteful instead of him? For *maybe* misplacing old magic items?"

"For being a sadistic pig," Aloise said quietly, resolutely.

Beau swiveled toward her. "What?"

"I've always liked Elias," she said, staring straight ahead along the road. "Always trusted his judgment. If he killed your brother, I like him more." She swallowed hard and met Beau's stare. Though her mouth was set, her eyes betrayed nervousness.

"Capu never trusted you; she never understood how you could punish all the *other* nobles on Mistress Dubois's list and defend Charmant. But I get it: you don't know what he was, do you?"

Tempest frisked, frightened by a bunny bursting from the bushes ahead, and Beau calmed her with his knees. "What are you saying? That Char belonged on Dubois's list?"

"Yes." She swallowed hard again. "Do you need me to describe why? Capucine and I can both give you a personal account." Her voice broke on the last word, and her throat tightened. He could see her pulse pounding wildly at her neck.

His mouth went dry. Beau shook his head. "No, you don't need to describe…" He reined Tempest in, bowing his head over her neck, and tried to slow his racing thoughts.

He's not lying about Char—he's just wrong. *He truly believes his brother was a good man who deserved the throne.*

His brother hadn't been a good man who was occasionally cruel to Beau. He was cruel to *everyone* with no power to stop him. Even Penny hadn't liked him, and she'd been a brilliant, well-connected duchess set to rule the kingdom beside him: someone Char should've respected, even by the most contemptible standards.

"Oh fuck. I'm sorry, Aloise." When he glanced at her, she nodded but said nothing, watching him work through it. Beau's mind whirled as he rethought *everything* in a more sinister light. Char had changed payments to other lords: why? What had he been paying them for? Char had made an entire vault of artifacts disappear. *Why?* Where had they gone? If he was willing to hurt people who were entirely in his power, what the fuck was he capable of?

I didn't have to kill him. But I wanted *to. Because I* hated *your brother, Beauregard. I fucking hated him and he deserved to die.*

What had Elias known? "Oh fuck. *Fuck.*" He wanted to ask why Aloise hadn't told him *sooner*, but unfortunately, he understood. She hadn't trusted him for the same reason Capucine hadn't, and of fucking course she didn't. Instead, he asked, "I'm sorry if this is rude, but...weren't you scared? Of me, I mean? To work for me?"

To his surprise, Aloise laughed. "Of course we were. Didn't you notice how on edge we all were the first few weeks? Uriel always hovering around. But none of the other lords liked you and the rumor was you'd murdered your brother. A vote of confidence." She shrugged. "And then you were so uncomfortable with us and so obviously pining after a guard you never said an inappropriate word to, it was clear you weren't going to pull the same shit."

Though Aloise and Penny continued to talk for most of that day's ride, Beau could only drag himself far enough out of the maelstrom of his thoughts to listen for short intervals, and to respond, even less. When they'd made camp, eaten a spartan dinner, and settled in for the night, Beau finally found the voice for his question.

"Pen?" When she made a small noise of acknowledgement, he asked, "Did I send Elias to his death for a brother I would've had killed anyway, if I'd actually known him?"

"You didn't send Elias to his death, Beau," she said, and though the words seemed intended to be reassuring, her tone was surprised, saddened. He could see the glitter of her eyes in the dark, the faint outline of the curve of her cheek.

She spoke gently. "Elias was dying of his injuries before he put that amulet on. He knew it; Vivienne knew it. I thought *you* knew. The amulet didn't stop that. It just kept him moving."

"Kept him alive."

"No, Beau. No." Gentle, so gentle, so sad, her voice. "He's not…he's not alive. He's a revenant. All the amulet does is delay his body laying down to rest."

Some part of Beau must've understood, because tears were running over the bridge of his nose, dripping onto the arm he'd folded under his head, but his mind refused to hear it. "He's still fighting. Still talking. So I have time to fix this. To get him back."

"Beau—"

"I'm magic. That's what he said," Beau said, voice breaking. "So I can get him back."

Penny's fingers found his cheek, brushed it gently. "He fought very hard to make you angry enough not to try that."

"I *don't care*." He sniffed. "You study magic, right? So you must have a book about it?"

"I have hundreds, but—"

"Then I'll find one that tells me how to get him back. I can do that. I can fix that." *He trusted me. He believed I was magic.*

Penny said nothing more to dissuade him, just curled up in his arms and held him tightly, rubbing devastatingly comforting circles against his back. Beau tried not to let that sap him of the last of his hope.

·𝕾𝕻·𝕾𝕻·𝕾𝕻·

"**A**nd you're sure those are your men?" Beau kept his voice almost silent, since Penny could hear him easily with the Perception Stone tucked into her bodice. The late afternoon sun set the gold of her nose ring and earrings on fire.

She sent across a wave of quiet reassurance, then stepped out of the tree line with Nightbird. The Veritelutte sentries saw her at once and lowered pikes, but at her greeting, they relaxed again, bowing. After a quiet conversation, one took her horse's reins and Penny held a hand out toward Beau, an offer for him and Aloise to join her.

Aloise strode out first, patting her roan and muttering, "See, boy? It's fine." Beau was not proud of how much willpower it took to emerge from his own hiding place in the trees.

The sentries didn't recognize Beau, bowing their heads with a casual sort of deference for what must be a nobleman traveling with their lady before continuing their conversation with her. "Yes, those who are traveling have been assembling on the north end of the estate for the better part of two days. The dowager queen, her retinue, and the generals of her forces have been put up in the manor—"

"My—the queen is here?" Beau cut in. His mother was alive. That was a relief, even if it meant she'd betrayed him.

"Yes, my lord. Do you have business? I can have her informed of your arrival."

Beau hesitated. "No…no, thank you." He exchanged a glance with Penny, who squeezed his hand lightly before releasing him.

"Thank you, Master Denis. We'll make our own way in."

They handed their reins to the second sentry to be taken to the stables and strode through the colorful gardens of Penny's manor grounds. As they neared, a small, dark-haired woman in a seafoam dress bounded out of glass-paneled double doors, squealing at the top of her lungs. When Penny saw her, she kicked up her own skirts and ran. The pair collided, hugging and spinning so aggressively they collapsed to the ground, laughing.

Feeling like an intruder, Beau approached at a statelier pace with Aloise at his shoulder.

"Gods, Vic, you're lucky the tri-west aldermen have dragged their feet, or we'd have been on the road already," the younger woman was saying, "but I was *this* close to hanging the three of them from the battlements by their bootlaces, I was so impatient."

"I appreciate your restraint," Penny said dryly. "Get up so I can introduce you to someone."

"Someone?" Lianna scrambled to her feet and brushed off her skirt. Her head cocked to the side as she studied them briefly. "Is it the brother-in-law Uncle Alphonse keeps insisting is dead or the *gorgeous* woman whose name I need immediately? Hello, darling." She held her hand out to Aloise, who gave a startled laugh before taking it and curtsying.

Penny smirked at Beau, then shook her head. "All right, fuck propriety, I suppose. Lady Lianna Penamour, this is Aloise..."

"Aloise Degland, my lady, and it's an honor to meet you. I'm His Majesty's guard."

Lianna brushed a kiss across the back of Aloise's hand, patted it, and then turned to Beau, eyes inscrutable. "So it *is* His Majesty, then. You look awfully lively for a dead man."

"King Beauregard, very much alive, and hoping to stay that way with your sister's help. It's nice to finally meet you. I've heard quite a bit about you."

Lianna said nothing, just stared at Penny with a look that communicated whole libraries of text Beau couldn't decipher in the least. Beau's wife laughed a little, low and uncomfortable, and said, "Yes, really. Let's go inside. There's *much* to discuss."

"Do you want me to send for baths? No offense, uh, *Your Majesties*, but you smell like the horses dragged you here." Lianna managed to make the titles sound both dryly sarcastic and completely suitable. He supposed he should've been offended, but he found Lianna's energy infectious and delightful.

The sisters exchanged another glance, and Beau realized they wanted to talk without him. Fair enough; he supposed when they'd last spoken, Penny was planning to force a confession out of him and put him on a ship. "I could use a good scour before I see my mother again. I'd hate to hear what she has to say about the smell of sneaking here from the isles through every wood and swamp."

Lianna drew up to a sudden stop. "Oh! Oh, gods. I'd completely forgotten that—Your Majesty, I'm so sorry for your loss."

"Thank you," Beau said, hoping to forestall any further commiseration. His father's death gave him a pit of guilt in his stomach, worrying that he wasn't grieving as a son should.

Lianna nodded and continued, speaking with deceptive lightness about minor things around Veritelutte, which Penny responded to equally casually. Every now and then, a word or name was emphasized in ways Beau didn't follow, but the sisters acknowledged each other's arcane insinuations with quiet *hmm*s and occasional laugher.

As Beau was led to a mosaic-tiled room where steaming water filled a deep copper bath, he caught Penny's eye and she smiled, sending warmth and calm and comfort in a wave. He smiled back and enjoyed a bath so hot it nearly peeled his skin from his bones.

He rebandaged his wounds and dressed in silence, for the first time in his life missing his staff. Uriel's quiet competence, Aloise and Capucine's cheerful chattering, and El—Beau's stomach jerked, threatening vomit.

The stand-mirror in the corner showed him a tall man, reasonably broad in the shoulders, with dark hair growing too long in his eyes and an uncharacteristically gaunt, grief-shadowed face. His beard was overgrown, his clothes wrinkled from being shoved in travel bags. Not how Beau imagined a king.

He straightened, tugging the creases out of his shirt and rubbing a hand over his scruff. He pictured a crown on his head. The image felt ridiculous.

"Excuse me," he said, sticking his head out and meeting a liveried man's eyes. "Could you bring a shaving kit, please?"

"Of course, my lord," the man said, bowing deeply. Word of who Beau was had not spread through the manor yet. "Right away."

Minutes later, Beau wielded a freshly sharpened razor, soft-bristled brush, silky-foaming soap in a polished horn mug, and a matching pair of silver scissors and comb. He lingered over the basin, taking more care than normal over grooming. He trimmed his hair so it wouldn't poke him in the eyes and fell more respectably over his brow. Stepping back from the mirror, he was pleased to see the process had dramatically improved his kingly perception.

When he donned his jacket, which had been hanging in the bath steam and lost a few of its deepest creases, he looked rather smart. Artifacts in his pockets, knife at his belt, wedding ring on his finger—all he lacked now was a crown.

He was led to the east wing, where the dowager queen had been given rooms. Beau tapped each fingertip against his thumb in turn again and again, practicing what he'd say to her. He hadn't formed a coherent script when they reached the rosewood doors and the man asked Beau how he'd like to be announced.

"Uh…" Beau cleared his throat. "King Beauregard will do."

The man's eyes widened drastically, but he was too well-mannered to do other than say, "Yes, of course, Your Majesty." He knocked, stepped in, and called the name in a clear voice.

"Beauregard?" His mother's voice was confused, disbelieving. "I think you must be—"

Beau stepped in and Acier stumbled up out of her seat, sending the chair bouncing across the floor. "Beauregard! You—you're—" Her eyes flicked to the servant. "Thank you, that will be all."

As the man hastily bowed out, she breathed, "You're alive."

Beau waited for her to look relieved, to cross to hug him, to show any sign at all she was happy to see him. Her face had gone deathly pale, her lips compressed to a thin, anxious line. At her sides, her fingers plucked idly at the lacy overlay of her gown.

"Yes," he said simply. "I'm sorry about Father."

"Yes," she said, swallowing and recovering her composure. She bent to right her chair and sit, letting the action hide her face. "A great tragedy, to lose the last of one's family."

"The last?" Beau said quietly, scanning the room for a seat and deciding he'd rather stand for this. "I still have a mother. You still have a son."

"Yes, of course," she said, looking down at the table as though chastened. "What are you doing here, Beauregard?" She looked up past him. "And where is Elias?"

Vomit threatened, and Beau swallowed repeatedly. "My guards were killed, along with many people of Leau, defending me from Lord Courdur's attempt to assassinate me on the isles."

"And you came out unscathed?"

He couldn't understand her tone of voice. "No, certainly not." His fingertips brushed against his hip, which ached. "But notably more alive than I would've been without their sacrifice. And significantly angrier than when I left."

"Angrier?" She made a small, incredulous sound. "Hard to imagine. I suppose you're making your escape over land instead of taking a ship? Risky, without guards. Or did you come to beg a few swords from the Penamours?"

"Interesting that you think I came to ask the Penamours for help and not you," Beau said. "Did you bring no men with you?"

She cleared her throat, and he could see in sharp relief on her face her decision to lie. "I had quite enough challenge getting out of the palace with my own life, let alone an army. After your father's death, things moved rather quickly."

"I imagine they did," Beau said. "What an impressive woman you are to have made it out to Veritelutte with an entire retinue and the—what was it the sentry said? 'The generals of your forces'?"

Acier took a deep breath, chin lifting, eyelids dropping like shutters over her eyes until only the faintest glimmer of her irises were visible. Caught.

Beau shook his head, a faint exhalation alluding to a laugh. "You're bracing yourself for me to ask for something. I shouldn't have to ask. You're my mother. You should've offered help." He tucked his hands behind his back. "I should've heard about Father's death from you, not from my enemies attacking me. You could've written, told me to come here. That you were here. That you were safe. *Anything*."

She said nothing, every inch cold composure. Beau wanted to shake her. "Do you give a single shit about me? Have you ever?"

"Beauregard, don't be vulgar," she said dismissively.

Beau boiled over.

"There is a woman on Leaurepit who I've called Ma my entire adult life. She has fed me, housed me, worried for me, put me to work—she encouraged me into the man I am. You don't even know her name because it never occurred to you to wonder if anyone was doing those things for your son, since you weren't and never have," Beau said, staring levelly at his mother.

"When men came to kill me, do you know what she did? She picked up kitchen knives, and she *fought* for me. She called her friends and neighbors to fight for me. To *die* for me. She risked everything she had to keep me safe and put me on the throne. My Ma.

"You and I, we've been given the gift of *everything*, every comfort and power and opportunity. Don't you think it's a fair exchange that as nobles, as royalty, we should be better than the common person? We should be kinder and stronger and braver, more honorable? More accountable. More generous." Beau found his voice hardening until his words fell out like stones. "But here's a common innkeeper, a woman with none of your power or luxuries—and she's outdone you a thousand times over."

Acier made a small sound in her throat, and though tears gathered in her eyes, they were cold, ice chips in a frozen sea. Beau stepped forward until he towered over her.

"I am your son, and I love you, no matter how ashamed I am of you, or you of me. I'll see you protected from what's coming with Lord Courdur. But I do demand of you this *one* maternal act: support me in securing my throne. It is *mine*, and Lord Courdur will not have it."

She started to stand, but Beau took another step forward and she cringed back in her seat. She shook her head, something like derision twisting her mouth. "Beauregard, this is your opportunity to run. I'll give you enough men to see you to a port, and you will leave. Granvallée will be in good hands—they need not be yours."

"You already promised the men to Courdur." Beau watched her face, saw the flinch.

"Lord Courdur is not an evil man, whatever you think. He'll be a good king, and—"

"*I am king!*" Beau shouted, quelling her. "Lord Courdur tried to kill your *only remaining son*. He is *your enemy*, or he should be! I'm not running, Mother, and I'm not giving up my throne to this usurper. I'll have my crown, and I'll have it with the help of your men."

"If you do love me, as you say—as your mother, I'm asking you not to put me in this position." The face she turned to him was unyielding, unsoftened by his words.

"Commit the men to me. All of them," Beau said coldly, "or I'll have you imprisoned."

She shifted her jaw from side to side, watching his face. "I'm a guest of Lady Lianna Penamour," she said, "and you're a wanted man. You don't have the power to have me imprisoned."

Beau grinned, a horrible, humorless thing. He leaned down to press his hands against the table, putting his face level with hers.

"Actually, Queen Acier, you will find you're now the guest of Lady Victoire Highput née Penamour. *My wife.* Her men are mine. This manor is mine, should I ask for it. And I have the power to do whatever the fuck I want with you."

He wasn't sure how to feel about the fear in her eyes. It wasn't what he'd been looking for. He wanted a mother, not another noble to strongarm into doing his bidding. But it was slightly validating, having the muscle. He turned to leave. "Think about it. I'll see you at breakfast tomorrow, and we can discuss your decision."

·ℜ·ℜ·ℜ·

Penny and Lianna looked up, conversation cutting off abruptly, when he entered the sitting room. Lianna studied him, taking in his freshly groomed face and clean clothes, and a smirk broke across her mouth. "Okay. I get it now."

Pen shot her sister a silencing look as Beau asked, "Get what?"

Lianna laughed secretively. "I'm glad you availed yourself of a bath and shears. Anything else I can provide? Dinner will be here in the next few minutes. Since Vic called for a stay on our march, I had the cooks unpack some of the better food."

"A few thousand good soldiers would really hit the spot right now," Beau said lightly, lowering himself into a seat at the round tea table. His hip and thigh howled at him, despite how gingerly he sat. When he shifted, his stitches pulled horribly.

Penny's little sister tapped her fingers against her lower lip, amusement glimmering in her dark eyes. "I'll have to see if the cooks have any prepared."

As Penny reached over to flatten his chest bandage more neatly, tugging his collar straight, Beau asked, "Have you successfully persuaded your sister that you're not possessed, mind-controlled, or otherwise under duress?"

Penny glared good-naturedly at Lianna. "We resolved that sufficiently, yes. We were just discussing how very good your position is looking currently."

Eyebrows shooting up, Beau said, "Oh?"

The door opened to admit a stream of servants bearing trays of food, goblets, and carafes. When they'd arrayed it on the table and bowed out, Lianna said, "To be honest, Beauregard—I can call you that, can't I? Seeing as you're my brother now and all? I was very firmly your adversary until about an hour ago. It may seem strange that that's a good thing, but it is."

Beau sliced ham, laying some on each of their plates silently while he waited for her to continue. Lianna smiled rather smugly as she poured herself a glass of wine. She seemed to enjoy the drama of dragging it out. "You see, when news of your father's death broke, Lord Courdur reached out immediately to the three families most loyal to him and asked for our support: the Penamours, the Abadies, and the Tivelyns. I knew Vic's theories about you, so it was an easy yes to Courdur."

Beau's face fell. Lord Abadie and Lord Tivelyn controlled the two counties within Chudeau—his father's duchy. *His* duchy, now. All the men he'd hoped to have in the capital were in those two men's hands. He realized Lianna was waiting for a response. "*Easy yes* to supplanting the rightful king? Not a great vote of confidence."

"Actually, it's a significant vote of confidence—for my sister," Lianna said. "The Abadies and Tivelyns awaited our answer. When we swung for Courdur, so did they."

"So," Beau said, meeting Lianna's eyes as her brows rose significantly, "now that Penny's married and declared for me..."

"*That* changes nothing on the surface, *yet*. We'll bring the other families around, but it will mean Vic reaching out to each of them herself."

"They'll have received my letters from the isles," Penny said, reaching over to rest her hand on Beau's. "But now that I know the lay of the land, I can be more direct. It's clear Courdur was expecting to depend heavily on Chudeau's men. At least a third of his are still at the border."

Beau nodded, staring into his wine as he swirled it. "He's expecting to have most of his own men, yours, the Abadies', the Tivelyns', and my mother's. So if you're successful—and my mother answers the way I hope she does tomorrow—we'll steal the better part of his forces out from under him."

"See?" Lianna said, grinning. "Your position is good."

"*If* you can convince the Abadies and Tivelyns. *If* my mother commits her men to me. *If* any of the Houses I wrote to show up for me. *If* I can get anyone from Verdmont here in time. *If* the Macabries don't elect to join Courdur against me and the Lamonts don't try to stop you marching your men through Estforet to the capital. Quite a lot of variables."

"What do you mean, *if* your mother commits her men to you?" Lianna asked. She ignored Penny's quiet warning murmur of *Lili*, continuing, "I assumed the only reason she handed them to Courdur in the first place was because you were supposed to be dead. And I guess because she used to be an Abadie, so she sided with them. Not worth it to die on principle when there's no winning. Now that you're alive…?"

With an uncomfortable lift of his shoulders, Beau contemplated how to explain something he didn't understand himself. "My mother had a favorite son. It wasn't me." He winced; that wasn't what he wanted Lianna to take away from the conversation. "She assumed when my father died, I'd run. She was wrong, but she had reason to believe it."

"Now that you've shown you aren't running, though?"

She hates me, Lianna. Eyes fixed on the table, he said, "As you said, not worth it to stand on principle when there's no point. If it'd just been me, she definitely wouldn't have supported me. But since I married the most powerful woman in Granvallée, I may not be a lost cause. That will be the deciding point."

Lianna sat back in her seat, brows high and mouth downturned. "Cold."

"I suppose royalty doesn't get to be sentimental," Beau said, feeling an inexplicable urge to defend his mother's choices.

His sister-in-law sparked up, voice raised. "I hope to hell you don't actually think that. Sentiment is all that's going to win you the throne, *Your Majesty*. Do you know how much easier it would be for us to just kill you? How many favors we'll have to pull in to bring the Abadies and Tivelyns to your side? How much goodwill we're burning with our own family—the Courdurs are our mother's peo-ple! You got married in the middle of nowhere: it would be nothing to throw your body in a ditch and pretend it never happened, an-nouncements were fake. We're supporting you because Vic loves you, and that's *it*, Beauregard. If you mean to be as cold as your mother in exchange, I'll kill you for a tyrant, make no mistake."

Penny hastily reached out to grip Lianna's arm, but he spoke first. "If I become a tyrant, Lianna, you have my full permission to stake me through the heart. I'm *immensely* grateful for your help. I won't forget it."

"Lili," Penny said, "there's no one I know who adheres more closely to the precepts of taking care of those who care for you. Honestly. You'll see."

Lianna's dark eyes cored him like an apple. She ignored her sister's remarks entirely. "I'll hold you to that, Your Majesty."

"At knife-point, I'm sure," he said, a grin tugging at his mouth as he nodded to the blade peeking out from her sleeve.

She nodded seriously, then speared a hunk of ham on her fork and popped it into her mouth. They ate for a while in silence, the sisters exchanging occasional glances. Beau got the distinct impres-sion that they were somehow fighting with one another, though none of the looks that passed were especially angry or intense. He poured himself a second glass of wine and vanished it down his throat too quickly for polite company.

As he polished off the last of his food, he said, "Pen, those magic books?" He tried not to beg; it wasn't very kingly. But the urge to find some way to draw Elias back to him, to remove the amulet, to fix what was broken crawled maddeningly under his skin, made it feel claustrophobic to be doing anything else.

She nodded and wiped her mouth, swallowing her last mouthful, but Lianna was faster. "I'll walk him to the library. You need a bath, Vic, and I need to chat with my new brother."

"Do not kill my husband. I'm rather fond of him," Penny said sternly, kissing her sister on the cheek.

Lianna looped her arm through his to pull him along the hall, and Beau snuck glances down at the small woman, trying to get the measure of her. "We're taking the long way," she said as they emerged into the cool gardens, now growing dark, "so you can answer the questions for me Vic wouldn't answer properly."

He laughed uncomfortably. "All right."

"What happened to your lover?" When Beau's step faltered but he said nothing, she pressed, "The pretty boy everyone was talking about? Good fighter? Macabrie wanted to buy him? What happened to him? Because the way people were talking, I assumed you didn't even *want* a wife, and here you are with my sister, theoretically besotted. I want to know what happened to the other man."

Beau stopped, stomach churning, and Lianna planted herself in front of him. She crossed her arms and stared, implacable.

He opened his mouth, but he couldn't bear to repeat the same thing he'd said to his mother, that his guards all died on the isles, to *summon* that. Bile burned at the back of his throat. "He—he's—"

Her attention was too sharp. Beau turned half away, shaking his head. "I can't talk about him, Lianna. I love your sister, I have immense respect for her, and I will take care of her. She's my wife; she's my future."

The small woman's expression softened. "That's pretty much what Vic said when I asked her. Did he die?"

Beau squeezed his eyes shut. "I don't know," he said quietly. "They're all telling me yes, but he doesn't feel dead to me. That's why I need the magic library." Something else tried to claw its way up his throat, a sob or a gag or more answer. A small hand took his arm.

"I'm really sorry," Lianna said. "The library's all yours, if it'll help you get answers. Or…closure. But Vic is the best person I know. I need to know you're not treating her like a second choice."

The king didn't trust his voice. He shook his head seriously, and Lianna squeezed his arm. "Good. Tell me what you love about her while we walk."

"Is this a test?" he asked hoarsely, trying to summon a smirk.

"Absolutely," Lianna said, smiling teasingly, though her eyes were sad. She looked so much like Penny, but her eyes were lighter than her sister's, faintly greenish, and her face was quicker to change, flicking from expression to expression.

Beau cleared his throat. "She's brilliant. Always curious. She says what needs to be said, asks good questions. She—" He breathed an almost-laugh. "She somehow managed to call me an ass and also say some of the kindest things anyone has ever said to me in the same breath. She's compassionate, she's funny, obviously she's beautiful." He shrugged. "Everything. It was always going to be her. It couldn't have been anyone but her."

Lianna looped her arm through his and laughed. "You missed a few attributes," she said, "but I'll say you passed for now. You said brilliant first, which is good—that means you know better than to ignore her advice. She could run circles around you politically."

"Don't I know it," Beau said. He squinted down at one of the flowerbeds. "You grow so many tulips here."

"Yes, they were my father's favorite, and we've kept to the tradition of growing them in the Penamour family gardens. I don't know if you know flower language, but tulips stand for—"

"—familial love. Unconditional." Beau smiled. "Penny told me. They're beautiful."

He patted Lianna's arm, enjoying the ferocious, bright energy she put off. "I'm glad she has you, Lianna, and Natalie too. A tulip kind of family is something special."

"You don't have to sound so envious, Beauregard," she said, elbowing him teasingly in the ribs as she released him. "You have a tulip family now, too. Are you as obsessed with dusty old magic stuff as Vic is? Because if so, you're going to like this library."

"I've always been fascinated by it. I wish I'd spent more time on it, but there wasn't much in the isles. A whole library just about magic must be..." Wonder lit in him.

"Ugh, you sound almost as excited as Vic. You two *are* made for each other. The library's just up here. I'll leave you to get to know all the ancient mages she obsessed over growing up. Just close the door before you have a wank over them, okay?"

Beau laughed, shoving her a step away from him. Being around her made him wish he'd grown up with a sister. He'd thought he understood what having more siblings would be like, but this was infinitely better than he'd imagined.

Later that night, a knock as he settled into the deliciously comfortable bed and watched his wife brush her hair brought a folded note. The outside had been formally addressed to King Beauregard Mylan Adelard Tristan, but it was unsealed. Inside, three simple lines in his mother's handwriting:

> *My men are yours. I will not be receiving visitors for the remainder of my time in Veritelutte, as I am in mourning. When you no longer have need of them, my men will escort me to Corinon, where I will retire.* —*Queen Acier*

"What does she say?" Penny asked as she slid into bed next to him, snuggling in against his chest. "Do I have to imprison my mother-in-law?"

Beau pulled her tighter, breathed in her hair. He tossed the note on the bedside table and blew out the lamp. "No. She said her men are mine and she never wants to see me again."

Penny's wash of concern drew a hollow sort of happiness out of him. "It's all right," he said, kissing her hair, her forehead, her lips. "I have a tulip family now."

WE DO NOT KILL MESSENGERS

Penny and Lianna didn't need him for the politics, so Beau buried himself in a frantic consumption of magical knowledge. In the back of his head, he could feel a constant tick like a clock counting down the seconds of Elias's life.

He's dead, the rational part of his mind insisted, but the rest of him didn't believe that at all.

Deep in the most beautiful library Beau had ever seen, amongst the carved wood shelves and tiny art niches and cozy chairs piled with soft, tasseled pillows, the king sat surrounded by books and manuscripts and scrolls dealing with the Maurilel.

He'd begun, on Penny's advice, in a thick book with a much-creased spine and dozens of pages marked with small scraps of paper, as if it had been referenced a thousand times, *The Families of Maurilel Magic: A Definitive Guide.*

He hadn't even known there *were* different types of Maurilel magic, but each of the strangely named families seemed to have created their own kinds of objects. Spiriters, Fallacists, Smiths, Lifebinders, Carvers—each family had pages of illustrations and names of famous mages who'd made great discoveries or inventions for their branch of magic.

In the margins, Penny had made notations in neat, tiny script of dates, alternate names, and lists of things that must be artifacts attributed to each family.

It was the Tradelords who made Revenant Chains, and according to the book, they were unequivocally evil artifacts.

> *The Tradelords, sometimes called simply Traders—or Traitors, depending on who you asked—wielded the most controversial magics of the Maurilel age. Scholars who staunchly maintain that magic is inherently neither good nor evil, but dependent on the will of the mage, nonetheless agree that most artifacts created by the Tradelords can serve no purpose but a malevolent one.*

> *While the other families of magic paid the cost for the creation of spells and objects in their own blood, the Tradelords paid in the blood of others—and in some cases, such as with their infamous Revenant Chains, their unholy bargains bartered prisoners' souls.*

An image of Elias, pulsing with dark magic and grinning like a stranger as something laughed with his vocal cords sent a shudder through Beau. He paged through more books until he found an illustration of a jade-green necklace around a man's throat, not carved in the same shape as the one Elias had put on, but pulsing the same dark energy from slashes like wounds in the man's flesh.

Beneath the image, in small text: *Prisoners, once enslaved, remained animated long enough to complete their business in less than a quarter of instances.*

"Enslaved?" he muttered. The pages that followed were one horror after another.

> *...preferable to select physically strong candidates, as the individual's physical health equates to the durability of his revenant form. However, a strong will may substitute.*

> *...consider carefully the complexity of business required of the revenant; higher intelligence candidates may be able to accom-*

*plish more challenging tasks, but will also be more capable of
exploiting loopholes in the master's commands.*

*...the difference between 'alive' and 'animated' is distinct. Can-
didates perish immediately upon donning the Chain, but may be
animated for up to a month afterward. The bargain is complete
when the revenant is no longer animated, which will occur a) at
completion of business, b) when the revenant is too damaged to
sustain form, or c) when the candidate's will is expended.*

Beau was running his finger over that one line—*candidates
perish immediately upon donning the Chain*—and choking down the
urge to cry when Penny found him.

"Oh, Beau," she said, sinking down next to him. She had a
riding dress on and gloves shoved in her waistband, ready to travel.
"He knew what he was doing. He did it to protect you."

Beau tipped his head up and took her hand. *She* was leaving to
protect him, too, traveling into Chudeau to meet with families who
could just as easily have her imprisoned or killed as help. He couldn't
lose any more people he loved. "I should go with you," he said. "If
they *don't* side with me, you'll be—it's not safe. Don't go alone."

"They'll try to kill you on sight. Your presence would be a
needless complication," Penny said with finality, kissing his nose. "I
have to talk them around. I'll return with an army, Beau."

Beau captured one of her hands, cupped it in both of his, and
pressed it to his lips, then his forehead. "Please be careful. *Please.* I
need you more than I need an army."

"I beg to differ," she said with a laugh.

"I'm very serious."

She sighed, fond exasperation spiking through the ring. Sitting on his lap, she leaned against him. "I can see that. I *will* come
back, and with an army. Stop underestimating me. I've been playing
politics with these people since I could speak full sentences."

And Elias was the best fighter who ever lived, but look at him.

Still, he had to let her go. He didn't watch her leave; he was afraid he'd be memorizing his last look at her.

Lianna came into the library an hour or two later and found him still touching the same line in the same book, staring off into space. She sat beside him. "So. Found a lot of good news, have you?" she asked lightly. She pulled a handkerchief out of a pocket and scrubbed it roughly over his face, which was how Beau found out he'd been crying.

"The Chain took his soul," Beau said. "Enslaved it."

"*Fucking Twelve*. Can you reverse that? Cut him loose?"

Beau turned to stare at the shelves. "Maybe? If I could find another artifact that deals in souls. Tradelords, Spiriters, and Life-binders all did things with—" He waved his hands nebulously in front of him. "—spirit sort of energy. Penny doesn't have much on the Tradelords because their shit was fucking evil, but maybe..."

Despair overtook him. Even if he found a description of the perfect artifact, something specifically designed to reverse the process of making a revenant, what did it fucking matter? He didn't *have* it. Every artifact he had was sitting in his room right now, useless in this endeavor.

"All right. You stick with the scary evil ones and I'll start looking at Spiriters, hmm?" Lianna said, hopping up to run her fingers along the spines of the books as she perused titles.

"You're going to help me? I thought you found the Maurilel unbearably boring?"

Lianna rolled her eyes and yanked out two books, stacking them on a table. "Ah, yes, good reminder. Being entertained for the evening is *drastically* more important than saving the soul of the man my new brother's been in love with for most of a decade. Phew, close one. I was almost bored!"

Beau let her draw a chuckle out of him and began to read again in earnest.

They'd found descriptions of at least a half-dozen artifacts that would almost certainly help, and Beau was no closer to any solution he could bring to bear. Those that dealt in souls would do nothing for his wounded body, and those that healed the body didn't touch the soul. And, of course, he'd never even heard of any of the artifacts mentioned.

Abruptly, he realized they were working backward. "I'm such an idiot," he said aloud, standing and crossing for the library door.

"I'm sure you're right," Lianna teased, "but why?"

"Need to research what I *have*, not what I need."

He darted down the hall to Penny's room, shooed a servant out, and pulled the artifacts out of their drawer, laying them out on the bed. He turned the Perception Stone in his hand as he looked over the others, enjoying its strange tug of magic. The stone feather, just as sharp and finely crafted and utterly useless as it always had been. The butterfly pin—he didn't need to change his appearance. And the Orb of Tethering.

Beau tossed down the stone and picked up the small glass ball, running his thumb over the gold wire. What had the vault card said—extends life? Penny had mentioned something about conditions when she'd pulled it out of Elias's pocket in the forest. Extends life. Maybe…

He tapped it against his mouth and felt it buzz faintly on his lips. It smelled like magic. Not the awful kind of the Revenant Chain, but something like a rainstorm, like the ocean, like snow falling off a mountain in sheets—monumental and uncontrollable.

Leaving the rest of the artifacts, he marched back to the library. The Orb stayed cool in his hand however long he held it, absorbing no body heat. While he looked over the books, he found himself setting it against his lips or rolling it between his palms. Something about its magic was soothing.

Crouched or sprawled on the floor, he reviewed every book that seemed likely to hold information about the Orb of Tethering. He found dozens of different orbs described, and a handful of tethers. Every time he started to doze off, the glass in his hand sent a cool pulse through his fingers, like a nudge. Like it wanted him to understand.

"I'm trying," he muttered to it, picking up another book.

He dug through everything from the spirit-magic families. He tossed book after book about war magic aside. He flicked impatiently through magic of illusions, of transportation, of domesticity. Finally, he trudged to the end of the shelves, to the section devoted to the Swains. The Swains were, in Beau's opinion, useless. The 'romance mages,' *Families of Maurilel Magic* had called them—magic of beauty and love. Nice concepts, but not what he needed now.

He was so certain they'd be useless to him, he was utterly stunned to recognize some of their magic immediately. On the first page he opened in the first Swain book he tried was a drawing of two familiar rings, though the illustration was labeled *Rings of the Shared Heart*, not Rings of the Throne. The text described them exactly, down even to the different ways people experienced emotions, from physical sensations to visual color distortions to musical notes.

"Strong Swains were known to be able to manipulate emotions through the ring?" Beau read aloud. Baffling. He could do that, and he wasn't a mage at all.

He took hold of the pages and flipped them with his thumb, letting his eyes unfocus as they rapidly thrummed by.

Wait—

He stopped, creasing a page as he slapped his palm down on the spread. Too far; he flipped back frantically.

There! There it was, the Orb of Tethering, illustrated in precise detail down to the gold leaf laid to make the dainty wires glimmer like the real thing. What was it doing in a book on the *Swains?*

> *The Orb of Tethering is one of the most beautiful celebrations of commitment created by the Maurilel. Devilishly complicated to create, they're even more challenging to use, as the magic demands perfect and complete dedication on the part of each end of the tether. History is littered with tragic tales like Arkan and Visolde,*

*where orbs are shattered uselessly because one party is unwilling
to meet the other's sacrifice.*

*Honest communication is key to a successful tether. When each
partner understands what the other offers, they can find shared
ground and hold these expectations in mind while shattering the
orb. Only equivalent offerings can form a successful tether.*

Beau read on, blinking the blurriness of exhaustion out of his
eyes and rereading as much as he needed.

As he understood it, the orb had no guaranteed effects at all.
If—and it was a big *if*—the users were able to tether their souls, the
effect depended on the tether's strength. Some people reported small
things, like feeling calmer, breathing more easily, sleeping better

Others found, once tethered, that they didn't get sick, and injuries healed more quickly. A few legends spoke of people who lived
two or three lifetimes with their loved one, health extended far past
the norm by the tether.

No one spoke of bringing anyone back from the dead with it.
And while it certainly dealt in souls, none of the books mentioned
anything about stealing a soul back with it.

Beau went back for the Tradelord books and searched for
information on where Elias's soul would be. He felt—though he
wasn't sure why, as it wasn't described quite that way—that the Revenant Chain must be another sort of tether, binding the soul of the
one who wore it both to their failing body and to some other plane,
where it would go when the bargain was complete.

If Beau's tether were stronger...

A sudden sharp, sour-yogurt taste of shock resonated through
his head. He froze as it began to grow more bitter, the acidic and
herbal flavors of fear.

"No, no," he muttered. Through the ring, he sent his concern,
his worry for Penny. Two flavors assaulted him. The first seemed
involuntary: a spikier, more astringent panic.

The second was an intentional push of honey and lemon, the taste of her calm.

"What's wrong?" Lianna set her fingers on Beau's arm.

Beau tried to sort through Penny's pool without changing anything, wanting to understand the layers of her fear. With his focus so internal, it was hard to speak. His words came out halting and quiet. "Something is wrong. Penny was surprised, and not in a good way. She's...she's afraid. Or anxious. She's not terrified. She's not...I don't think she's in danger. She's telling me to be calm."

"You don't *think* she's in danger?" Lianna repeated. "I'm not crazy about that level of certainty."

"Neither am I, I assure you." His mind raced. Penny would be in the capital by now, and he'd barely slept since she left. If she *was* in danger, he'd arrive days late and too exhausted to stand. He could feel every healing wound pulse in time with his heartbeat.

"All right, what are we doing?" Lianna's expression was fierce.

Beau pushed his questioning, his worry, harder through the ring. Penny's response slammed into him: calm, determination, a flicker of anger, protectiveness, certainty. The latter was so strong, he coughed on the taste of stone dust.

He didn't look at Lianna as he said, "She doesn't want help. She's certain she can handle whatever it is."

He heard the snick of a fastener, the faint whisper of metal on leather; Lianna messed idly with the knives she kept on her forearms. The grim set of her mouth and the faraway look in her eyes suggested the same mental calculations he'd been running about the likelihood of being any help to Penny. "And yet..."

Beau nodded. "Yeah. We're going to the capital."

·༄.༄.༄·

Riding at the head of an army did not make Beau feel as powerful as he'd thought it might. For one, it moved *painfully* slowly.

And though it should've made him feel safer to be surrounded by swordsmen, he couldn't stop thinking about how easy it would be for any one of them to be a Watcher, to slip into his tent at night and knife him in the neck.

They gathered gossip as they rolled out of Veritelutte and into Estforet: Lord Courdur, it seemed, had been reunited with the poor Lady Penamour, Duchess of Veritelutte, and she was now enjoying his protective hospitality.

Weeks ago, they heard, the late Prince Beauregard had kidnapped the duchess and tried to solidify his claim to the throne by faking a marriage to her. She'd foreseen this treachery and solicited Lord Courdur's generous aid in ending a threat to her life and the security of the throne. Humbly and with great regret, Lord Courdur had accepted the burden of the throne in the prince's stead.

More than once, Beau had to recite the mantra, *We do not kill messengers*, in his head to still his hands. Lianna was no help; her temper was worse than his, and she despised lies almost as much as he did. He kept her from violence, but she'd spat on a tavern keeper who said, "Shame King Alphonse is already married. Would've been better if he married Penamour and took Veritelutte under his wing. Ain't right, a woman holding all that land."

Long, empty hours gave Beau too much time to ruminate on Elias, on Penny, on the isle folk, on Courdur, on the lurking danger of an assassin's knife and the looming war with Courdur.

"I don't want war," Beau admitted to Lianna as they rode. "The only reason I agreed to be my father's heir originally was to prevent this, and here it is. I won't give Courdur the throne to avoid a fight, but I hate that our people will die for a power struggle."

"Thought you wanted retribution for the isles? Didn't you tell them you were going to make 'such an example no one would ever try to piss in your pot again' or some such?"

Beau shot Lili a wry look. "I want to make an example of *Courdur*. Not hundreds or thousands of our people. We'll need them when the Destiny Riders decide to cross our borders."

"Uncle Alphonse won't back down without a fight." Lili popped a boiled peanut in her mouth from the small sack in her lap. "His move against you in the isles failed—now he's not fighting for just the crown; he's fighting for his life. He knows you'll strike back. He'll eliminate anyone and anything necessary to protect himself."

Beau swallowed. "Penny?"

"Vic's smart, and the people she was going to meet *are* friends. I don't know if he'll quite dare trying to kill her." Lili grimaced. "Unless she's pregnant. He'll have to do something then. Can't have your spawn running around."

Beau hadn't considered that. The blood drained from his face.

"Oof, he forgot how babies are made," Lili muttered. "See, Beauregard, when a prince and a duchess love each other very much—"

"You are *exhausting*, Lili," Beau said, rolling his eyes, but he was grateful anyway; her teasing managed to keep him from dropping into the deepest terror and despair. As he did every few minutes, Beau delved the pool of emotions and reassured himself that Penny was still connected to him, still calm, still resolute. And as she always did back, Penny sent him warmth and reassurance and love.

"Thank you," Lili said, grinning brightly. "Now *where* is your guard? I haven't flirted myself hoarse yet today."

"Leave Aloise alone," Beau warned. "She has a job to do."

"Quit hiring such gorgeous guards and you'll have to fight fewer nobles for them," she teased, sticking out her tongue. When Beau's face fell, her shoulders dropped. "Oh, fuck, I sent you down the Elias hole. I'm *sorry!* Think about something else. Hey, what kind of tree is that? The acorns say oak, but I'll be damned if those aren't the maple-est leaves I've ever seen."

His fingers trailed to his pocket, where the Orb of Tethering sat wrapped in a handkerchief. Though he'd spent every night of the ride contemplating how to use it for what he needed, he still had no real *plan*. And the little voice in his head that always doubted him loudly kept saying, *Are you sure you even have magic? Fat lot of good it*

*will do you to smash that thing and waste it without any way to make it
do what you need.*

"Would you help me with an experiment tonight when we
make camp?" Beau asked abruptly, and Lili raised an eyebrow.

"Ew. Sorry, even if you weren't my brother, I've tried men. Not
for me," she teased.

"*Ha* ha," Beau said. "I'm serious. I need to test magic, and I'm
going to do something stupid. I'd like someone around who can at
least call for help, if it goes wrong."

"That sounds *way* less boring than reading about it. I'm in."

Hours later, after camp setup and dinner and half a bottle of
wine for courage, Beau stood in his tent with a knife in his hand, his
left sleeve rolled up above his elbow, and his sister-in-law sitting on
his cot, watching him doubtfully. "You're going to…cut yourself?"

"Maurilel magic is in the blood," Beau muttered, staring down
at his arm. Before he could think too much about it, he swiped the
knife along one of his old scars, reopening a thin red line. Beau
made no sound; the pain was so familiar and so strange.

He tilted his arm so blood would run down into his palm and
gathered it there messily. What would a mage do with this blood?
Probably not hold it in their hand like a child with a skinned palm.
Probably have some sort of dedicated ritual bowl with a matching
jeweled dagger. He felt a giggle rise up in him and suppressed it.

"Should I be, uh, seeing anything?" Lili asked.

"Hold on." When he felt there was enough blood in his palm,
Beau lifted his hand out in front of him. Feeling silly, he closed his
eyes. "Elias," he whispered, but he *willed* the word out as hard as he
ever had. "I need you. I need you to come to me."

He squinted one eye open. Nothing had changed with his
blood-streaked arm. How did the blood come into it? Did he need
to do something with it? Was this all stupid because he actually didn't have magic at all? Perhaps the Rings of the Throne were
simply more attuned to him than most people because they'd been

passed down in his family for so long. Perhaps the gold light they thought they saw in his eyes was just reflected light on hazel irises.

Elias? he thought harder. A drop of blood ran ticklishly down the side of his forearm toward his elbow. Fuck, he felt like a fool now. He wished he hadn't done this in front of Lili. She'd roast him mercilessly for this.

"That wasn't a command," Lili said. "Just a statement of fact. Maybe you need to *command* him to come back."

Worth a try. He didn't close his eyes again. He couldn't take another second feeling that silly.

As he spoke, he shouted in his mind, shoving the command out toward wherever he imagined Elias was just as he pushed his emotions through the ring. "Elias! Come to me."

The blood in his hand *boiled*.

Beau yelped, trying to shake it out, but a cold, green flame ate through the pool of blood in his palm and started to climb the drip streaks up his forearm like a fuse. He grabbed at it with his other hand, but the flames freeze-burned through his fingers, climbing irrepressibly to the cut.

And then they burrowed into his arm.

"Fuck! *Fuck!*" Beau shouted, the ice-spike of green fire driving into his veins.

As quickly as it began, the flames extinguished, leaving Beau panting and grabbing at his arm. His skin was spotlessly clean of blood, and though he still bore a cut, it didn't bleed. It faintly glowed green, as Elias's wounds had.

The verdant energy crawled visibly but painlessly back down the inside of his arm toward his hand, tracing out his veins. "Oh no," he breathed. "Oh *fuck*, what is it—?"

Lili appeared before him, reaching out to grab his arm. He jerked it away and stumbled back a step. "Don't touch it," he said urgently. "This isn't my magic. This is...Tradelord magic, I guess? It feels bad, like the Chain did."

"Is it hurting you? What's it doing to you?"

He ignored the question, staring with horror at the corroded-copper color of every vein in his forearm and left hand. Just above the cut, where the green had tried to spread, his skin was *hot*, faintly glowing gold.

"Is that your magic?" Lili pointed to the aureate flare that cuffed his forearm, seemingly holding the green fire at bay.

"I don't know," Beau said. "I don't know. I didn't expect…I don't know what the fuck is going on. I don't know if this means I actually do have magic, or if it's just the Chain responding to me trying to fuck with the commands I've given it, or…"

She brushed her fingers tentatively over the gold glow. "It's burning hot. Does that hurt?"

"No." He turned his arm to see every angle. "None of it hurts now. It's just…unsettling."

When it seemed his arm and whatever strange magic had infested it had reached equilibrium, Lili laughed. "*Gods*, Beau, when you say you're going to try something stupid, you *really* go for it, don't you? Vic'd be slicing you to ribbons right now for trying that."

"Yeah," Beau said, chuckling slightly, but his chest was filling with a buoyant, giddy sort of hope. "But if I can make magic do whatever the hell it just did by instinct and happenstance, I can definitely make an artifact work a little harder than it's expecting to. This proves I can do it. And as soon as Elias gets to me, I'm going to. He and I can get Penny and the throne back."

22

A LEASH, A CROWN, AND SIGNET RINGS

The capital was so deeply surrounded by soldiers, it looked to be under siege. Beau tapped his fingers on the saddle horn, impatient as Lianna argued with Courdur's representative.

"Come on," he muttered, "all I want is to see my wife." This was, apparently, a great deal to ask for, if the representative's shocked face was anything to go off of.

The green glow of his veins had steadily drained down toward his fingers, ticking like a countdown for the entire march. All that was left was an awful verdant cast to his fingertips. He thought it meant Elias was close, which made his impatience even worse.

When Lianna rode back, storm clouds in her face, Beau braced himself for the news.

"He said you're welcome to come to the palace, where Vic will await you with all the other gathered nobles in the throne room," she said. "I suspect he thinks you've come to surrender, now that you've seen his forces."

Beau nodded. Their own force was barely a quarter of what Courdur held the city with—*if* Courdur commanded them. With no way to communicate with Penny beyond bursts of emotions, Beau couldn't ask her how the conversations with the other nobles had gone. He didn't know if he could expect a single one of Courdur's men to turn.

Beau's fingertips tingled with the soul-chilling magic. Tugging off his riding glove, he eyed them: barely even a hint of green to them, and the space between his first and second knuckles glowed brilliantly gold. He pulled his glove back on and clicked his tongue at Tempest, riding not toward the city, but past his men toward the treeline, scanning the space between trunks for movement. A breeze kicked up, cooling the morning and tossing the branches with gentle shushes. The birds were strangely silent; in fact, he could hear nothing of nature over the clang and chatter of the soldiers.

There—

Beau reined up hard, making Tempest grunt.

What emerged from between the trees was not Elias. Half-staggering, half-floating, a noxious black-green shadow in the barest shape of a man moved steadily toward Beau, two piercing green dots for eyes fixed on him. Undergrowth curled away from it, and where it touched the trees, sizzling pale patches of ash were left.

As it drew closer, Beau could see the pieces and parts of real flesh, barely bound together by a bilious torrent of magic. Twenty feet away, it filled the air with such horrific, nauseating pressure that he had to fight Tempest to keep her from fleeing. She screamed and kicked anyway, all but bucking him off in her terror.

Beau felt the last of the green magic trickle away. In a thousand voices, the creature opened its mouth and spoke. "You called."

"Elias?"

"You are not yet king."

The magic in the air was ravenous. It grasped at Beau, at Tempest, the trees beyond. The sky grew darker.

"No, Courdur is sitting on my throne." Beau pointed toward the palace, and the revenant's eyes followed his finger. "We're here to take it from him. Will you…help me?" He had to choke the words out. He didn't want this thing's help. He wanted *Elias.*

"It is my business. There is little time. This body is broken beyond the limits of magic."

Beau hesitated, then slid off Tempest's back and took a step toward the revenant. Tempest yanked her reins out of his hands and backed away, squealing and blowing, eyes rolling. She was too well-trained to bolt, but for every step Beau went closer to the shadow creature, she took several away.

"I can help you with that," he said, holding a calming hand out. "I have a different kind of magic. Something to help you help me. Help you finish your business."

"This body is broken beyond the limits of magic," it repeated.

Beau shook his head, edging closer. The Tradelord magic fog crushed his chest, brought bile up his throat, made his eyes burn. "No, it isn't. I can fix it. Let me…" He reached into the densest part of the deep green cloud, his arm lighting up with stinging cold, buzzing like a hornet. His fingers traced the edge of the amulet.

The revenant slammed its fist into the center of his chest, knocking him back and off his feet. Beau gasped and rolled, clutching at his breastbone. It felt burned, broken—but his skin was whole and unmarked.

"Please," he choked out, "just let me—"

"The bargain is almost complete. It is time." The revenant walked in hideous, staggering, too-fast movements past Beau.

Standing, the king dropped his voice to command the creature. "Stop." It came out too hoarse; it was so hard to breathe. He tried again. "Elias, stop. Let me fix you."

The words shuddered through the creature, bursts of green and blood-red energy sparking in it. It turned and looked over its shoulder at Beau, and one hazel eye showed through the darkness. Its mouth worked, a shriek pouring out. And then Elias' voice, distorted and strained, said, "Let's go get your crown, Highness."

The revenant staggered on toward the palace, its slumping, amorphous form growing in size with each step. Gasps and screams rose from the soldiers, who broke formation to scurry out of the revenant's path.

It ignored the swordsmen, walking through the clear corridor its malevolent presence carved for it. Beau followed as fast as his hip, still twinging from the half-healed slices, would carry him. He caught Tempest's reins and led her behind him, ignoring the way she tossed her head and shied to be free. Soldiers who had unsheathed blades or lifted crossbows hesitated as the creature neared, then simply broke and ran.

The revenant reached the front doors, raised its hands, and smashed through them with a screech of magic that sent a shock-wave back through the fighters. Guards poured out, ready for an attack but not ready for the thing that stood before them, billowing choking clouds of dark magic. They fell in pieces, most too quickly even for screams.

Chaos roiled behind, Beau, too, but he kept his eyes fixed on the revenant. He *had* to command it. If it carved its way through the palace, through the throne room, it might kill Penny. It would certainly wipe out most of the peerage. *I brought him here. I have to control him.*

But the revenant moved fast, faster than the king could travel. Gut churning, Beau darted into the hallway, following the trail of bodies. Distantly, he heard screaming as more guards died, and the pulsing infrasound of the magic driving Elias forward. Slipping in puddles of viscera, the king sprinted toward the throne room.

The creature's repulsion of his attempt to heal Elias had torn open the wound in his shoulder. It bled heavily, and his fingers felt weak, less responsive than before. To the blood soaking into his shirt, he whispered, "Wait for me, Elias. *Wait.*"

This flash of magic, more expected and less dramatic, was nonetheless excruciating as it sizzled, cold, across his chest and stabbed ice into the cut in his shoulder. He ran faster, throwing himself against the double doors of the throne room and flinging them open. Beau fought to recover his footing.

He couldn't stumble in like he was dragged; in a room full of nobles, he needed to be visibly in control of the magic he'd brought in. He needed to be kingly.

Gold magic burned through the tear in his sleeve at the shoulder, brighter and hotter with each effort to walk slowly, steadily. He managed a brisk but regal entrance, barely taking in the crowded room before his eyes went to Elias.

Nobles were crammed against the walls, lords holding swords toward the massive, hulking creature in the middle while the ladies crouched behind them or held jeweled knives in white-knuckled fists. Archers in the towering window niches above fired a constant rain of arrows on the revenant, which writhed and screamed but took no action, held about the neck as it was by a leash that Beau could see, now, originated from him.

The screams, to Beau's horror, were in Elias's voice.

Where is Penny? There—she was using the chaos to edge around the room, making her way toward Beau. As Beau found her, an arrow meant for the revenant ricocheted in her direction, and she narrowly dodged. "Elias, take out the archers. *Only* the archers."

A cloud of death erupted up from the mosaic tiles of the throne room, spinning and tearing. Its path through the soldiers summoned a dark rainstorm, blood spattering down on the nobles below, who shrieked and cowered. Then Elias was stalking back toward Beau, dead archers dangling from windows in pieces and parts.

"I deeply regret what you've brought our kingdom to, Lord Courdur," Beau shouted, spotting the man crouching behind a small knot of guards at the far end of the room. He wore Beau's father's crown—*his* crown. "You've been given everything, more than any noble in this room, and still you send men to die to scrape and claw more power for yourself. You foul, disgraceful *toad* of a man, pissing on my father's grave and telling every peer of the realm it's rain." Beau turned his attention to the nobles, who were deathly still.

"Courdur lied to you. The rightful king lives, and Victoire Penamour chose me. My wife. My queen." Penny slid in next to him, threading her fingers through his and staring the rest of the peerage down alongside him. "I would've preferred to put on my crown as my father intended, with no blood spilled, but make no mistake—by right of my blood and the spilling of my foes', I'll hold what's mine. I protect Granvallée from its enemies, inside and out."

Still, no one moved. They watched him and they watched the revenant and they trembled with horror and anticipation. Courdur did not answer; he licked his lips nervously, eyes darting around the room, weighing reactions.

Beau's eyes did not dart, but the same nervousness filled him. What more could he do? Did he need to unleash Elias to bring these people around?

Penny nudged him through the ring, and Beau realized she hadn't been holding his hand—she'd been handing him several small, heavy metal *somethings*. Beau cupped them in his fingers as he pulled away. Signet rings.

Beau lifted the first, which bore an eagle in flight over a mountain peak, the symbol of the Abadies, then held it out for the room to see. "The Abadies—" He began, and Lord Abadie swallowed hard before raising his voice.

"We stand with the rightful king," he said.

The second ring, with its sunburst and three stars, prompted Lord Tivelyn to say, "The Tivelyns stand with the rightful king."

The lion head of the Robens drew a proud smile from Lady Roben: "The Robens stand with the rightful king."

A pair of ravens facing each other for Lord Blanchet, Lady Roben's fiancé. "The Blanchets stand with the rightful king."

Lord Gandinne, with his pretty dimple and a ferocious look at the room, stepped forward with no prompting from a signet and said, "The Gandinnes stand with the rightful king. He stood with Durebord when Lord Courdur would've starved us out."

"Poulinpont stands with the rightful king," Lady Ovanne said, nodding to Beau, and Beau thanked every star in the heavens he'd made his father rehear her proposal in court after digging for the funding amidst the mess Char had made.

"And of course," Penny said, lifting her own signet ring and placing it in Beau's palm. "I stand with the rightful king."

Elias shuddered, and despite the smoking leash that tied him to Beau, he began to advance on Courdur. Beau stepped with him a half-second later as if advancing had been his intent, and the crowd parted before them.

"I know you believed those Houses sworn to you. But they lied. Those forces outside are *mine*, not yours," Beau said, pouring rage into it, and something pulsed from him, a wave of force that passed through the nobles and rattled Courdur's teeth. "Did you truly think to stand against the royal line of Granvallée, Courdur? Do you have any idea the magic at my disposal?"

Courdur gritted his teeth, fear and fury battling for control of his limbs. But to Beau's surprise, it was Lord Macabrie who stepped into Elias's path. He stared at Beau for a moment, ignoring the revenant with a truly heroic show of control.

Then he bent his head, his body, his knee—he knelt. "The Macabries stand with the rightful king." When his eyes flicked back up to Beau's as he stood, the man's face said he expected Beau to remember that he'd spoken without being approached, without being asked. "My family and I will leave you to dispense your justice, if we may?" It was barely a request.

Beau nodded, glad to have people leave this charnel pit.

The Macabries fled, and as if a dam had broken, other nobles knelt, muttering their family names and their loyalty to him. They evaporated, slowly at first, then faster, until most were simply running from the room.

Elias continued his menacing march toward the crowned usurper, moving as if slogging through waist-deep water. Magic-shrouded pieces sloughed off onto the floor as the revenant continued forward, and Beau realized with a horrific jolt that Elias was coming apart at the seams, that he might not even make it to the end of the hall. The tug-of-war between his purpose and Beau's commands was too much for his will.

"If you wish to swear to me," Beau called loudly, "return to the throne room tomorrow. For now, I want the usurper alone with the weight of my displeasure."

The remaining nobles bolted, trailed by guards. No one wanted to be in the same room as the visibly unraveling magic creature boiling its way toward Courdur.

Lord Courdur's face paled from the violet of fury to merely red, and then to pink. By the time his heels hit the wall behind him and his head thunked into it a half-second later, he'd gone waxen-grey. "Beauregard," he said, licking his lips, "I was made to understand you had no interest in the throne. Had I realized—"

"What did you call me?" Beau tilted his head to the side, genuinely stunned that the man could watch his roomful of supporters go up in smoke, face down a Maurilel revenant, and still speak to Beau as if he were a child interrupting the adults' conversation. He snatched the crown off Courdur's head. "*Try again.*"

Falteringly, as if it cost him dearly, Lord Courdur said, "Your...Majesty. Forgive me."

Beau looked into the man's terrified, unrepentant eyes. Maybe the Tradelords' magic had burned away his compassion. Maybe he'd simply found his own well of hate, with the memory of Maisie's empty eyes and Nicky's body and the rest of Leau's dead fresh in his mind. Whatever it was, he could summon no mercy for this man.

"No, I don't think I will. Elias?"

The revenant did not *kill* Lord Courdur. It shredded him.

Beau stepped hastily back out of the spray of gore, stomach churning and new fear lighting up his head. This was it—the deal was done. The enemies were dead and the throne lay clear before him. If he didn't act now, Elias's soul was gone forever.

Dropping the crown, Beau pulled the Orb of Tethering from his pocket. With his other hand, he reached blindly into the whirlwind of collapsing magic. His fingers found the cold, awful necklace. It scorched his flesh away, drove slivers of ice under his nails, carved chill into his bones, but he held on.

Howling with the effort, he peeled the amulet away from what was left of Elias's chest. It sucked at the flesh, pulling an all-too-human cry from what had been Elias's mouth. Where it had lain, Beau slammed the Orb against El's breastbone.

It shattered.

From somewhere deep in his chest, Beau was wrenched out of his body and into hell.

HELL

He stood in a room chiseled entirely out of the green stone from which the Revenant Chain had been carved, air so cold it ached to breathe. From his chest, a thin, gold line trailed off toward a floating form Beau didn't have time to identify.

Another figure, half-again as tall as Beau and dripping unholy magic, stepped in the way.

"You are very far out of your depth, little heart-mage," it said.

Beau took a step back, fighting to get his bearings. This… creature…was humanoid, but its strange, otherworldly form defied any categorization his mind tried to fit it with. Terrible, dangerous, fiendish, and beautiful in an awful, unbearable way. The voice was the same, flaying and chilling him as its magic did, but simultaneously drawing him in.

He had no idea how long he had stared, silent. The creature gave no sign of impatience. "I'm—" His voice broke, and he swallowed hard. "I'm not a mage."

Its smile made him ache. "Oh," it breathed, "I *do* love a liar, and they are so rare among your kind. But you need work no harder to intrigue me, heart-mage. Such sweet, sweet offerings. Put the taste of you in my mouth, and then follow an offering straight into my home? You have my fullest attention." It advanced on him as it spoke, delivering the last few words as a whisper that curled along his neck. Beau shuddered, frozen to the spot, afraid to breathe.

Though he had no idea what this entity was, he knew in his bones that he did not want its fullest attention.

"I didn't come here for you. I came for Elias."

Its eyes flared, and it turned slightly so it and Beau both could look at Elias's form, floating slumped in the air behind it. Every wound Beau had seen on the revenant was present on him; his body had been cut and pierced so many times he was simply a mess of red in places. A pool of blood and entrails filled the floor beneath him. Aside from Courdur, Beau had never seen a more viscerally destroyed corpse.

"The offering?" The creature chuckled, a dark sound that vibrated through Beau's chest. "You would attempt to retrieve him? Do you mean to tell me he spoke truth when he said he put the Chain on himself? He tried to tell me, but he is such a beautiful liar, I could not give it credence. I was too cruel in my disbelief."

It stroked its hand tenderly across one of Elias's cheeks as if in apology. Elias twitched and groaned. His eyes moved beneath the lids fitfully.

Beau staggered toward him. "You did this to him?" A sob caught in his throat: relief that Elias was alive and horror that he'd been mutilated so completely and was *still alive.*

The creature cast a sharp, sidelong glance at Beau. Its clawed hands moved continually over Elias, and where it touched, flesh stitched itself together, reassembling into slopes of muscle and skin Beau remembered. "*You* did this to him, heart-mage. Some of the heaviest business I have seen a revenant bear."

It studied Beau for a moment, then narrowed its eyes. "The necromage slavers built the deal to ensure their prisoners would feel in their soul whatever torment their bodies endured. Once the deal is complete, I prefer to give them their relief."

It ran the tip of a claw lightly along the gold thread between Beau and Elias, and Beau shivered as he felt it distorting the tether's magic. "I do not expect a heart-mage to understand necromage bargains," it said, "but I must wonder what has happened on your plane to produce a heart-mage who does not know well enough to leave slavers' magic alone. You offered your own blood in a necromage's trade. How is it you do not know better?"

Everything in Beau's mind was telling him not to trust this creature, even after the mercy it had shown Elias's broken soul. But he found his mouth opening regardless. "There are no mages anymore. Only the objects they left behind. We study them to try to understand how to use them, but books can only tell us so much."

The creature bent toward him, bringing its face close to his and sucking air in as if inhaling his words. It closed its eyes, mouth working like it was tasting, savoring. "So honest. So earnest. Like your magic." It leaned close and whispered, "May I have your soul? I have never consumed a heart-mage soul. It smells *delicious*."

"No," Beau said, stepping back. "I'm going back to my plane, to my body, and I'm taking Elias's soul with me."

"It need not be now. I am happy to pluck your soul at the end of your mortal life. His as well. You could spend eternity together, in a way. Poetic."

When Beau only shook his head in fervent denial, it smiled again, and its unholy allure drew a gasp out of him. Its fingers found the faint gold thread again. "I could tear this so easily," it breathed, "and the one that ties you to your plane as well. Keep you here just as you are. You are so, so far out of your depth. Do you know what is required to make fast a soul tether?"

Beau nodded, trying to look more certain than he felt. His knees shook. "He has to agree to my terms. And it has to be strong enough to repair his body as well."

"Indeed," it said. It studied him, eyes cycling through colors he'd never seen, colors he hadn't known existed. There was so much he'd never known existed.

He stared helplessly back at the entity, trapped in numb awe. "I have made a decision, heart-mage."

It tugged on the gold line, pulling Beau closer hand over hand with no visible effort. When he stood less than a foot from it, it bent to put its eyes level with his. He could feel its breath, cold and searingly painful against his face. "I will not tear your tethers and imprison you here. I will allow you to touch him and attempt to complete it—on two conditions."

Beau couldn't move. The constant, inexorable pressure on the gold line where it was rooted in his chest was on the edge of tearing it, an awful, sickening almost-pain. "What conditions?"

"First: if the tether fails either in binding your souls or in repairing his body, you will both stay with me. You will give me freely whatever I desire, heart-mage, for as long as your soul dwells in my home, and then I will consume you and let you rest."

Its voice promised pain and pleasure and torments he couldn't begin to imagine. He wondered fleetingly what the alternative was; where was his soul *supposed* to go? Beau couldn't bear to look at it anymore. He shut his eyes and said, "And the second condition?"

"You will permit me to visit you."

Beau blinked his eyes open again, frowning. "Visit me? On my plane? In the flesh?"

It smiled again. This close, he could see each long, glistening tooth was etched with runes. "Yes. A single visit is all I ask."

What choice did he have? He had nothing at all to bargain with. "I would choose the time. You'd have to be invited—called. And you couldn't hurt anyone."

"Oh, do not limit yourself, heart-mage. If you call me, you may want to take advantage of the damage I can do," it said, chuckling with deep, devilish mirth. "I will submit to being called. I will not cause harm to you or to Elias."

"You will not cause harm to anyone I care about."

"Care is too broad. A heart-mage can trouble himself over half the world," the creature snapped, and for the first time, Beau felt the devastating hint of how powerful the thing truly was, how much it had softened and gentled to speak to him. "I grow impatient."

Its claws pressed into the tether until he felt the magic wither and peel. "I will not harm the ones you love personally. You will place no more restrictions on me," it hissed.

Something much more vital than magic from a glass orb was starting to shred under this creature's claws. Beau fought down a whimper, every corner of his being vibrating like glass about to shatter. "I agree," he gasped out. "With those conditions, it's a deal."

When it released him, relief drove him to his knees. It had already turned away from him, reaching out to run the backs of its fingers along Elias's jaw. "Wake, morsel. Wake deaf and dumb, and despair to see your heart-mage risked himself for you."

Elias's eyes slitted open. When they met Beau's, they went wide with horror. He thrashed in the air, and though he wasn't bound in any way Beau could see, he hung as if tied in place with rope. He tried to shout, but no sound came out.

Beau didn't know if any of the gods could hear him here, but he prayed with the entirety of his soul for this to work. He didn't try to speak; the creature had said Elias would be deaf. He reached up toward Elias so the gold line of the almost-tether lay along his palm.

The books had spoken about all the necessary terms, the things that needed to be held back and the things that must be offered. They'd recommended couples lay out detailed documents, memorizing them so they could *feel* them when the orb was broken.

Beau didn't know what was required to make a tether strong enough to bring a body back from the dead. He didn't know how to communicate carefully delineated terms to someone who couldn't hear or speak to him. And, truth be told, he didn't know how to hold anything back from someone he loved.

So he didn't.

Everything, he willed into the tether. *Everything is yours. All of me. It's yours. I'm yours.*

Elias looked at his offered hand, the gold line that lay on it, and Beau's face. He shook his head; he didn't understand. His mouth formed questions he couldn't ask. His eyes flicked to the creature standing over Beau's right shoulder, and raw horror played over his face. He turned back to Beau's hand.

I'm giving you everything. Beau willed the thought toward Elias harder than he'd ever tried to send any magic command. *Give me all of you in return.*

Elias nodded. He licked his lips. He swallowed hard. He grabbed Beau's hand, gold line lighting up hot between their palms.

The tether pulled tight, jerking Elias down out of his floating imprisonment, and then Beau and Elias both started to slide away, the room blurring around them. *Did it work?* Beau's mind fired frantically. He held his breath.

The creature's hand closed around Beau's arm, and he felt the tether tighten painfully. "My name is Vensharice, heart-mage. When you speak it, I will come." Its fingers uncurled, and Beau let Elias's unyielding grip pull him back toward reality.

·❦·❦·❦·

B eau was too big to fit back into his body. Folding, crushing, sliding himself into the ends of his fingers, the cavity of his chest, the length of his legs was the painstaking work of an eternity. When he had enough control to take a breath, the gasp shuddered and stuck like his lungs had forgotten their function. Puppeting limbs was too much, but he could manage eyes.

He peeled one open, then the other. A face swam into focus.

"Pen," he croaked. He tugged at the muscles at each corner of his mouth until they raised into a smile. "Did it work? Is he alive?"

Penny leaned forward, the brown of her eyes splintering and

glittering with tears. "Beau!" She turned away and said, "He's—"
Then her eyes refocused on his, wide and hungry, eating him up.
"You're alive. *Gods*, you're alive!" He became aware of pressure on his
chest and realized she had his shirt clenched in both hands.

With immense effort, remembering how tendon and ligament
bound bone and muscle, he lifted one arm, resting his palm atop her
hands. "'Course I'm alive. Just had to get this soul back in. Elias—"

"El is alive," she said, nodding. "You did it." Her voice broke
and she bent, pressing her forehead against their stacked hands on
his chest. She was shaking.

The other arm was harder to puppet. He lifted it eventually,
running fingers over her soft, soft hair. "I'm all right. Everything is
all right. I didn't have a chance to say it before I…went away, but
you were incredible. Thank you. Thank you. You gave me the crown."

He closed his eyes, opened them again. A blink, he supposed,
but a slow one. He was so tired. "I was afraid I wouldn't get back to
tell you I love you. I love you, Pen."

Penny pressed herself to him so hard it hurt, sobs wracking
her. Beau focused, leaking back into his own brain. He found the
pool of emotions there and peered down into it.

Relief. It was relief shaking her like a rabbit in a dog's mouth.

He examined the edges of the pool, saw how they stretched
away from him, gold and shimmering. *Ah.* The entity's words—*I
could tear this tether so easily, and the one that ties you to your plane as
well*—slid into clarity. "You were the other tether, the one that let us
come back," he said aloud. Something like a laugh coughed out of
him. "Holy shit, if I didn't love you, if we didn't have the rings—"

"Beau?" Elias's face appeared above him, whole and hale and
creased with worry, and an echo of Penny's relief rocked through the
king. "Does it hurt?"

With one hand under Penny's head and the other tangled in
her hair, Beau had no way to reach out for Elias, so he just let his
eyes drink him in. His clothing was a shredded mess, but the skin

visible beneath was almost entirely flawless. Beau could see glimpses of something on his chest, but it didn't look like a wound. "Hurt? No, nothing hurts. I'm just so tired. It was hard to fit my soul back in. Are you all right? You look perfect."

For some reason, that made El's face crumple. "Perfect," he said, nodding. He lifted his hand toward Beau, tracing a beautiful, opalescent line across the back of the hand. It caught the light, fragmenting into alternating pale and fiery colors as he pulled his scraps of sleeve back. The line ran up his forearm, along the back of his arm, up his shoulder and to the back of his neck. It was strangely familiar. He held his arm out closer to Beau's eyes; more glimmering lines hatched his forearm, straight and thin. Then he pulled his shirt aside to show his chest.

Beau jerked, sitting half up. Those were *his* tattoos on Elias's torso, though they were painted in milky, prismatic swirls instead of black ink. *His* scars decorating El's body in milk-and-fire lines. "What—?"

"We made a trade," Elias said, face grim.

Hefting himself up until he was sitting, one arm around Penny, Beau finally looked at himself.

Those opalescent scars were everywhere on his body, thick and ropy in places, thin and spiderwebbed in others, cratered like ragged holes in still others. He couldn't find a single square inch of himself clear of them. In most of his torso, he was more scar than flesh. Their pale kaleidoscopic light was hypnotic; he couldn't stop staring.

At length he muttered, "Even your *scars* are pretty, El. You should be studied."

A strange choking sound from Elias and Penny drew his attention away from his body. They were laughing, though their grim, tearful eyes made it seem a joke told from the gallows.

The throne room doors slammed open, and Lianna strode through, a lurid spray of blood across her breastplate. Behind her, Aloise entered more slowly, shutting the doors carefully behind her. When she caught Beau's eyes, her entire body sagged with relief.

"Everything properly went to shit out there for a while, but we've mostly got it sorted," Lili said. "What the *hell* happened in here? Why do you look like somebody carved you up and glued you back together with magic?"

"I believe I was, um, dead." Beau laughed. "A temporary condition. I've reconstituted."

"What a *stunningly* unsettling way to say you're alive," Lianna said. She gripped his arm and shook him slightly as if testing how solid he was. Then her eyes went past him to Elias. "And I see you've sucessfully un-revenanted the revenant. Hello, prince-killer. I've heard a lot about you."

"Duchess's sister, I presume," Elias said in his deep-gravel voice, bowing his head to her.

She grinned. "The very same." She winked at Beau and said, "I *fully* understand what all the fuss was about now. I mean, he's not for me, *alas*, but I get it."

"Lili, everything went as planned?" Penny asked.

Lianna shrugged. "Better, in fact. Uncle Alphonse was, shall we say, not much of a military strategist, and it seems the people advising him turned up dead a couple of weeks ago."

Elias's lips lifted in the faintest possible smirk.

"Most of his fighters surrendered as soon as the nobles rode out, shouting that Courdur was dead. Lord Tivelyn and I were just discussing what to do with them."

Beau swayed on his feet as they discussed the logistics. Penny was in her element, command pouring off her as she counted directives off on her fingers. Lianna, too, was entirely comfortable, armed and armored, relaying concerns and countering ideas. Granvallée's most formidable nobles, and they were on his side.

An arm circled his waist, holding him steady. "Sit down, Highness." Elias's voice: he'd tried not to think about it for the weeks of travel, but having it back was the first cool drink of water after a long stumble through the desert.

Beau let El walk him to the throne and ease him down onto the seat. It was just as uncomfortable as he'd always imagined it would be. "When you came back," the king said, watching the others talking, "was my body all in one piece?"

Elias hesitated. "No."

"Ah." Penny's visible grief and palpable relief made more sense. "Was yours?" Elias nodded. "Good."

Lianna and Aloise left again, talking quietly, and Penny turned her face toward Beau and Elias. There was something in her eyes, a sort of shadow when she looked at him, like she was still picturing him dead on the floor.

"Beau..." Elias knelt down next to the throne, resting his elbows on the carved wooden arm of the massive chair. "How do I thank you for what you did? How do I earn your forgiveness? How do I begin to repay you?"

"Repay?" Beau considered that. "You're mine to forgive as I please. And I do forgive you. I don't know that you owe me a debt."

Elias frowned incredulously.

"All right," Beau said with a shrug. "If you feel you do, you do. Here's my proposal: pay me in honesty. Never lie to me again for as long as we live. No white lies. No lies of omission. No oblique answers to 'protect' me. I gave you everything, which means somewhere in there, you have my honesty. Use it."

There was no trace of teasing or sarcasm in Elias's response of, "Yes, Your Majesty."

Penny crossed the room to them, setting a hand against each of their cheeks. "I cannot believe you're both alive," she whispered. "Lianna will work with the others to take care of things here in the capital if you need to rest. In a few days, we can announce—"

Beau grabbed her hand, kissed it. "No. There's too much work to do. A celebration feast, a coronation—then we should make our move on the Destiny Riders while our forces are gathered. Which means you and I need to visit Almeida, the sooner the better."

She blinked, and Beau felt her surprise and pleasure; it was exactly what she would've said, had she not been so worried about his wellbeing. "If you're able, but it can wait a few days, Beau. You came back from—"

"The dead, yes," Beau said, shrugging. "I feel fine. Come on. Let's get some servants started cleaning up in here."

For the next several hours, Beau was the perfect king. He cleaned up and redressed quickly, walked the fields to congratulate the fighters, assembled a hasty but sufficient victory dinner for the leaders, and sent wine and beer out for the soldiers to celebrate around their fires.

It was not as hard as it had been in the past to say the right thing, to smile the right smile, to offer a clap on the back or a shake of the hand or a regal nod. Whatever he'd given to Elias, he thought he might have taken some of the man's ability to play a part. Though his appearance gave everyone pause, it also called up some of the awe and fear Beau had always seen these people give his father.

When his strength finally gave out, he was already walking through the door of his bedroom and could collapse into bed with impunity. Elias sagged down on the end of the bed next to him, and Penny leaned against the bedside table to remove her boots.

"What a fucking day," Beau said into the mattress.

Elias lay back, arm warm against Beau's side. "Yes. Fucking day. Fucking month. Fucking eternity." Hoarse and humorless.

When Penny climbed onto the bed, the too-soft mattress sank in the middle, tumbling them together. Beau could feel all of their heartbeats; he couldn't pick his apart from the others. The pure, simple pleasure of warm bodies against him and lungs moving in rhythm with his lulled him into a syrupy, drunken sort of joy.

There were many, many questions to answer. Many problems to solve. Many threats at the door. But *tonight*, he had Elias and he had Penny and he had a crown. The world was right.

24

FACES OF POWER

It took nine days to pull together a proper enough coronation in the newly cleaned and repaired throne room. Most of the ceremony was rote memorization, a scripted set of lines and actions that every king in Granvallée's history had said and done in exactly the same way.

For this reason, older nobles were taken aback when Beau ended his vows to the kingdom by calling Penny to the dais. He'd warned her she'd be taking vows of her own, so she rose gracefully and took her place next to him with flawless, regal poise, the definition of a queen.

"Victoire Augusta Bridgette Penamour, do you swear to serve and protect this kingdom and its people?"

She dipped her head. "I do, Your Majesty."

"Do you swear to rule fairly and justly, to the fullest extent of your ability?"

"I do."

"And should your king fall, should I become unable to rule for any reason without an heir of age to inherit, will you accept the throne of Granvallée as its sovereign?"

Penny's eyes widened, and the ring exploded in a riot of shock. This was no part of the queen's vows. The queen did not—could not—claim the throne of Granvallée herself. Only a king could rule. But Beau's eyes were steady on hers, willing her to trust him, and she nodded slowly. "I will."

Beau smiled, placing the gold band of her crown atop her braids. "Then I crown you Queen of Granvallée, to rule and serve beside me." She took in a breath as if to say something to him, but he turned to the noble audience. "The role of queen under Queen Victoire will be different than it has been before, but I believe you will find it a welcome change."

He took a deep breath, caught Elias's small, encouraging nod where he stood against the side wall, and said, "I am your king, and all of Granvallée is subject to my will—except my wife. Your queen rules alongside me. She does not answer to me. You will hear her guidance, her commands, and her judgments as if they are mine."

Stunned silence hung heavy in the hall. Lord Macabrie, in the front row, was the first to break it. "She speaks with your voice, then, Your Majesty?"

Beau smiled at him. "No, Lord Macabrie. She speaks with her own. From this day forward, its weight in Granvallée equals mine." When the man pursed his lips as if to speak, Beau raised a hand and said, "I expect she and I will be aligned in nearly everything. However, if we disagree, a simple majority vote of the court will make the determination for Granvallée."

The buzz from the nobles resumed. A vote? Penny's hand wrapped his wrist, squeezed tight, and he felt the waves and waves of disbelief from her. She and he both knew she controlled the nobles, if it came to that; he was giving her *more* power than he held.

Affection was no part of the ceremony, but Beau bent to kiss his wife anyway. He reached through the ring, recognizing the action now as an outstretching of magic, enjoying the buzz of it. He pulled joy and reassurance and determination to the front.

As he pulled away from her, Elias nodded to him again, and Beau jerked his head toward the dais, calling the guard up to his other side. El hesitated; they hadn't determined what his role would be now, but there was comfort in the way he slipped into the space he'd always occupied at Beau's shoulder, his warm, steady presence returned to its rightful place.

The deadliest man alive to his left. The most formidable monarch Granvallée would ever see to his right. And in the center, a heart-mage, bound to both.

"Now," he said, raising his hands and commanding the attention of the room again, "let us turn our eyes to protecting our borders and our people. There's work to do."

Acknowledgements

I have had the privilege to build myself a tulip family, very few of whom share my blood. I owe a debt of gratitude to all of them.

First and foremost, my husband, the prototype for all my supernaturally devoted, violent-thoughts-and-gentle-hands love interests, whose support of my words has never slackened.

My sister, who reads every word with the kind of enthusiasm and commitment most people reserve for religion or boy bands, and who never stops talking about my characters like they're people.

My best friend, who keeps me on track, fights for my success and sanity, and will absolutely cut a bitch (literally or verbally) for bringing me down.

My amazing beta readers, who asked the kind of questions that spawn pantheons and inspire magic.

And my neurodivergent, oddball family and friends, who uncritically support even the wildest story ideas, social posts, and re-search deep-dives because they love me. (My cut-a-bitch bestie says this is too self-deprecating, and they would have definitely told me I was wasting my time if it was a bad idea. So perhaps their love is less unconditional than the 'tulip family' moniker suggests).

About the Author

S. E. McPherson has been a writer of fantasy and speculative fiction since she was eight years old, binding books with a hole punch and tied yarn. While she took a brief two-decade detour into the career of a marketing executive and won many boring business writing awards, she has found her way back to storytelling and illustration. *A King's Trust* is her first novel.

semcpherson.com | @semcpherson_writes | @semcpherson.bsky.social